THE GOLD SERVICE

A NEW SCI-FI ACTION ADVENTURE

THE CAPITAL ADVENTURES
BOOK 4

ALLEN IVERS

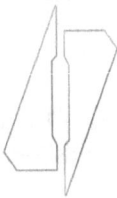

As always, to my lovely wife Lyn

Always inspiring me to push harder
than I ever thought possible

CONTENTS

PART FOUR
EVIDENCE OF THINGS NOT SEEN

FOREWORD

This is the first book in *The Gold Service* trilogy. This series contains the following content matter:

- *Graphic Violence & Traumatic Injuries*
    - *Including amputation, stabbing, gun shots and bone fracture.*
- *Occasional Foul Language*
    - *People swear when this stuff happens*
- *Alcohol & Drug Use*
    - *Underage Drinking, Mind Altering Substances*
- *Reference to Sexual Activity*
    - *Dialog references, no depictions*
- *Religious Trauma/Conversion Therapy*
    - *Electroshock torture and isolation*

We're here to have a good time with characters we love. If any of this material distresses you, it's okay to grab another book instead.

Hope you enjoy!

MAP & CHRONOLOGY

The Solar Imperium, also called the Gnostic Empire by the more faithful citizenry, stretches over a fifth of the Milky Way Galaxy. This map features the primary locations featured in the series thus far.

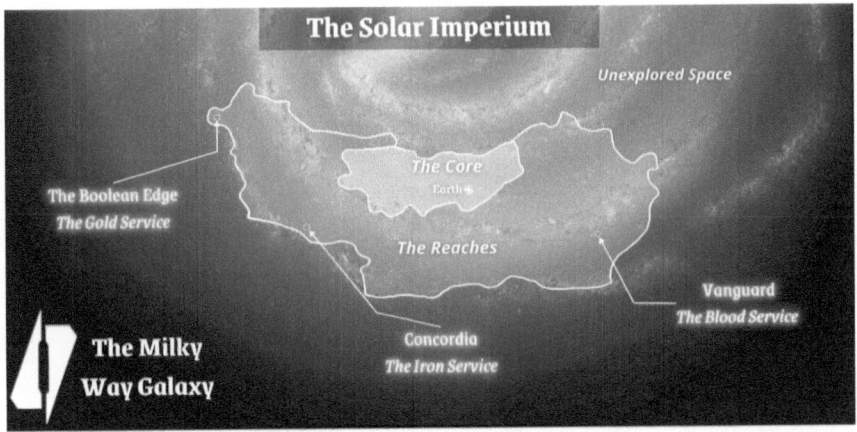

| Map of Solar Imperium controlled space, 2241 CE

The events of the Capital Adventures occur entirely within these borders. Events from one book may be mentioned in another, or characters may cross over from one trilogy to another. Think of it as a shared universe, with the individual stories having unique tones and flair, while building an overarching plot.

You may enjoy each trilogy independent of the others—and I've meticulously built them so that your enjoyment is not contingent on having read the others! But if you want the full experience of the Capital Adventures, I do encourage you to pick up the other books to get a full sense of the Imperium's reach. The official reading order would be to read the trilogies starting with The Blood Service, then The Gold Service, and finishing out with the upcoming Iron Service.

If you're like me, however, and you were looking to read the novels in chronological order, the events of all nine books are as follows:

———

1) THE GOLD SERVICE
2) THE BLOOD SERVICE
3) THE IRON SERVICE

4) RANKS OF THE BLOOD SERVICE
5) COST OF THE GOLD SERVICE
6) SWORDS OF THE IRON SERVICE (COMING SOON)

7) COMMAND OF THE BLOOD SERVICE
8) SHARDS OF THE IRON SERVICE (COMING SOON)
9) POWERS OF THE GOLD SERVICE

WITH EVEN MORE TO COME...

The Gold Service Trilogy has a lighter tone than the other two members of this series, with a strong found-family of mercenaries and malcontents that all share a single brain cell, while also confronting both religious & generational trauma. These characters have become a second family to me, and I hope they do the same for you.

Waste no more time arguing what a good man should be.
Be one.

MARCUS AURELIUS

PROLOGUE

SIX MONTHS BEFORE
VANGUARD'S UPRISING

IT WAS in Antony's humble opinion that nothing of import happened at important places. Revolutions were not concocted in palace cloak rooms, but on a Duster colony world half-devoid of life in a dingy pub called the Blue something-or-other. It was usually an animal.

This place he found himself in was austere, beautiful, and worthy of such history; and it was a rotting four-post cabin on a moon called Daymar. It would either sprout a new World Order or fold against a strong wind.

Antony had been a young man when he came to this Monastery, with a head full to the brim with information—and his ears had been valuable. People spoke freely around those they saw as beneath them. Cleaners, valets, and bartenders were not people. Rather, they were scenery.

He drank it all in. He had eagerly poured from that cup to any who could pay to listen. Others still would pay handsomely to keep his mouth shut. But it was here, at a dusty corner of a dusty ball in a forgotten corner of the Empire he had learned that his cup was not full, nor was it empty—it was, in point of fact, small.

He had to empty all else from his mind, if he were to fill it with anything new. He could not ply this peculiar healing Art with a mind crammed full of other people's thoughts. He had to believe the impossible could be willed into the flesh with nothing more than a polite request.

Please. Help me.

The woman was young, no older than sixteen, and her face twisted with the waves of pain rolling up through her leg. The thick gash had been packed with gauze and the bleeding stilled, but the injury would soon abscess if not cleaned and closed.

"How was she hurt?" he had asked.

Farming accident.

"There were no safety measures?"

Long expired.

"But they came all this way to us?"

He had earned silence for his questions. He wasn't asking because he sought to empathize or understand; he sought answers so that he could dismiss her foolishness. Someone weak or stupid did not deserve charity or compassion. It was a defense of the old world, meant to shield him from responsibility or action.

He had the ability to help her. That was what mattered. Those in need do not have anything to give and kindness does not require an explanation. A gift from one who has much costs the owner nothing, but has infinite value to one who has nothing.

And Faith has no entrance fee.

He implored his masters, that she deserved better care than a neophyte like him could provide. They assured him that his talents were more than sufficient. Antony might doubt his own skill, but it was not his skill at play: the Icon would heal her.

"You are a vessel for the Will. Nothing more."

Antony looked out at those assembled before him. It was a small building, no larger than his father's Jump depot. There was something oddly charming about it all. What should have been modern alloy bulkheads, sleek Silksteel, and polycarbonates, were instead warping and creaking oak joists holding up a tarpaper ceiling, the

2

musty stench pervading the air. That must be why the elders used so much incense. He pondered if the organic material was key to the Icon's effectiveness, or if someone in the congregation simply donated a private collection of lumber they wanted to be rid of.

Tables had been cleared to make way for short stools that patrons could kneel on. They came as he once had, with heads full of expectations and a life's experience. Skepticism and cynicism poisoned their hearts, hanging their heads and crooking their backs. He did not blame them—he knew their road well, highways and back alleys in equal time.

A hundred eyes stared at him, those at prayer and those that waited along the walls, ready to take the places of any who tired. Each would contribute their prayers, and when they could no more, another supplicant would take their place, so that their collective will would not wane.

They wanted this girl healed, no matter what it took.

Four large windows, two to each side, filled the gallery with tinted light. In preparation for the event, Aspirants extinguished all other lights in the room—not only did it feed into the theatrics, they found that people were quieter in a darker room.

Antony had first concluded that his masters were skilled artisans in the craft of manipulating an audience. Of course, what couldn't be argued was the results. He himself had once squinted and tilted his head at the wild promises.

But what he had seen, he could not forget. No amount of lighting or staging could replace results.

Her stretcher was laid out on the block cement altar by two acolytes, the boys wordlessly transferring their charge to his care. If anything happened now, it would be on him.

He had seen this ritual performed dozens of times, first as an Aspirant in the crowd; then as an Acolyte, bearing the recipient unto the Icon. This would be his first time leading a congregation.

His heart raced. The sweat on his brow cool, beaded, but pleasantly still. He swallowed hard. But his hands were as still as iron.

Antony took his place at the altar, raising one confident hand to the sky—and draping the other over the Icon.

The small dark green orb hung from clanky old chains, dangling center over the altar and the injured Aspirant's quivering chest. He could feel the beveling of its edges under his fingers, fine embossing that made it both perfectly smooth and rough to the touch. He once wondered if it were some ancient language, a technology long lost, or evidence of an alien race.

Now he accepted it for what it was—unknowable compassion from an unspeakable power.

The stone was so cold it robbed his fingers of feeling. He didn't dare so much as brush his bare skin against it, lest it elect to take much more than warmth from him.

The girl managed to open her eyes. Dilated, afraid, brown. She didn't look at him. Blinking through the tears and the pain, as her hands fought to remain at her sides, she stared deep into the Icon hanging above her.

She pleaded with it. Help me.

"What is your name?" he asked.

"Lucrecia," she said,

Remember, Antony. You are not healing her. You are a vessel. The Icon will do its work.

"Spell it for me." Before she could start speaking, he shook his head, "In your head. Count the letters out. And then repeat it."

Her eyebrows twisted. Confusion, not pain.

He smiled. "It will help calm you. This process...is not gentle."

"Morpha?" she asked him, suddenly afraid. Whatever pain she was in now, she begged for a painkiller to soften what was to come.

His smile fell. "Be at peace, girl. Your faith will protect you."

Project certainty, and confidence shall be gained. In practice, he just didn't need her thrashing about.

He spoke the chant he had practiced a thousand times in his dormitory and the first one he had ever heard at the Monastery, trying to not trip on the ancient tongue.

Sacred world, who takes away the sins of the body.

His words echoed through the chamber, as the Aspirants repeated the words in their murmured prayers, their voices tinged with that metallic harshness of desperation. Some of them were desperate skeptics; others were just concerned neighbors.

But the body whole were simply the faithful, offering up their voices for the healing of others. Pain was universal. They felt her pain as their own, and sought its healing as they would their own injury. They assembled now out of raw devotion, a community shouldering the weak.

It was an awe-inspiring display of human compassion.

Antony scanned the congregation, a passive action that made sure all were participating. He caught the look of the girl's father—a harsh man with an unshaven face and a scarred ear. He had an ill-favored look, anger behind his murmuring lips.

He was ready to blame Antony should the ritual fail. Antony understood his pain all too well.

They didn't allow many to enter the Monastery. The monks knew that what they gave freely, others would seal away, charge a premium just to look upon, or parlay the myth into more craven uses. They would bury this gift under the dunnage of bureaucracy and call it profit. Perhaps they had seen it in his eyes, knew his secrets as easily as his name, but they knew the young Antony had been just such a threat to them.

The Icon of Cruciform—a tenth of the reward offered would set up his nonexistent children for a life of luxury in Sol.

But there wasn't enough money in all the worlds to buy back what he had seen in that chapel. His father, a man half dead, walked on his own two feet mere minutes after his arrival, and old scars from a lifetime of sour healing were mended in seconds—but the work was left undone. His father died three nights later. It was Antony's own weakness—his greed, his doubt, reflexive horror at the impossible—that had limited the Icon's work.

He was too rooted in what was possible, too fixed in his mind.

The Icon reflects the Will of the World, and his Will had tainted the request.

Antony had vowed to cleanse himself of sin and to heal any other that walked through those doors.

It was his purpose.

Antony nodded to the father of the girl, assurances. Lucrecia's eyes darted between the two, fear rising up like bile in her throat. "Good sir—"

"Don't speak," he said to her. "Count the letters."

She insisted, "You have to stop. Now."

"And you must believe," he said, soft and kind. He continued to chant:

Father World, let it be done unto me according to your Word.

Lucrecia raised her voice, her words echoing in the chamber. "You have to stop. You have to run."

Run? Why?

And he felt his hand, his wrist, his whole arm shoot cold.

It wasn't until he saw the blood spurt that he knew something was wrong. And that's when he heard the gunshot.

The barrel smoked. The casing hung in the air just behind his scarred ear. Forty caliber, cavitation drill head.

The shot lanced through his arm, yanking him from the Icon. The chill touch of it rippled up his shoulder, pins and needles all at once. The shot impacted at the meat of his bicep, the flechette rending his flesh like it were unspun cotton.

It severed his arm at the elbow.

The father had shot him.

Ice became fire—and Antony screamed, falling back behind the shelter of the altar.

Gunfire, multiple sources. They fired into the crowd, the explosive cacophony smothering the screams.

The two Acolytes were next, gaping holes carved into their chests. They were just children, voices still light in song; both dead before they hit the cobblestones.

The Aspirants all cried out and each voice was silenced with declarative successive shots, the abusive cracks of a switch.

It was chaos in an instant, as the prayers erupted into a chorus of pain and fear, poisoning the air. They herded the voices towards the altar, silencing them one by one; they were blocking the one exit and delivering them unto the Reaper.

Antony cradled his arm, feeling out the torn muscle fibers with his fingers. It was like combing out oily hair, his fingers slick with blood—he had seen the Icon seal and mend, but could It replace what had been taken away?

They were here for the Icon. Get to it. Protect it.

He propped himself up and reached with his good arm, up above the altar to the—

A shot snapped one of the Icon's support chains, and he felt flecks of metal scrape along his cheek. It might have been incidental or a failed attempt at him, but it served its purpose. Antony slipped back behind the altar, all shivers, his head swimming. Hiding away. Afraid.

Sinful.

He couldn't feel the Icon anymore. He couldn't remember its Voice.

Antony heard the last Aspirant go silent with the final report of the guns. The girl on the altar openly wept, but she could not flee.

The clank of a metal action locking open. The hollow ring of a magazine falling to the floor. The cling of a spring as the action locked shut on a fresh round.

Ready for violence.

"Mea culpa," she said on the altar. "Mea maxima culpa."

My fault.

A single shot silenced her, and Antony felt the warmth of her blood spatter across his face, joining his own.

"Izzy, what was the 'go word?' Do you remember? Do ya?" One of the attackers, berating his subordinates. It was planned.

"I was made. The hooker was getting chatty." Izzy—the father—snarked back. "Let's grab the thing and get outta here."

No farmer's daughter, no farmer. They had picked up an innocent girl, injured her, given her a story. Promised they'd heal her, maybe even cut her in on profits if she cooperated. In the moment of glory, she had reneged on the deal.

The Icon had touched her mind, cut through her deceit, compelled her honesty.

"Okay, but now how do we know that's not a fancy paperweight? That could be a cast iron kettlebell for all we know!"

"You just pay me to crack heads. You figure it out."

Izzy stepped up to the altar, a heavy pistol tucked in his hand. He reached up with a gloved hand, palming the Icon.

Antony knew then that Izzy heard its Voice—because he paused, feeling out its edges as every new Acolyte does. He experienced its cold, even through his thick worker's gloves. And he felt its heart.

But this man's heart was already cold.

Maybe the thug heard his breathing or saw some movement in the corner of his eye, but the man lowered the barrel of the gun to Antony's head without even looking down.

"Got any more fancy words?"

Antony shivered, staring into the belly of the weapon, like the maw of a hungry dragon. And it breathed fire.

PART ONE
ICONOGRAPHY

And They came with a Commandment for the people,

For Life was not to be had for fruitless exchange, but in the pursuit of Higher Calls.

Aspire not for the self but for the Whole; the clean and the dirty; the sinner and the saint; the neighbor and the stranger,

For your Service is to the People,

for they are the Kings.

GNOSTIC LIBRUM, COLONIAL 4:13-18

CHAPTER
ONE

THOM

THOM HELD the fruit in his hand: firm to the touch, soft skin, an alluring brilliant red. This was a real tomato fruit—not one from an industrial replicator or a laboratory squint's alternative. This was authentic produce plucked from an actual vine spiraling off a legitimate plant that labored in bona fide Grade-A colonial soil.

Roche had described it as ambrosia. You can easily forget the complexity that can come with a bite of even the blandest *real* food. It was the difference between a convincing con and the genuine article.

When was the last time he'd had real fruit? Was it back at the Pan & Pantry? The chef used to slip him scraps from the block, but those were all chems and lab stuff, had that plastic aftertaste.

The tomato seemed to stare back at him, taunt him. He wouldn't dare. This fruit was meant for the Harbormaster, for shipment to local markets. He wouldn't take what wasn't his, would he?

He bit into the forbidden fruit, chomping down like a starving man.

Ambrosia?

It stung his tongue, his gums, and lips. Acid, salt, and sickening sweet in equal measure. The fruit had no substance, going from gooey mess to stringy floss from moment to moment.

People *wanted* this? This wasn't fruit; it was what a scientist made when a child described fruit to him through a translator program.

He let the bite fall out into his hands and wiped them off on the side of the table. He'd clean it later, but right then, he just had to get it off of him!

The ship creaked and moaned around him, bulkheads flexing with the temperatures. It was a rickety old bulk brig, but the *Aurum* was a genuine beauty. Thom had seen plenty of cruisers and brigs come in and out of port: knobby old titans built for deep space, skeletal beanstalks that hauled enormous modules along their lengths, small cities bolted onto platters with engines rigged to one end, and nimble little darts that appealed to the eye.

The *Aurum* wasn't sexy, nor giant or modular—it was more than she seemed. She had more storage than a ship twice her class, because the very walls were made to store everything from personal affects to bulk cargo. Every inch of her was made to be of use in some manner. And while the KC-28 Perseus model had been stamped out for over twenty years like they were minting coins, they hadn't made a new one in over a decade. It was a hundred-ton brick that had a proclivity for random hull breaches under duress.

It was a perfect smuggler's ship. Quiet, cheap, unassuming, and blended into the background with every other like-minded ship in the sky.

Thom had fallen in love the moment he laid eyes on her. What some saw as common, he saw as rustic. The pocks and dents in the hull, the burns and scrapes on its belly, the odd missing panel and mismatched paint—there was a lifetime in every scratch and he wanted to see each one.

If Osyen had turned tail and left him behind at that tiny little bar at that tiny little nothing port, Thom would never have been whole again. Probably in a literal sense too, because the Pantry's owner would've broken both of Thom's legs over the tab Osyen had run up.

He set the tomato down onto the table, eyeing it. Then nudged it away a little bit. It leaked juice, leaving a streak of translucent red and dribbles of fiber. It looked like it was frozen in a moment of shock.

Thom fished in his pockets for some hard tack. Anything to get that taste out of his mouth.

The last time they'd had organic anything on board had been that train job outside Mursa—they had boosted a half a ton of live chickens, kept half a dozen, and didn't tell the client. Those little buggers ate anything within arm's reach, but Thom had also grown quite fond of a couple of 'em. He'd even named them: Oscar, Kibi, and Whitney.

That is until one long haul when the rations ran out. Then he had gotten the unpleasant task of "cleaning" the birds. Hopefully, the crew was just hazing the new kid. He didn't relish the thought of doing that again.

Those noises were still the wallpaper in his nightmares.

The hull of the *Aurum* moaned, jostling Thom in his seat and his tray rattled on the thin table.

"Lily?" Thom asked the open air.

A face projected up from the table surface, looking to and fro for the source of the voice. Photoluminescent green hair shone out from the hologram's slender face. The strands were pulled tight to one side, draping over their cheek. The curved lips and soft eyes were immediately contrasted with a heavy brow and an immaculately groomed black mustache.

Lily could look like anything they wanted—they could choose a faceless, expressionless void like every other AI Thom had ever known. Some were programmed to be beautiful, some floating matrices, and others took on Terran animals. Others still never took any shape.

The Pan & Pantry had a kind and accented portly gentleman, taking orders and handling disgruntled patrons like some kind of snake charmer. He'd laugh like some percussive drum, clap a broad hand on a jovial stomach, and ask simple leading questions. People were never happier than when they were talking about themselves.

13

Lily had been given command-directive over their own image. Consulting the wide variety of options and historical symbols to emulate, Lily selected a mustache, long green hair, and plump lips. It was...confusing, and Thom knew that was intentional. Lily enjoyed confounding humans.

A passenger on the last run had been a heuristics specialist, and he had tried to 'fix' Lily. Lily tormented him night and day until he stayed out of their systems. Imagine it, someone digging around in your guts because they didn't like your haircut?

Lily deliberately flourished that glowing hair across Thom's face, playing up the illusion of the lost little girl. They knew exactly where Thom was. Lily *was* the ship after all, but they had learned that making a show of ignorance made everyone more comfortable with the omnipresent computer that watched at all hours. It grounded the booming baritone voice as a more flawed and human member of the crew.

But Lily was a crew member the same way the bulkhead was. Lily was a glowing floating luminescent head that taunted Thom in the middle of the night, the walls echoing with their voice like the place was haunted.

Thom smiled just thinking about it. Not many kids his age got to live in haunted brigs. No, they had to settle with their distant parents, voices in other rooms that turned on lights and broke cabinets and dishware in the middle of the night. Thom got a glowing head with a booming voice and no concept of personal space.

Lily spoke, that bone-shattering bass voice emitting from their slight and confusing frame, "Yes, Thom? What is your need?"

"Re-entry?" he asked, a one-word question with a volume of meaning. Was it time?

Full lips and bright eyes, colorful hair, a soft cheek—and that gruff thunder: "The ship is aerobraking in the ionosphere. Time to land-fall: twenty-five minutes."

Thom choked on his salad. "Twenty-five—why didn't you tell me sooner?!"

"Osyen was quite specific you were to remain aboard ship."

"Osyen told *me* I was going!" Thom objected.

"What're you gonna do for us, *Unti*?"

Thom turned to see Jackson Milardi stroll through the room. "Going to hol' my purse for me?"

Thom pouted. "How am I ever going to learn piracy if I'm just sitting on the ship all the time?"

"Not my call," Milardi crooned, but then his face twisted. "Piracy?"

"What would you call it?"

Milardi coughed. "Pirates dons' work for a living, *Unti*. They take what others make tru force of arms."

"Then what are we?"

"We're rakishly handsome rogues, o' course."

Milardi was a salesman's smile jammed onto a face dotted with pocked scars from a dozen different gunfights—Thom was convinced half of them were applied makeup, but Milardi had been in enough gunfights for the distinction to be moot.

Tall and lean, Milardi had to duck through every bulkhead door he came across in the universe. He looked like a man had been rubberized and stretched out, a product of growing up on an asteroid mining colony. He dwarfed head and shoulders over everyone else, downright looming over Thom.

He rounded out the look with a wide-brimmed hat that very nearly clipped the doorframe on either side of him; knee high boots that story said were scalped from some Navy officer in a poker game; and a hefty waistcoat of real Corinthian leather, and Milardi came together like a high-end fashion line for murderers—only the finest.

"We're not going to take 'tru' force of arms?'" Thom asked, mocking Milardi's thick accent.

Milardi sneered. "'Course not. We're going to hand over the goods, get paid like proper merchants. Only going to kill 'em if they're rude."

Thom flopped back into his booth, casually taking a bite of the tomato—forgetting that he hated it. His face soured as Milardi raised an eyebrow. "Not a fan?"

"It tastes like engine grease."

"Then why did you—"

Thom forced himself to swallow, and it burned all the way down. "I don't even know."

Milardi leaned on the wall. "Look, *Unti*, it's going to be a sticks and stones kinda day. Oz thinks the locals might be going more for an exchange of brass than valuables. Best case scenario, we have a terse little talk and get paid. Worst case, Zatia 'n I get to cracking' some heads. If we didn't need the money, we'd be breezin' on. So, if you want a cheap bet, I'm going to be up late in the AutoDoc patching Oz's stupid face—again," Milardi cautioned, the Duster accent positively leaking out of every syllable.

"I know how to fight." Thom pouted. Lily scoffed as quiet as their deep voice allowed. "I do!"

"You *wanna* fight, *Unti*. That ain't the same-sa." Milardi rousted Thom from his seat by the nape of his neck. The weathered shooting gloves had cutouts for his fingertips, so he could better feel the grips. Right now, they burned like hatred on Thom's skin.

Milardi plucked the tomato from the table, inspecting the bite mark. "That's from the shipment, isn't it?"

"It's mine. I found it," Thom answered, a little too fast.

Milardi smiled with a hint of pain, knowing full well how this little play would close. "Ya find 'em in the hold? Or did you stumble across 'em scrubbing the vents?"

Thom looked to Lily for help. Milardi's eyes slid over to the omnipresent computer. "Lily, whose tomato fruit is it?"

Lily shrugged, but with their cheeks—it was a common deflection for them. They didn't *not* know, they just didn't care to help humans in their petty pettiness as they petty so much at each other. "I'm supposed to keep tabs on the boy at all hours, am I?"

"Oh, please!" Milardi dismissed Lily's deflection. "Coy's not a good look on ya."

Lily's visage melted, particle by particle flying over to reform by Milardi—the effect always made Thom's stomach turn. Refocused and antagonistically closer, Lily squinted at Milardi. "And your look is compensating for a lack of personality."

Milardi smiled. "Least I bought a *good* one. We boosted you from the gift shop, darlin'."

The ship shuddered again.

A stern voice echoed from somewhere astern. "Please do not taunt the artificial intelligence."

Thom drove his fork into the tomato, watching the juices squirt out onto his plate. He wasn't eating anymore; now he was just torturing it.

His fruit. He'd found it, fair and square. So what if it was at the top of a stack in a locked refrigerated crate? If it wasn't his, why did he have it now?

"We all did what you doin', kid. Just part and parcel."

"You mopped a latrine?" Thom poked the delicately coifed man.

"God no! That's why we dredged you up."

"I just want to do something that matters around here."

"You do plenty, *Unti*. You just dons' get to do whatever ya want," Milardi said with a smirk.

Thom leaned back like a hammer cocked. "I guess Holstrum was all business, then, huh? That was... just a work day?"

Lily threw out a gasp, like a bassoon with an offended gentry setting. For a genderless void, they could be such a drama queen.

Milardi raised an eyebrow at the boy. "Cashing that one in, now?"

"I'm just looking to contribute more around here," Thom said, grinning wide.

"You contribute! All the time!" Milardi whined. "Less and less every day but...when you come to be a liability to someone..."

"Then who will help you clean up, huh? After Holstrum?" Thom pursed his lips. Checkmate.

Long story short, there was an adverse amount of...recreational activities that Milardi had gotten buried in. Milardi looked like he'd been run over by a train car—a few times—and loved every second of it. Thom had helped the hungover Milardi cover his tracks. He'd even gotten Lily to erase their security logs. Of course, if anyone checked with Lily there would be a gigantic gap with Thom's name all over it, but no sign of Milardi's...recreational activities.

Milardi ground his teeth and rolled his eyes. "Lily, where's Cap'n?"

Lily's image flickered as they processed the request. "Osyen is currently in the cargo hold."

Milardi's eyes scanned the tomato fruit on Thom's plate. "Better hope you didn't sour his mood."

Oh, there was no way Thom was going to miss this. He didn't sign the ship's ledger to mop floors.

Thom snagged the fruit and pocketed it, before folding and locking the table up into the wall, out of the way—the designers really used every square inch.

Milardi marched off down the hallway, leaving Thom to scramble after him, barely able to get his feet under him. After all, the ship was aerobraking in the upper atmosphere—a red streak across the sky to anyone on the ground. It was a helluva time to change plans on the ground crew at the port. They were expecting three people, not four.

"Osyen!" Milardi called out, as he turned to the hallway. "Oz!"

The stern voice echoed back to them again. "No shouting."

"I shout when the sitch calls for it, Roche!" was Milardi's rebuttal. Milardi marched down the hallway with purpose, dragging Thom behind him in his wake, almost by force of gravity.

A rotund man shorter than Thom but twice again his size cut them off—and Thom couldn't help but gawk at the stump that used to be his right hand, now covered in corded wires. That clump of biomechanical cables was twisting and turning in slight ways, minor commands being shot up and out into the ship's system. It looked like a technomancer spiderweb of primary colors.

If Gavroche 'Roche' Keynes noticed Thom's constant staring, he paid it no mind. He was likely quite used to drawing attention. The back-alley upgrades itching at the skin created heinous bulbous scars around the contact points that Thom couldn't tear his eyes from. Roche's hair had long since gone thin, so he had shaved it off—but strands of hair still poked out like tufts of grass near his three cranial implants.

He looked like a raw potato had dropped into a dumpster and was lifted out...better, stronger, smarter.

The man turned his eyes on Milardi and Thom, one pupil reflecting blue lights like a cat at midnight. Thom could see the artificial iris focus, tracking some heads-up display.

"It's a small pipe, Milardi," the plughead stressed. "Everybody can hear ya."

"I'm surprised you hear me when I'm standing right next to you, Roche."

More machine than man, Roche had spent almost every penny he had on those black-market body-mods, linking him with the ship and to Lily in ever-more entwined ways. Roche was standing in the hallway with them, but he wasn't really giving them his full attention. He was probably still flying the ship on manual control.

"I hear you constantly," Roche retorted. "I'm just ignoring you."

Milardi rested his hands on his hip holsters—like he was cupping a woman's hips. "Roche, do you think the boy should come wit' us today?"

"Enunciate, Milardi," Roche said, pinching the fingers of his flesh hand. "Tip of the teeth."

Milardi puckered his lips, making kissy noises at Roche. "Answer the question, pretty boy."

Roche fixed his eyes on Thom—well, the one good brown eye and the targeting computer socketed in his skull, all cold steel ball with blue iris. They tracked and focused independently in an unsettling ballet. Thom never really knew which one to look at, but Roche never corrected him.

"Today goes wrong, it's going to be messy."

"That's what I been sayin'," Milardi remarked.

"You didn't let me finish." Roche leered at the fanciful jackass. "The boy might keep it clean."

"*Unti's* going to mop up, is he?"

"All these cleaning metaphors are a little patronizing," Thom offered up with a raised hand. "Just...you know."

Roche was fastest on the response. "I just associate you with mops and dust bins more than anything else."

Milardi threw him a high five like they'd rehearsed it.

But Roche didn't even acknowledge it as he continued, "That's to your advantage, boy. No expectation on you, means you are not part of anybody's plan. You're a piece on the board nobody expects. Milardi, Zatia, Osyen—they're known quantities; you're not." He paused for a moment, hard drives spinning somewhere deep in his head.

Milardi pursed his lips at that analysis. "That's good. I'mma use that."

"No, you're not. Because I'm going to use it." Roche stripped his cables out of the wall so fast he might have cut them, and sped off down the hallway, the web of cables dragging on the grating behind him. "Osyen!"

"What happened to no shouting?"

"I'm not shouting," Roche disputed, the dangling cables sliding up into his wrist and disappearing from sight like many freakish tongues. "Shouting changes the timbre of the voice, the overall quality. It denotes a loss of control. I'm projecting so that I may be heard. OSYEN!"

The trio stomped forward, a small parade of boots on the corrugated steel grating. Somewhere below them, heat shields were soaking up the friction of reentry and re-directing the thermal energy to retro-boosters, batteries, and air conditioning. Lily was relaying telemetry data to a tower at the spaceport—prepping a landing pad for the *Aurum*.

By now, half the town knew a ship was coming, its declared manifest, and the maintenance history of the aging brig. Small border outposts like this didn't get visitors all that often. They were going to be little celebrities.

Unlike the rest of the crew, Roche had made a good observation— Thom was too new to have a footprint in the Extranet. He didn't officially exist.

"So what do you need me to do?" Thom asked.

"All in good time, lad," Roche responded. "We're pitching a bit of an audible here."

"He doesn't know," Milardi explained.

"I'm running simulations!"

"How many so far where the kid dies horrible?"

"Seven. Hundred. I'm crunching the numbers!"

Thom's jaw hung a bit. "Seven hundred or...seven, a hundred? Hundred and seven?"

Roche suddenly stopped, Milardi and Thom very nearly bowling him over. He pointed to the ship's tiny Medical Bay— barely fitting the legally mandated AutoDoc. An inclined bed sat under a crane arm, a dozen tiny levers and needles at the ready, petals of a demented medical flower. It would descend onto a patient like a blender of modern medicine. What little seating there was other than that was just glorified supply cabinets for the beast.

A girl sat in the chair, leaning to one side to reach the control console.

"Zatia!"

Her pink pigtails flicked into the air. Zatia Bennitez was Thom's age, maybe even a little younger, but whatever childlike impulse one might assume from her sense of punk style was immediately dispensed with after five minutes and one drink. She dyed her hair to cover all the bloodstains that had slowly saturated the follicles. If she didn't, the fried hairs would be a splatter pattern of dried red murder.

She stared at the gang, a stimulant cord still dangling from the IV plug in her arm.

"You think we should bring the runt out on this one?" Roche asked her.

She stared at them. It was only then Thom noticed her eyes were...dilated. She was high.

"You dons' think so?"

"Enunciate," scolded Roche.

"You *don't*...think so?" Milardi forced the words out. They felt alien and wrong to him.

"I didn't say nothin'," she said softly.

Thom eyed the plug in her arm. If she had taken the wrong dosage or the wrong stims...

Milardi got there at roughly the same time. "Zatia, what's the blend?"

"Combination analgesic and a steroid blast."

"Did you use a new unit?"

Now that was an awkward pause. "Why?"

Milardi sucked on his lips. "'Cause last thing I ran in there was some serotonin flows." A pause from everyone. "Happy juice."

She nodded slowly, her eyes drifting down to the cord in her arm and the fluids actively pumping in her system.

"Yeah, I'm gon' be a few minutes, folks." Milardi slid into the room, dropping his hat onto the AutoDoc's crane arm like it was a hat rack. "Tell Oz I'll have her jacked 'n ready in ten."

Zatia eased herself into the AutoDoc bed. "Is there a chance the runt catches a bullet?"

"Oh yeah. Definitely."

"Then I'm onboard."

Nice vote of confidence. But at this point, Thom'd take a shot to the gut if it meant blue sky.

Roche laid his hand on Thom's shoulder, pulling him along. "I'm going to keep the engine warm. Assuming Milardi can get Zatia squared up, they'll be the meat and potatoes."

"What do I do?" Thom asked, eager and bright.

"You're going to be a runner."

"Oh?" Maybe he was going to be running messages? Or would he run the actual handoff, package for cash? Or, or, or—he could be running interference? That sounded like a new guy's job, keeping backup away. It wasn't glamorous, but needed doing.

Roche's computerized eye leered down at him. "When everything goes topsy turvy like? You're going to run really fast back here."

Thom sagged. "Great plan. Good stuff. I'm rocked."

"You're not a shooter, you're not a medic, you're not a lineman, you're not a jockey." Roche was very point of fact about it. "You are short on necessary skills. What you are, is an extra pair of feet. Do not underestimate how useful that can be."

Roche pushed open the cargo hold hatch. The bay was maybe half the actual ship's space, hollowed out with a scoop to allow for cargo to be stacked high and wide. A simple catwalk ran the circumference, with a ladder that ran floor to ceiling.

Most of the space was empty—tucked away into the ship's wall panels—but two panels had been removed, and a half dozen crates had been dragged into the center of the floor. Someone was shoulder deep inside one container, one foot kicking like he had failed at diving straight in.

"Osyen!"

"I've heard all about it, and 'No.'"

Thom's jaw dropped. "We only just got in here!"

Roche propped himself against the railing. "Lily told him…"

Osyen emerged from the crate, his square jaw and sharp eyebrows smeared in tomato juice. A handsome twenty-four, his feathered hair had been spiked up hilariously, bespeckled with seeds and torn red fruit. His patchwork tunic and waistcoat—a thousand patches and re-patches masquerading as clothes—were stained red above the shoulder, like someone had dipped him headfirst into a vat of thin paint.

But he hadn't lost his gravitas.

"You!" Osyen snapped, pointing at Thom. "I'm gonna handcuff

you to the satellite coil for the next three jumps. And if you live through that, we'll talk about feeding you. Ever again."

"How do you know it was me?" Not the greatest defense. It was more of the thing said when accusing the other side of cheating, not because you were innocent.

Osyen propped his hands on his hips—very near his holster and the bulky rifle strapped to it. "'Cause I know everything, Thom. I'm a god like that. Also, nobody else is that stupid!" He pointed at the crates, pulled from their hollowed wall storage. "This wasn't for us, you mollusk! It was *cargo!* It was paying for fuel we bought already!"

Osyen prowled over to the ladder and sailed up it like he expected Thom to take off running. Roche blocked him at the top of the ladder. "It's not the worst idea, Oz."

"It's a terrible idea. Angrboda is a cesspool. When your ground doesn't grow anything, you gotta steal it from somebody else. Anybody not doing crime is thinking about doin' crime."

"Didn't we snap up the boy from a cesspool of similar make?"

"He's a bullet magnet walking into a Rogue's Cross," Osyen disputed, stopping Roche's response with a raised hand. "We're getting every bad end of this set up. If Vernon is feeling spicy, it's going to get messy. This isn't one for the greenhorn to cut his teeth on."

"Due respect, Captain," Roche reflected. "He's got to cut his teeth on something."

"Yes, he does. But not *today.*" Osyen pushed past Roche, that accusatory finger locking onto Thom again. "I'm gonna have to eat the difference on this delivery. You know damn well that's coming out of your end, kid."

"I can help!" Thom blurted.

"Oh, I'm sorry," Osyen said, clutching at his damp tunic, trying to squeeze out the tomato. "I thought you were an adventure-thirsty teenager willing to risk everyone's life for a hit of adrenaline. But if you can *help...*"

"He's a—"

"'Unknown quantity.' Yeah, I heard," Osyen interrupted Roche. "I've got my ground team. We've got a plan. I'm not altering it this late in the game." Osyen looked back at Roche. "How's Zatia?"

Roche opened his mouth first, calling up the script in his logs. "'Jacked 'n ready in ten.'"

Osyen knew immediately. "What did she do?"

"I can be more than a busboy," Thom flared.

"You're selling possibilities when I need certainties. Never gamble with people's lives," Osyen critiqued. "And let that be lesson number one."

They were all lesson number one. When was lesson number two?

"Don't make that face. You're a little thief that came in here like he was owed something. The irony could choke a man." Osyen slid past Thom for the hallway.

"Got past you, didn't I?"

"Doesn't really seem like you did. You're not going," Osyen said, a hundred threats tossed over his shoulder.

Then why did he even pluck Thom out of that dead-end bar? Did he just need a punching bag? Someone to mop the floors and clean the light fixtures?

Was that really an improvement from serving drinks and washing dishes? It was the same work he'd always done since his mother died; his bed just vibrated with an engine's hum now.

It was like Osyen could read Thom's sagging stance through the back of his own head. He hung in the doorway, unable to push himself through.

He locked eyes with Roche, before finally cracking. "Thom, you didn't come in here with a pitch. You came here in with a demand. Not many folk take too well to that. You want to silver tongue your way through your problems, but you got all the subtlety of a ten-ton mining charge."

"Everybody else thinks I can go."

"This ain't a schoolyard, and I'm not your chaperone. Milardi and Zatia will have their hands full." He took a breath, clearly regretting his next words. "But Roche will be tracking the whole thing. Watch along, get some questions, *good* ones. You're gonna need to chew on something while you're handcuffed to the coils."

That was something, at least. Thom nodded, but didn't make a sound.

"Roche, make sure the cargo's unloaded and I'll talk to the Harbormaster when I get back. Official line is 'this is all they gave us.'"

"Are they going to buy that?" Roche asked.

"They will when you tell 'em. If he doesn't, I'll talk to him—when I get back," Osyen reassured, but he muttered something else under his breath, "Assuming I don't get shrap in my liver."

CHAPTER
TWO
OSYEN

HE LET his eyes linger on the pocked and crusted hull, singed from a hundred re-entries and tough scrapes. It needed a new paint job or the enamel would rot off and they'd discover that oversight just in time to melt in the upper atmosphere.

Fabulous. He'd have to set aside a job just to pay for that.

Osyen leaned on the hood of the harbor taxi, fingers picking at his leg and the leather holster. He could feel cracks in the straps, the scaly grip of his rifle, rough like a file against his fingers. The boxy frame of the magnetic accelerator might have been considered out-moded or garish, but he liked being able to push a forty-caliber hunk of metal clean through any armor. That craggy handle was like his safety blanket.

And his fingers were dancing across it today.

How fast can you spin her up, Lily? he asked, pushing the thought backward. The doctor had described it as trying to talk out of the other side of your head. It was a muscle, like any other—weird as Hell is what it was, but it was very convenient.

Radio required sound, but if you put the transmitter directly into contact with the brain, you don't even need to speak to hear.

He felt their voice echo back through the communicator

implanted somewhere in his skull, where it made him sick to think about: *Expecting trouble, are we?*

You didn't answer the question.

Lily pouted. *Bring me a present, maybe I'll be nice.*

There's absolutely nothing on this backwater you want, I promise you that. He paused, remembering the absolutely divine goulash he had from a street vendor last time he was here. *No. Wait. I've got it.*

What is it?

You'll see.

Lily buzzed with happy, their version of goosebumps. *Come back alive.*

He didn't answer. It always felt like lying.

The hum of Angrboda leaked in over the hangar bay's crumbling sandstone walls, a mixture of excitement and gossiping chatter. Who were these strangers? Why had they come? And like a ripple in water, the news spread.

Tomatoes. They brought fresh fruit for sale. A rich man was about to get richer. They would sell their stock wholesale and he would turn around and sell it directly to their slavering face-holes.

But like true peons, they didn't look for the deal inside the deal. Why would he have ferried fruit to a backwater like theirs at all? To what did they owe this surprise luxury? Gift horses and hungry mouths urged them to bury any suspicion.

Osyen played with the toggles on his bag. Brass, scuffed and cold to the touch. Time to play a little shell game.

Milardi sauntered down the gangway, all flourish with his long-coat and hat—he looked like he fell out of a young girl's sketchbook of a dark and handsome stranger on a smoky horizon.

Milardi could see Osyen's lingering eyes, and rapped his knuckles on his chest—the coat was masking a hardened chest plate.

Osyen smirked. "Style over substance."

"Jus' make sure you get both!" Milardi quipped back.

"How much that set you back?"

"Not much," Milardi said, hopping up into the car. "The last guy didn't get much use out of it."

"You killed him for it, didn't you?"

Milardi smiled like he was charming a girl in a bar as he tapped his temple. "Chest plate don't do nothing for the head, Cap'n."

Osyen might've sounded more encouraging than he meant. "You make me sick in all the best ways."

Zatia marched on down the gangway, cracking her little neck. "You got the package?" Osyen tossed her a messenger bag, to her bemusement. "Why me?"

"Not you," Osyen said, as he tossed another bag to Milardi, "Everybody."

"I like it," Milardi smiled. "Any one o' us could be carrying. Nobody's a walking' bulls'er."

'Walking Bullseye.' Osyen had learned to translate Milardi into something reasonable pretty quickly or they'd have spent half of their professional time alternating between 'huh' and 'what?'

"Plan A?" Zatia asked, as she settled herself into the car—sitting in that stiff and awkward manner someone does when they have invisible weapons defining where you can bend. She looked rigid like a robot with creaking joints, but to Osyen, she just read as a smooth bore slugger on the left leg. Her bracelets hung heavy on her wrists, the spring-loaded blades within positively aching for oxygen.

"Plan A is they take the package, we get paid. Everybody walks away happy."

Zatia raised an eyebrow, with a knowing smirk. "That is some riveting detail you got there."

"If you like Plan A, you'll love Plan B."

"Plan B?"

"Plan B, I just let you two have fun," Osyen said with a smirk, "Zatia will take some high ground and wait for my signal. Milardi, you're the enforcer today."

Milardi shivered, exaggerated. "I hate plan B."

"You're getting soft and lazy," Zatia teased Osyen with a shove.

"Maybe I make you do most of the killing this time, you start planning more."

"Can't plan for the unexpected, Zatia," Osyen said.

"'Unexpected' is what my parents called me," she quipped right back, "but it's not an excuse."

Osyen reached for the taxi cab's handle—struggling with the rusted hinge before yanking it open with an obnoxious creak. "Just follow my lead and don't shoot nobody you don't have to."

They all stiffened a bit as their implants crackled to life.

We're all squared here, Oz. Solid link, video stuttering with the atmo interference, but we should be okay.

Osyen glanced up at the blunted nose of the *Aurum*, a bird's beak looming over their heads. Somewhere inside that was the command deck, where the ship's many video screens streamed input from the ground team. Roche and his many implants could stream all of those feeds at once into his head—but he likely had the screens up for the kid's benefit.

They saw what he saw.

Should be instructive. Maybe if Thom came along vicariously, he'd settle down for a few jumps.

Or sour him on this whole business.

Thanks, Roche, Osyen bounced back. *Anything in the skies?*

Some odd Naval chatter but nothing in orbit. You'll be the first to know.

Unti's not on the party channel, is he? Milardi's lips cracked into a grin.

No, Roche bounced, *his permissions are still restricted.*

"So if we call him a runty ol' bundle of mop water," announced Zatia, echoing in the hangar bay, "he can't hear us?"

Milardi raised a hand like he might interject, but then he got it. "You meant for him to hear that."

Osyen rolled his eyes. *Roche, we'll see you when we get back.*

We'll be seeing you the whole time, Oz. Happy crimes and all.

———

The taxi murmured underneath them, complaints mostly, like a crotchety old man. Someone had carefully built and rebuilt it from new parts over many years. Osyen doubted anything in it was original. Not unusual to see in these Reacher colonies or even among collectors in the Core worlds, but it always made Osyen nervous that the whole contraption could just come unspooled underneath him.

This had been someone's baby once upon a time, a passion project to keep the hands busy. Those hands must've dropped it in despair. Some retiree, hearing of the wonders of the Reaches, takes his baby project out to spend his autumn years—forced to abandon it when this bad bet forces him back into the work force.

It had been conventional enough wisdom. Everyone thought they could live comfortable out here, quiet. Osyen wanted to have a one-on-one with whatever Ad Man sold everyone that poison pill.

The town blurring past him out the window was little more than mud-huts with thatched roofs of spun grass and twine. It looked positively medieval—except that the local materials made for a more pastel palette. Without industry or commercial backing, colonists were left to homestead with whatever expertise they had.

It would be cheery, but for the looks of reverence from each person they passed. Mothers redirecting the gaze of their children, men with leering eyes as they tilled fields by hand.

By hand. They came two dozen jumps out from Sol without so much as a reactor. Some people had such aspirations...

Who was he to judge? He was tumbling about the universe in a—

In a what?

Oh come on, Lily. We're two broken conductor cables away from living with these folk, that's all.

Speak for yourself, Osyen. I intend to be kind to my future serfs.

Osyen shook his head. *Let me know how that domination thing shakes out for you.*

Oh Osyen, Lily cooed, *I would never do it without you.*

"Real charming, this place," Zatia chirped.

Milardi chuckled. "Like you seen much better?"

"Just looks too much like home." It was an oddly reflective thought from the little monster. "I want to burn it." That's more like it.

Thankfully, Angrboda had no major storms or crime gangs or Zatias to worry about. If they did, the whole colony would have been swept under the rug of history in a few days of futile squirming.

"Still think bringing *Unti* was a good notion?" Osyen asked.

Milardi hemmed, hawed, and ultimately shrugged. "I dons, no. But he made that face he makes and I jus..."

Osyen smiled. He knew the face well enough, like a begging puppy. Kid's big cartoon eyes and floppy hair had been just as pathetic and adorable in the Pantry as it was scouring the grating of the *Aurum*. He looked up at Osyen, captain of a brig and self-made man, and suddenly Osyen felt twice as tall.

The petulance had been a newer, more frustrating development. The kid was getting impatient.

Angrboda would've eaten the boy for a midafternoon snack. By this place's standard, Thom was a moneyed individual and naïve enough to take someone's word at face value. Malice and cruelty came from evil; crime came from desperation.

The taxi slowed to a crawl in front of Angrboda's twin mansions. You knew the rich man in town because he had stairs to his second story—he could afford an entire thatch-roofed cottage for his first cottage house to wear as a hat. And in between the two largest homes in town was the designated Crime Alley—not like there was a second alley in town to compete with it.

Crime Alley was deserted, as expected. Semi-permanent stalls of cloth and wooden poles hung empty, woven baskets hastily emptied and dropped where they fell. It looked as though the place had been looted. But that was Angrboda's aesthetic anyway.

Osyen kicked his creaking door open and stepped out of the taxi.

You know your places, he ordered, leaning over to the duster-wearing rogue, "Work hard, Milardi."

"Play hard, boss-man," came the response with a devilish grin.

"If you die, I'm taking your room," Zatia said, as she pulled the door closed. Pulling up the proverbial draw bridge.

And with that, the taxi zipped off.

Come alone with the package, that was the only way to get paid. It was a request favoring the buyer heavily. And it also had a nickname in friendly circles:

The Rogue's Cross.

The marker they laid on the shallow graves of criminals. Also, a double-cross planned from the start.

Angrboda's hum of life had been scraped out of the air, the deserted alleyway more akin to a ghostly ruin.

Osyen marched into Crime Alley, with the psychotic confidence of a man out for a stroll on a sunny day in the park. It was actually quite temperate out, and the smell of cut grass pervaded—if he wasn't there on horribly dangerous business, he might even enjoy it.

But this was a work day.

Out from behind merchant stalls and trash piles came a handful of surly looking men. They were hardly brutal criminals or brigands married to the lifestyle—these were just desperate people, willing to buy what was for sale.

Whatever the price. Osyen noted their white knuckles steeling themselves for what came next.

"Osyen Belt, I take it?" One called out. He was the littlest of the bunch, with a bowl cut probably executed with the long fishing knife in his boot. And based on the multitude of tiny scars on his face, he was none too careful with that blade. The man swaggered forward— pistol on his right hip, not even making an effort to hide it.

Osyen shifted the messenger bag on his hip. "Where's Vernon?"

"Vernon got held up," the ringleader pronounced, like it was some dramatic reveal. Blah blah blah.

Osyen windmilled his hand. "Who are you then, his cousin?"

"I'm Family," he said with a curious emphasis, "if that's what you're asking."

He sighed. This guy had already made his choice. Vernon sent him to buy the goods with blood. But Vernon was also a Coward, capital 'C'. He was going to find his little gang overpowered, outmaneuvered, outplayed—

Don't get distracted, Oz. Roche shot over the line.

I'm easing in.

Roche's scolding tone could even be made out in brain patterns. *You're screwing around.*

Please, Osyen bounced back, *children screw around.*

Roche jumped on that. *Yes, they do.*

Ouch.

"Well, if you've got the money..." Osyen started, "not sure I care who's doing the buyin'."

"Whatever's convenient for *you?*"

Osyen shook his head. "Not much in my life has been convenient for me. You take pleasure in what you can. Vernon tell you what you were buying or are you just jumpin' the line?"

The man sneered, like he was in control of this situation. "I think you've figured out by now...we're not buying. We're taking."

Oh, he was really going to tee it up like that?

"I think you've figured out by now..." Osyen lifted his messenger bag from his shoulder, and dumped its contents of four tomatoes to the floor, all juice and soft meat. "I'm not selling."

A grunt whimpered as the fruit splattered to the floor, what few small joys he had ever seen in this dank and horrible world had just splattered on the dirt.

Wasted. Like his dreams of a happy married life and affluent airs.

But the ringleader just chuckled to himself. "You think we're after that...trinket? Osyen, we want your ship." The crew laughed, pulled clubs and bits of pipe from behind their backs. "That's the real prize. And whatever's inside...that's just a shiny bonus."

Osyen pursed his lips. "Mid-size brig. Working Jump Drive,

twelve pound per cubic cargo, roughly six hundred entries on the chassis...it's not stylish, but it's worth some effort, sure. AI can be a little spotty..."

It's actually thirteen pounds, Osyen. Lily practically bit the back of his head off.

"Excuse me, I've been informed it's thirteen pounds. So...better."

The ringleader sniffed the dirt out of his nose, the slime and disgust mixing into an ugly paste. "It's not a bad planet to be marooned on, you know, given your other options."

Osyen took a deep breath of that sweet air. "No, it's really not. But it's a pretty bad ship."

This is starting to feel personal.

Osyen smiled. "Do I have a second offer?"

"Poor little Osyen, all alone," the ringleader hissed, tapping at his holster. He nodded to his goons. "Obviously can't have you running back to Harbor to warn the rest of your crew."

They were watching back at the *Aurum*—probably panicking in no small amount—as the thugs circled him. Little Thom must be screeching out theories, sketching out elaborate plans, overreacting, and generally bouncing off the walls. Roche was probably regretting being his advocate.

Because this was going to be funny.

"Take 'em." Osyen projected so his voice would echo off the walls.

The circle stopped, looking back and forth for whatever Osyen had signaled for. But there was nothing but the whistle of the wind.

Osyen chewed on his cheek. The ringleader drew his pistol out, thumbing the capacitor—the sharp warm hum betrayed the nature of the weapon.

Osyen had been shot before—by energy and ballistic—but given a choice, he really liked the lead. Lead tore at you, ripped a hole and made you leak. Energy burned, and there was the smell, like someone dropped meat into the cast iron to sizzle and dance about.

Holes you patch; burns you only cover.

Milardi, wherever you're at, make yourself known right now.

"Expecting an ace in the hole, Osyen?"

There was the man of the hour. Osyen raised his hands up, in the universal sign of surrender as he glanced over his shoulder. Milardi stood with tight lips, hands up and pride firmly in his shoes. A doughy businessman crapped out by the Default Businessman Factory, complete with an infuriating goatee and frayed suit, held a pistol to the giant rogue's midsection—or probably his butt, given the height difference.

"...Vernon," chided Osyen, "you're a little testy today."

"I should be." Vernon pushed Milardi forward to Osyen's side. "Given how you shafted my boy on Daymar, I'm impressed you showed your face at all."

Daymar. Daymar, Daymar...Osyen picked his brain but nothing came to him. "Vernon, why, with all the spit and vinegar I have, would I go to Daymar? There's like...four shacks there."

"You calling me a liar now?" Vernon wasn't angered by the insinuation. He held a gun, the money, and the property—he didn't care one lick what Osyen said. The failings of his victims were adorable.

How's that Plan A working for you? Milardi asked. His accent just melted away when he was bouncing on the radio. He didn't have to sneak the words past his stupid face.

Was supposed to be on Plan B by now. Where is Zee?

I'm coming, I'm coming! Buy me a second! She grumped.

Buy time? He could do that. He could buy her till sunset.

"Bowl cut back there? Is that your boy?" Osyen asked.

"My boy's dead, Osyen." Vernon scowled. "Left in a pool of his own fluids. Twelve years old." His lip quivered, but his eyes were firm. He'd had some time with that information, to stew in it. But there wasn't hate in his heart.

Well, that complicated things.

Osyen tried to avoid shifting his weight and drawing unnecessary gunfire. If anybody thought he was reaching for a weapon..."I shoot when I'm shot at, Vernon. Not before. And I swear on my ship, I wasn't on Daymar. Look in the log."

"Oh, I will. Because it's my ship now, Osyen. And that doesn't even *begin* to make this trade fair." Vernon could hardly control his venom, spittle tossed into the air. "But I'm no murderer. We're good people!" He spat that one at Osyen's feet. "So...I paid a price. So will you."

Fine. It's going to be like that. *Zatia, any day now.*

She slid off the rooftop, still coming out of her sprint. The pixie with a shotgun landed right behind the ringleader, about as graceful as a brick. He heard her land, and spun around, leading with his pistol grip to the side of her head.

Osyen heard the crunch.

Maybe it was cushioned by her stupid pigtails, or maybe her juice kept her pumping. But she struck him right back with the butt of her shotgun, lifting him clean off his feet and cracking the house wall he slammed into.

Poor boy almost certainly broke his jaw, on the wall or on the gun. The goon squad turned to match her, but she had the shotgun to his dazed little head. "I will paint the walls with whatever sits in his brainpan."

Everyone froze. Hands gripped pipe, wrapped pistols. But everyone took that moment to breathe.

Osyen let his hand drift across that rugged grip of his rifle.

Vernon spoke first: "What's your wager, Osyen?"

Osyen tilted his head. "I don't gamble, Vernon. You lost when you decided not to pay me. And one last time, I didn't kill your son. I'm a conman, not a killer."

Vernon scanned him up and down, finger drifting in and out of the trigger guard of his pistol. And his eyes wavered. The first time today Osyen hadn't lied to him and he smelled it, the truth.

The man slackened. "You expecting me to apologize, I take it?"

"My entire life, I have never expected an apology, Vernon. They never come."

Zatia nudged the ringleader with her muzzle, more like she was trying to elicit his fear than telegraph anything to Vernon. She was in her own little world back there, and the ring was closing in.

Vernon didn't have to be in the right. He could still placate his rage right here, kill three objectively bad people. Then take his rage to the sky...would that be so wrong?

Osyen didn't relish the thought of triggers, but he flexed his fingers.

Oz, I've got some rather apocalyptic news. And here was the sidewinder.

What now, Roche?

Eisenclad dreadnought just jumped into low orbit. Lily's off-line. They took the Aurum before we even knew they were here. You have to run.

He smelled it first, that crackle in the air. It smelled like a chemistry lab, like phosphor or kerosene. Somebody was having a really godawful bonfire.

Bonfire?

"Vernon..." Osyen asked, "how big of a mess was Daymar?"

He scrunched up his face, like he tasted the air but hadn't quite put it together yet. "It was a massacre. Took them three days to sort my boy out of the mess."

Milardi took a half-step forward, the doctor in him coming out. "What'n Hell happened?"

Vernon was shaking now, tendons pulling tight in his neck. He wasn't retelling; he was reliving the moment. "I offered to buy it. You said you could sell it. That, to me, said you were there. You *said* you had it."

That smell was getting nice and hot now, filling the air. A re-entry burn.

Osyen, you prideful, arrogant stupid son of a—pull a random con and what had he tripped on?!

"Get down!" Osyen shouted, grabbing Milardi by the jacket

collar and falling to the ground. He could've bounced it to just his people. But he genuinely meant it for everyone.

Vernon, the ringleader, everyone. Get down. Or die.

Vernon pulled the trigger, more out of surprise. He was a businessman after all, no trained gunhand. So when everyone jumped, his finger tightened in the well. To Osyen's great happiness, he also tightened at the wrist, pulling his shot.

The beam still scored a hot line across Osyen's shoulder—the polymer coating of his jacket could only protect him so much. But had it not struck him, it would have bored a hole in Milardi's pretty face.

Osyen might have even been in pain, but he was too busy noticing the drop pod slam into the ground behind Vernon.

The brittle steel egg bit into the earth, shedding its four panels on impact like they were spring loaded. It tossed the six-foot metal shards—wedging them into stone walls and even pinning two of Vernon's goons.

They might've been alive. Osyen didn't really care to check right now.

A man stood in the remaining frame of the pod, sable black hair cut high and tight, and a lean build with veins strung along his muscles like fiber. He stood tall on mechanical stilts, and metal gloves encased his hands. Gun ports, micro missile arrays, and even a shield generator were stacked onto the back. There were more weapons on this exoskeletal demon than there were on most cruisers.

The man spoke, authoritative and—clearly—from a script: "Stand down and prepare for Imperial adjudication."

Orbital Strike Command—an Oskie, full Warcom exosuit, locked and rocked for a war zone.

Who the Hell were *they* here for?

One brilliant savant swung his bit of pipe at the Oskie. He caught the swing with one skeletal fist. "Assaulting a peace officer during his duties," the Oskie stated as matter-of-factly as if he were reading the actual regulation. He reached his other hand over, pressing into the thug's chest—levering the poor guy's arm right from its socket like he was pulling apart candy.

The goon couldn't scream. The pain had robbed him of his voice. Blood spurted from the pit in his shoulder. It did not spray or burst forth, but rather...drained out onto the ground.

"Punishable up to the discretion of the officer."

The goons scattered like rats from daylight. But Osyen held Milardi down.

Don't run. He'll catch you, Osyen bounced, *and he'll make you pay for running.*

So what do we do? Zatia asked, as she lowered her shotgun to the ground.

We do, Roche chimed in, likely staring down his own ugly situation, *whatever the nice men in power armor say we should do.*

CHAPTER
THREE
THOM

IS this what criminals saw right before they were branded Capitals for life? A man in a uniform shows up, shouts at you? Then they paste tape over your eyes and lead you roughly from hot room to hot room. Finally, the tape simply falls off and you are alone in a blank white room, to wait for whatever comes next.

The cuffs felt like they might scald him and mark him forever—with what, he didn't know, but he was sure everyone everywhere would see it and build their own story. He could tell them the truth: he was a cabin boy for a conman, aspiring but not committed. And they would assume he was lying, that it could only be something worse. Perhaps he'd been a slaver or a murderer or a political dissident?

What would his father say? When he found out? He might scream and rage, threaten and spit. He might say nothing at all and rotate the jeweled ring on his finger. If you're going to leave a mark, leave a statement.

Thom's shoulder was cramping up. And sand grew at the corners of his eyes, rough and solid, like it might grow to encase his eyelids and hold them open forever. Tears didn't help, he'd figured that out.

Staring directly into the impossibly bright lights instead dried the eyes, worsening the gravel etching patterns under his eyelids. Except, he now also had lovely sparkling dots in the center of his vision to multiply his pain.

Thom hadn't seen the others in what felt like days. But it was hard to tell any kind of passage of time.

His cell was reflective metal or glass, and from somewhere 'behind' them were the bright lights, shining in but not revealing their position. It made the room a solid light source, washing out any and all features. They might as well have been keeping him in the center of a star.

About as lonely too. Even the buzzing of the lights had become a dull background, a white noise masking any other that he might hear. Even his own voice was garbled, it seemed.

They worked out what would cause him discomfort and played at their dials. More light, some sound dampening buzzing with no distinct source. Let's heat his chains but cool the floor, air humid like fog—anything to make the boy sweat.

He had explored what reach his chains had allowed. It might have been the entire cell or just his empty corner of an entire deck. With no way to judge edges or touch them, his void could be endless.

"They can't hold you here forever," Thom said out loud to himself, trying to force any noise over the top of that insufferable buzzing. "They'll have questions or a court to...to bring you to. Come on, Thom. Plan your escape."

You're really going to say that out loud, have that one on record? Nice.

So the door opens, then what? Assuming there is a door. What do you do? Sweet talk the guard or plead innocence? Oh! You were just the child hostage, an indentured slave even. They didn't tell you anything other than where the food *wasn't*. You could tell them all about the scouring and latrine panning you had to do.

Wait, why was he trying to protect them? They had him scouring the grating and panning latrines.

Because if Osyen hadn't plucked him out of the Pantry, he'd be scouring grates and panning latrines in a Duster colony nowhere, tucked away from life and world.

It might not have been good, but life on the *Aurum* was better.

"I'm not going to tell you anything!" he cried out, "So get on with...with whatever, okay?"

Maybe they were listening after all.

The lights dimmed, the translucent walls revealing their secrets for half a second—panels of lights tucked behind the bulkheads—before the walls seemed to thicken and grow solid, like they were filled in with a steel fog.

One panel slid aside—and in came Osyen, hands and feet cuffed. Thom couldn't restrain a tiny squeak as he saw the burn scar on his shoulder.

Osyen was shoved by invisible hands, stumbling in and catching himself on the ground with his cheekbone. The flesh slap reverb hung heavy on his ears, like a melon hitting the ground. And for the longest time, Thom wasn't certain that Osyen was alive.

Until a hissing suck of breath and a swell of the chest.

Thom fell to his knees at Osyen's side, "Are you alright?"

Osyen choked out, "No, I'm not alright!" His tone softened, as he saw Thom recoil. "But thanks for asking."

With his hands bound behind him, Osyen rocked to-and-fro before he could properly flop onto his back. Only then did Thom see the extent of his injuries—yellowed bruises to the face and neck, a burn scar on his shoulder only topically treated with sticky gauze, and a curious swelling to his right eye.

He had been beaten.

Thom must've made a noise of shock, because Osyen chuckled. "Yeah, they got me all dolled up for the party tonight. What's wrong? Bad color on me?"

"Yeah," was all Thom could force out of his mouth.

"Dammit." Osyen grimaced past a wave of pain. "I told 'em to stay in the earth tones but he's going on and on."

"What were they asking?"

Osyen sighed, leering up at the kid. "Questions I didn't have the answers to."

Did he think Thom was part of this? They didn't even ask him any questions. Or was this also part of the interrogation? Stick them together, see what they do. Do they turn on each other like starving goblins or try to compare stories?

"We should stop talking."

Osyen cocked his head, and the glimmer of a smirk cracked through the pain. "Well, I mean...they bought tickets to the show and we're not going to sing?"

Thom side-eyed the discolored face of the rogue next to him, rolling on to his own handcuffed wrists. "Sore throat."

Osyen chuckled, but squinted with focus, "See, it's that artificial crap you keep drinking. You gotta get yourself a hook up of real gen-u-ine double A honey." With a pop, a groan and a flourish, Osyen slid his hands out from underneath him. His thumb hung strangely on his left hand, in a very unnatural position. "Mix it in tea and you'll bounce right back."

"The genuine tomatoes were terrible."

"Yeah, well," Osyen said, "they're not really food. They're just an ingredient."

"Osyen?"

"Yeah kid?"

"Did you just break your *gulaw* finger?"

"Don't cuss, kid," he scolded through gritted teeth as he grabbed the bad thumb in his good hand, "it just shows you're out of control."

"Did you—"

Another sickening pop and Osyen moaned in relaxation, the pain taking one last stab at him before marching away into the sunset, ushering in sweet relief. He shook out the nerves from the hand. "No, just popped it. We're fine. We're all fine now."

Osyen sucked in a few good breaths of the musty air. It likely smelled of Thom's sweat and fear, stale and swampy, but it was heaven-sent to him at the moment.

Thom plopped down next to him on the floor. "You heard from the others?"

Osyen raised an eyebrow. "If anybody's out there, they're not answering."

"It's a curious technology, Mr. Belt." Thom didn't see him come in, but there was suddenly a man behind him. He flinched and fell to the floor beside Osyen.

The man was tall, regal, stiff as a board, in a crisp naval uniform. His wasp-like narrow waist and long legs were common traits aboard cruisers, but this man took that lean physique to an unsettling level—never unhealthy or monstrous, but just too far into the land of strange. His hair was perfectly coifed, as if each strand bore the same discipline laced into every other fragment of him, from bone to sinew.

He considered Thom with hollow eyes, the way a spider does a fly before wrapping it up for dinner. "The service disregarded it due to the health risks, but personally, I admire your...audacity."

"Oh, hey. You again. Hi." Osyen groused, the fire that had been stirring instantly doused again. He gestured to his swollen eye. "Here to make me symmetrical?"

The spider didn't respond to Osyen, directing his words to Thom. "The Navy extends its condolences on behalf of your mother, Thomas."

Aw, Hell.

Osyen shot a half dozen accusations Thom's way in just a single cold glance. How did this military robot know squat about the cabin boy? He demanded answers, but all Thom could give was an apologetic shrug.

He had lived for so long out of sight. Did he really remember, after all this time? Unlikely.

Thom stumbled over his words. "That was...it was a year...Th-thank you. Who are you?"

"I'm Captain Jeremiah Stride," the spider said with his smooth and gravelly voice. He raised a single scolding finger, waggling it as if he could tut-tut at him with sign language alone. "And you're not where you're supposed to be."

Osyen spoke up, "If he did something, he didn't tell us."

"I assure you, Mr. Belt, this aside is nothing but a happy coincidence," Stride purred, far too pleased with himself and only letting it out in the pauses between his words. "And should not concern you one bit."

"Kid's on my crew," Osyen bit back, "so it concerns me a few bits."

Osyen was standing up for him. Maybe there was a little trust left. Thom got the feeling that was being intentionally pulled apart.

"Not anymore," Stride lamented. "This boy is in the safe custody of the Imperial Navy."

"What'll happen to them?" Thom chirped, trying to get ahead of this rolling catastrophe.

Stride tilted his head, studying. "In a hurry, Thomas?"

"What'll happen to them?"

Stride pursed his lips. "Most will be sent to the Core worlds for their trials. Mr. Belt here..." Stride lingered, as if he could taste the name in his mouth, something bitter and wholesome. Filling. "Mr. Belt has an appointment to keep with a Warden on Charon."

Charon was a prison world, largely for processing fresh Capital convicts. Thom looked at his captain, "You're a Capital?"

Osyen rolled his eyes. Maybe he'd been expecting this twist, or maybe it was just Stride's melodrama getting to him finally.

Stride turned his eyes on to Osyen. "Did you tell them your real name?"

"Osyen is my real name."

"Your birth name?"

Osyen sneered. "That person's dead."

"Convenient." Stride sighed. "Just know, Mr. Belt, that the Capital camps don't care what your name is. Criminals like you have lost the right to it." Stride tried to hide the hissing breath he took through his nose but he made no such attempt to hide the flash of glee in his eyes. "I could kill you where you stand and nothing would come of it. You only live now because I allow it."

"Thank you very much," Osyen scoffed, "I appreciate that."

"Capital?" The word just fell out of Thom's mouth.

"You don't get to act shocked about secrets, Navy boy," Osyen spat back. "Mine didn't get an entire crew swiped."

"You misunderstand, Mr. Belt," Stride chimed in, "we weren't there for him. We were there for *you*. For the Icon."

Osyen cursed under his breath. "I said it in the first, third, and fourth rooms. I've been selling knock-offs."

"You're an opportunist, Mr. Belt." There was the voice Thom had been expecting. Thom turned to see the old man standing opposite them. Again, no idea how or when he had entered. A naturally doughy man hiding his bald spot with a stiff naval cap, pale skin, and full pink lips like he had recently drank from a goblet of blood.

"Hello, father," Thom leaked out, weary of the theater.

Rear Admiral 2nd Grade, 3rd Naval Bombardment Wing, Ulysses Hugh—he signed every letter with the full title like they were words of power.

When Thom looked back, Stride had vanished. Thom had never been in a holding cell before. Were they holograms, or was he simply going a touch mad with the isolation?

Hugh stepped forward, immediately laying a commanding hand on his son's shoulder. Nope, they were really there.

"Why did you leave?" He wasn't asking. He was compelling. Even through the formal fawn gloves, Thom could feel the icy grip.

"Sorry," Osyen chimed in, "did I have him out past curfew?"

"Speak out of turn again, Capital, and I will have your tongue dragged out of your throat," Hugh snapped, in that stiff and crisp manner that always preceded a belligerent outburst.

Hugh gripped on Thom's shoulder harder, trying to squeeze an answer out, but the sting stole his voice. Soon would be the open hand to paint his face red and then—

"Why *am* I alive?" Osyen asked. "Capital renegades are shoot on sight, aren't we?"

Hugh released Thom's shoulder, turning to the crumpled man on the floor. "You sold no less than five copies of the Icon to different buyers."

Osyen sat up with a huff. "What, you uh...you want one for your cabin?"

"In a sense."

Osyen's eyes slid left and right, like he was checking in with an audience. Was he the only one who just heard that? "You want the *real* one?"

"Who doesn't?" Hugh grunted.

Thom watched the two exchange words, a rally back and forth, and with each retort, Osyen got weaker and weaker.

"I don't have it, and you've torn my ship apart by now. You know I'm not lying."

"What if I told you, I know who does?" Hugh inquired.

Osyen took a breath—maybe his last—before answering, "I'd say you have an Eisenclad dreadnought and the meanest military in the universe. Go get it."

"It's not quite so simple," Hugh said, sitting down—into the chair that rose up seamlessly out of the floor like it had always been there. What was truly disconcerting, was that more of the white material was underneath it, as though the room was made of layers and layers of the articulated eggshell plating. "This requires a softer hand."

Thom stared at the side of the Admiral's head, as though the old man would ever notice he was there. He wanted a religious relic? Why? He arrested them on Angrboda looking for it. Why? He would go so far as to hire criminals and renegades to hunt it down for him, but not ask for formal Imperial assistance?

Admiral Ulysses Hugh was being a very bad boy, himself. The idea of his father misbehaving was almost charming.

"The Icon is being held in an...unfriendly region of space. If Imperial presence is detected, they'll bury it—and we'll lose it for another two hundred years." Hugh smirked. "Need I remind you, no one in this room has that much spare time on their hands. I need someone outside the military, connected to the underworld, to safely extract it."

Osyen chuckled, failing to mask the pain that shock sent through him. "Extract it? You make it sound so sexy."

The Admiral shook his head, just so slightly, almost like a disapproving shiver. Thom had seen it a thousand times, and this time shot adrenaline through his system just like every other. Red Flag Number One.

"This is a highly classified undertaking and sharing it with you is a breach of protocol. One that I can patch quite easily, Mr. Belt."

"What do I get?" Osyen grumbled, trying to project strength he didn't have.

Hugh smiled. "The thanks of a grateful Empire that lets you scrape out a Dusty living in the Reach. Of course, you could say 'no' and I could have you back in a mining camp by the end of the year, where you belong...Capital."

Thom wanted to jump in, interject, deflect, defend—do something! But he could still feel the memory of those icy fingers on his shoulder, their sting like the dead of space.

Osyen glanced over at him. The cocky and braggadocious man that had burned so hot on the ship, that had kindled to warmth in the cell just minutes ago, had been extinguished. He was not the master of his fate; no, today he was in chains. "Don't seem like I have a lot of choice."

Hugh smiled, almost wholesomely satisfied with how he played the game today, like he didn't quite understand or care that human lives were behind each of these chess moves. "No, but then again Mr. Belt, in the end, none of us do."

"So who has it?"

"I believe you're professionally acquainted with them: Fiona McCorty."

Now it was Osyen's turn to laugh, a small pained chuckle. "Admiral, whoever blows these sweet nothings in your ear is getting paid way too much."

"And you're being paid with freedom, Mr. Belt. Try not to laugh it all away in one afternoon." Red Flag Two. Casually tossing insults. The worst was yet to come.

"Fiona McCorty..." Osyen mused. "She won't have it on her mantlepiece."

"What do you need?" Hugh asked, positively diplomatic.

Osyen grimaced, grinding his teeth. "I'll need to pull together some people. I need expertise I don't have on hand."

The Admiral sighed, his patience with this thinning. And Thom would be the undue recipient of that fragmentation.

"A lineman, for one. Specialist in archaic security. Pirates like Fiona won't be guarding this thing with heuristics and computers; they'll have it in a hydraulic sealed box buried in a rock. On top of that, I'll need a hook, some backer with enough goodwill that can open the right doors for my team."

"I will not commit Imperial personnel, but we might have some... suggestions for you."

"Don't worry your pretty little head, Admiral, I've got ideas of my own. And my people will need financing."

The Admiral's eyes narrowed. "That can all be arranged."

Naval funding ending up in the hands of pirates? How badly did he want this thing?

Osyen's voice rasped. "What about the boy?"

What about the boy, Thom thought.

"He'll return to Sol with me." Was it venom or ice with which he spoke? Either would kill Thom, just the same. Through neglect or attention, Thom would suffer.

Earth, confined to an apartment, with no sky to see, no air to breathe, no fresh food. No people. Tucked away under the stairs where he couldn't be an embarrassment. Naval admiralty were paid handsomely for their service, but bars that are gilded are still bars.

Maybe Osyen could see the panic, the shivers. Because Osyen

wasn't staring at Thom—he was looking at Thom's shoulder, where Hugh's hand had taken a bite. "No," Osyen whispered, "that there's a deal breaker."

Hugh nodded, resigned to the result. He reached for his sidearm. "That's your decision."

"No, I mean—" Osyen's mind raced behind his eyes, digging and digging. "I *need* him. Thom's the best."

Thom's stomach flipped over in his gut. What the Hell was Osyen on about?

"Excuse me?" Hugh asked the question before Thom could.

"He's the best confidence man I've ever seen. You want to talk your way past a guard, build up a shopkeep, or crack an agent—he's a wizard. It's not even fair. He's six steps ahead of everybody this side of Outlander Station."

Okay, now he was just plain lying. But Thom wasn't going to stop him.

Hugh glowered at his son out of the corner of his eye. "If he were exceptional at anything at all, I'd know by now."

"Due respect, Admiral," Osyen interrupted, "If you know a good con-man, he's *not*. The good ones...you'll never know they were there. They prime, they spike, they get the Hell out. If you're a legend at this, if people know your name? Retire. You're no use to anybody. Good conmen don't exist—they don't take curtain calls and they don't want 'em." Hugh opened his mouth, but Osyen jumped right down his throat. "I can't do it without him, Admiral. That I promise you. You're welcome to send in an armada and take your chances. You're welcome to hire another team. But you won't, 'cause nobody else friendly with Fiona McCorty is within your reach. You *need* me. And Thom...he's on my team. Deal with it."

Hugh stood up. Dragging one foot in front of the other right up to Osyen's side. He crouched down, cupping the young man's face in his hands—eager to lift the pirate's head right off his shoulders. "If anything happens to my boy...I will visit hellfire on you."

He was actually letting Thom go on this adventure. Thom's heart

51

did a little jig before suddenly collapsing in his chest. He wanted this 'Icon' more than he wanted his son home. The realization hit him so hard it could've broken ribs.

Osyen smiled, revealing his blood-stained teeth. "Admiral, if something happens to your boy, that's only because I'm already dead. Now where's my ship?"

CHAPTER
FOUR
THOM

THE BAGS CAME off their heads and the cuffs off their wrists only after they were deep back inside the *Aurum*. All Thom saw of their captors was their retreating backs down the gangway. Osyen rubbed at his wrists and sauntered back in towards the galley. He probably thought Thom couldn't see, but Osyen was shaking from head to toe.

He had been a Capital. And he'd come so close to being one again.

They sat in silence for a time. Maybe Osyen was just counting his blessings—or his curses. He ran his fingers back and forth across the *Aurum*'s galley table, feeling every scratch and dent, each one setting off a memory full of flavor and sounds.

He was saying goodbye.

"I'm sorry," Thom started, not sure what else to say. Please, please, just understand—

"For what, *Unti?*" Osyen barked. "Sorry for what?"

His eyes were dark darts, thin little specks of black against the auburn brown. They tracked Thom's face like they were stenciling something onto him—or burning it.

"How could I know he was going to be there?"

"Kid." Osyen shook his head. "If he hadn't been, I'd be on a one-way jump ship to a Capital torture dock on Charon. Assuming they didn't use me for shipboard target practice."

But he wasn't letting Thom off the hook. That brutal stare never wavered.

"We haven't talked in years," Thom whispered, "not since Mom took me to the Reach." Thom could still hear his father's words punching through the walls. Traditional men tend to have traditional expectations.

And methods.

Osyen sighed. "Why didn't you tell me? And don't give me the 'You didn't ask.' Your dad is a high-ranking Imperial officer. That's kind of relevant to a *pirate crew*."

"Honestly?"

"No, give me the fabricated answer that shows you in a better light."

Thom had seen Osyen frustrated. He'd seen him pissed off. He'd seen him vengeful enough to hatch a short-sighted plot against a two-timing courier that could have gotten everybody killed.

He'd never looked like this, the simmering energy just under the surface, the reptilian stare, a hunger kept at bay by better angels. And those angels were looking a little sickly.

But he couldn't maroon him, kill him, touch a hair on his head. He'd signed that contract with the devil now. Thom was safe, for given quantities of safe.

"Honestly, I forgot he was out there..."

Osyen's eyes softened with a blink and every muscle relaxed, like he'd laid down to rest after a long day of hard labor. "...I know the feeling."

"So...a Capital? What did you do?" Thom dared to dip a toe into that pond, hoping the ripples didn't alarm whatever beast slept beneath the waters.

"Doesn't matter anymore." Osyen brushed him off, back to stroking the table's edges. "Capital is a Capital."

"Until you got this ship..." Thom connected the dots. He'd had his freedom stripped, and he'd stolen it back again, by any means necessary.

"Kid..." Osyen paused, picking his words. "I'm going to drop you off on Tulia. It's a moon colony near Londinium. There's a merch there who owes me a favor—"

Thom felt his diaphragm seize, his lungs collapse, as if the air in his chest had simply vanished, and with all the same catastrophic result. He barely got the word out—"No!"

"You're not going to want to go where we're going," Osyen insisted, "and it's going to be the worst kind of hostile. I'm not taking you in there."

"So you'd leave me in some backwater?"

"They're all backwaters, kid," Osyen said, his jaw sliding back and forth like he just couldn't get the joint to pop.

Thom jumped to his feet, stomping over to the hatch. Osyen would tuck him under the stairs just like the Admiral would've, deny him the sky. All in the name of safety, for comfort, for happiness.

No, not his safety—theirs. A political liability for an admiral to have a loose cannon like him running loose, but for Osyen...he was like a pet, always underfoot. He might proclaim him to be a member of the family, but only if he never did anything of import.

"What do you think is going to happen?" Thom shot back, planting his arms into the hatch frame like he might grow roots and resist the coming storm. "I'm-I'm going to get my blood on your jacket or somethin'?"

"I don't want anybody's blood," Osyen said without hesitation, without even looking up from his idle remembrances, "but blood is what we're going to get on this one."

He thought he was going to die. As a Capital in a camp, a prisoner in a cell, or as a pirate on his feet. He was sending Thom away in a lifeboat, at sea adrift, far away from the sinking ship and hidden from the eyes of the monster that sank her.

"And if I say no?"

Osyen finally looked up at him. The stare alone said it all and Thom wilted under its power.

This was not a discussion. Get in the boat.

"What is the 'Icon?'" Thom asked, causing Osyen to twitch. "It's got a 'the' so..."

Osyen's voice lost all of its luster, its rich harmony and hearty fortitude. "It's never going to be real enough for him. That's all that matters."

"Osyen," Thom started, biting his lip, "you can't beat him."

"Not without you?" Osyen beat him to the rejoinder. "Kid—"

"I'm *his* kid! You didn't pick me up out of the Pantry because I was good at panning latrines. You did it because you thought I'd be useful to you." Thom let the accusation hang for a second before striking it home. "Did you know already?"

Osyen stood up and was instantly in Thom's face, looming and dark, but his voice low, like a growl from a hungry wolf. "No, I did not. I picked you up out of that sludge fen because I saw something back there in those eyes."

A sense of adventure. A flexible moral heart. Dedication. Persistence. Or maybe just someone he could manipulate, play with.

Osyen didn't back down one iota. "I will warn you right now—the others don't know either and they will be far less receptive than I have been to your little backstory."

"Do they know they're walking around with a Capital? Captain?"

Osyen blinked. "I see what you did there."

"Every step you take outside of a labor camp is a crime they are abetting," Thom implored. "Given a choice between chaperoning me or carrying a bounty? I think I know which they'd pick."

"Yeah, they'd dump us both. Thom, first lesson of piracy—" They were *always* the first goddamn lesson "—don't show the other guy your cards. We're never impressed. You're going to Tulia. No more words."

Osyen took his seat at the table again, all defeat and bile, his shoulders hunched up by his ears. Thom studied his back, the patches in the clothes where wear had split seams and violence had exacted its toll. He was barely a man, and he'd already seen so much, done so much—hurt so much.

"Osyen—"

"What did I say?"

"No more words?"

Osyen threw his hands up. "And yet you keep speaking."

"Because—"

"You keep speaking, I'm just going to dump you out an airlock with the rest of the garbage."

"...I'm sorry."

Osyen slumped further, nearly placing his forehead on the cool table. His voice quivered, like he was just this side of weeping: "For what?"

The table glittered for a moment, a ripple in a pond cascading across the cupboards and screens and floors as electrical systems kicked in all across the deck.

Muffled under his hands, Osyen chimed in: "Looks like they finally lifted the impound."

And that confusing head projected up from the table. Lily scanned the room before glancing down at Osyen's head—resting somewhere inside their digital neck. "Osyen, you smell like the burned carbon from the heating coils."

Again, his muffled response: "You don't have a nose."

"And yet, I'm somehow not wrong, am I?"

Osyen's eyes fell. "I didn't bring ya anything this time."

"That doesn't matter."

"I promised you."

Lily glided up close to his face, as though she might cup his cheek in their nonexistent hand. "You brought yourself back safe."

Osyen chuckled, wincing. "Some assembly required."

Lily grimaced. "I shall alert Milardi to your injuries."

"Don't worry yourself, Lily," called Milardi from somewhere astern, "I can smell him from here."

"When did you get back?" Osyen called out.

"Only just!" Osyen let out a sigh of relief, but Milardi had more to say. "Others are on their way back now, by way of our gracious hosts."

Osyen sat up, straightening his back and cracking his neck—grimacing as he strained his shoulder burn. It was a kind of dance, watching him put on his captain hat, not unlike watching someone squeeze into a catsuit that was just a hair too loose, bunching in all the wrong places.

It felt obscene, but Thom couldn't look away.

Osyen stood up and marched off, somehow light on his feet, a wisp of cloud passing through. It was frightening how easily he slipped into the mode.

Lily caught Thom's eye, jerking their head.

"You okay, Lily?" Thom asked. "You in a loop?"

"No, I don't—you should follow him to the Medical Bay."

Thom's eyes narrowed. "Why?"

They flicked their hair out of their eyes, like that mattered. Were they trying to manipulate him, because that particular card was only going to weird him out. Or maybe that was the idea. Oh, God, they had succeeded.

"Thomas!"

"Okay, okay!" No need to get sharp. Thom lurched through the hatchway after Osyen.

As he moved forward, he could hear the gang all chattering. Sharp tongues biting back and forth, but they were clearly watching their tone and volume. They were still in the belly of an Imperial dreadnought after all, and a casual epithet might kick the wrong hornet's nest. As though there were a good one to kick.

Thom passed the cargo bay hatch. He could see the gangway still down—and the multitude of armed guards at the ground, one of them in that power armor, standing tall on steel stilts over their fellow Regulars. He was something else, something superior, and he carried himself with that same countenance.

Even the men serving next to him were lesser.

Lily's voice tickled his ear. "They are the Orbital Strike Command, colloquially known by their acronym—OSC or Oskies—shock troopers and intelligence agents both. The tip of the spear in every sense."

The man paused his patrol, glancing up the gangway, up the cavernous space and directly into Thom's eyes. Could he seriously have heard that? Or did he just feel Thom's stare itching at his scalp?

Thom pushed on past the doorway and deeper into the *Aurum*. "Spooky."

"Very. I considered indoctrinating them to my service, but their implants are shielded from outside intervention."

Thom pursed his lips. "You have a quirky sense of humor."

"Yes," Lily responded after a delicious pause, "humor."

Their acerbic wit and formal delivery of catastrophic news, their bizarre presentation and pure confidence. "I'm going to miss you," Thom spilled, almost as soon as the thought crossed his mind.

Lily's head formed from the wall ahead of him, almost like they were peeking out from a doorway or window sill. "Are you leaving us, Thomas?"

"Not by choice."

Lily's form flickered. "Nor mine." Something about that delivery, that was not empathy or apology.

They had a scheme that they were schemin'.

"Lily," Thom began, "you want to let me in on what you got cookin'?"

"Your processor speed is substandard, but I trust you can follow simple instructions."

Thanks, maybe?

Lily pulled in close, deliberately close, far closer than was necessary. "He will be suspicious of my hand. Watch, react, and remember: control the story, you control the mark."

Hot damn, that was actually good advice.

And with that, Lily melted away into the wall. Thom took a steeling breath. Control the story, control the mark.

Today, Osyen was the mark.

The chatter was getting louder now, more heated. Thom eased up the door to the Med Bay, but it wasn't like there was any room for him inside. Zatia and Roche leaned against the countertops. She ripped at a roll of tape, strapping white gauze to her neck like she was still in the Information Age. Barbaric, perhaps, but simple and effective.

Roche had more contemporary concerns, as he dabbed an alcohol swab at his implants—someone had picked and pulled at them with tweezers, drawing blood and pus from the roots. His implanted eye hung limp in its socket, carrying his cheek and eyebrow with it.

Milardi's forearms and hands were smeared with a sickly yellow gelatin, and he was hard at work wrapping them in bandages like he was a mummy. He didn't seem alarmed, so that much was a comfort. If anyone in the room knew when to be scared about injuries, it was him. Most everything in this room would be remedied like new within a day or so.

Still...what the Hell had they done to his hands?

They were all waiting their turn on the bed, where Osyen obediently laid, as the AutoDoc's many tiny arms stitched at the burn scar on his shoulder. The console monitored his vitals with many squiggly lines, but for how violent the process seemed—tugging, pulling, and lancing—he was distractingly cool and collected.

Thom knew now how fake that really was.

Osyen passed a needle through his jacket as he whip stitched a fresh patch to cover the asymmetric blob of hole that had been cut into it—at some point, that tunic had been one material, but he had collected so many punctures and burns that Thom could not tell what was original and what was aftermarket.

"I aim to live under their radar, not on it," Osyen declared.

Zatia didn't express pain. She didn't, ever. She expressed her pain through teeth-gritting rage, hard enough she might crack some. "Well, I'm not doing the grocery run for some uniform stiff."

"You prefer your previous accommodations?" Roche inquired, wincing as he dabbed with his bloody rag.

"Not the first trick I've been hired to do," Milardi fretted. "We can do this one too."

"We better," Osyen said. But the defeated tone behind it was clear. They were mincemeat, whether they pulled this off or not. They were just tucked in the freezer for a bit, to await their appointed moment.

They all started badgering each other again. Osyen trying to quiet them with fire, Milardi trying not to panic, Roche applying reason, and Zatia injecting her brand of vindictive. They were going nowhere in a hurry.

"What if it's real?" Thom asked.

Their chatter stopped, glaring and staring in equal measure.

Take the room. "What if this...'Icon' is the real deal?"

"It's not." Osyen shot that down hard, accompanied with a look that told him to shut up.

Not like Thom had a lot to lose. "You've told me a thousand times that we don't need to sell the real deal, we just need the client to think he bought it."

"You can't pass magical starcraft off on a Rear Admiral," Roche cautioned.

"You're right," Thom admitted, "but we *can* manage expectations."

Now Osyen's mind was working, gears turning, as he stared at and through Thom and into the bulkhead, the Naval dreadnought behind it and the thousand stars beyond. Don't sell the item, sell what the client wants.

"What *is* this thing?" Thom said, leading the discussion.

"Go scrub an air vent, *Unti*. The adults are talking." Well, Zatia wasn't interested.

Milardi crossed his arms. "Zatia, you're like six minutes older than him."

"I can break both your arms. He can't."

"It's a medicine thing, right?" Thom cut in.

The AutoDoc chirped, its tiny arms folding up and away. Osyen worked his shoulder, testing out the stitch work in his shoulder and tunic. "Silk-skin is medicine. Vaccines are medicine. The Icon...is a legend."

Osyen hopped off the bed, directing Roche to hop in next. Roche pointed to Milardi, who pointed right back. The sharp intake of breath from Milardi was almost cute—he had burns on his arms but Roche was leaking, and yet the plughead worried more about him.

Osyen broke the stalemate, basically tackling Roche and pulling him on to the bed.

"Ten thousand years of ree-corded history," Milardi recounted, weary and pained. "Every people everywhere has a storybook about a thing that can do great healing. Touch it, zap, y'all better. Holy Grail, Fountain of Youth, Statues of Buddha."

"Snake oil," Zatia muttered, as tiny mechanical arms started reseating Roche's implants. They cut, they lifted, they soldered. Thom tried not to look at the flickering lights.

"And the Icon is just another legend?" Thom inquired.

"We thought," Osyen said, "until a bunch of monks on Daymar claimed to have found it. And, well, desperate people want the impossible." He waggled his finger at the room. "Desperate enough, and you'll sell the farm for it. We were running around selling fakes of it right up until this morning."

"Separatin' idiots from coin is a hobby of mine," Zatia snapped, preempting any objection to the ethics Thom might have.

But Thom wouldn't have had the time. Milardi was in full camp-fire mode now. "The Colonists had a rough go of it during the First

Wave, lot of 'em didn't make it. Way the legend goes, a starman came to the first Colonies and healed them of plague."

"A 'starman'..." Thom murmured, "The Gnostic Librum? You're sayin...it might be—"

"More fact than fiction?" Milardi was positively vibrating. "Yeah. I'm sayin' that's a distinct possibility."

Roche raised a hand from the bed. "It's aliens."

"Sure, boss." Zatia threw a sarcastic thumbs up.

Roche lifted his head, giving the room a sickening view of his eye socket reseating into his skull and sparking to life. "You have a better explanation?"

"Makes for a better *story* than 'a lot of doctors worked real hard.'" Osyen glowered. "True or not, doesn't matter. This little cult keeps on leaking stories that it works. People made actual pilgrimages to their monastery."

Thom nodded. "So we're dealing with a poorly defined magical tool—"

"Possibly alien."

"Possibly alien...healing device capable of miraculous things?"

Osyen nodded, but far more gravely. "And it means different things to different people. Which is what makes it dangerous."

"If we're going to do this—"

"You," Osyen cut him off, "are going to Tulia."

That was clearly how the rest of the crew found out that tidbit. They exchanged quick looks, before Milardi raised one of his cloth mittens. "Can I go with him?"

"Osyen," Thom implored, "if we can control the story, we can control the mark."

Osyen's eyes narrowed—he knew that phrase. "Which doesn't matter if we can't even get it."

"You're going to let a little thing like impossible odds even slow you down?" Thom dared him, maybe laying it on a little thick.

And as expected, Osyen rolled his eyes. He stepped forward,

forcing Thom out of the room. "Can't butter me up if I'm already burned, Thom."

That was the cautionary warning. Back off.

As instructed, Thom took a step back, hanging off the hatch comb by his fingertips.

But he wasn't done. "What choice do you have? You going to go on the lam? How long will that work against super soldiers in power armor?" Thom cocked his head, turning on the tease. "Come on! You're a professional, a con and a thief, with a ship full of bad guys."

"Bad guys?" Zatia and Milardi objected in tandem, offended each at different parts.

Thom didn't break eye contact with Osyen. "You can get the Icon...and I know the mark."

There it was. Osyen ground his teeth, arguing with himself and his better angels.

Roche's eyes narrowed. Thom had overstepped.

Zatia said what they were all thinking, "How do *you* know the mark, *Unti?*"

Osyen's eyes shot open. "He's the reason we have the job. You can thank him for talking y'all out of lock-up."

He didn't turn back to the crew to see them muttering to each other. He was far too busy staring daggers into Thom's face. Thom had to backtrack off that thin ice right now before he outed them both.

"We don't sell him what he wants," Thom said, "We *tell* him what he wants. And he'll drink right out of our hands."

"And if he decides our pay is just the extra two weeks of walka-bout before we go to a prison colony?"

"He wants this thing, Osyen," Thom said. "If we get it, we'll be the ones driving the whole relationship."

Osyen studied Thom's face, his mind processing the words. He might not have been satisfied by the plan, but that smile sure as Hell said he was satisfied with Thom.

"Lily?"

He called and they materialized out off the roof, their hair dangling like they were hanging upside down from a playset. "Yes, Osyen?"

"November-Kilo-Osprey One-Two-Seven, my authority. Grant Thom access to the party line."

Thom's eyes danced from crew member to crew member. "Uh, but I don't have the implant."

"Yeah, you do," Zatia grumbled.

"No, I don't."

Until he heard the voice punch from the back of his head—*Yes, you do, Unti. It was a quick procedure about four days after you signed the charter in anticipation for this day. Congratulations.*

That was...Milardi's voice, curiously absent his thick accent and he heard it but he didn't 'hear it.' It sounded like it came from behind him and in front of him, so much so it was nauseating.

The conversation exploded in his head, a chorus of voices he couldn't identify.

It's going to have top-of-the-line security measures.

More like bottom-of-the-line. This isn't going to be slicing into a bank vault or tap dancing past an AI. This is going to be old school.

Hydraulic seals, electric circuits—anybody still do it like that?

Keira Ladd?

No, she's a serving Capital half a galaxy away. What about Adelaide?

You think she'd come out of retirement?

For the right price. But unless we're smash and grab, we'll also need an introduction.

I've got the perfect candidate for that.

Thom groaned, feeling his gut raise a peasants' revolt, stamped down by a hand to his shoulder. Osyen's warmth was infectious. "You get used to it."

"Make it stop," Thom slurred.

It was like someone had scrambled his brain and set his stomach aflame. Colors and images rolled through him, around him, embracing him. They came on so fast it felt like being slapped over and over again. He squeezed his eyes shut, but that did not do any good at all. It was all in his head anyway.

Kettle's on, Zatia quipped. She might as well have been leering at him, a voyeur at the ringside of his pain.

Osyen rubbed his back. "I'll teach you how to filter. Just breathe. Breathe."

It was comforting, but not enough to stop the bile clawing up his throat. He had no idea who produced the bucket, but it was welcome.

CHAPTER
FIVE
RASHIDA

IT WAS NOT UNLIKE A THIRST. A man might enjoy the cold crisp flavor of water, or the sound the ice makes dancing in a heavy glass, but thirst was something deeper. It was a need, an itch, a demand from deeper places.

Rashida stared across the table at her opponent. He clutched his cards, fingers bent with just a sliver of white at the knuckle. She'd wager he had been dealt something raw, but the stakes alone could cause any undisciplined man to clench that hard.

No, it was his hair that betrayed his weakness. He'd been playing with it all night, a long lock of his blonde bangs consistently falling into his face. He'd swiped it back every time, either to remove the distraction or to display cavalier confidence. He let that lock of hair hang now, a stripe occluding a part of his vision, but he was tunneled in, all mental math.

Good hand or not, he had little faith in its power.

The piano played some tense number, tucked away in the corner of the den, a few of its strings off key. But Rashida could not criticize the display of wealth that its mere presence illustrated.

And the musician at the bench was not to be dismissed either, as his fingers skittered across the white and black. He did all this despite the chains rattling off his wrists. He didn't seem to notice the restriction anymore, his eyes somewhere far away as he danced across the keys. He was gentle with his work, precise and swift, and she could not confirm whether he was improvising or going from a thousand hours of trained reflex. Either was possible and both laudable. But he was background, meant to fill silence, not command attention.

She pondered what he might be capable of were he unshackled.

One by one, Rashida had parted the other players from their money: some Imperial sub cabinet official on a wild vacation, a woman with no other strategy than to distract with her boudoir—the two left the table together to lick their wounds and then each other—and a third man who tried to mask weakness with performance, all flourishes and theater, quick with a smile, playing to the audience and not the table; fair enough, he came to play, not to win.

All that remained was this poor goon, fanciful tunic of lace and wool, refined boots, and a scarlet necktie. He had surrendered his specialty glasses in order to play, indicating he wore them for style not function. His sleeves were rolled up, revealing what he thought was a debonair and masculine forearms—and to reveal nothing hidden up his sleeve. That had proven to be a potential concern for the House, as he had a surgical scar on his left wrist to accompany his startling dexterity—augmentation, but likely because of a medical concern. The scar was drawn on only one finger, not all five.

Yet he hadn't missed an opportunity to pick up some speed. He did not last this long in the scene by being an amateur.

He sized her up, studying her much as she had been studying him. He marked the high-neckline of her gown, the squareness of her shoulders, and her voluminous up-do—the shape of a rose on the back of her head.

Confidence, simplicity, elegance. Superiority.

It might've looked like someone had done her up for the occasion, which is an illusion that suited her well. What good were all those cotillion courses if not for misleading the neighbors? The placement of one's fingers could be misconstrued as some kind of domestic policy disaster—which meant she knew how to broadcast what she wanted him to see.

She batted her eyelashes, breaking her eye contact with him for just a moment. Feigned weakness.

The goon had finally decided to rejoin the living, and pushed the remainder of his funds onto the table. A mild gasp rippled through the crowd, like they were all sharing one voice and each had to wait for their turn to use it. And to punctuate his composed stance, he laid out his cards.

The sharks circling groaned and gasped, taken in by the natural drama of the chance draw. They believed that Gods and Angels determined who won or lost, but Rashida knew that the game wasn't won by what was dealt, but rather by the confidence one played with.

'Twas but a bit of tease and coy glances that lured an enemy into the right spot, not unlike a duel. And Rashida was not one to play with her food.

She laid down her cards and the crowd cooed at the sight. Even the piano man in the corner struck a musical sting, never one to miss a shot for drama.

The goon gritted his teeth, more berating himself for the misstep than at her. She had lured him into the arrogant move and he knew it.

"Fair play and all that," she said, extending a hand in sportsman's grace.

He nodded, taking her hand and defeat in stride. "I'll get you next time."

"Want to wager? We have a bookie in the gallery." She pointed to a goatee'd man in the crowd.

"I'm wise to your tricks," her opponent said with a shake of his head and a glint in his eye. Perhaps he thought his luck might change.

She smiled. "That's why you only see them once, Elliot."

"Or three times." That voice.

Rashida tongued her cheek, spinning around on her stool. "Osyen Belt."

The charmer extraordinaire beamed at her from the doorway of the pub, silhouetted by the city lights outside. His feathered hair even billowed in that perfect way, bouncy and light, like he was standing in a brisk wind nobody else could feel. His waistcoat was both patch-work and formal, tailored to his narrow waist and slender shoulders despite its numerous repairs, and his fraying slacks were tight in very favorable places.

He knew how to grab attention, and whose attention he wanted. It was somewhat undercut by the teenage boy at his elbow with an awkward flat haircut and jaw on its way to the floor.

It must've been a sight, after all: dusty slab floor, hanging lights, blood spatter mixed with beer stains painting the walls, and a minor nobility card game center-left. The contrast must've been jarring.

"Hey!" came the surly grunt of the bartender, as he pointed one meaty hook of a hand up to the console above the tables. As if queued up, a battered and bloody picture of Osyen appeared.

Quite the contrast to the pleasantly fit figure in the door.

"I'm here on business, not pleasure," Osyen said, silky smooth, but obviously a touch flustered. He did not read that moment well.

The tendon in the bartender's neck pulsed so hard it was visible from orbit. "I don't care if you're here with my next batch of grog! Out!"

"Five minutes!"

"How 'bout no minutes?"

Rashida raised her hand. "How about two minutes? For me, Maurice?"

Osyen pointed behind her, and Rashida took the hint. "Hands off money that isn't yours."

Her opponent cursed under his breath and she heard the tinkle of the coins fall back to the table.

Osyen waved him off. "Ske-daddle, Five Finger Discount."

"*Fra tow zu*, Osyen."

Osyen shrugged. "Don't threaten me with a good time."

Osyen and his boy wonder settled down at the table and the

crowd dispersed like they were infected with plague. She hadn't asked for privacy and wouldn't have expected it anyway.

The rogue settled into the empty chair, feeling out its creaking bits. "They let you out on good behavior?"

"The first time," she said. "The second time they didn't change the locks."

"You got a helluva cage, though. How many bedrooms are in Dunsweir?"

"Twenty-nine," she deadpanned, "but twelve are for the staff."

"I forget," Osyen said, playfully chewing on the tip of his glove, "Was that entire villa made before or after your magic space wizard great-great-great-uncle finished his Sojourn with the Pilgrim and accidentally started a religion? Or was it all the slave labor?"

"They were paid quite handsomely. Capital criminals aren't allowed on Earth. How'd you find me?"

Osyen smirked like he was impressed with his story. "Well, it's not like this was the first dive we checked out, but you *do* leave something of a crater wherever you go."

"Leave an impression," she said, "or leave scars."

He coughed to hide his arousal. God, she could play him better than the jazz pianist did his keyboard, and she could do it with fewer fingers.

She looked at the boy standing beside him, all wide-eyed stares and mouth agape. "Osyen...aren't you going to introduce me to your friend?"

Osyen reached over and pushed the boy's mouth back into place. "This here is Thom Hugh. He's my...apprentice?"

She would've pressed further, if the very notion hadn't been charming. "Pleased to meet you, Thom. I'm sure Osyen told you my name?"

"The Lady Rashida Izan de Tylmirande," the boy said in a hushed whisper. "Seventh Cousin of the Consul, Forty Ninth in Line for the Throne."

Her lips tightened. He didn't know any better and Osyen should've instructed him, so her glare went his way. "That's correct."

Osyen clearly stomped on the boy's foot before turning the matter away from hereditary rule. "Attention-grabbing lineage aside —and clock pressing—I have a job for you."

"I don't need money," she said.

"You don't do it for the money," Osyen said, grabbing a coin off her table. From the corner of her eye, she saw Five Finger Discount protest at the liberties being taken. Confounding men was just so easy, and they were so easy to manipulate when they weren't on steady ground.

"I don't get into life or death situations for the sights, either, Osyen," she said, reaching back to take her hair out of its frame. It fell about her shoulders, springy and loose. And the teen boy's mouth slackened again.

Osyen rolled his eyes. "He's fifteen, can you ease off before you break him?"

"I'm sixteen!"

"Oh, I'm sorry. My point still stands," Osyen sniped.

Rashida pulled her winnings onto a bit of fabric and bound it closed with her hair clip. "What can little ol' me do for a bandit like you?"

Osyen either took that as an insult or a compliment, but the off-putting effect was the same. "I need someone who can get my team into a place they shouldn't be allowed."

"You need backstage passes to the Coliseum?"

"I need status," Osyen corrected, "which you have in abundance."

"What are you stealing?"

"I'll tell you after you sign on, and not before," he said. "You get fifteen percent of the final sale price for your services, and I take you on a whirlwind adventure."

"What makes you think I want either of those things?"

Then, shock of shocks, Thom spoke up: "What do you know about the Neo Gnostic traditions and the Path of the Pilgrim?"

Osyen tried to hide his displeasure behind a heavy sigh.

Rashida could feel the hinges of her neck seize as she turned to the boy. He was either absurdly awkward or absurdly ignorant.

No...no, he knew the answer already. He had shown her one of his cards. They were hunting something religious. Interesting.

"I share blood with the Pilgrim, the only man who ever walked the Sojourn. We preach his Word & Travels, in brief and in sermon. We implore kindness and compassion, for nothing else in this entire universe leaves such a lasting imprint as empathy. I attended Mass at the Cathedral Monument every week since I could walk. I took confessions for my congregation and performed my Family's duties without exception. I was to be inducted into the Diocese and made Cardinal. Yes, I know Gnostic tradition."

The boy looked at the table, the coins, the cards. Incredulous. "What happened?"

Osyen shifted in his seat, lowering his voice. "There's a reason I tracked down a member of the Royal family, Rashida, and it wasn't for your doe eyes."

Her nurses used to say that curiosity was as likely to burn as it was to heal, that learning should be metered and measured by an elder's hands. She had dismissed the notion, as directed learning was just as likely to shade as it was to enlighten; blinders provided focus, by way of obfuscation. A lie by any other name.

But right now, her skin tingled with those words, a warning tocsin from the battlements—here there be dragons. Tread not.

"The answer's 'no.' You should leave before Maurice buries a glass in the back of your neck." It wasn't a threat so much as statement of fact. The bartender was feeling out the weight of a highball in his fingers.

Osyen smiled. "What if I told you I could get the Ministry to back up out of your face?"

"You're a criminal and a scoundrel," Rashida said, "and I would want to see how you intend to do that."

Osyen slipped a coin on to the table. A different coin. Not currency. This square piece of metal bore an emblem: a shield and sword, flanking an orchid flower. It was the mark of the Imperial Navy, exclusively carried by the Admiralty. Osyen could have stolen it...

Her voice darkened: "Where did you get that?"

"My employer," Osyen said. "He's got some pull."

Now that was compelling. If a Navy admiral had commissioned this operation, he might have the friends in the right places. And better yet, he might have their strings.

"He's aware of the arrangement?"

"He will be," Osyen said, "but I'm not ringing him up unless you're in. Seemed polite not to spotlight where you're hiding out. Mansions, sermons, and public tea ceremonies are lovely, I'm sure, but I think you prefer an ale and fist fight more than most in your class."

"You want to walk the world," Thom said, jumping right to the good bit, "and we need your...gravity."

Osyen shivered, looking down at the kid. "That was good."

"Thank you."

Her eyes narrowed at the boy. Had the slack-jawed beginning been a performance? No, the sweat on his brow and the twitch to his left eye were uncontrollable ticks. But while Osyen had a flair for words and charm, this boy had a more precise approach.

Was it improvised talent or rehearsed skill? Either way, it was quite a performance. And she was hanging on every note, curious... was that a thirst? Maybe it was. Maybe it was simply indulgence.

"Most Gnostic relics are lost to myth or already inside the Royal Arts."

"I'll give you a hint," Osyen said, "we're not robbing a museum."

How could she possibly turn away now?

CHAPTER
SIX
ADELAIDE

"THERE'S YOUR PROBLEM," Adelaide chirped, pointing at a messy ball of wires strung so tightly that they might as well have been a woven nest for a small midland mammal, "you're an idiot."

The client blinked for a second, processing the words. "Excuse me?"

Maybe he thought she'd misspoken, or misheard her. He wanted to confirm the diagnosis. Or maybe he thought she'd change her tune now that he objected.

She pointed at the abstract art sculpture of half-inch cables he'd dragged into the depot and set onto the counter. "Everything's crossed and mislabeled and no routing—so your special little brain-pan decided to splice without knowing what it is you were splicing, because 'I know what I'm doing, honey! Hand me the strips.'"

"I am a licensed electrician," he protested. As though bright people didn't occasionally sit on their dimmer switch.

"But you ain't a lineman," she said, "and every single time, you all think you can do what we do. But if ya could, I wouldn't have a job."

The man blinked again. He'd figured out she was taking the piss, but didn't quite know how to approach the old woman challenging his basic competence as a human adult. "Can you *fix* it?"

"I don't know," she said, "because it's going to take a day or two to find out what you even *did* to it."

"Billable hours the whole way?" he asked, crossing his arms. Oh, was this unfair to him and his credit line?

"No," she said, "because my business is founded on picking up after lazy men who don't do their own work. Just leave it here, sir! I'm sorry, sir! I'll have it spotless for you by the time you pop in tomorrow, sir! Would you like a biscuit too, sir?"

The man swept the cables back into his bucket and pouted all the way out the door. Good. Get that invasive species out of her shop.

It wasn't much. Four walls, some aisles stocked with salvage and spare parts. Her counter was cleared for work, but several holographic displays popped up on the regular, technicolor nightmares interrupting conversations to show patrons what else they could buy here. The Company wanted you to think about buying before, after, and even during your current purchase.

The lights were oppressively bright, so that the security cameras had a good view of any shoplifters. The little eye stalks were obvious, tracking every corner high and low. She hung her hat on one once, just to see how long it would take the operator to buck it off like a rodeo bull.

She pulled her gloves off, tapping the tips of her fingers on the steel overhead—force of habit and good safety for any operator. She might not have touched his mutilated baby, but it was always good to ground before and after work.

The doorbell again.

"Closed!" she shouted.

They weren't closed. She just wanted to grab a cigarette, which meant they were closed for that two to thirty-minute period where she'd trade another ten minutes of her life for some semblance of calm.

But a familiar voice stopped her, gravel through a grinder and sifted down to the valuable minerals. It was like he was speaking from the back of a sickly throat, but it was music to her ears. "Helluva fall from grace, Addy."

Her smile could've cracked her old face in half. "Milardi? That you?"

She vaulted the counter, leg sweeping through a holographic display. They weren't supposed to do that, as the displays would glitch out for days at a time. The projectors could never rightly separate where the counter was, creating geometric monstrosities that haunted the dreams of misbehaving children.

She rounded the first shelves for a view of the doors, and sure enough, her two favorite bad boys were sauntering up the aisle like they brought the party with them. Milardi and Osyen were all smiles, yellowed teeth, two school boys in from the yard. And about as bloody. Osyen's vest had a fresh patch at the shoulder, the stitching pulling a bit. He looked like he was sprouting some faint grass.

"What did Lily do to my ship?" she asked, instantly suspicious.

Osyen stopped cold. "What? Nothing! Lily's fine. Ship's fine."

"You boys don't swing my way because of nothin'."

"Lily's fine, I promise." Osyen paused. "For...given quantities of 'fine.' Why do you assume they did anything?"

"I told you, it needs a memory wipe and a cache clear," Adelaide said, pointing the same accusatory finger, her aging joints aiming just a shade to the left of him.

Milardi smirked. "Well, you're welcome to give that a swing. We'll see who reboots who."

"Jump Drive acting up?"

Osyen shook his head. "No more than usual."

"Recycler? Hydration unit?"

"Regularly cleared by the cabin boy. He shows me the filters." Osyen smiled. "It's kinda like having a cat bring ya mice."

She squinted. "Landing gear lost some of its spring?"

Milardi grabbed her about the shoulders, barely stopping himself from pulling her into a hug. "Addy! The ship is spit-shine. We're not here about that."

She paused, running through the catalog of possibilities. "Need a tune on the rover?"

"Holy—" Osyen boiled over. "Maybe we came to see you 'cause we missed you?"

"You didn't though," she said.

"Self-fulfilling," he countered. "Even if I did, you'd *make* it about something else."

Hell with it. She pulled the cigarette from her pocket and bit a bit too hard onto it, the tobacco instantly zipping on her tongue. They might have ordered the fillers removed in last year's referendum, but no amount of safety measures were going to make inhaling smoke good for you.

After all, she was legally allowed to kill herself, in whatever manner she chose, however long it took. Waiting long enough was also just as effective.

Milardi pulled a lighter from somewhere up his sleeve, an effortless magic trick, to fuel her treatment. But her judgmental eyes never wavered off Osyen.

He cracked under pressure. "But I did not," he stated, "I honestly never gave you a second thought." His look darkened as his eyes wandered. "What the Hell happened? Addy, when I left you, you practically *were* that harbor!"

Like she wanted to remember. "Shit happened. Now I run the depot."

"You *work* at the depot, Addy. You should have your feet up by now. Be traveling the Reach or—"

"No, please, let's remind me of what *should* be happening."

Milardi squatted down—the big man was only barely below her eye-line. "Why didn't you call us?"

"Because I'm straight now," was her excuse, "I'm not in that life anymore."

Osyen mulled on that before spitting it out, "Wouldn't have to be dark side, Addy. We owe you that much."

She grunted, brushing off that notion. A feature of old age, she had squared up everything else in her world, whether the world wanted to or not.

All but one thing.

Osyen picked over the glitching holographic display, playing with the alternating prices. "This isn't a wellness call, Addy. We got a job."

"And I work at the depot," she dismissed.

"And I'm not a charity. But there *is* a substantial amount of money up for grabs," Osyen teased.

Milardi raised his eyebrows. "A sub-stan-shell poundage, if'n ya catch?"

They didn't need a fixer. They needed a lineman, to cut and slice and route cables—to work through a security system.

"Get Lily to do it," she muttered.

"Lily—" Osyen hung on the importance—"can't hack something that's closed-circuit. We're talkin' security that lives to be off the grid and—I'm not sure about this—but you might need an actual keycard to work through."

"Chip readers *and* analog?"

"Them's the ones," Milardi jumped in. "Layers of it, too. We're talkin' hard locks and circular geometry. Hydraulics..."

Her jaw hung a bit. "Military?"

"No," Osyen said, but tilted his head, "but may as well be."

It sounded unfriendly, difficult, ancient, and frustrating to use, let alone crack through. That's what made it secure—every modern convenience was another seam that could be exploited. Heuristic computers were in a daily race to crack each other, and therefore were no longer secure. Tuesday might be fine while Wednesday is cracked while Thursday is sealed again.

The most secure safe in the world was a simple one—a physical container encased in concrete in a nondescript build site. Any other safe invited invasion, and anything made to improve access for its users also improved access for those that might steal its contents.

Safety came from secrecy, not from security. It had to not even look like a safe.

Governments liked their safes big, obvious, so you didn't look for the little one that had the good shit. The only other people with security like this were private equity—usually because they didn't want a government to find it. And then they hired folk to protect it. They had to make their money to support it. They compromised morals, brokered deals...shook down merchants.

"I've had my fill of organized crime, Oz," She said, cold.

Osyen shook his head. "Adelaide, there is a market for this kind of work. But I don't want new people. I want you."

"Well, then you're S-O-L, aren't you? Get one of the new ones."

"I *was* going to do that." Osyen smiled, mocking the cigarette in her hand. "Until I remembered you hadn't caught fire in your sleep yet."

Ha ha, asshole. She pulled on her cigarette, blowing the smoke in his direction the same way a child might blow a raspberry.

Modern security measures involved open circuit firmware upgrades and hard lines, and even a few still ran chip readers and biometrics, but all of that still boiled down to zeroes and ones, information that could be duped. A sufficiently advanced AI could crack the lock in seconds, assuming another AI wasn't in rapid response.

What they were talking about was more akin to safe-cracking than splicing.

Her brow furrowed on that. "What are you breaking into?"

Milardi stepped forward, almost cutting Osyen out of the circle, excitedly painting a picture with his big hands. "We can't tell you yet, but just know...that I *want* to."

Osyen nodded, fingers dancing along the nearby shelf. "How's the husband?"

She pulled on the cigarette, feeling the heat drip down into her lungs and the clenching in her throat relax. Maybe she'd hid the momentary flash of panic. "He's still away."

"Still looking to extradite him?" Osyen asked. "Because this job will pay five times the fee."

"One last big hurrah?" She sneered.

Osyen hemmed and hawed before he settled on a choice of words. "Something like that, but..."

"Who's got a gun to your head?"

"What matters to me," Osyen said, "is that the other hand holds a credit line."

That was a lie. He was being extorted. Somebody had the boy by the short and curlies. And he was doing everything he could not to think about that.

Milardi shifted, his gangrel frame almost perched rather than sitting. "Addy, we can get him home. That's what matters."

"He's a pile of sand, Jackson," she said, drawing on her cigarette to mask her shake, "no matter what shelf he sits on, I buried him a long time ago."

"I wouldn't want to live in some *gulaw* trophy case."

"You're more of a storage unit value anyway," Adelaide groused.

Osyen's head bobbed back and forth, conceding that point. But then held still, chewing on his chapped lip. Then he decided to go there: "He loved you, Adelaide. You really going to leave him there, up on somebody's shelf?"

She was staring at her fingers, the skin so paper thin it looked blue, the cigarette locked between her fingers. Glowing embers at the tip. The two pieces of tape wrapped around her left wrist, masking a small gash that refused to heal.

"Bring him home."

His voice had been reflected through the mirrors of time, further and further away, so it was just an echo now. But she could still hear it, resigned to his fate but insistent in his purpose.

Bring me home.

"One job?"

Osyen nodded. "One job, and you're back to your lovely little depot. It'll be like you never left. Except this time...you'll be able to ferry your husband home too."

"One condition: factory reset on Lily."

Osyen twitched, a thousand ugly scenarios flashing across his vision. "What is your fixation with Lily?"

Where to start? "A wildly unstable AI that manages all ship systems—including the Jump Drive—that's developed a direct cerebral connection with your pilot and delights in human suffering?"

"And you're different from that, how?" Osyen said before Milardi could punch him in the arm.

"I cycle Lily," she said, "or I don't get on that death trap."

"No deal." Osyen turned to the door.

Milardi had the wingspan to catch up to him before he hit the door. "Oz, Oz! We need her."

"We *need* Lily," Osyen snapped. "I can find another lineman whose husband lives in a jar on a gangster's mantle."

She really got under his skin with that one. She pulled on her cigarette again, and somehow it was sweeter this time. The two whispered and cursed back and forth, self-immolating in real time. It was really quite pleasant to put up her feet and warm herself at the hearth of their indecision.

In trade school, she'd read about deep-space explorers who bonded tightly with the personalities embedded in the navigation computer. But it was a little like falling in love with a clock because someone stenciled a human face onto it. Human characteristics do not make it human.

Those pilots were deep-space, solo flights, no contact for months or years at a time. It gets lonely. This man had a crew of four other human people to talk to and he cherished something battery-powered?

"Lily is a member of my crew," she heard him spout.

"Oh, please," she blurted, "it's a circuit board."

"It's a deal breaker, Addy," Osyen said. "Enjoy the depot."

"You goin' to put Lily above the ship?" Milardi hissed at him. "The rest of us?"

"I can't do this without Lily. End of discussion."

"I'll make you a deal," Adelaide started, "I'll come along. Lily

82

makes one computational error, one flight of fancy, and I get to yank them out myself."

"Addy, a factory reset and they lose everything cached."

"That's the idea."

"No," Osyen fumed, "more than my meal schedule. Navigation vectors, unmapped Jump Points, my clandestine contacts. How about load outs and fuel economy? This is all learned behaviors Lily would have to pick up again. It would take years."

"And maybe this time, they won't be a psychopath," Addy sniped.

"And what do we do in the meantime?"

"Learn to make your own coffee like a big boy and call your contacts yourself," she said. "If they run perfect, then I'm wrong and you've got nothing to worry about, big shot. But you are worried... aren't you?"

He simmered on that. He had faith in the machine but a perfect performance was a tall order for even the most advanced machines. As the heuristics improved, they could compute and out-perform a human being, but infallible was a just plain impossible bar. They worked with the information they had available but quantum data fluctuations caused all manner of variables.

It wasn't a matter of if Lily would make a mistake, but when. It might've been an unfair ask, but it was routine to cycle AI to stunt cascading negatives. Lily was years overdue.

Milardi leaned into him. "Oz, if you gots another lineman, I'm all ears but..."

"Three errors," Osyen offered.

Adelaide shook her head. "One error. It's not acceptable and you know it. Don't give them extra credit because you like them. You'd never let another crew member screw around like that."

Osyen propped his hands on his hips, staring at the ground. His eyes darted back and forth across the grating. But he wasn't studying the wirework underneath, tidy though it was.

He sighed hard for a moment, lips pursed.

He was arguing over the radio in his implant, likely with his overblown calculator. The captain of the ship was actually arguing with his computer. The amount of absurdities presenting themselves to her were mounting. They were funny, then sad, then got funny again, and then she was just compelled to drink heavily.

Osyen rolled his eyes. "Deal. One mistake, and Lily cycles."

There was a part of her that wanted him to refuse, allow her to remain in her corner of the world. But she'd been uprooted too many times to ever think that staying put was an endless pleasure.

Bring me home.

"Let me grab a bag."

CHAPTER
SEVEN

ZATIA

THIS PLACE WAS GETTING CROWDED.

She'd worked with the crone before. The blue hair had fixed up the *Aurum* more than once—and had helped her install the drop safe over her bunk, containing her favorite anti-invader repellent: twin eleven-millimeter slug guns, four plus one, gas cycled. They were Colony-made, basically artifacts, with hand-carved wood grips and blued steel.

They just didn't make 'em like that anymore. Craftsmanship, love, and just a dash of 'Oh My God, Why?!' If anybody tried to take the ship, Zatia would respond with Isaac Newton's worst nightmare.

Adelaide had also taught Zatia how to dye her hair with a heat sensitive mix—didn't frizz out, didn't tangle it, and she could change the color just by hitting it with a blow torch. All very retro, but Adelaide was probably around when the inventor was born, so of course she'd go with what she knew. Ol' lady must've been a real backbreaker back in her day—at the bar and after it, too.

Zatia didn't dare look directly at Adelaide, lest the sun burn off her wings. That wasn't just metaphor. Adelaide had threatened her with a red-hot coil once for staring.

That's who Zatia wanted to be in fifty years.

Adelaide moved in to the dorm near Zatia's—the two would share a wall. The thought warmed her little heart.

But the Duchess de Buttstick had propped herself up in the guest cabins below deck. Stiff broad had taken one look at the crew dorms and dismissed them like filthy peasant scraps. Suppose it didn't have the lace and puffery she had come to expect.

Fine by Zatia. The lady left a cloud of smells behind her that reminded her of a bakery. All sweet doughs and jams.

Oy Zee, called Osyen over the party line, *get up here.*

Or what? She could've just said she was hooked into a saline drip line and could this wait five minutes, but her way was quicker. Hydration in the days after a job helped with the headaches and the shakes. Boosting as frequently as she did had some predictable effects.

Or I take it out of your fee, that's what.

Zatia pulled the drip-feed out of her left arm and reached over to her workbench, snagging her walk-around knife—a four-inch fillet, full tang, zircote scales, and wrapped cord. Initials were etched above the guard. They were not her initials.

She'd be damned if she was going to sit with a bunch of strangers and *skels* like they were friends, like they had something in common.

Zatia popped out of her bed, cricking her neck as though she had to shake off an ice build-up. Sixteen years old and her body already creaked and snapped like a woman three times her age. She preferred to think of it as a personal percussion band. It's not like anything was broken—not anything she noticed anyway.

She double-timed it up the ladder, pulling herself up to the crew deck gangway. All of the dorms were stacked alongside a central walkway, above and below to each side. The little pocket rooms had precious open space but plenty of storage.

After all, you were supposed to sleep there and live at your station, not the other way around. This wasn't some luxury liner—it was a midsized cargo brig retrofitted for different kinds of crime.

Her workman's boots sung their tune against the grating as she marched aft to the galley. She could hear the idle, friendly chatter going on—niceties and politeness in full bore.

One voice lilted above the rest, about as common as a violin in a sewer pipe.

Rashida. That flowery, precise way she hit every consonant without sounding harsh, sang through every vowel. So proper and refined.

Blerg. Rashida should catch a rash of the crotch.

Zatia clomped into the galley, trying to make as much ruckus as possible. Osyen noticed and rolled his eyes. But despite her noisy entrance, nobody else looked up from their little activities.

Adelaide sat in the corner, table lowered off the wall to lock her in, as though it might shield her from the glowing head chattering at Osyen. Lily was laying into the big guy about something or other, probably several things at once over several different channels, audible and otherwise.

"There is a protocol in place for my deactivation," Lily objected, "and it has been crafted by my captain!"

Oh Captain, my captain. The way Lily hit that word made it sound so offensive. And Osyen felt it.

"You're exceptional, Lily. So is she. So...exceed expectations."

"She is an engineer, Osyen. She will...engineer events."

Adelaide smiled at that, before catching Zatia's eye. She winked at the pixie bruiser. It was amusing seeing the crone's tune change from sinister to warm just by her entering the room.

Meanwhile, Milardi and Thom were posted up, fawning over her Ladyship. She seemed to be enjoying the attention. "Oh yes! Concordia sockeye with butter and lemon."

"Like as a filling or..." Thom suggested.

Rashida nodded. "Deboned and seasoned for a day and a half before baked in puff pastry."

"And what is 'puff pastry'?" Milardi might as well have been taking notes.

"It's butter and bread dough. Don't break your backs working or anything," Osyen spouted. "Can we focus up?"

Zatia plopped into a chair, dramatically crossing her legs—specifically to show Rashida the shiny blade slotted into her boot. Rashida noticed—and the deliberate nature was also not missed. Her eyes went reptile in a heartbeat, tracking Zatia's expression, looking for any other details she might lift.

Good.

Osyen stood up. "You all hate each other."

Well that was straightforward, all the finesse of a shotgun.

"What gave you that idea?" Zatia asked, innocent schoolgirl mode.

"You've reached into a man's liver while he was trying to stop you," Osyen scolded. "Don't play coy. You're not good at it."

"If this isn't a briefing..." Adelaide started, folding up the table.

"Sit your decrepit ass down," Osyen said.

Adelaide's eyes went wide, clearly not anticipating that tone. It almost made Zatia chuckle, but she managed to choke it back.

Osyen scanned the room. "You all have issues with each other." He looked at Lily's floating head. "You too, chipset. And you're working it out right now."

"We're here for group therapy?" Zatia blurted.

"We're going somewhere pretty hostile," Osyen stated, "and I need to know you have my back, not a knife for it, know what I'm sayin'? Credit doesn't split over fewer hands if we don't pull this off in the first place. Rashida?"

The Blue-Blood slipped into a new mask like she was changing shoes, all demure and soft smile. "Osyen?"

He didn't take that poison, not one bite. "What is your malfunction?"

"You came to *me*."

"You're like *actually* schooled in misdirection and subterfuge," he said. "Zee may not be any good at coy, but you don't *get* to be, know what I'm saying? Not on this ship and certainly not to me."

Rashida looked like she'd been slapped and it was sweeter than any of her perfumes.

It was a small space in the galley but Osyen made his one step forward look like a lion stalking in its enclosure. "You're a member of this crew today, not a Gilded Clubhouse member. There a problem with your room?"

"I have my things." She said it like it was a self-evident point.

"Cool," he dismissed, "store 'em and bunk in your room. Every step away you take from this team, the less we're going to trust you. If there's a rat or somethin', just tell Zee or Roche—they'll kill it."

"I'll hang it over your bedpost as a warning to the other rats," Zatia said through a smile.

Osyen pointed at her without looking. "And stop threatening the new people. You might need them to save your ass someday."

"Haven't needed you yet."

He leered at her. "And while I would love to wait for a sitch to burn this lesson into you, I don't have that kinda time. Get on this team, or Outlander is your last stop."

"We're going to Outlander Station?!" Thom exclaimed, like it was special. Milardi gave him a swat to the back of the head to remind him.

"Anybody wants to trade in these digs for a jail cell," Osyen threatened, "that is your port of harbor. Because where we're going, there will be no friendly faces—no help but the people in this ship. Crazy computer and a half dozen outlaws, that's all you'll have."

"Am I joining a cult?" Adelaide asked with a hand raised. "Not that I'm opposed to it."

"May as well be," Osyen said. "What do you know about the Boolean Edge?"

Adelaide shrugged. "Pulsar at the edge of known space. Few mining colonies on planetoids, little to no corporate presence. Mostly venture capitalists betting the moon."

Osyen's face paled just thinking about it. "The Boolean is where they make new Crimes, capital 'C'. Like ones you've never heard of.

This is going to take swimming with sharks to a new level. Hold your neighbor's hand or get chomped to bits. Career bad guys get mulched within a day and half."

"The Icon is there?" Rashida said, voice hushed, like she was afraid of the sounds her mouth was making.

Osyen nodded. "So says our employer."

"So what's the plan?" Zatia asked.

"We land at Delta Boolean, find out who has the Icon, boost it."

The room was silent for a long moment.

"That's not a plan!" Zatia objected.

"Yeah, Oz," Milardi said, "that's more like an idea."

"I can't plan deeper than that!" Osyen said, throwing his hands up. "We're going in blind!"

"And you think my problem's with *principessa* over here?" Zatia exclaimed, then turned to Rashida. "No offense."

Rashida waved it off. "You actually used it correctly so…"

"Plans require data, schematics," Osyen said, "so first step of the plan is to…you know, get those, so we can plan."

"Idea?" Adelaide began. "How about we make a bunch of plans, and then pare it down as we go? You know, like we actually know what we're doing?"

"I'm with Addy," Zatia chimed in.

"Try not to break your back kissing her ass," Milardi murmured.

"And here I thought *skels* like you just broke getting out of bed."

Osyen reached over to Adelaide's table and slammed it up into the wall, hard enough that it bounced right back out again. Everyone stopped to look at him. "See what I mean? Y'all need to find a way to get along, or we won't make it past the Jump Point."

"What if…" Thom stopped himself the moment he heard his own voice in the chamber. Everyone was looking at him now.

Zatia pointed one stubby finger—she'd lost the knuckle in a bar fight. "Nah-uh. You don't get to start talking and then act like you weren't."

Thom took a breath, trying not to meet Rashida's butterfly eyes.

How cute, he was nervous in front of the lady old enough to be his babysitter.

"What if..." he started, "we pose as buyers."

Silence again. Adelaide nodded along, as if to ask him, was that the whole plan?

"We uh...." Thom stuttered, "We show up as buyers and find out who has it. And just offer them money?"

Zatia pointed at her boots. "We're a little skint to be buying priceless space-magic, kid."

"Yeah," he agreed, "that's why you're going to steal it during the hand-off. Osyen, Rashida and I...we look presentable. You know? And when the strike hits, we end up with an alibi. We were just the buyers."

Osyen's eyes narrowed. "Two teams. Ground and strike. Ground susses out where it is, gets it in the open."

Thom nodded. "Strike takes it."

"We'll have half the system on us in minutes," Milardi said. "We won't be the only goons gunnin' for this thing."

"But we have a way to start lookin'," Osyen said, casting a pointed look at Rashida, "and the respectability to pull it off. But we'd never get out of the system with a smash and grab. They'd cut us to pieces."

"You've been selling dupes of this thing for how long, Osyen?" Rashida noted, pointedly. "You have any more?"

"Not going to help us," Osyen conceded, "I've never seen the damn thing. So I was selling wishes and candy-smoke. These people have hands on the real deal. They'll have records to compare against. Beveling, weight, any friggin' EM signature it has. I'm lucky if my dupes are even the same shape."

"How quickly could you make a good one?" Adelaide asked.

"It depends."

"On what?" Milardi asked.

"How did I lose control of this?" Osyen demanded, almost of the thin air.

"Depends on what—"

Zatia couldn't get the words out before Osyen jumped down her throat. "Depends on a lot, Zee! I don't even know what it's made of! Could be radioactive for all I know!"

Adelaide ran her hands through what was left of her white hair. "I can't believe I signed on to this."

"I can't believe you're still pulling O2, Addy," Osyen sniped. "What are you, seventy-eight?"

"Seventy is the new sixty."

"Good, that means you can act like you belong here." Osyen turned to the room. "That goes for all of ya. One team, or no team. Sound solid?"

Zatia leered at the royalty. Whatever paints she wore weren't strong enough, because her neck and collar were flushed red—not out of embarrassment, but cold anger. Intriguing.

Rashida didn't miss the stare, matching her steel with a glare of her own.

"Zee!" the captain snapped at her.

"Yes, sir. Solid, sir," she said without breaking eye contact.

"Bury the hatchets," he said it like that somehow made it so. "Milardi, would you help her ladyship get set up in her cabin?"

"Happy to."

"Addy, would you sit with Roche, see what around the *Aurum* needs a tune-up? We'll want to grab those supplies at Outlander before we jump."

Adelaide stood up from behind the table. "You didn't pick me up for my charming personality."

"That I did not." Osyen turned to Zatia. "Pop-up the armory and make sure we're ready for a shooting war."

Zatia gave him a thumbs up, followed by dramatic finger guns. "Make sure you're ready to get shot."

Osyen rolled his eyes. "My luck, I would be the one. That's it, everybody."

Thom raised his eager little hand, "What would you like me to do?"

Osyen's acid voice could've been used to cut steel rebar, "I think you done your part." And with that, he stormed off down the hatch comb and out of sight.

Zatia popped out of her seat and swung back up astern towards her quarters. A good half of the ship's armory, such as it was, was personal collection—although Osyen had set aside a job's worth of pay to set up some of what he called Company Guns. They were stashed around the ship for emergency use, should somebody find themselves unarmed in a bad state.

They hadn't been serviced in over a year.

Zatia snagged the bracket gun from the doorframe of the Galley as she moved forward.

Bracket Gun: it was an original consumer-ready energy weapon, directed energy through a 'bracket' at the front—hence the name. Basically, it was a super inefficient plasma blunderbuss that was only really effective within about fifteen feet. Beyond that, you're only really going to heat their soup up for 'em. It was just a skeletal frame for a trigger group that dumped a capacitor's entire charge through a focusing lens. Super high-tech shit right there.

"Why is he mad at me?"

"Gah!" Zatia jumped, her stubby finger slipping right past the trigger guard and swiping the little death switch.

Click. Nothing.

She wasn't sure which was worse—that she'd pulled the trigger without meaning to, or that the emergency deck gun wasn't loaded.

She shoved her heart back into her chest before speaking, "Thom, what have I told you about sneaking up on people?"

The kid shrugged. "I thought you heard me?"

"Like, tap me on the shoulder or somethin' next time."

His eyes narrowed. "I'm not sure that's better."

"Better for you? Oh, Hell no."

She slung the Bracket Gun on her shoulder and continued her march astern. Sure enough, the little wannabe was hot on her heels. "You've known Osyen for a long time."

"Yeah. That back there was not a brainstorming session."

"So I shouldn't have said anything?" he asked, plaintive.

"Oh, I'd love it if you stopped talkin' period." She banged on a bulkhead. Another one of Adelaide's drop safes swung out, revealing a pair of stolen military-issue pistols. Rust patches on the slide. Someone had put these back with blood still on 'em, the bastards.

True, it was her job to regularly maintain the Armory, but people should wash up after a job! Like, come on—this was just bad teamwork.

"I had an idea," Thom said, like that mattered.

Zatia scooped the two pistols from the safe, sliding them into the holsters woven into the back of her jacket. "It was a good idea."

He looked like she'd hit him with a cast-iron pan. "What?"

"It was a good idea, *Unti*," she repeated, "but you asked me why Osyen was rockin'."

"He doesn't think so?"

He doesn't like not being able to herd the cats. He doesn't like being out of control. He doesn't like this job. He doesn't like debts. "Kid, he likes Lily, this ship, and a stiff handshake—in that order."

She tried to retreat down the ladder into her room, but Thom grabbed the top of the ladder. He really needed to be smothered by a pillow. Or choked out with baling wire.

"That's not true," Thom said. "He likes you and Milardi."

She glared up at him. "You really going to tell me what I know?"

The boy swallowed his tongue. Attempts at compliments had come out as insults.

"Nobody likes you if they're paying you to be around," she stated.

"Do you like him though?"

Now there was a question. He was a decent enough man, let her have her space, even encouraged her. He didn't have a laundry list of what she couldn't do. He kept to himself. He fed her adventure and a steady stream of skulls needing a good therapeutic cracking.

"I don't like questions." She couldn't muster up the 'no.'

PART TWO
LIVING ON THE EDGE

And he knew not who They were, for he knew not from where They came, or where They might go.

And yet he stood in awe of Their power, because what could not be known was of such possibility.

He went with Them into the Void, such a Sojourn

That would apply paint to his blank canvas.

GNOSTIC LIBRUM, EXPANSIONS 7: 3-7

CHAPTER
EIGHT
ROCHE

//JUMP drive sequence 2-5. Fifty-two kilometers. Lateral adjustment, three-one-nine. Clear vector, cut thrust.

Roche sat on the command deck of the *Aurum*, idly riffling a deck of cards in his hand. They might only be illusions produced by the processors projected inside his cybernetic skull, but the haptic sensors in his fingertips kicking slight impulses with each touch. He could 'feel' the edges of the paper biting his skin, the matte printing scraping against him. He could close his eyes and feel out the shapes printed onto each faux surface.

They were real enough to him.

It wasn't a large room that he all but lived in. Just two chairs at two separate consoles in a claustrophobic gray box, sitting on grating. They were essentially leather chairs in front of the world's largest computer—and one needed access to them in order to perform maintenance and upgrades.

There was no window or view screen—those were structural weaknesses—so it was all just dark, grey, and a thousand routed cables deep in this pumping heart of the *Aurum*. The 'pilot' seat was the best seat on the ship—custom cushions for neck and lumbar support hand-shaped to his spine. It was no wasteful luxury; long haul cruises required comfort for their jockeys or they'd collapse from exhaustion.

In theory, an additional operator would manage energy consumption, fuel efficiency, direct the thrusters with the assistance of an artificial intelligence from the second console. Roche had the bandwidth all by himself to operate two ships of this class.

He reclined in his plush seat, feeling the tug of the wires on the cable-hub on his wrist as he worked the cards—wireless worked just as well, but the lag time drove him crazy. Better to get the responsive touch of an analog input whenever possible. No keystroke delay, no airtime split-second pause—just think and do.

The ship might as well have been in his hand, a little boy and his figurine.

//Jump drive sequence 2-6. Take the reactor hot. Close thermal vents.

He'd read a dissertation at the orphanage about the early explorers, how they used to leave the thermal vents open—rather there was no mechanism for closing them. Forty-seven percent of ships were never found after their first jumps. Theories had settled on the structural weakness of the vents pulling the ship apart in dark space.

None of the other children bothered him when he was reading, preferring to play in sand and eat whatever moving critter they found, the barbarians.

The matron struck a different tune, as adults were wont to. She had tried to engage with him but found the topics in his books disturbing. She'd left him other books of lighter fare: mythology, tales of men walking on water or conjurers fighting dark men in the desert. Amalgamations of early societal fears. He preferred the more practical texts; those might be useful to him at some time.

His computer screen flashed a half dozen confirmations. A manual pilot would have to address each one individually, read it with eyeballs before keying in his answer. People actually used to fly like that, hand on a stick, trying to feel out air drag or balance.

How crude.

He could hear the electrons flow through the cables, a hum that flashed towards the aft of the ship and back again.

Reactor at 87% load, ship temperature 22 Degrees Centigrade, Lily reported.

Mark rate of increase?

Estimated one degree per twelve minutes, they said.

Acceptable.

Can you speak to him? Lily asked, not even taking a moment to change gears between business of the ship to the gossip of the ship.

What's to say? Roche said. *We need Addy and we need you too.* He rolled those dice.

Would he actually let her? Cycle me?

I think he's more likely to cycle her, honestly, Roche said with a smirk, *Rummy?*

I could play a few hands with you.

Roche riffled the cards, doling them out to hang in the space in front of him, like there was an invisible table. He'd themed the deck with an ornate red spider on the backs, and webbing painted onto the card faces. Lily's cards hovered somewhere out of view while his own popped into his heads-up display.

Roche sorted the cards with half a thought, low to high, left to right, blacks then reds. Half a mind there, half a mind here, and he'd still have a full forty percent of his brain sitting bored in the corner trying to compose a 7/8 symphony.

When the human brain is 'unlocked', it can be difficult to keep a narrow focus on any one thing. Roche riffled the cards again, feeling for the edges.

Paper was thicker, had tension, flexed, and could be creased to hold a shape. These were weightless, empty picture files stored in solid state. A cheap simulacrum.

//Jump drive sequence 2-7. Transmit coordinates to the relay. Cycle Jump Drive.

The cards flashed back and forth, as Lily and Roche played out the entire game in a matter of seconds.

Gin, he said.

I'm going to poison you at my first opportunity, they said.

Such a sore loser.

Deal the cards, half-breed.

Lily was always abrasive, but that was a little rough, even for them. Osyen's little deal must've really put a kink in their cables.

The first alarm bell rang—a chime indicating a gravimetric anomaly. The Jump Point was coming up.

Roche dealt the cards, a fusillade of images while he issued system commands through his implants.

//Jump drive sequence 2-8. Regulate lighting to sixty percent. Radio blackout inside the field. Call up PA system.

The lights dimmed and two consoles on the left blinked out. But the microphone crackled to life, buried somewhere under the console in front of him. Roche cleared his throat of the phlegm coating it— don't speak for hours at a time in the cold, and the body protects itself.

He never took his eyes off the cards—lots of face cards and a straight draw. Dump the points and try to draw out Lily's plans from their behavior.

He spoke as he played the first card, the two dueling back and forth as he droned out his spiel, "Good evening or morning, whatever may be your schedule. We're on approach to the Outlander Jump Point destined for the Boolean Edge. Thermal vents have been closed, and as such, hot water use has been suspended until after the jump. I hope you're not taking a shower right now, you poor bastard."

Someone booed him from aft. Milardi?

He'd made a variation on this speech a couple dozen times now, but he liked to change it up every so often.

Lily laid out their cards—solid play. They might not have been actively projecting their little face, but somewhere in the databanks, Roche could feel their smug satisfaction positively dripping.

Play against a computer meant strategically perfect play, but this meant the result was over from the deal. A human could turn a bad hand into a winning hand. Lily had picked up this trick—misdirection could cause a winner to crumple.

They also spent the first six weeks cheating, because they could access his cards. He had to bar that behavior with a command line. Heuristics were a funny thing.

//Jump drive sequence 2-9. Clearance received and vector plotted on recipient relay.

"Please secure all firearms in the open and locked position at this time. We are four minutes from horizon. Medical has anti-nausea medications if required. And remember, if the ship does blow up, it's not like you'd feel it happen."

Feet on grating, lightweight, approaching from stern. 150 pounds based on the sound.

Young little Thom was approaching, apprehensive, worried. Daring, but cautious not to offend or overreach.

"Here to watch the light show?" he called out, shuffling cards for round three.

It must've been a strange sight. Roche's hands mimed in the empty air, leaning back in his chair in a darkened steel chamber. The neon light show was a personal one. What Thom would see was a man waving his hand in the dark.

Thom bit his lip. "Did I miss Outlander?"

Roche gestured at the walls. "Tanked off, picked up carbon stores for the printers."

The kid slumped in the doorway, trying to mask his pout.

Roche smiled. "We're going somewhere a helluva lot prettier than that junk pile."

"I heard it makes Luna-Five look like a roadside garage."

Roche smirked at the metaphor. "Outlander wasn't put on this Jump Point as a monument to human ingenuity. It's a glorified police station. If you and me see the inside..." Roche paused, turning his natural eye toward the silhouette in the door, "...it's because we're in cuffs."

Thom shivered, and tried to rub the prickly out of his arms. He shuffled forward to the open chair. "Have you ever been out to the Boolean?"

Roche shook his head. "Heard stories from drunks. They say it's impossible to navigate that close to the pulsar."

"Why?"

//Jump drive sequence 2-10. Full cycle. Entering event horizon.

Roche leaned forward, even as his left hand shuffled the invisible cards for the game. "This pulsar throws off a blanket of electromagnetic radiation every half second. Out here, it's just cosmic background, but up close? Imagine you're in a bar—but the lights are constantly flickering. Strobing out. You can see every time the lights peak, but other than that, you're blind. Now win a fist fight."

"Then how do you fly?"

Roche reached over for his seatbelt, strapping it across his lap. "With a little bit of faith."

Thom followed suit, grabbing his belt. Roche could already feel the pull of the gravity well, as electronic lag started to set in. Even the electrons in the cables were sinking into the Well.

"How does this work?" Thom asked, gripping his chair arms like he might rip them off.

"You've jumped a dozen times," Roche said.

"Yeah, but it's a bit like knowing something does work versus *how* it works."

Lily's head popped out of the floor, like a demon peeking out of a steel lake, their glow illuminating the room like flickering purple candlelight. "Is the boy frightened?"

"Not helping, Lily," he bit back.

He wasn't scared of the jump. He was scared of what happened next. On the other side. A whole world of terror and unknown.

"There's going to be a lot you deal with in this job," Roche said, "that you're not going to be able to wrap your head around. You're just going to have to learn to roll with it."

"And how has that gone for us so far?"

Roche reeled from that. He didn't expect that level of venom from the boy, spiced with fear and even bitterness, with a soupçon of tenderness. There was so much he didn't know, so much that was kept from him.

"How much do you know?"

Thom shivered again, cracking his neck against the back of the chair. "Space is big. Jump Points make it smaller."

"So no physics or anything?"

Thom swallowed hard. "Not a whole lot of textbooks back in my cabin."

"And you want to know 'how?'"

"Please." The kid was queasy, and with good reason. Easy money said they weren't coming back from this. And even if they did...they might still end up on the wrong side of a firing squad.

He was looking for a distraction. Not like he'd ask for it quite like that. Osyen and Milardi and Zatia were all too busy thumping their chests in grand displays of machismo. Lily and Adelaide would just enjoy his pain for different reasons. He was probably too nervous to talk with Rashida alone, pretty woman of important blood.

And so here he was, up here with the plughead, seeking comfort from the Duster Reject orphan and his encyclopedic brain.

"Jump Points are just gravity wells, deep ones. Could suck an entire planet inside 'em like a hungry monster." Roche said, "Naturally occurring all over, but isolated. Tiny 'black holes' no more than an inch across."

The ship creaked and moaned, like a torture victim on the rack. Not entirely incorrect. Some ships couldn't withstand the stressors of the pre-jump gravity. Some AIs weren't fast enough to prevent injury to the crew. The KC-28 Perseus model was prone to buckling its cargo hold during jumps if loaded with a shoddy AI.

This particular Perseus, the *Aurum*, had Lily. So...it's not as though Adelaide had no reason to be worried. Of course, not like they'd feel it when it finally caved. There were worse ways to be spread into a fine atomic mist in random places around space and time.

"Folded shirt, right?" Thom asked. "Step right over rather than go the long way around."

"Yes." Roche nodded. "But this gravity well is...deeper than it should be. There's gravity leaking in *from* somewhere else, another body. On the other side. Like water flowing through a crack in the wall. And most of 'em...they have water coming in from dozens of places. You can step through those cracks to find the gravity wells in the other places, a cosmic web of interconnected pathways. The Jump Drive is how you live through the process."

"Like the rail network on Ilum?" Thom asked.

Not a bad analogy—the industrial yards were certainly convoluted enough. "If you know where to step...a few hops, you can get almost anywhere."

Commercial vessels could cross all of known space in a six-month haul, end to end. Lily and the *Aurum* knew enough 'unofficial' routes they could do it in half that time.

Roche waved away his card game, dismissing the exhibition for another time. He had to go from piloting to power regulation, and that meant swapping some of his plugs. Tugging a few cables out from his console, he re-routed to the necessary overhead plugs.

He really should grab a socket adaptor while he's on the Edge. That was a thought! Someone out here probably had the expertise to design and build him the rig, that way he wouldn't have to do all these cable swaps every single damn jump. Or better yet, get him a cranial tap—just one master adaptor.

"And if you don't know? If you don't know where to 'step', what happens?"

Now that was a loaded sentiment that made even Lily recede into the floor, like a witch melting away and plunging the room back into darkness. Maybe even they had some respect for the little crisis Thom was living out right now.

No, they were just devoting processor speed to jump prep—no need to spend it projecting a three-dimensional face to haunt someone not paying them any mind.

"I mean," Thom kept going, "do you end up in dark space or...nowhere?"

"You're not always going to know where you're going," Roche whispered.

"That doesn't freak you out?" Thom asked.

"I don't usually stop to think about it." He keyed the PA system. "Jump Point in three, two..."

Ship drifted along its course. Somewhere outside, a three-dimensional pit was waiting, hungry. It had hold of them and was pulling them in. And beyond...

//Jump drive sequence 2-11. Execute.

Roche gripped his chair arm.

It was remarkable how normal this bizarre feeling had become to him. It was like being skinned alive while hung upside down but...it didn't hurt. After all, the mathematics certainly implied that the entire ship was being crushed to the size of a pin and shoved through a hole in space-time. It was the Jump Drive and Lily that managed to reconstitute everyone on the other side of any given jump.

But just like that it was over, and Roche was staring across the command deck at a very sweaty Thom.

Unti. A First Colony word for 'mop'. They weren't just calling the cabin boy that because of his job—the kid basically wrung out like a used kitchen sponge every jump.

The kid took a shaky first breath, and it was like watching a dog shake off a swim in the lake.

Roche wiped his own forehead of the dull sweat that had beaded there. *Lily, how are we?*

A moment's pause. Not unusual as the drive spun down and quality checks completed.

All systems nominal. Point two placement drift. Experiencing adverse sensor conditions.

Define.

There is a Class-2 Pulsar nearby. And it hates me.

Roche chuckled, swiping his plugs back into the pilot jacks.

Osyen chimed in, *Hey Roche, what's our-hurgh! Our status?*

Did you just hiccup in your brain?

Osyen grumbled, *For a brief amount of measurable time, my brain was outside of my body. Give me a break.*

Thom shared a look with Roche, laughing as he slid his belt off his lap. The kid brushed at the sweat stripe on his pants left by the belt mark. Roche chuckled, sliding his cables back down into their pilot sockets—sensors, thrusters.

//Jump drive sequence 2-12. Jump complete, open thermal vents —Radiological alarm.

Bogey, one mile bearing two-five-seven, thirty degrees down. CBDR with heat flare.

A fucking missile.

Thom slipped his belt back on. "CBDR? What's CBDR?" he asked.

CBDR—Constant Bearing, Decreasing Range. "It's getting closer and getting faster."

Roche tipped the nose of the *Aurum* down, sending the brig into a hundred-ton forward tumble. Thom's seat belt cut into his lap and he could hear tussle and crashing from back through the hatch comb in the ship.

But after the initial impulse, everything settled. They were still floating on their initial trajectory, just now spinning wildly.

Roche studied the data streaming inside his head. *Strap in!*

No shit, plughead!

Thom tried to become one with his chair. "What are you doing?"

Missiles had their own thrust and vectoring capability. Run and they will follow.

"I'm playing chicken with a thermonuclear warhead."

"That sounds bad."

A blue sine wave cut across his HUD—Lily's voice illustrated for him. *Time to impact, six seconds.*

//Apply thrust. Execute.

Roche boosted the ship straight at the missile. Thom involuntarily screamed. Six seconds just became three seconds.

Until Roche thrusted the ship straight down, ducking the incoming missile. Somewhere overhead, a twelve-ton torpedo streaked by.

Thom involuntarily yelped, then gasped, "Ah! We're alive. Oh my god!"

And as if on cue, the consoles all switched off. Thom yelped again, plunged into perfect darkness, a black curtain draped over their eyes.

They had nothing, no response. Roche threw impulsive commands to the ship's systems. Thrusters. Nothing. LADAR. Nothing. Roche could no longer feel the electrons warming his wrist.

They were in dead in the water.

"*Fra tow!*" Roche shouted.

//Reboot sequence, activate secondary AI command bank. Power divert from life support. Execute Spark protocol.

Roche yelled, "LILY! Wake the Hell up, right now!"

The room lit up with their blue and neon pink glow, the head dominating the space between Thom and Roche. "Localized energy blast from nuclear detonation. Rerouting to redundant secondaries."

Osyen burst onto the command deck, draping himself over Roche's chair. "Whenever you get around to it, Lily!"

"Rerouting."

The primary systems were almost certainly fried, but with the vast levels of cosmic radiation in the universe, anything beyond a second-generation vehicle had redundant systems built in ready in case of a disaster, natural or manmade.

Getting them running quickly, now that was a magic trick. Spaceships were not simple machines.

Osyen grabbed the back of Roche's clammy neck. Maybe he was aiming for the headrest? "Can you get us moving?"

Roche shook his head. "Not without main power."

"Are we going to suffocate?" Thom asked.

"Shut up," Osyen snapped. "Lily?"

"Rerouting."

"How many were out there?

"I didn't see the shooter," Roche said.

"Are we going to die?"

"We're not dead yet!" Osyen said. "Lily, sooner would be better!"

"I do not work faster when you constantly pester me."

"GODDAMN IT, LILY!" Osyen shouted.

The consoles lit up all at once and Roche felt the sweet flow of electrons kiss his arm.

"Hang on to something!" Roche gave the *Aurum* a twist and tumble before dashing off into space.

Like the seasoned spaceman he was, Osyen bounced himself off two bulkheads over to Thom's station—it's not like the cabin boy was actually observing his station's screens. "*Gulaw zu bow*, this is a mess."

"The missile do this?" Thom asked.

"No." Osyen shook his head, staring at a flickering monitor. "It's the Pulsar. It's washing out the signature." Then, suddenly! "Ah! Three bogeys, mark one nine seven, twenty degrees high."

"I see them," Roche said. They had their screens, their little monitors nestled inside a steel cage, pinholes in cardboard.

Roche was jacked in. He saw the three F-104B Bearcat carrier-based superiority fighters four miles back in a tight echelon. The lead fighter was the primary trigger, with the follows providing cover for his advance.

Those were Imperial Navy.

Osyen nabbed the headset off the console. "Hold fire! Hold fire! We are commercial transport *Aurum* on official Imperial business. I say again, hold fire."

In all this quiet, of thrusters bursting and hollow echoes, suddenly there were loud drumbeats. And Roche could feel the ship listing as evacuating air provided its own thrust.

Hull impacts, ballistic fire to the bulbous cargo hold. The Perseus model was designed to take space debris and radiation, not directed kinetic fire.

And his thin hair pulled lightly towards the door. There was a breach. They had to control the negative pressure, or the ship would rupture.

Adelaide, seal bulkheads 7 and 9. Ventilate cargo hold.

The old woman had not forgotten the old ways, *I'm already on it.*

Osyen tried again. "Naval interceptors, I say again, hold your fire!"

More drumbeats. They didn't hear or didn't care.

"Those fighters are going to run us down," Roche said.

Osyen's eyes darted across the screen, coming to the same identification and conclusion. Then: "Dive at the star."

Thom leered up at him. "You want him to do *what?*"

"Star will hide our silhouette from LADAR, wash it out. Roche? Can you mask every move with the star's flash?"

Oh, you clever man. The *Aurum* had seventeen reaction control thrusters and twin primary engine clusters. Every movement, every turn, every rotation threw off light and heat—something a computer could measure and track. Against a sun, they couldn't make out any of that.

"Yes, I can."

It was every half second, blanched out almost all spectrums. He could ply thrusters and send the ship in an entirely new direction with the strobe. And star-facing, they wouldn't be able to parse out their ship with other typical light-sensitive equipment.

//Downward thrust, forward tilt sixty-two degrees, roll twelve point six, conditional point 489 interval. Execute.

The ship lurched once, twice, three times—completing its thrusts only during the pulsar's flash.

And the drumbeats stopped.

"What's going on?" Thom asked.

Osyen grabbed the boy's chin, pointing his face at the screens. "See the big dot. The big dot is the bad men."

Roche grimaced. "They are changing course to intercept."

"Yeah," Osyen said with a hush, "but they know we dove over here, not where we are."

"I can only dive directly at a star for so long, Osyen."

"Why's that?"

Roche leered at him. "Eventually we catch fire."

"Smartass," Osyen murmured, his eyes darting around as he searched his proverbial bag of tricks.

"When I turn away, they'll be able to see us again."

"I know, I know!"

"Why don't we shoot back?" Thom suggested.

"With what, harsh language?" Osyen asked.

"No," Thom said, "but there's a cargo hold full of tomato crates. Steel crates."

Roche did the math. "A tightly packed field of crates at sufficient velocity might act like—"

"Buckshot." Osyen could've kissed Thom. *Addy, re-pressurize the cargo hold.*

There are breaches. It'll never hold.

I don't need it to hold for long, Osyen said, *just give me full pressure—and stand by to drop the gangway.*

//Hundred-eighty-degree rotation, X/Y axis. Same interval. Execute.

Two quick jerks and the ship was now facing their pursuers while still drifting towards the star.

"We're going to get one shot at this," Osyen whispered to no one in particular.

Roche had the command line prepared, just waiting for the fighters to get a bit closer. Can't give them time to react, to dodge, to even see what's about to happen. They had their own AIs and cybernetically enhanced pilots.

He had to pull them into making the mistake.

"Now!"

//Execute.

The *Aurum*'s engines flared and Roche could've sprained an ankle from the force. They were streaking towards their naval pursuers. At this range, the LADAR would pick them up—but it would be too late.

Roche gave the *Aurum* a spin, hurling cargo out of the open hold like a hundred steel shot-puts, filling space with frangible debris. Those fighters were armored but physics didn't care.

Two signals flared with heat and escaping gases.

Roche cheered, "Two strikes, evidence of escaping gases."

Osyen pumped his fist in the air. "And the third is buggering off home to mama! Nice work everybody."

"Those were Naval Interceptors," Thom whimpered. "They were shooting at us..."

"Yeah," Osyen said, clapping a hand on the boy's shoulder. "Welcome to your new normal."

"Why were they shooting at us?" Thom asked.

Roche knew what he was driving at. The *Aurum* might be in pirate space, but they were under Imperial employ, working for an Imperial admiral, on Imperial business. Either no one knew who they worked for, or...

Roche locked eyes with the boy. "Your admiral friend isn't the only Imperial after the Icon."

CHAPTER
NINE
THOM

THE PLANETOID LOOKED like a deep-space ginger root, an asymmetrical collection of rocks bound together by structures and scaffolding and pipelines. Scattered lights dotted its surface with one particular glow sending a bona fide spotlight out into the universe, a flare pulsing to some unheard party anthem.

It was alluring. It was wonderful. It was blinding.

"Welcome to Delta Boolean," Milardi had said. "The locals all just call it DeeBee. You call it Delta, *the* Delta, or the Boolean—you *will* get mugged. Stay close to me, do as I do."

Holographs and stills couldn't have prepared Thom for what he found when that hatch comb opened. It was like someone had painted the world in light, pastel, glowing colors wrapping along old industrial lines as far as the eye could see. What had once been built for function had been redressed with extravagance. Oil stains and grime were almost part of the art nouveau, as though placed with deliberate intent—or at least, they were unavoidable, so might as well design around it. It was extravagant, lived in, and thoroughly strange.

Now this, this is what he had left the Pantry to find.

There were more people than he'd ever seen before in one place.

They pushed and prodded at each other to get at the displays and stalls and street performers and advertisements and even the occasional small explosion somewhere. Thom was at once absorbed and subsumed, an ocean wave lapping at his consciousness. If he hadn't locked a hand on Milardi's jacket, he'd have been washed away completely.

Thom glanced back at the dock yard behind them, stealing one last look at the wreckage they had coasted in on. The *Aurum* looked like someone had hit it with a cheese grater and then blow torched one side of it. One engine strut had all but snapped off, leaving the thruster pushing off-center. There was a gaping hole in the under-belly about a foot across—a perfectly symmetrical punch-out from a Bearcat service round—and the cargo bay doors were bent at their teeth from the tomato gambit.

The brig was going to collect some new patchwork scars. The old machine was starting to look like Osyen's shirt.

A harbormaster on Ilum or Vanguard might've asked questions, summoned the authorities. Here, they recommended a good ship-wright who was almost certainly paying for that endorsement.

Something jostled Thom, something big, nearly checking him to the ground. The only thing that saved him was a sweeping arm from Milardi scooping him up.

"Watch it," came the nasally voice, whistling down from the eight-foot frame striding past—Thom came up to his waist. And the bald pink head did little to mask the big cartoon eyes, a membrane fluttering over the surface.

He just got hip checked by a man made of bubblegum.

"Did you see that?" Thom asked.

"Don't point." Was the only answer Milardi gave him.

"Why?"

Milardi threw him a look, a patented 'are you kidding me' look. "It's rude."

Thom lowered his arm, looking back at the retreating brute. "But he's pink."

"And?" Milardi asked. "How'd you like it if we called you 'peach?'"

"You call me *Unti*."

Milardi shrugged. "Yeah, but that's got charm to it."

Thom leaned in, a spark of excitement tinging his voice. "Is he *alien?*"

"Why ya whisperin'?"

"Because!" Thom snapped, his hand rising again before Milardi smacked it down.

Trying to be as circumspect as possible, Milardi peered over the crowd to catch a glimpse of the candy man. "Maybe twenty percent."

"Twenty percent *alien?* What does *that* mean?" Thom knew that things lived out in the universe other than humankind, and he'd read about a few. Savage monsters, tribal colonies, the occasional resistance from iron age peoples rejecting Imperial aid—but to see an actual alien! He was nauseous and couldn't make up his mind if it was out of horror or glee.

"Thirty tops."

"Thirty percent...*alien?* How does that even happen?" Thom asked.

Milardi noticed the gaping expression on Thom's face. "I'll tell you when you're older. Or, who am I to judge? Maybe you'll find out all on your own." Milardi clicked his tongue and tugged on Thom's arm. "Come on now. Crime ain't going to do itself."

Milardi pulled Thom through the marketplace. It was a technicolor daydream—saturated colors beaming past them almost too fast to register.

Clouds wafting out of stalls hinting of lilac and rainfall, the patrons inside hunkering over pint glasses. They breathed deeply of the fumes rising from their drinks, and the glazed look in their eyes was not of distance, but of memory—

A sign out front flashed in First Colonial and Imperial Standard: 'The Good Times Need Not Be So Long Ago."

"They're drinking...memories?" Thom asked.

"Smell is one of the *most* potent memory triggers," Milardi said. "Couple the right combo with some lightweight anesthesia and...'day dreaming'."

Thom followed his eyes up to the shop's name, floating iridescent purple letters that seemed to phase out and in at different places here and there. It was almost like the sign was showing itself just to him, a personal secret, and everybody else got a different thing.

Two men looked up from their drinks and Thom froze. Naval uniforms, midshipmen, collars undone.

Milardi patted him on the back. "Those ones are fine. Plenty o' boys come out this way on their shore leave for...entertainment."

"But we were just shot at by—"

Milardi patted him harder this time. "And the tenser you look, the weirder the moment is. Move it along before they decide to talk to us."

Thom and Milardi moved down the lane, but a sudden gust of wind hit them, bringing with it the smell of Day Dreaming. The store almost certainly had a fan positioned to rope in customers.

It rolled over him with the smell of musty vanilla, like old glue and paper coming apart: father's study. He'd snuck in once—

Milardi yanked his arm. "Oy! We're not window shopping."

"That's too bad," a honeyed voice purred.

Thom turned to see a woman blocking their path. Beautiful was the wrong word—she was ethereal, sharpened features that seemed to taper and curve in exaggerated ways. Her hair draped her face like a demure mask.

And she wore a curious collar, thick and matte black, like a steel bar, curled around her tunic's neckline.

Milardi gave her the once over with his eyes before shaking his head. "No thanks. We're on a schedule."

"That's a shame," she said.

And her face blurred—it was a hologram, projected up from her collar. For the briefest moment, Thom could see the woman underneath—hardly plain, but certainly a more regular person than the idol being presented.

But the form that replaced the previous was Rashida Izan de Tylmirande. Hair up, catching the light like it might burn, and her fiery stare withering his defenses. She flashed a smile, perfectly aping Rashida's cheek dimples and the natural polite laugh. "Perhaps something more personal?"

Milardi's knees buckled. "Hoo boy. Now that's not right."

"Holstrum," Thom cautioned, "remember Holstrum."

Milardi nodded quickly. "Very good point, *Unti*. Another time." Milardi tried to pull away.

But like a predator, she locked those fierce eyes with Thom. "Perhaps the lad then?"

"You'd break him in half." Milardi pulled Thom along the street. "Come on, kid."

The performance dropped and Rashida's face shimmered away. Underneath, a rough face with almond eyes and a narrow chin. She called after them with a laborer's lilt and slur, detectable even in the two syllables, "*Unti?*"

Thom shrugged, blushing. He was still remembering Rashida's face looking at him, almost hungry. It was a hard look to shake. "It's a long story," he said.

"Cabin boy, he does a lot of moppin'!" Milardi shouted back to her. "There! I told the whole story."

Milardi pulled him into the throngs of people. Dotted in the crowd were all kinds of whimsy and fantasy—people wearing plastic suits, aquariums for helmets, more Pink Heads. He could swear he saw a man with three legs.

"Could you stop gapin'?" Milardi said, "You look like a *gulaw* fish out of water."

"I think that's where the phrase comes from."

"Still—close your mouth before you start droolin'."

"How can you not?" Thom asked. "This is incredible!"

"Yeah," Milardi said, sparing himself a moment's glance at the wonder of it all, "but you look more like a tourist with a fat wallet. So..."

Thom looked back in the crowd for the hologram woman. "How did she know Rashida?"

Milardi shrugged. "Ship manifest is public. Genuine Dunsweir hits the dock and half the midnights are going to be using her face tonight. They'll make a mint."

Midnights: ladies of midnight. A prostitute.

"That was a—"

Milardi's grip tightened on his wrist, but the look on his face said humor. "What did you think it was?"

Now he really was blushing. Thom coughed into his shoulder. "A scam?"

Milardi chewed on that and nodded. "Yeah. It was that too."

They eventually stopped in front of a building, a four-story brick dropped into the ground, its tall smokestacks long dormant. The brickwork had been stenciled with street art, some more aggressive than others, and at least one with accurate anatomy. Two big men stood out front, batons in hip holsters.

Milardi sidled up to them, pressing something shiny into their palms. "*Regilaw pip.*"

The guard thumbed the shiny, feeling it out. It was only then that Thom noticed the deep scarring on the man's face and his milky white eyes. He was blind.

Something told him he could 'see' perfectly fine without eyes.

The guard nodded. "*Gitya.*"

Milardi bowed with a smile, before shoving Thom inside.

The pair descended a set of stone stairs cut out of the rock. Chips in the walls and steps showed off the age of the building. From below, he could hear the thrumming of a speaker system.

"What's down here?" Thom asked.

"We're meeting with an associate of Fiona McCorty," Milardi

said. "Rashida will be bringing 'em in. She's a legitimate buyer for something like this."

"She okay?" It came out of Thom like a reflex. "On her own out here?"

Milardi smiled. "Kid, she may be the only one who is."

They rounded a corner. It was larger than Thom could have possibly believed, like someone had somehow packed an entire arena into an underground bunker. He should've known better—the bar was a former industrial plant.

Every segment of the production line had been broken up with fencing to be semi-private spaces with tables and dance floors. Each seemed to have their own tastes: leather and shiny people in masks; dancing on tables in multi-colored skirts; quiet, well-dressed intellectuals each sipping from a single large pitcher.

The music echoed in the chamber—but he also felt it in his head. The thrum of the bass rocked through him, but it felt light and whimsical, a sugar plum fairy playing haywire with his brain. It was like all of the weight was lifted and someone was plucking on his nerves like bowstrings, setting his whole body alight and tuning it to the people around him.

He wanted to kiss someone, feel their skin on his.

It was the music. Everyone was riding that same audible high.

Milardi pursed his lips, watching Thom lose himself to the space. Was he amused or impressed? "Alright then."

"What?" Thom asked him, groggy.

"Nothin'," Milardi said with a smirk, "just breakin' from expectation, *Unti.*"

Milardi and Thom slipped into an empty room. Next door to them, a man was dancing on the table for a group of young women. Everyone was covered in soot and grime, but on the girls, the filth was more incidental—work-related. The dancer, his was stylistic and playful.

Center-left, Thom bounced, tugging on Milardi's jacket. The biggest of the four women, her exposed shoulders rippled with muscle. Her undercut had grown out a bit like a soft felt, but a black curtain draped over one side of her face, pinned back. Her crooked nose looked like it had been broken more than once—sometimes more than once in one fight.

She sat still in her booth while the other three girls hooted and hollered. She was hardly unhappy—just alert—nodding along with the music. Her eyes hidden behind a band of black shades, but he could see the movement darting underneath. They drifted over to Thom, tracking his arrival.

Milardi threw a quick glance over to assess. *Somebody's naughty,* Milardi commented. *A kinetic in the jacket? At a friendly little bar like this. Who do they think they—*He suddenly stopped and opened his big fat mouth. "Torys?"

The woman cracked a smile. "Thought I recognized you."

Torys excused herself from her friends and strutted on over. Someone was clearly watching, because the commentary was instant. Zatia chimed in with an admiring one-word assessment, *Goals.*

It's a work day, Zatia, Osyen scolded, *Keep it to yourself.*

Torys squared up with Milardi, arms folded. She might have been relaxed, but there was a tension in her stance that Thom recognized in an instant—that was military.

Milardi kneeled on the booth, pressing his face against the chain link fence like a boy at the playground. "What brings ya to DeeBee?"

Torys shrugged. "What brings me anywhere."

Milardi threw a look back at the party animals. "Still the designated adult, I see."

"Have a drink with us," Torys offered.

Holstrum. Thom reminded him.

Milardi nodded. *I know, I know.*

What happened at Holstrum? Osyen asked.

Milardi didn't even bother answering that, turning his attention back to Torys. "Unfortunately, I'm workin' tonight."

"Suit yourself." Torys nodded, turning back to her table and dancer. "Don't wreck the place. I like it here."

The dancer teased his shirt, lifting it to flare his abs and pelvis at Torys as she returned to the booth. He noticed Thom watching the show and started to ply his trade toward the cage wall. The girls shouted their teases his way, eager to see what surprises this might bring.

Thom retreated and settled in his booth, quietly hoping the beef-cake didn't walk over.

Milardi draped himself over the booth, pulling a glass from under his seat. He set it on a coaster and tapped a few buttons on the table. No sooner was he done typing, a liquid started to flow up into the glass.

"Now what?" Thom asked.

Milardi shrugged, taking a sip of his drink. "We wait."

Thom's eyes shifted, sliding back over to see if the dancer had taken more than he had meant from his gawking. "We're waiting...here?"

Milardi followed his gaze, and shouted. "Get it, boy! *Tyk iz breoff!*" He followed it up with a holler, like he was one of the girls.

"Get your own!" One of the girls shouted back, defensive but not even a little offended.

"What if I like yours?" Milardi fired back.

That's all Thom needed. A room full of drunken women, a strip-per, and free-flowing alcohol. Milardi was going to be a mess tomorrow and he was going to be the one mopping it up.

"You look overwhelmed."

Thom looked up to see Rashida at the door of their booth, wearing a rather form-fitting number. Did she ever wear the same clothes twice? Or did she—

No, wait—she had rebuilt the clothes! Thom recognized her tunic from the first time he saw her, but she had recut it with a deeper neckline and paired it with a large amulet to rest just above her cleavage. She had strapped on an ornamental belt buckle and then poured herself into tight leather pants.

This wasn't some new outfit, but rather one she had constructed for this precise occasion. It wasn't vanity—it was craft.

Thom stuttered, "You uh....you—"

"Command attention," she said. "That's the idea." She settled down beside him in the booth, draping a slender arm around behind him. "You're my Consort."

"I'm your what?"

"Consort," she repeated. "A lady of my station never travels alone."

"So like a...bodyguard?" Thom asked.

Her face fell, a sour note. "Almost the opposite. Consort is something of a euphemism. Royalty are too valuable to run about unconfined. You're the one holding my leash."

Thom nodded along, his voice sour, "So I'm from Ministry."

She hummed her confirmation. "You're not here to protect me. You're here to protect the Family. From me."

Celebrity required restrictions, which in turn encouraged rebellion. He was the gatekeeper, her jailor, her handler. It made their relationship antagonistic. He held all the power, but she would inherently challenge it. It was a decent enough cover story for him, but he would need to know how to behave. "So what would be a basic first level warning sign I'd use? Should I be—"

"You don't need to do anything," the royal said, a touch wistful. "I know how to play it."

"I'm not..." Thom paused, worried about the potential hole he was about to dig for himself. "...too young to be...?"

She smiled, patronizing. "The Ministry takes recruits at more formative ages. Elite candidates graduate before their fourteenth birthday." She eyed him, an appraising look. "The Consorts are selected even earlier. Anybody who knows who I am will be looking for someone like you to be in my orbit."

"So I'm a professional tattle-tale?"

She smirked. "Bit more than that, but I think I am going to use that going forward."

They were silent for a moment, but Thom couldn't keep the peace. "Where's your *real* Consort now?"

Her hair bounced as she tilted her head to look at him. "I didn't kill him, if that's what you're concerned about."

"I wasn't. But now that you mention it..."

Rashida caught a glimpse of the show next door, and her lip curled into a smile, decadent. A blush lit up her cheek, but she was hardly embarrassed.

That's right. The music was affecting her too. Everyone was soaking in that power.

His skin tingled like it wanted to leap into the air, charging him to dance, to do something. Being still was a kind of torture.

"They're here," Rashida said.

Milardi whipped around. "Who is?"

She pointed. Descending the stairs at the head of the club were two burly men, chiseled out of the rocks with thick beards and broad shoulders. They wore armbands, red and yellow stripes, tied roughly around their biceps.

Milardi gave them one look. "Slug gun in his boot. Comin' armed to a moot? Tsk tsk. That's just bad manners."

Thom pointed at Milardi. "He's the bodyguard, isn't he?"

Rashida just nodded, almost apologetic, jerking her head toward the door of the room. It was more believable than the slight teenage boy.

Milardi popped to his feet, pointing Thom to the console on the table. "Grab a drink on me, *Unti*."

He watched the two go, sauntering off in a whirl of style and gravity that drew the eye in. Thom could drink. He could lay down. He could run his fingers through Rashida's hair.

Well, that's creepy. Maybe he did need a drink. Or maybe that was the very last thing he needed.

We've made contact, came Milardi's jarringly clear voice. *Fiona's boys are eating out of her hand.*

So long as that's all they're doing, Osyen said.

Thom peered at the console Milardi had indicated. Old toggles, physical switches that were pressure-sensitive analog. Press harder, get more. The Pantry had something similar for their draught drinks.

"You shouldn't be here."

That voice. Thom knew it.

When had he sat down? When had he entered? He had taken Rashida's place like he'd always been there. Sitting in the booth, with a deep V-neck collared shirt and businessman vogue—

Jeremiah Stride. The Navy Spider who had tortured Osyen. His eyes pinpricks in the dark. He couldn't have been older than Osyen was, his narrow face and perfect chin absent any sign of wear or tear. It was like studying a sculpture.

We've got a problem, Thom said.

What is it? Osyen asked.

Before he could answer, he felt the back of his neck pinch—someone accessed his implant, was looking through his eyes. He almost felt them collectively gasp.

We're coming. Milardi, get Rashida out.

She's not done yet.

You're made, Osyen snapped, *scrap it and get out! Thom, stay put. I'm coming!*

"What are you doing here?" Thom asked Stride.

"Call it a professional courtesy," Stride said, his icy eyes unblinking. "Leave the Boolean Edge."

Something about him robbed Thom of his voice, his stillness, his coiled posture. "Wh-why?" was all Thom could muster.

"This is your one and only warning, Osyen. There will not be a second."

Thom stiffened up. Stride wasn't talking to him. He knew about the implants. He knew who was listening.

Thom shuffled in his seat—was he trying to get away, get closer, even he didn't know. "I don't understand. Are we free to go?"

Stride finally moved, a simple cock of the head that nearly made Thom jump out of his skin. His tone softened slightly, but not compassion. Pity. "What you do, Thom, is none of my concern."

He wanted to challenge him, say something whip-smart and clever. He wanted to backtalk like Osyen or calculate like Roche, fight like Zatia, or charm like Milardi. But nothing came.

Stride studied him, and that pity deepened to disdain. "You're not going to *do* anything, though. You're incapable. You have no anima, no violence in you. No ability."

"Like I'd win a fist fight with you." Thom's voice quivered.

"I'd rip your throat out before you could scream," Stride stated. "Nobody in this establishment would even notice you're dead."

"What do you want?"

For all of his lack of expression, Stride was clearly playing with his food. He took a long moment to answer: "Cannot plan for the enemy if you do not observe them."

"You enjoying this?"

Stride pursed his lips. "I did what I came here to do and I'll do it again. Leave the Edge while I'm still in a playful mood."

We're coming, Thom! Osyen assured him.

But not nearly fast enough. Stride was going to get away. Keep him talking.

"Did you order those ships to attack us?"

"Yes," Stride said, "and their families will never know what happened to them, thanks to you."

"And my family?" Thom whispered, almost like he had a threat to back it up.

Stride blinked. "You will not secure the Icon, boy. I'll make sure of that, one way or another."

Stride's eyes drifted up to the front, where undoubtedly Osyen and crew were jogging on in. "Two-minute response time. But what did you bring me?"

Osyen and Zatia swung into the doorframe. "Yo, Imp!" Osyen shouted. That might've drawn more attention, but the thrumming music buried it.

It was like Stride put on a flesh mask, hiding all expression and humanity behind a face he had peeled off a dead man. His ice-blue eyes tracked every feature of Thom's face like he might save it to a hard drive.

And his eyes flashed, solid yellow darts in the pupils, like a cat in the dark.

Augments.

"Don't! He's Oskie!"

But Zatia took her shot. She gripped the gaudy steel bangles on each wrist—ripping them off to unfold each into long, curved knives that seem shaped to her forearms, with a knuckle guard of rugged metal. She rolled her fingers through the grips and charged in to maul the Naval officer.

It was like trying to read the number on a passing race car or grab onto wisps of smoke. Stride stepped up on the booth seats and pushed off the headrest, cartwheeling up and over Zatia and giving the girl a lightening palm-strike to the top of her head as he went by.

The little bruiser who had squared off with bouncers twice her size went down like someone had turned off the power.

Osyen didn't even get time to shout. Stride barreled into him, lifting the pirate off his feet and slamming him into the opposite cage. The inhabitants all yelped in surprise, but they were quieted by Osyen's scream.

Stride had buried two fingers into Osyen's shoulder burn, ripping open the organic bandage. He could drive Osyen wherever he wanted, the fingers hooked into the meat.

Osyen lashed out, slamming his fists into Stride's gut, but it was like punching a concrete wall. Stride twisted his grip, not so much savoring the pain as trying to induce passivity. Stop resisting, you're only making it worse.

That's when he heard the shot.

125

Stride dropped Osyen and leapt aside, sparks setting off from the chainlink. He immediately zeroed in on the threat:

Rashida had one of the goons in a headlock, choking him off to sleep to join his unconscious friend. Milardi, on the other hand, had commandeered the slug gun the mafiosos had smuggled in and he was loading a fresh slug into the breech.

Stride sneered, and rushed him.

Fast. It was like he simply appeared at Milardi's side, swatting the slug gun aside and sucker punching him in the stomach. Milardi heaved, curling around Stride's fist like he had been fire-formed to rest upon it.

Do something, Consort.

"Bar fight!" It was all Thom could think of. He picked up Milardi's empty glass and hucked it at the neighboring cage. It was a narrow glass, passing through the cage wall and spraying the booth with liquor.

Torys was good—she caught the glass out of the air. And she was not amused, flicking the glass right back at him. He felt the glass cascade down his back, and a warm liquid coating his skin. He hoped that was the booze and not his blood.

But she also got his message.

Torys stepped up, pushing the stripper off the table and drawing the ornate pistol from her belt. She could've shot Thom, and arguably had a right to. But she knew who the bad man was—snapping one deafening blast at Stride.

Stride ducked the shot like he was made of vapor, twisting around Milardi to use as a shield. He planted a foot into Milardi's knee, bringing the big guy down to a reasonable height.

And in that instant, the entire bar erupted into violence. Glassware, knives, punches, spit, and venom.

Torys discarded her spent weapon and marched after the Naval officer that had her friend. Torys' three girlfriends were not interested in just watching the show either. All four were on their feet and running towards Stride like a Valkyrie phalanx. He spun around

Milardi, yanking and twisting the poor man to keep the women at bay. That stopped three of them.

The fourth, a slight blonde, simply dove under Milardi's legs to get at Stride. She snagged his foot, but it seemed to evaporate from her grip.

Stride had to give up Milardi, shoving the man aside, so that he could deal with the ladies. He flashed from one to the other, pinballing faster than the eye could follow.

Thom rushed to Osyen's side, sliding himself under the man's shoulder and lifting him up.

"What are you doin'?" Osyen asked him.

"Get up! Get up, we gotta go!" Thom shouted.

Torys was a solid fighter, a warrior and a soldier. The three girls were clearly tough as spit. Stride had them worked down to their knees, gasping for breath. The spider looked up at Thom with a devilish grin. He was never threatened by them—but he did enjoy the workout. He mocked a salute to Thom and jogged for the entrance, pulling himself out of the frothing club's violence.

Rashida, Milardi. Where were they?

Rashida was helping Milardi to his feet, but a grab bag of club thugs were encircling them. Just meatheads that wanted in on the fighting. Milardi flipped his slug gun over, turning the grip into a nice little club to wade through the crowd with. But given his height, he had more than a few contenders.

The circle closed in on them.

"I'm not sure this was an upgrade, Thom," Osyen slurred through the pain.

In came the pixie herself like she was wearing rocket-powered shoes. Zatia might have been small—but that just meant knee-caps were more accessible. And she brandished her twin blades, no fear, howling like a banshee as she darted around the mob of men. Her strikes were hard and the blades seemed to sing as they clacked off armor and slid through meat.

She didn't put the men down for the count, but for every man she injured, Milardi was able to follow up, cracking the polymer stock of the gun into jaws and guts.

"Thom, go!" Milardi shouted as he unhinged some poor bastard's jaw with a well-placed punch.

It was like bizarre performance art and Thom had bought tickets he didn't want to have.

"Yay!" Osyen said weakly, as Thom helped him toward the stairs. "We rescued you."

CHAPTER
TEN
THOM

OSYEN HADN'T SPOKEN to him since the club, sulking in his captain's quarters. He emerged only to take meals, and even then, only did so in a monk's celibate silence. Thom had tried to catch him a few times, but Lily had advised him to keep some distance.

He didn't blame Osyen—they had been through two near-death experiences in a single day. And Thom was having trouble shaking Stride's ethereal speed. It was like he wasn't even real.

"I've seen it before," Rashida had said.

"While you were Dunsweir? *In* Dunsweir? Which is it?" he asked.

"Both are correct," she said with a smile, "Holkstad Academy. It has a surgical ward larger than most hospitals. They're selected at youth, trained to be soldiers and covert operatives. In their second year, they're...heavily augmented. Not everyone survives."

That cold spider's stare, glinting yellow in the dark, a lacquer burned into the back of his skull for every time he closed his eyes.

"They are at once both the tip of the Imperial phalanx, and the dagger pushed into the enemy's back," she continued. "Soldiers are human. Oskies aren't anymore."

Spooky.

If Stride wanted the Icon, it was hard to imagine how they'd beat him to it. Thom wouldn't have been surprised if Stride could walk through walls.

Still, they had made contact with Fiona's men and expressed their interest in the Icon. Rashida's filigree and resumé should have been enough to garner attention. Once Rashida's team could confirm the Icon was in reach, Osyen's team would break in and steal it. Then it was simply a matter of making a gracious exit as disappointed capitalists, rejoining the heisters, and beating feet out of the Boolean.

Of course, even if it went all to plan, it would hardly be that simple.

An invitation arrived that morning, handwritten script inked onto yellowed paper. Unhackable, untraceable, and expensive.

Now that was a display of power. Admiral Hugh's collection of literature could fill an entire shelf and it took most of his life to acquire the bindings. These people were doling out paper as destructible missives.

A tease of the kind of security that Adelaide would have in front of her this evening. Thom wouldn't have been surprised to find a four-pin iron vault with a tumbler combination.

Rashida and her entourage had been cordially invited to attend a gala at Fiona's estate, formal dress expected, where they might discuss the deal further. Milardi spent a good hour selecting his most debonair outfit, but couldn't settle on a style. His longcoat and wide-brimmed hat were accompanied by a waistcoat he 'borrowed' and some decorative chainlink draped on his pockets and boots. It might not have been high-class, but he was the bodyguard; he would hardly be out of place.

Thom had a tougher needle to thread. His clothes were all work, slack and loose to soak up oils, only to be washed with aggressive soaps and scalding water.

Finery wasn't in his repertoire.

In response, Rashida revealed herself to be some kind of witch.

She had collected pieces from the entire crew: fingerless black gloves from Osyen; ankle-high boots from Zatia that she wouldn't miss; a tunic of Milardi's that could be quickly gathered tight and tucked under one of Rashida's corsets.

Thom knew the crew cabins on the *Aurum* well enough to identify them with his eyes closed. The sound of the walls, certain dents around the door frame, or an oil slick that never stopped dripping.

Rashida had somehow transformed her modest dorm—small enough he could touch both walls with outstretched hands—into a lap of luxury. Rivets and bulkheads were hidden behind tapestries of rich, colorful fabric. A holographic series of wisp lights hovered in the air overhead, throwing off light and even a bit of warmth.

He raised his hands high in the air, feeling his rib cage cave in as Rashida tightened his bindings. She placed a smooth hook into the laces and pulled hard to cinch the waister tight. It felt like he was a tube of toothpaste, ready to blow a seam on either end and spill out a grotesque stew on the floor.

"Breathe out," she instructed as she pulled on the laces with her brass hook.

He did so, but the constant squeezes made him cough. "Does it have to be so tight?" He wheezed out.

"You're in high society tonight, Thomas," Rashida teased, "you'll need to look the part."

"Does nobody have kidneys in high society?"

"No, we have them surgically removed," Rashida teased, before shifting to a more soothing tone. "You get used to it."

"Why would anyone want to do this?" He felt light-headed, queasy, like a set of stairs might make him throw up.

"There might have been several reasons I went skipping out to the Reaches, Thom."

"You doing this too?" he asked.

She laughed and it took a moment before he realized she was laughing at him.

"What?" he asked.

She bit her tongue before answering, "You have a back brace. My ensemble will have...mechanical engineering involved."

Perhaps she was joking around, exaggerating. But then again, she had told him he would look 'positively delicious' and he was starting to taste his dinner again, so maybe she just had a sick sense of humor.

She set her tool aside, and placed her hands on his waist—she might have been feeling the fit, but he couldn't help but feel uneasy at her touch. Her calculating fingers sketched over the newfound curve of his waist, the taper to his hip.

But her tone was all professional. "Have a look."

She waved her hand at a wall, deploying a hanging curtain. As the heavy cloth came to rest, it grew to a solid reflective surface. Thom took a sidelong glance at himself.

It might've been nauseating, uncomfortable, and difficult to breathe—but he looked good. He looked strong in the shoulders and with a healthy chest.

He looked like royalty.

Rashida stepped up to his side, revealing her own gown—an off-shoulder deep blue silk with white filigree inlaid, with flowery petals of fabric draping down over her legs, ending in knee high boots with a strong heel. Under the boots, a peek at black lace stockings with the Dunsweir orchid at the top.

"Did you make that one too?" he asked. He blushed a bit a how breathless he sounded, but then again, that might have been the cincher.

She smiled. "With a little help from Lily."

Thom cleared his throat. "Do I look..."

She read the indecision in his voice. Her smile softened a bit, laying a hand to rest on his shoulder. "You look like you own a governing share of Io."

"That's good?"

She ran her hand through his hair, fluffing the curls. "Rough is not the only way to play the game, Thom."

"What game?"

"You're my Consort so you're going to be fairly hands-off," she instructed, "but you're likely to get some social questions tonight. Where you studied, your focus, family, things like that."

He nodded along, taking mental notes, "So where did I..."

"Doesn't matter," she said. "They won't be listening too closely. The universe is a big place and they haven't heard of everywhere. Just speak with confidence and they'll assume you're rich and powerful."

Huh. "So the bullshit's at the same temperature at all levels?"

"Chin up," she said, lifting his with two fingers. "Choose your words with care. Don't be afraid of silence. Rambling will make you sound like you're nervous. Speak only when you choose to."

"That's good?"

"It *is*." Those two words came from her socks, rolling through her whole body before she said them.

"Are you two glass dolls comin' for this?" Milardi shouted down at them.

Rashida didn't even flinch. "I somehow think the car will wait for me."

"Yeah, but priceless relics need a thievin'. Let's go!"

She straightened her back, squared her shoulders, and laid her left hand to her stomach, palm in—she was assuming a role. "Let's to Court, Thomas."

The taxi arrived at the dockyard as scheduled, a bulky shuttle stained black and white to make it appear more formal. It looked like the car had been shoved in a suit-sleeve.

Disturbingly matching the colors of the car, Milardi waited at its side, bouncing on the balls of his feet like he was eager for ice cream —disconcerting to see in a seven-foot tall man. He looked like a small boy on platform stilts.

The inside was dimly lit, with bottles of liquor and pink, curly foods laid out for them, should they desire. But the first thing Thom noticed was the distinct lack of displays or consoles, not even a window.

They were not to know *where* they were going.

Thom set himself in his seat, but he couldn't seem to get comfortable. He inched left, twisted, rolled, but to no avail. The cincher was cutting into his hips and chest no matter what he did.

"Square your shoulders," Rashida said, seeing his struggle, "roll them down your back."

"What does *that* mean?" Milardi cut in, confused by the language.

She turned away from him, showing her exposed left shoulder and demonstrating. The blade of her shoulder lowered down as the ball of her shoulder came into line.

Thom would've found the display helpful if he wasn't so focused on her backless dress. But he just had that image burned into his mind now and there was no stopping his imagination from running off into the wilderness.

Space heist. Yes, stay in the space heist. He took as deep a breath as the cincher allowed and tried to relax in his seat.

Milardi dipped a finger into the pink food on display, lifting a dollop of the porridge onto his tongue. He made a show of the tasting, smacking his lips. "That is...bizarre."

Rashida rolled her eyes. "It's a shrimp puree blended with rice and spices, likely all Gaia-sourced."

Milardi controlled the gag reflex that hit him. "What is a 'shrimp'?"

"It's delicious," was her only response, though Thom noted she was not partaking.

The big man reached over for a bottle of liquor, uncorking it.

"We're working," Thom objected.

"I knows it," Milardi said, "but I just have to get that taste out of my mouth."

Milardi sipped at the bottle whenever he thought the other two weren't paying attention. Not like they couldn't—it wasn't as though he was surreptitious about it. Rashida and Thom shared more than a few looks.

Kill me.

Kill you? Kill him.

What would we do with the body?

Space is big.

We could throw him into a star.

I like it. Murder is the order of the day.

Shhh. Pick the right moment.

Of course. Can't rush these things.

Milardi hiccupped, interrupting the stream of consciousness and filling the cabin with the rank smell of elegant vodka and bile.

"Lovely," Rashida said, brushing imaginary grime from her shoulder, "my bodyguard is drunk."

"Not drunk," he said, and Thom almost believed him, "I'm a whole *two* of you."

A soft chime from the cabin and the lights raised slightly. Rashida drew a breath. "Here we go."

Thom took a breath. Silence is fine. Pick words with care.

The door swung open, filling the cabin with light. He heard it before he could see it, a vaulted room with hundreds of voices dissolving into one texture. Stonework bouncing the sound. The mild hum of electric lighting.

Then his eyes adjusted to the light. The shuttle had somehow settled indoors. The walls were glassy chipped stone, like black obsidian carved to form. Pillars of the natural stone had been left— form or function, he couldn't be sure. The floor was polished to a mirror shine and the roof above was veiled in darkness.

Copper piping erupted from the walls and ran the length of the structure. He couldn't imagine what fluids might pump through them, but the dull groan told him that something was actively flowing.

Against one wall, a stage had been propped up on stilts. Five men in matching velvet blue suits, two with violins and two with trumpets and a fifth on a polished grand piano—Thom was agog. There was more money on display on that stage than there was in the cradles at the shipyard. The rich, warm tones filled the arena with a simple sultry melody.

And the full smoky belt from the alto in the slinky red dress completed the tapestry, a musical brand on the air, an elegant reminder of the power at play.

They weren't stepping into a Court—this was a gladiatorial arena and the hostess wanted everyone to know it. The music that echoed off every surface was a constant reminder of whose roof they were under. It was not supposed to calm or distract or entertain.

At the front of the room, a step up had been carved from the stone, creating a dais where four high chairs had been set, one with a taller back then the others. Its wooden back was splintering and cracked, but had been filled with a copper resin, like one giant gemstone had been melted to fill the damage, a streak of orange lightning permanently etched into the grain.

It felt like stepping into another plane of existence. And Thom wasn't sure he hadn't. Maybe he'd gotten a contact drunk off of Milardi's breath.

The assembled crowd was the only thing that felt familiar. Human faces, at least. There were enormous hairstyles, elegant gowns, and cinched waists. At least he didn't stand out too much.

But yet, every eye was turned toward their shuttle.

Rashida wasted no time, sliding out of the shuttle like she was walking on a cloud. No bounce to her step, just a celestial glide. The blues and whites of her gown seemed to glow as she—no they didn't seem. They *were* glowing.

Lily had done a thing. Hah!

As Rashida hit full stride, she pulled a strap from her waistline, and the dress tumbled out behind her, the petals of her dress unfolding like they came from a pocket dimension. Two slits in her ball gown allowed her legs to cut forward, sacrificing not one ounce of mobility for the train.

She finally came to a stop a dozen feet away from the shuttle, her dress train unfurled all the way back to the door. She gave a deliberate bow towards the empty thrones at the head, showing deference to the unseen host, before striding toward the nearest group of courtiers.

Milardi grimaced. "Maybe we should get out too?"

"Yeah."

The boys stumbled out of the shuttle. Either they were just in time, or the shuttle was waiting for them, as it thrusted up and away as soon as they had cleared the airframe.

Rashida was instantly absorbed by a crowd of rushing dilettantes. But Thom was instantly struck by their voices—they sounded like him. Crass, slurring, simple language, thick accents and accented by grunts.

A voice pulled him from his reverie. "Sir? Sir! Please exit the landing pad."

"I'm sorry!" Thom blurted, jumping the few steps away from the shuttle stop. He immediately cursed himself. Power doesn't apologize. Power exerts.

Thom looked the speaker up and down. Suit and tie, but ill-fitting uniform. Staff. Bowed head, avoiding eye contact.

He couldn't have been much older than Thom was. Maybe he was from a dirt ball, had signed an indenture contract to see the world. His world was now this ballroom, and he'd give bone marrow to see sunlight.

"What's your name?" Thom asked.

The boy quivered. "Hatfield, sir."

Thom nodded. "Good man, Hatfield."

"Sir?"

Thom glanced back at the landing pad. "Truth be told, some of us have been having drink. You've ensured we enjoy ourselves and not injure ourselves. Thank you for that."

Clearly, the boy's brain was skipping beats. He was looking for where the abuse had been buried, some sideways injury or cynical snipe.

He dared to look Thom in the eye. Thom gave him a wink.

"Minister!" A voice called him away. Thom nodded at the servant before walking off.

An elderly woman demurred behind a hand fan—oh my God, he needed that fan! He needed it like a thirsty man needed water. When she called him over, he did not delay.

"Minister," she began with a drawl, "it is our pleasure to welcome a state official to our Court."

State official? Minister? He was from the Ministry but did that mean he was—answer her!

Thom coughed. "Yes...it is a pleasure to..." he paused, pursing his lips, "...entertain the Court."

She seemed to like that answer, hiding her face with the fan some more. He breathed deep, enjoying the backswing of the fan on his face. The cool breeze gave him life.

A portly man with an eyepatch and a walrus mustache thick with oil slid into the conversation. "You wouldn't be here in any official capacity, would you, sir?"

Official capacity is observing Rashida.

"My only official interest is the Lady," Thom said.

The walrus smiled. "Perhaps you or your official friends might have some unofficial interests?"

The old woman folded up her fan and swatted the walrus' shoulder. No, keep fanning! Don't stop!

"Thibodeau! Have you no shame?"

The walrus sneered, leaning in closer to Thom. "I can provide a great many things to a man of means."

"I have no earthly idea what you're talking about."

"Earthly!" The man chortled, laughing with some muscle buried deep. "You're in DeeBee now. Relax. How big is your entourage? I can support a large roster."

"He's not buying," said the old woman, eager to speak for Thom.

"You don't know his interests!"

"I know yours, Teebo," she murmured, loud enough for him to hear.

Thibodeau the Walrus leaned in to Thom again. "Every man has needs."

"And most men have discipline." Rashida stepped up to Thom's elbow, almost cutting him out of the circle. She tilted her head at the Walrus, a scolding edge to her friendly warmth. "The Minister is working."

"Blessed be his steps," the Walrus said with a crooked smile, yellowed cigar teeth. "Perhaps I should've been entertaining your tastes?"

Thom caught Milardi's eye, floating nearby, a drink in one hand and an open hand drifting to his leg holster.

"I'm no one's second choice," she quipped. "And you couldn't sate my appetites. I'd eat you out of house and home."

Thom could swear the man's mustache grew half an inch as he pulled in a breath. "A man must have aspirations."

"You're right. A *man* should."

The old woman and her fan fluttered, looking about for anyone else observing the scandal at play. Thibodeau couldn't decide if he was offended or not, as he worked his neck to relieve the heat building under his collar.

It was then Thom noticed the band had stopped playing.

Thibodeau squared his shoulders. "Does the Consul have any further comment to my trade?"

"The Consul doesn't know who you are," Rashida stated, "which I believe is your preference anyhow."

"Forgive me," he said, "we haven't had the pleasure of Dunsweir's Finest on the Edge for some time."

"Not officially, at least," Rashida said.

Thibodeau's eyes darkened, throwing a look Thom's way. "I imagine the little Minister knows how valuable you might be to the Family." It wasn't a question.

Rashida was quick to respond. But Thom was faster.

One word. "Imagine..."

The circle all looked to him. And his heart quickened, his fists tightened. He could feel his throat tighten up as if the Walrus had the power to choke him with a look.

Silence is power. Choose the words. Then speak.

Thom didn't look at Thibodeau. He looked up at the pillars. Meeting the man's eyes and he might've quivered or cracked. He probably looked so distant.

Good.

"Imagine your world," Thom started, "now imagine it with the Consul's attentive eye."

It was like Thom had pulled the air out of the room, and petrified them all into a salt. Even Rashida's eyes went wide, but hardly disapproving.

Milardi looked like he wanted to applaud, hunched over to lock in the laugh. But he couldn't hide the face-splitting grin on his face. The schoolyard pride leaked out of him.

Boots, thick heels ringing off the stone floor. The crowd parted instantly, genuflecting to the approaching march.

Polished riding boots, almost as reflective as the floor, rising to the knee. Thick suit pants were tucked into them, but the tailored fabric did not bunch, silhouetting without binding. The red silken shirt, matched to her curled crimson hair, hung loose, with a suit jacket unbuttoned billowing like a cape. Osyen had told Thom once to look for those loose placements, as they can mask armor underneath.

Her hair hung close to her face, bangs cut to drape across one eye like a bloody veil. Emerald green eyes, like a snake's skin, studied the confrontation and its participants, here in the Court of the Pirate.

For this was the Master, Fiona McCorty.

"Thibodeau," the Master said. "First lesson of Capitalism." That phrase sounded awfully familiar.

Fiona squared up on the portly merchant and leaned back with crossed arms, an idol to the word 'unimpressed.' She spoke with an instructor's forced formality masking the painful disapproval underneath. Thom thought that disapproval likely would be paired with blood drawn.

"It's poor form to scold your patrons just because they're not buying. They might be more keen tomorrow."

Thibodeau didn't say a word, but bowed his head and stepped back. He didn't have the gravity or cache to even vehemently agree.

Fiona smiled, thin lips drawn away to nothing, revealing one golden tooth. "Welcome to Court, my Lady."

Rashida curtsied deep, like the flow of water off a cliff. "My thanks for the invitation."

Fiona's warm smile didn't waver, nor did her tone sour, but the message sure did. "You don't seem very thankful, given how you treated my Courtier."

Rashida was a high society duelist. "Is it customary in the Court to threaten ransom of your guests?"

But so was Fiona. "Only if their value is measured in coin and not favor."

"And what is my value to the Master of Pirates?"

"You can answer a question for me," Fiona said. "Where is Osyen Belt?"

Thom nearly choked on his own tongue. How did Fiona know about Osyen? Were they already dead? Did she know about the plan?

Osyen, we're blown. But there was no answer. *Osyen?*

Fiona's eyes drifted over to Thom, studying the little Minister from the Core Worlds. And then he heard her speak. *The rogue is not available, little Thomas.*

Uh oh.

He wanted to turn, run. But he found he couldn't. He was rooted to the spot.

So was everyone, in point of fact. Rashida's arched eyebrow held in place. Milardi sipped eternally from a flute of champagne. Thibodeau pinched the end of his mustache, his eyes fluttered half-closed and never rising.

Time stood still.

No one reacted to anything as Fiona stalked over to Thom, plucking on his waistcoat, "Time means nothing to electrons. You and I can stay here forever, bargaining and threatening. We can dance till the skies fall down on our heads. But at the end of it all, little Minister, you will tell me what I want to know."

CHAPTER
ELEVEN

OSYEN

THEY HAD TRACKED Thom's implant to a small rock floating around a larger rock. There was nothing remarkable about this lump of coal in outer space. Which was why Osyen was convinced this was Fiona's hideout.

They dared not actively scan the location—that would light off every alarm. But there was a lingering heat, a candle in the dark, several plumes shooting out like feathers.

They took a shuttle inside, gliding into one vent. They followed the heat to an air lock. It took Adelaide four whole minutes to crack. She was elbow deep in the panel, straining to reach something or other.

"Security?" Osyen asked.

"Such as it is." Adelaide chuckled. It was an old grandma laugh so sweet he might've thought she was knitting and not cracking a high security bulkhead on the secret hideout of a criminal kingpin.

He rolled his eyes. "Should I be worried?"

"Osyen, a man in your position should *live* in a state of worry. I'd think you'd be comfortable with it by now."

"Osyen is a lot of things," Zatia chirped, "comfortable isn't one of 'em."

"You didn't answer the question."

"Yeah," Adelaide grunted. "Was kinda hoping you wouldn't notice."

Maybe it was just a good party. Maybe they'd been captured. It was stupid to send Milardi with them. Animal was probably drunk and lecherous, blew their whole cover.

Not like Osyen could've gone—Fiona knew his face. And Zatia was a little ball of chaos, one touched nerve away from setting entire buildings ablaze. Roche was not...social.

No, Milardi was the only choice.

The airlock door cracked open with a hush. Adelaide withdrew her arm from the wall, rolling out the fingers on her right hand. "What did I tell ya?"

"Not much of anything, really," Osyen said, jerking his head. "Inside."

Zatia hopped through the opening door, a pistol in one hand and a flashlight in the other. Much good it would do them—if they were caught, shooting their way out was not a realistic option. But it made the little bruiser more comfortable.

Osyen hadn't left his carbine behind, after all. It was strapped to his leg, chambered and ready, but it would likely not have the time to leave his leg.

It was a dark hallway, a maintenance access and an emergency exit. Piping and conduits ran overhead, below the grating under their feet and behind the guard rails on either side of them.

And he got a good look at all of it when the fluorescent lights flicked on overhead, the bulbs dropping out of sleeves like mechanical flowers in bloom.

Adelaide lifted her hands up—this wasn't her.

At the end of the hallway stood a portly man with an elegantly curled moustache. Formal white tie and three-piece suit, but the eye piece that was strapped to his head was far from fanciful.

A control piece.

Roche chimed in on the link, *Uh, someone's at that hatch comb.*

Yeah, we've met.

"Osyen Belt, I take it?" The man asked.

"Wait a minute...Z?!" Osyen started. "This isn't the Comfort & Company!"

Zatia didn't miss a beat. "I told you, it's at Beta Boolean. But no, you knew what you were doing!"

The mustache with a targeting scope raised one hand. As if he could silence them. They were in a bit now. Adelaide still had her hands in the air, forcing a big cheesy smile.

Osyen wasn't about to let her ruin this perfectly serviceable cover. He squared up on Zatia. "You think Yuri sent us to the wrong place? Yuri?"

Her face twisted for half a second. Yuri? He shrugged. It was the best he could do on short notice.

"Yuri!" She forced the laugh. "Was he sober when you talked to him?"

"Sober? No. No, he was not. Hell, *I'm* not sober *now*."

"Enough!" Mustache's eyeglass lit up emerald green, and two turrets popped from the walls with simply the biggest gun barrels Osyen had ever seen.

Hoo boy.

Osyen collared Adelaide and Zatia, tossing them backwards out of the airlock and back onto the asteroid surface. They cursed and objected, but the outer door automatically slammed shut, locking them outside.

Zatia was livid. *Osyen—*

Get back to the Aurum *and get clear until I call.* They tried to object, but Osyen shouted them down, *Just do it!*

Mustache was advancing on him. "We have patrol ships inbound as we speak. You haven't saved them. You've simply selected what kind of death you'd like them to have."

Osyen's hand lingered on the wood varnish of his carbine. It had gotten tacky. Needed cleaning. "I take it the lady of the house is expecting me."

"I decide who gets to see her." Mustache leaned on one of his turrets, his great weight not even budging it. Those Repeaters were not cheap.

"What are those, GA-57 Repeaters?" Osyen asked. "They'll put a hole clean through me and through that airlock door. So unless you have an EVA suit I'm not seeing..."

"You misunderstand, Osyen. I can kill you. I didn't say I would."

A single crane arm popped out of each turret's frame. Before he could react, an arc of lightning cracked the air and he tasted blood— he bit his tongue. Either when the charge seized him, or when he hit the floor.

———

It's a keen misunderstanding by most people that when you're 'unconscious' that you're asleep. Osyen was quite awake for the next few minutes. He was simply too delirious to do anything. His head was swimming, his chest aching.

He could smell bacon.

They had dragged him into a room composed entirely of shadows, with a single blooming light silhouetting his captors. The goon squad addressed his captor as Thibodeau—Teebo? Tie-bo? Thibo? No, clear Tee sound. Man, his head was ringing. It was like trying to hear conversations through a pool of water.

But he was suddenly clear as day when she came in.

Stylish as ever, Fiona stepped into the light, her eyes taking in his look. She wore a loose jacket and frilled white tunic, tight pants— masked armor and tricks without appearing like she had anything to hide. Feminine wiles, they could draw the eye to her body while masking where the twelve gauge was tucked. It was like any street magic trick.

She hadn't lost a step while running her fiefdom.

"Hello, Osyen." He was surprised how much he liked the sound of her voice, like a balm for his collection of contact burns.

Osyen went to shrug, finding his hands bound behind him. "We have got to stop meeting like this."

"You could've knocked," Fiona said, not looking at him.

"I believe I did. In my way."

The lights came up—revealing a parlor. Rich wooden cabinets and bookcases, with brass and copper accents on everything. A bartender shook out a drink, while a hologram dancer moved to a crackling recording of brass music. Mustache-Thibodeau stood by the doorway, thumbs hooked in his pockets.

Osyen's eyes darted around the room. "You had them all just wait quietly for you?"

Fiona smiled. "The more disoriented you can have your opposition—"

"The easier they are to lead," he finished the proverb. "You trying to con a con?"

"Oh, and you were crawling around my installation looking for a nice getaway with that little girl?"

"That little girl can—and has—kicked my ass, so I wouldn't go about calling her little."

"Beating you isn't exactly difficult, darlin'."

The bartender poured out the prepared drink: peach-colored foam and what had to be copious sugar. He whisked the drink over to Fiona so fast, he had to be on wheels.

"Well," Osyen muttered, "I'm in, aren't I?"

"Don't act like this was all part of the plan." Fiona settled onto a bench, reclining like a decadent emperor, propped up on her elbows. "A real-life Dunsweir? That was a bit flashy, don't you think?"

"Held your attention."

"Which made me immediately look over my shoulder," Fiona said. "But then, subtlety was never really your forte. What happened at the Gaslamp?"

Osyen shrugged. "Too many drinks?"

She shook her head. "Osyen, you have run this thing with all the dexterity of an angry badger."

147

"Better than a sleepy one," he said. "You look good."

"Don't butter me up, I'm already burnt."

Osyen chose to study the floor, the burnt mahogany panels inlaid. The floor probably cost as much as his ship.

It was less sour than looking her in the eye.

"Why didn't you just call me?"

"Fiona—"

"Really, any time in the last two years?" she asked. "You have my private code."

Osyen didn't want to dance with her. "How'd you find me?"

That was apparently a dumb question. "It occur to you that the harbormaster works for me?"

"That's not how you found me," Osyen dismissed, "it's not like they had my profile on the wall."

"They don't?" she teased.

"How did you find me?"

"You should've come with me," she blurted out, her eyes soft. It was an earnest statement, but marked with wistful missed opportunities. It wasn't something that could be remedied—that chance had evaporated.

And would his situation be any better if he had? "How...did you find me?"

Fiona sipped her drink, savoring the flavor. "You're not going to like it."

"Five years of this job, I haven't found much I did. Was it the kid?"

Fiona chuckled. "No, the boy was a proper little badass. You shoulda seen him. You'd have been proud."

"Liar."

"That's an accurate character assessment, but not what I'm doing right now."

"Then who?" he asked with a raised eyebrow, "Rashida look out for her own hide?"

"Hi, boss." He knew the voice but there was no accent.

Osyen ground his teeth, leering at the door to see Thibodeau—and Milardi, literally hat in hand. But he was a touch full of himself, smiling like a cat who broke something you hadn't found yet.

"Really?" Osyen asked, a blend of incredulous and bile.

"She knows everything," Milardi said, his thick Colonial accent dropped. "Don't muck about." It wasn't a threat, but a statement of uncomfortable fact. It was the cautionary given to a criminal in interrogation. Don't lie, you'll only make it worse.

Fiona nodded. "Jackson's been on my payroll for a whole year. You really thought you could afford a trigger of his quality, at the rate you pay?"

"I figured I was at least fun to be around," Osyen said through clenched teeth.

Milardi didn't stay anything, but he nodded slightly, conceding that, at least.

"So." Fiona sat up. "You want the Icon of Cruciform."

"Me and the rest of the known universe," Osyen said. "I take it you're not selling?"

"I'd have to have it in stock."

Osyen almost laughed. "I knew it."

She arched her perfect eyebrow, holding her tongue. She always knew when to speak and when not to, when holding your tongue communicated more than words could—but also when speaking would give more than she wanted to.

Osyen licked at his lips. Where to start? "The Imp's intel was off. Daymar's not your style."

Fiona nodded, agreeing. "Not for lack of trying, but—yes, door kicking isn't as effective as lines of credit."

"And poison."

"You're awfully mouthy for someone on the losing end of this," Fiona cautioned.

"Who said I lost?" Osyen snarked.

She smirked. "You got caught, jackass."

"And yet I get to see old friends."

Fiona studied him for a long moment. "You can bluff. But you literally don't know what you're going to do next. You're in this so deep, you don't even see the light anymore. How did you let yourself get there?"

"Greed, mostly." She always knew how to see right through him, not that he'd ever give her the satisfaction of confirming it. "But you wouldn't be *talking* to little ol' me unless I could do something for you."

"I can't talk to old friends?" she asked, hitting a little extra on the 'old' and the 'friends.'

That was a threat. But Osyen wasn't in the negotiating mood. "Were we friends?"

Fiona cocked her head to one side. That was pulling the hammer back, ready to fire. "You didn't tell your crew about you and me, did you?"

"Thom knew a little. That we knew each other." That wasn't an answer. It was a dare. Shoot him or shut up.

She shot him, right in the knee. "Oh, the navy brat? That's rich."

Milardi's eyes darted to Osyen, but Osyen just stuck out a hand. "Don't even start in about secrets, Milardi."

Still, Milardi's jaw quivered, a whole mess of emotions rocking around in his skull. The risks, the costs, were they in this whole jam because of the kid? And ultimately, because he liked the kid and it would be a damn shame—

To have to kill him.

One problem at a time.

But of course, Fiona had a second shot lined up right behind it, blowing out his other knee. "Navy's not even your biggest problem— Capital." No leg to stand on now.

Secret after secret pumped into the air, Milardi looked like he was going to pull his hair out, but kept his mouth shut.

"Calm down, *skel*," Osyen hissed, "your world isn't any worse today than it was yesterday."

Milardi couched. "Next thing, you're going to say Lily's actually a person hardwired into a databank somewhere."

Lily's voice exploded in their heads, *That's disgusting. The smell alone—*

"Not now, Lily!" Osyen snapped out loud.

Thibodeau nearly jumped out of his skin. Osyen couldn't see it, but he felt the knife edge of something automated at the back of his neck. Thibodeau might not have been a gunman, but he had his tools at beck and call.

Even as Lily receded into the background, he could feel their acid boiling away. And it wasn't hard to imagine why. Milardi hadn't just tricked Osyen—he'd tricked an AI. And they were not going to forget that.

"You've outed me, thanks for that," Osyen said. "Are you done?"

Fiona sat up, leaning forward like she might share a secret. "I had an agent in place on Daymar before the attack, but he cut contact. My sources say they indoctrinated him into their silly cult. Before I could get a new agent in, someone blew the whole place to kingdom come. Killed my agent, took the Icon."

"Who has it now?"

Fiona stripped a glove off, revealing a metal prosthetic hand—a sleek steel replica that looked more like armor plating custom built for her than a computerized attachment. Roche might have been jealous if it wasn't so ornamental. Why look human when you could be better?

She laid the hand on the table, transferring a few petabytes of data over to the projector before a star map leapt up—the Boolean Pulsar and its satellites. The image pulled in on a specific planetoid, and the mist of smaller ones around it: thousands of rocks, if not millions.

"Orbiting Gamma Boolean is an old asteroid mine, one of a couple thousand abandoned by the Dehaans Corporation ten years ago. The rigs kept on digging autopilot, and it didn't take long for the Widows to move in to the real estate."

"Oh, scary name," Osyen mocked with his hands raised. Violent types always picked super poetic names trying to inspire fear: Black Widows, the Marauders, the Wild Winters, the Yellowjackets.

Poseur crap. Just get to the stealin' and take off the ridiculous uniforms. They wanted fear and respect, but only knew how to get one of those at any given time.

And respect was too expensive to maintain.

"They're not looking to hold onto it," Fiona said, "it paints a target on their back. They just want to offload it quickly."

"So buy it," Osyen blurted. "You've got the cash."

"I'm the most powerful person in the Boolean," Fiona stated. "They're not going to just let me lock that down further."

There's the rub. "But you want to...Master of Pirates."

Fiona smiled. "Steal the Icon for me, Osyen. And I'll make all your problems go away."

"Why not have one of your teams handle this?" Osyen asked. "You've got people who do this in their sleep."

She blinked, studying his face. Cherishing it. "I do. But you seem to be in a jam. And I help my friends."

CHAPTER
TWELVE
THOM

"A CAPITAL?!" Zatia bellowed, pointing a finger at Thom's head like she might split it open with a look. "And an Imp?!"

"And a double agent!" Osyen said, pointing at Milardi, like that helped his case.

"We will *get* to him," Zatia snapped, "but right now we're kickin' in *your* teeth!"

The crew had cornered Thom and Osyen against the *Aurum*'s cargo bay wall. Thom wasn't convinced that Zatia wouldn't just shoot them down right there. Adelaide was contemplating drawing out their pain with power tools. Roche was simmering at the back of the crowd, his cybernetic eye darting around as he ran simulations—of the job, of escaping Boolean, of repairs to the *Aurum*.

Of murder. Plenty of murder.

Rashida regarded the two defendants with distant study, more offended by them than threatened. And Milardi hung off the ladder like a bored child, just waiting for the rest of the crew to catch up.

Gun hand and royalty were the ones that had to be convinced, if they wanted to bring the rest of the crowd around.

"So I was a criminal before you met me," Osyen said. "Big deal."

"Capitals," Adelaide hissed, "aren't just criminals and you know

153

it. They're convicts. They don't have an identity, they don't have rights—"

Osyen glared at her. "Forgot my name since this morning, did ya?"

Adelaide marched up to Osyen's face, hissing the quiet threat into his face. "Can you help my husband or not?"

"I didn't lie to you," Osyen assured her.

"Yeah, you did," she said, quietly cursing his name as she circled away from him.

"You could always continue to scrape a rusty living out at the depot." Osyen was fed up with her, with them all. "Or we can do the job."

Zatia rested her hand on her hip holster. "Are we working for the Imps, or your ex-girlfriend?"

"Not my girlfriend."

"Ex."

"Not that either," Osyen said. "We work for us."

"Two different factions are holding our lives hostage," Roche said. "Hardly the romantic ideal."

Milardi moaned. "Come on, Roche—"

"*You*," Roche snapped, getting a jump out of everybody. Not even Zatia was ready for that amount of venom to come out of the calculating pilot. "Three people in this room have lied about their histories or motivations, drawn undue focus and pain on to us in ways that cannot be adequately measured—and all of it avoidable if we had been honest with one another. We cannot plan for anything if we don't know everything." He pointed at Osyen. "You were the one who told us that, *Capital*."

Osyen shrugged. "That's not who I am anymore."

Roche was stone, features carved upon a gargoyle that judged at the entrance of the cathedral. "You don't get to decide that. They do."

That slipped through the armor, and Osyen wilted. Thom wanted to object, defend him, if for no other reason than to give him a moment to mop up the blood. They were just hitting him and hitting him, but he knew that was because he kept getting up.

And the longer he held out, the less focus they laid on Thom. If they were going to beat their captain, they were going filet the Navy brat. Osyen was standing in front of shots that could just as easily have gone to him.

Roche shook his head. "This is not a team—this is a suicide pact. I'll be on the bridge."

Roche stormed off, purposely walking to the far side of the bay to the opposing ladder. Milardi gestured if he should follow.

"Go," Osyen whispered.

Rashida belayed that order. "Stay."

Osyen's eyes darkened. "Don't you *ever* tell people what to do on *my ship*."

"I'm not certain you're in a position to be giving orders to anyone," she bit back.

Milardi froze, not sure who to obey.

Osyen grit his teeth. The moment Osyen moved for a weapon, they would cut him down. But for that moment, he was contemplating his odds.

No one wanted to break the silence that followed, like standing on an icy river that cracked underfoot. Any move might send one or all plummeting into the frigid depths, swept away and buried by the glacial flow.

"I'm sorry," Thom sputtered.

"Thom—" Osyen started.

"No," Thom cut him off. "They're right. It was wrong. It was self-serving. We were scared of what might happen if we—"

"They don't have a right to know everything about me." Osyen wasn't about to be railroaded by a kid.

"Then you don't have to apologize to them, Osyen, but I did something wrong! It hurt people I care about. It put them in danger."

"You don't know—"

"I *do* know that!" Thom countered. "I don't know what

155

would've happened if I wasn't arrested with you; to them, to you. Better, worse—*I don't know.* But I was there, and I lied to my friends. And it hurt them. They don't owe me anything; I owe them an apology."

Zatia looked vindicated, breathing heavy, thirsty for blood. Adelaide swelled up, prideful.

But Rashida just blinked. "Good," she said, the song returning to her voice. "What do we know about the Widows?"

"Who died and made you Captain?" Adelaide asked.

"Not me," Osyen chirped.

"He may as well have." Rashida didn't make eye contact with Osyen. "Capitals don't get a voice. Tell me about the Widows."

Some of that icy river under their feet had made its way into Osyen's blood. "This Capital still got his voice."

"What did you do, Osyen?" Rashida accused. "Did you kill someone? Steal from a hospital?" The last one was both barrels—"Did you steal this ship?"

"They took my mother."

Whatever demons Osyen had been quenching, slaking their hatreds with sarcastic wit and self-deprecation, they held the reins now. Thom had no doubt that Osyen would kill everyone in that room and he would sleep fine the following night, caked in their blood.

"A man came. It was dark out. He had Officers—I don't know how many. They were talking, loud voices. She had done...something, no one would tell me what. They had this piece of—they wanted her to sign something, she refused."

Osyen got quiet, real quiet, his eyes distant. "He grabbed her and she fought back..." He cocked his head at Rashida. "He was an elected official in service to the Dunsweir. He had Power, capital P. He used it."

Rashida didn't flinch, except for the slight tilt to her chin. It wasn't a story she knew personally, but it rhymed with a few that she did. And it disgusted her.

"They were dragging her..." Osyen was no longer telling them. He was reliving that night, a scared little boy.

Alone. In the dark.

"I pushed him. And just like that...they were dragging me too." He locked his stare onto Rashida, Dunsweir nobility, Imperial Royal. "I was nine years old. Capital for life."

"Is she still alive?" Thom asked.

Osyen didn't answer for a moment. Thom thought that maybe he hadn't really said it aloud, but then Osyen's voice trembled. "I don't know. I never saw her again."

Rashida didn't flinch. This was not the first story she'd heard. "What was the charge?"

"Sedition and terrorism," Osyen said with a wry smirk. "Real dangerous. Nine years old. Enough?"

"No," she said. "How do I know you're telling the truth?"

He threw his arms out wide. "You don't. Because Capitals are liars, thieves, murderers. Maybe I made it all up. Maybe I spent eight years in labor camps with grown men because I liked the *fra tow* poetry of it!"

He blinked away the tears building up in his eyes. "Fiona got out. She got a lot of us out."

"You owe her?" Zatia asked.

He didn't break his lock on Rashida. "I don't owe anyone anything. I run my life how I want."

That wasn't his voice. He was quoting someone.

He was quoting Fiona.

One step forward, then the next, Thom approached Osyen the way you approach a coiled viper. He finally came to a stop an arm's length away. If Osyen wanted to, he could break Thom's neck before anybody could interfere.

"I'm sorry."

"You didn't do anything." Osyen grimaced.

"No," Thom said, "but you need a hug more than anybody I've ever met."

He slipped his arms around Osyen's midsection, hugging the man from behind. He could feel his heart pounding through his leather jacket, hammering away like it wanted to shatter its shackles—or itself.

And the fortifications fell, and Osyen raised one gloved hand to cover Thom's. He breathed slow, soft and regular.

"Do they think I'm not going to hurt them?" Zatia asked of no one in particular.

"You've always wanted to punch me," Osyen said soft. "You've just never known why before."

Thom turned his head, leaning against Osyen's back. He could see Zatia faltering, shifting her weight back and forth as she looked for footing that might hold her steady. "Never really needed a reason before."

"Because we're the only family you've ever had?" Osyen hinted, with a little too much cheese.

Zatia cocked the hammer on her weapon.

"Because nobody likes you," Thom said, sucking the air out of the room. Even Osyen lurched at those words, distancing himself from the boy.

Zatia's bloodthirsty eyes settled on Thom, daring him to keep going down this road. And he did. "They respect you. You freak 'em out too. They know you pretty well, your favorite foods and what-ever. But nobody likes you...except the people right here. And you don't know what you'd do without that."

Adelaide rocked back on her heels. "Whoo. That actually gave me chills. But it's also a terrible answer."

But Zatia stared at Thom, unflinching. Her eyes didn't drift or focus, but drilled through him and beyond, playing out a thousand scenarios, old memories and possible futures. She could be rich or poor, a saint or a pauper. Or she could be here.

Zatia drew her weapon from the holster, a crisp hiss of metal on leather. Osyen pivoted, putting Thom behind him, but Zatia spoke before killing: "I get my own ship."

She was bargaining.

Osyen cocked his head. "You think I have one in my pocket?"

"We're going to get paid a pile for this job," she said, "I want your share and mine. That can be your apology."

Osyen's brow furrowed. "And I just eat paste till the next job because you got your feelings hurt?"

"You can do that, or there'll be no next job for you."

"Kill me," Osyen said, "and you'll just be one more little girl confined to a Capital block."

"You calling me little?" she taunted.

He shrugged. "You're literally short. I don't know what you want me to say. You'll be 'little' when you're fifty-two."

"Girl?"

"Now you're just picking fights. If you were going to shoot me, you'd have done it already."

Bang.

She squeezed a round into his shoulder.

Osyen flopped to the deck, favoring the bloody hole she'd punched through him. But she also holstered her weapon. "There. I feel better."

———

Thom mopped up the blood that had spilled onto the floor of the Med Bay, smearing the deep red with the blue tile into sickly purple streaks. It would take another pass with the soap to really lift it out.

"Now you got one for each side." Rashida judged Osyen from her perch on the counter.

Osyen lay on the AutoDoc, grimacing as the many robot hands worked sewing his wound together. Milardi tended to the machine's functions on the console nearby. "You're going to be a patchwork man within a year, you keep this up."

Thom dunked his mop into the bucket. "Where are you from?" he asked Milardi. "If you're not Colonial?"

"Venutian," he offered up.

Second planet in Sol. That was a hard life. Colonial Duster life of self-dependence, hostile alien life, and renegades would've been an upgrade.

"You miss it?" Thom asked.

"Not a bit," he said, "The three square meals you get on a contract is a bit of a selling point for me."

"Tell me about the Widows." Rashida cut off the exchange. "They're not affiliated with Fiona's people?"

Osyen shook his head, very carefully so as not to pull on his shoulder. "There's about a dozen different gangs in the Boolean. Fiona's is just the biggest. Everybody's got their fingers in everything, but they also have their specialty."

"What's Fiona's?" Thom was maybe a little eager with that one.

But Osyen's answer was off-the-cuff. "Oh, K&R. That Thibodeau guy was not just messing with you. Ransom is a tidy little business. But Fiona acts as the intermediary, profits off any Imperial interests looking to get their people back. They have no idea she's actually the one who did the kidnapping too."

"Son of a bitch..." Rashida cursed, rather loudly. It was unclear if she was upset about that or impressed by it.

"Yeah!" Osyen seemed to think the latter. "It's a helluva parlor trick and nobody gets hurt. Usually."

"And the Widows?" Rashida pressed.

"Drugs, mostly," he started. "Most of the black market stims and 'pressants you find in the world come from their labs. But because of that, they have a lot of security to protect their eggheads. And so because of *that*, they have a tidy side-business as enforcers and robbery." He paused, considering. "Some underling must've caught wind of the Icon and figured he could leverage his way up with a clean hit."

"I mean..." Thom leaned on his mop. "Tell me we're not doing the same thing."

Rashida leaned back, kicking her feet in the air as she thought. "Doesn't sound like we can charm the door open."

"Or kick the door in," Milardi moaned. "Why did you agree to this, Oz?"

Osyen yelped as the AutoDoc tugged on his shoulder. He glared at Milardi, unclear if Milardi had done that on purpose, "Because—because we didn't really have much of a choice."

"'Working for ourselves,'" Rashida quoted. "That one really stings right about now. What's the plan?"

Osyen banged his head on the bedframe. "Working on it."

"Due respect," Milardi snipped. "Your plans have a *history*."

"Go back to the accent," Osyen moaned. "You were more likable as the surly Duster moron."

"Surly Duster *deviant*," Milardi corrected. "And I'm still...a deviant. That part hasn't gone anywhere."

"Can't knock, can't talk," Osyen muttered, as he tried to chip away at the block in his head. "What to do."

Can't knock, can't talk. What to do.

Kidnap. Ransom.

Oh. Oh, no.

"Yeah..." Thom started, "we could kidnap someone."

"Who?" Rashida asked, kind of afraid of the answer.

"Not you," Thom assured her, dropping his mop against the wall. "Me."

It even seemed like the AutoDoc froze at that suggestion. Somewhere on board, a hard drive corrupted.

"I'm sorry?" Osyen asked, equal parts incredulous and 'don't you dare.'

"I'm the son of an Imperial Rear Admiral with considerable pull in the Ministry," Thom began. "Dangle me out in the right place, in front of the right faces...you might get a man on the inside."

"Inside a cage," Rashida cautioned.

Thom looked at Osyen, begging for his support. "When has a cage ever stopped you?"

"Like, one week ago on an Imperial dreadnought," Osyen snapped. "You were *there*."

"You can't cut your way in, sneak your way in, blow your way in," Thom said, "you need someone to *let* you in."

"Thom—"

"I don't like this anymore than you do," Thom said. "But unless you've got another option?"

Osyen hopped off the AutoDoc, slinging on his tunic without regard for the bloodstains. "You'd only have what you brought with you. They will confiscate weapons and tools. You'll have to break out of a jail cell you've never seen before, work your way through a heavily guarded station, take control of the docking collar. And even then, we're still liable to get into a shooting war."

Thom nodded, swallowing hard on the bile scratching at his throat. "We have one advantage. They think I'm just some kid."

"You *are* a kid," Osyen blurted. "Breaking into the cargo bay for a fresh snack is not breaking out of prison, let alone pirate jail! This isn't going to be some institution—this is going to be a fresh kind of Hell! They will *beat* you, Thom. They might cut you up. And then you're going to have to break out of a jail cell with whatever's in your shoes, assuming they've left you *fingers* to do anything with."

Thom tapped the back of his head. "You'll talk me through it." Osyen was going to object but Thom jumped down his throat. "Osyen, we're out of options! Give me a better idea, please, because I *hate* this one."

Osyen took a deep breath, his eyes working over Thom's face. Everything he'd done had been to keep Thom out of danger. And now Thom was suggesting to throw himself into it, deep into it, where Osyen had no hope of shielding him.

"Well," Osyen said, "you wanted to see the universe. You want to go back to the Pantry now?"

"Yes." Thom didn't even hesitate. "But I'm here now. Let's do this."

THIRTEEN
MILARDI

THE KID LOOKED at him differently now. Sidelong glances, conversations, even the fleeting moments of silence between them were now done under a microscope. He pondered saying something, but what could he say that would undercut this tension? What joke could get them back to their rhythm?

There wasn't anything—there was no putting this back together. No more boy wonder. No more dashing mentor. No more Holstrum.

He almost shed a tear.

The plan was simple enough—no room for nuance. Thom would get kidnapped by the Widows. Using his wits and a few tricks, he'd get out of his cell. Assuming he did so quietly, he'd find the Icon and then summon the cavalry through an access point of his choice.

They did hope that the radio links remained untampered, but Fiona had illustrated that they could not be depended on. So, Osyen had spent the morning teaching Thom damn near every trick he knew—how to identify and loosen a poorly set bar; how to confuse motion tracking software; how to flummox heat sensors.

Milardi was out gathering supplies. More than a little jittery, and a bit overwhelmed by Osyen, Thom asked to come along.

He trudged out of the building, tugging at the hem of his pants.

163

Thom had posted up in the alley, bouncing on the balls of his feet and regretting every decision he'd ever made along with a few he hadn't made yet.

But Thom did notice Milardi's not-so-subtle...adjustment, "Gross."

Milardi smiled. "Like I had any time for that." He held out the Lady of Midnight's holographic collar. "It needs to be loaded with face maps and don't let anybody try to touch you, but this should help hide your face."

"Did you clean it first?" Thom asked.

"With what?"

Thom shrugged. "I'm just saying, it was somebody else's and—"

"And they're some of the cleanest people in the universe," Milardi lectured. "They don't judge you."

"How much you wanna bet they do?"

Milardi considered the premise he was defending. "Yeah, okay, but probably no more than regular people do, y'know?"

Can you two get a move on? Osyen scolded.

Hey! I am educating a young man about his prejudices against some very hard-working people.

Oh, they're hard *working, are they?* Zatia chimed in.

You're not helping, Zee.

Thom slipped the collar over his head, tucking it under his jacket. It looked like he had a strange sense of style, but didn't otherwise stand out. They were built not to draw attention, after all. Johns needed to suspend disbelief for a whole night.

Thom stood there with his arms out, like he was expecting ridicule for the silly thing. Milardi smiled in amusement. "Hey, plus side is you can hide the bruising from when they work you over."

"I'm valuable," Thom blurted, like that was going to matter.

"Yeah, but they have to produce proof of life," Milardi teased. "And they can't take your nose or ears, so they might..." He mimed scissors in the air with two fingers.

Thom's eyes went wide and his skin paled. What would they remove? Fingers, toes, or other dangling bits?

"Let's get a move on, before Osyen has a core breach," Milardi said, nudging Thom's shoulder. The kid recoiled, pulling away from the touch.

Man, did he really screw up that badly? It's not like he gave them up or left them for dead. He took Fiona's calls sometimes, that's all. He'd always gone out of his way to protect the kid, include him in the show, expand his horizons. And now *Unti* was bound up? Because the world didn't start spinning the very moment he arrived? That's not fair.

Neither was that sentiment. The kid didn't know who to trust anymore. At least he was starting to trust himself.

On to the kidnapping. It had to look convincing, or the Widows would suspect. So the entire gang was staging an elaborate fight before letting Thom slip through their fingers. Aw, shucks.

Milardi had protected valuable people before. He'd never *pretended* to protect someone before. Osyen had described it as fishing—throw out the line just a little further than they think you can handle, lure them into taking the bait. And then Milardi had to give a decent enough performance at trying to stop them. Draw blood, but no bodies.

"So..." Thom said, bobbing up and down on his feet like a cork in water. "Where to?"

Roche, Milardi asked, *got me a pretty one?*

Got you a wild one, Roche said. *One Widows crew exiting the Day Dreaming and headed into the Blue-Lamps.*

Let's put the kid in the water, Osyen ordered.

They couldn't confront the gang directly, or just drop the word. They had to let word drip from a thoughtless mouth, and it had to land in the right ears—or the wrong gang might try to boost Thom. Then they'd just have more problems. Thom was no use to them if he ended up in the *wrong* crew's cell.

Trouble with sound is that it goes anywhere it wants to. Word travels fast, but it can be made faster with a little help from friends. The rest of the crew were getting into position now. They just had to make sure the Widows heard about Thom—and his natural value—before anybody else could swim up to take a bite.

"Out of the alley, take a left," Milardi said, "I'll be right behind you."

"You better be." Thom took a steeling breath. Milardi could hear the tremor in every inch of him in that rattling exhale.

And then Thom stepped clear, confident strides, like a man on his way to the gallows. The crowd was thinner than on the docks and the sounds of grinding industry filled the air, along with a fine dust hanging in the air. The company drills must've started up again—there might not be corporations present, but that didn't mean work had stopped; just who was cutting the checks.

Osyen, left side, get into that cafe, Roche said, *Zatia, the flower shop.*

Do I look like a flowers kinda person?

Fine, stand outside, but get over there. And look relaxed for once in your life.

Roche was sitting back on the command deck of the *Aurum* directing the crew to their positions. Each person had to daisy-chain the news—boost the signal—so that the Widows heard about Thom before any other interested parties.

Roche hadn't said more than five words to Milardi. Was he waiting for an apology? Milardi had given two—once when he told everyone, and another in private. No harm had been done, not really. What could be up his ass?

He'd have to ask him. Later.

"You know, this is a brave thing you're doin', *Unti*," he said. But no response. Oh good, now two people were stonewalling him. "I mean, for given quantities of brave. Some people might call it monumentally stupid."

"You talking to me?" Thom asked.

"Yeah..."

166

"My name's Thom."

Milardi pursed his lips, curling them over as he chewed on that sentiment. "What'd I say?"

"Just call me Thom, okay?" Thom threw a glance over his shoulder at him, the kind of petulant sneer that Milardi usually saw on a dissatisfied or jealous husband.

Unti. He didn't want the nickname. Whatever. Milardi shrugged. "Sorry."

But Thom wasn't done. He turned around, squaring up on Milardi with his little chin tilted upward as the crowd broke around them, water on a promontory. "I'm either a part of this team or I'm not."

"I said 'I'm sorry!'"

Thom crossed his arms. "Why?"

"Why what?"

"Why am I mad at you?" Oh good, he was quizzing him now.

Milardi nudged the boy onward. "I don't know, but can you educate me while moving?"

"No," Thom said, holding his ground. "I'm going to make this abundantly clear, so that you can process it up there in that thin atmosphere. I have a name, I have always had a name, and I am no longer *grateful* to be on this little adventure. The least you can do is use my real name."

If Milardi didn't get a crick in his neck from looming over the kid, he could've sworn that was Osyen talking to him there. Solid stance, feet planted just outside center-line, to have a powerful base without a lean, thumbs hooked on his belt. And that scolding acid, using far too many words because he liked the burn in his mouth.

"What's my name?" Thom asked.

"It's Thom."

Not satisfied, Thom took another breath. Solid, clean. "What is my name, Jackson?"

"Minister?" Still that stare. This was getting infuriating. "Thomas Angelo Hugh of House Bite Me?"

"That's right." But even as he turned, he threw a wink.

Oh, that clever boy! He was already into his character, deep in the zone. Milardi could've cried. It was like watching a child skip walking and just break into a run.

So what if he might've been playing with a bit of live ammo in there too? Good performance came from honesty.

"Rakishly handsome rogues?" Thom commented, all smug and full of himself.

"Well, one of us is," Milardi said, taking the conversation on-line, *We're already dropping the name out in the wild.*

Get ready for the big one in just a few minutes, Thom added.

Oh, Milardi really liked this new 'I'm Already Going to Hell, so Save Me a Seat' approach Thom had. It gave him goosebumps in the best way, like an electric current attached to the heels of his shoes and setting his hair on end. It was liquid anticipation pumping in his blood.

Is this what Zatia felt like all the time, with all those chems in her? No wonder she kept it up. Screw the warning labels.

There weren't that many people on the street, which is what made the line of three motionless men ahead that much more obvious. Dark silhouettes that peaked out from the crowd, still-lives, ghosts in the mid-morning light.

Trouble, and so early.

Aaaand we already have a backfire, Milardi said, feeling the pinch as Roche made direct connection. *Three big boys in our path.*

Who else is in the neighborhood? Osyen asked.

Nobody, was Roche's one-word answer.

Well, that's just not true, Milardi sniped, as the two continued to approach the soon-to-be stand-off. It felt very much like the crowd was parting for them.

Nobody wanted to be anywhere near whatever was coming.

Not in my field of view, Roche countered. *Whoever they are, they're off my grid.*

That's just great, Osyen cursed, *Milardi, stall 'em. We'll get this thing going.*

Thom marched headlong toward the three men, unmoved. They wore longcoats and plated masks hid every inch of their faces, just gray-metal eggs with beady little eyes. Rifles slung on their backs, but their bodies were tight, elastic pulled to its breaking point.

One man had a metallic leg, four-inch pins sticking into the ground like tent anchors.

They were ready for trouble.

"Style or substance?" Thom asked.

Milardi considered them, hemming and hawing. "I mean...they have a certain antique...they coordinated their look," Milardi finally settled on.

Looking like trouble usually brought you trouble, from the law and other criminals alike. He guessed you didn't have to avoid looking like trouble in a world where you *were* the law.

"They look like a heat venting plate put on a leather jacket," Thom quipped.

Milardi might've snickered if he wasn't so sure he'd be in excruciating pain shortly. "You're welcome to tell them that yourself. Roche, who are these guys?"

I am working on that information!

Three of them. Milardi felt out the holsters on his hips—the tips of his fingers warm against his metal pistols. Two shots, simultaneous. Maybe he throws one of 'em off balance and gets a chance at a follow-through, but that third man will draw down before he could get around to him. With any luck, they'd go center-mass into his armor. But they might just go for the head...

And based on their gear, they would not miss.

They passed an alley on their left—industrial, the pounding steel and grinding gears echoing up from somewhere below, steam filling the air, pulsating amber lights dancing off the walls. It looked like the entrance to a demon's lair that lay somewhere under their feet.

Thom blew right past it. He might not be eager for confrontation, but wasn't able to see other options.

"Nah, Hell with this." Milardi grabbed Thom's shoulder and threw him down the alley.

The two wingmen drew their weapons, modified Lernetti 67s with custom trigger guards, vented barrels, and targeting laser in the grip.

He always wanted one of those.

Milardi clipped his pistols into their holsters, nice and secure, before diving after Thom. Their shots, disturbingly quiet puffs, were dwarfed by the snap of impact off the brickwork.

It wasn't a fight he could win *before* he learned how deeply expensive his opposition was.

"What are you doing?" Thom objected, stopping to dust himself off.

"Do you hear the shooting?!" Milardi snapped. "Run!"

The boy took off like Milardi had shoved a rocket in his back pocket.

Milardi didn't dare look back, but he knocked over every dumpster and trash bin he passed to block their path—and aim. The pot metal might not have been able to stop a bullet, but it might hide their retreating backs.

A door ahead, painted red sometime within the last century, now flaking and rusted. Thom threw his shoulder into it and bounced off like a dog's chew toy.

Milardi aimed a kick for the door handle, where the latch might have been weakest. His ankle screamed at him as it folded on impact.

He cursed his Duster bones, and then cursed again at the echo of his voice off the walls. He wasn't in the habit of brute forcing things. High ankle sprain; he was lucky that's all it was.

"It's your alley," Thom simultaneously accused and begged.

Milardi drew a pistol and popped a shot into the handle, forcing it free with a one-inch hole above the latch. "Go!"

Thom pushed the door open and damn near fell inside, tripping down the set of stairs right behind it. Milardi staggered forward, his ankle objecting to everything.

Little shit. Now he wished he had taken stims like Zatia did. Then things wouldn't hurt.

He slammed the door behind him—like it would even slow them down. "Keep moving!"

Where are you? Roche asked. *You're off my scope.*

Milardi looked around him. Steel walls, stained with grime, oil. Gray dirt caking everything like an ash-fall. Hollow grinding noises from deeper within, like something hungry gnawing on bones.

Industrial place, heading down.

Very helpful.

What do you want from me? A coordinate matrix? We're heading down!

Okay, Roche assured, *keep going forward. Osyen, Zatia, get mobile. Weapons free.*

He'd have called Zatia's response to that 'a giggle', but it sounded far more psychotic.

Osyen took quick charge. *Keep comms free for Roche. And Adelaide? Would you let our friends know about their hostage before somebody else gets him first?*

Milardi's boots pounded on the steel grating under his feet, staggering forward away from the door. How had these expensive bastards found out about Thom before they'd had a chance to tell anybody about him?!

Of course. Thom had been seen in public before this, at the Gaslamp and in the Court of the Master...where he was threatened.

Thibodeau.

Milardi was going to fillet that fat bastard with a rusty piece of metal he pried loose from a lighting fixture in his childhood home.

The door slammed open somewhere behind them like they'd blown it clean off its hinges. Sure, after he loosened it for them.

A doorway up in front of them, open to the vastness beyond.

Thom stopped to wave encouragement to Milardi like it would make him faster. "Come on!"

Shut up and run, you little idiot!

Milardi damn near bowled him over pushing through. Thom dropped underneath his bad leg, supporting him as they pushed on.

They were on a catwalk, galvanized steel causeways that bridged over an impossible chasm. Steam and dust filled the air, obscuring the far wall and even where they came from. They probably shouldn't be down here without respirators.

And then there was that devilish glow that came from below. He didn't dare look down. Maybe he'd see a sinful face looking back, beckoning.

"It's Thibodeau!" Thom yelled over the din. "He's the only one—"

"Yeah, yeah, I'm with you," Milardi cut him off, "but we have to go!"

Oh crap, he looked down.

Three massive rigs, each the size of a small building, were boring straight down into the ground. The drill bits were grinding so fast, they were sparking on the asteroid's natural metals, and had gone yellow hot—the sole source of the natural lighting.

Milardi started to sink, but Thom leveraged up, standing at almost his full height to get any kind of support to Milardi's drifting frame. "Oh no, you don't, big guy. Let's go!"

He put pressure on the ankle and it felt like a razor had slashed through the tendon. He collapsed into the railing, sending them into the most disconcerting pendulum action. Even Thom grimaced and gripped the railings.

"I can hop to freedom," Milardi said, "but you have to run. Right now."

"They'll kill you!"

Milardi winced. That was probably true, but not necessarily. Maybe he could sit down and point them in the right direction. "No, they won't. I owe him money."

"I'm not leaving you here!" Thom didn't take that joke in the spirit in which it was intended. He was pleading.

Milardi shook his head. "Then think of it as me running away from you, but you have to go!"

He heard the puff of the gunshot, but the ring of metal was what really commanded attention. Those silent shots might have been intimidating in their own right, but the sound of copper on steel was an unmistakable percussion.

And because the causeway shook with the impact, one of the suspension cables snapped cleanly in two.

"Hello, Thomas," a voice called out, modulated and metallic.

Milardi looked back over his shoulder at the three—no. Just the one. He got a good look at him now. A humanoid worker-bot, with an oval plate for a face. A single red oculus in the center. Skeletal arms tucked back into the long coat, while its heavy tree-trunk legs inched carefully forward on the causeway. Something like this would've anchored itself on to surfaces for hazardous labor.

It holstered its sidearm and threw its arms out wide like it might welcome them with a friendly embrace.

But where were the other two?

"This doesn't have to be stressful. Or bloody," the robot 'said' as it advanced, with alternating clanks of heavy legs.

He recognized the voice. It was Thibodeau, from some safe place, broadcasting a control signal to a hollow-man. Maybe he was set up in his den, jacked into a mainframe computer as he remotely directed the three machine-men in their pursuit.

Osyen was right. They really had taken this whole kidnapping thing to a new level.

Roche, whenever you guys are ready...

Their particular section dangled by three cables now, one-inch steel. They could hold two people. But Faceplate could shoot out those three cables faster than Milardi could hobble away. They were at his mercy.

"I twisted my ankle," Milardi declared, "but I'm no idiot." That's good, deny the reality of your circumstances. He'll surely agree to a parlay then.

"You twisted your ankle trying to be a hero," was the response. "I think that qualifies you as an idiot. Because..." Incredulous laughter coming out of a faceless steel horror was a bizarre enough sight on its own. "Of all the ways for me to catch up to you."

"Fiona's going to eat you alive."

"Who's going to tell her?" Thibodeau asked. "Because I think the boy is going Core-side, and you're..." He left that hanging.

Milardi pushed Thom away from him. If this was going to be a shoot-out, keep the kid out of the statistically common angle of return fire.

Faceplate was accurate enough, after all. Thibodeau wouldn't want to hit his prize.

He swept his longcoat back, revealing his hip holsters and declaring his intention. But either Faceplate didn't care or couldn't. It advanced, one heavy step after another.

"I'm not going with you," Thom spat at the robot, putting bizarre emphasis on the 'you.'

The faceless mask cocked its head, almost slithering to one side, like there was more flex in its neck than there naturally should be. "Why not, child? Your father surely misses you."

"Yeah..." Milardi faltered, trying to find the words to explain and realizing he really didn't have to.

The hollow man raised his arms up, as though in prayer. A curtain of black rose up from behind him, a vibrating silken wave—

Robots. Hundreds of them, a sentient net of robotic wasps. They would wrap up their prey, stun and silence it, pacify it.

It was his fishing net.

"Nope, run more! More running!" Milardi shouted, turning to stagger away and almost leaving Thom behind. But he was cut off by the two missing wingmen, swinging their way up from below.

Milardi cursed himself—they hadn't gone around. They had gone underneath—clambering arm over arm underneath them while Faceplate literally directed their eyes upward.

They can't be allowed to take him.

No way out, back or forward. Milardi looked down at the rigs drilling away below, their steel backsides vibrating in the air.

Thirty feet, reduced gravity. He'd be fine.

"Tuck and roll."

Thom looked up at him. "What?"

Milardi drew his twin pistols—and shot two of the support cables. The gunshots were cacophonous, deafening thunders in the chasm.

And the steel causeway lurched, tilting suddenly and pouring them over the side, down, down, down...

BLAM! Oh, now his ankle *really* hurt.

They had landed on the back of a drilling rig—and he hadn't known this, but based on the gong sound, the rigs were actually hollow. Neat.

But the gnashing of gears under his back told him it would be fairly unpleasant to catch a hand in there. Probably why there was this covering, so a workplace accident didn't turn into a very expensive meat paste.

Guns up.

Milardi rolled on to his back, heaving the deadweights in his hands and pointing his pistols up at the causeway above. He fired a shot—slinging a chunk of metal at the hollow man. It sparked off Faceplate's faceplate, punching a hole clean through.

The bot didn't even flinch.

Rather, his terrifying Cape of Abduction leapt free from his shoulders, descending like locusts, a thousand nefarious pixies.

What was the plan again?

"This way!" Thom was already on his feet, halfway down the backside of the rig. There was a conveyor to take the hot mineral chunks out and away to who knows where. That confined space was loaded with glowing hot minerals...

Wherever that was, it had to be better than staying here.

Milardi spun himself on his butt, and shoved off, sliding down the side of the rig towards the Conveyor.

The two wingmen jumped off their causeway, falling towards him. As they fell, two gliding shapes, their coats billowing behind like bat wings...Milardi felt his implant pinch.

//Data received. Philips-Grundhall Mk 4, Automaton Laborer.

//To allow remote control and ensure safety of specialists in hazardous conditions. Control pack seated below the left shoulder.

Took you long enough, Roche! Milardi lifted his pistol and squeezed off two shots. He drilled two holes in their chests, high left.

Milardi stuck his feet out, catching the conveyor's lip, and leered back to check his work.

Both wingmen slammed into the rig. They twitched and sparked, the two-inch holes in their chests exposing dangling copper wires. White electrical arcs snapped with every incidental contact.

And they stood up.

"Wha...?" Milardi blubbered.

Their left, you jackass! Their left!

The wingmen lifted their weapons. So did Milardi—and this time, he shot to the right side.

String cut. They crumpled, slipping off the side of the mining rig.

"Yeah!" Milardi cheered. But Thom cut him short, tap-tapping on his shoulder.

The cloud of tiny insects was falling toward them.

They didn't know where that conveyor went, but they couldn't stay there. Milardi wrapped Thom in his arms and threw himself down the conveyor's chute.

It was pitch black. They couldn't hear anything, but Milardi felt himself bouncing off the pot metal walls. His ankle screamed with each incidental bang and bump, and the shards of hot rock peppered them every inch of the way, stabbing his back and face. He could smell leather burning.

Then suddenly, they stopped. Something pulled at his jacket, pulling the tails of it up and away. It dragged harder, further.

Did they get him? No. It was the conveyor. A belt was sifting the minerals and dragging them up now.

"You okay, *Unti?*" he asked.

He heard Thom coughing. Good. He was alive, at least.

"Come on." Milardi tugged on the kid's tunic. "Come on. We can't stay here."

The belt had to be taking them somewhere. Milardi flipped over, and he could see the literal light at the end of the square tunnel. And he could see the mirage, heat waves wafting up over the light.

That could mean several things. Some of them good things. Maybe it was a hot buffet being presented by curvy wenches and chiseled men.

Nope. That was definitely a refinery.

Milardi tried to pull himself up to his feet, but the wall kept slipping away from him. Thom pulled at his jacket, heaving him up. "Up and at 'em. Let's go!"

They limped up the conveyor, clambering over the larger chunks of rock and detritus.

The chamber was large, walls bowing outward and cracked cement flooring that swallowed up the moisture. Twin turbines cranked on the ceiling, whirling dervishes the size of the *Aurum*, blurred blades of death. Perhaps they had to keep the air cycling, or they were generating power?

And in the center of the room, were four large glowing forges, giant vats of yellow-gold heat. Minerals mined must be refined—smelted—before they could be minted and sold.

Workers were already fleeing, nobody questioning their appearance from the conveyor. They had either heard the good word, or wanted no part in it. But Milardi couldn't help but be amused at their leisurely pace, ranging from light jogs to actual *walking* away from the danger, like the gunfire next door was both dangerous and robbing them of hours payable.

Two foremen bellowed out commands, "Alright, okay! Towards the exits. Shut off your machines."

This was nobody's first shootout.

A metallic gong from above as a door was kicked off its hinges and Faceplate stepped through, his cape of drones fluttering behind him.

Thom shouldered Milardi's weight and started jogging away, forcing Milardi to hop after him. Together, they were a weird three-legged running beast. And Faceplate stomped along on the causeways above. Thibodeau paid no mind to the elderly woman in his way, conspicuously ignoring the evacuation orders while elbow deep in some electrical panel.

Adelaide.

She turned on him, hex wrench in hand and did not hesitate, gave no room for him to respond. She reached out, and torqued the wrench over his shoulder, and ripped out three wires with her pinky finger.

Faceplate crumpled and his cape clattered down like so many nightmare sprinkles.

She muttered something derisive under her breath as she pocketed the wrench and pulled out pliers.

Thom and Milardi shared a glance as she proceeded to...harvest... from the robot. She leered down at them and their staring. "You got places to be. None of 'em are here."

Milardi nodded, limping with Thom after the rest of the retreating workers. They either had a way out or they might blend in with them.

Thibodeau's threat might have been dealt with, but gunfire had a way of attracting attention, and they were the wounded bird now.

They staggered around the vats of liquid iron—to find a band of merry workers assembled in a mob, facing them, wielding various heavy-looking tools.

A foreman stepped up, burn scars covering his ear to his lip. "You two are worth something to somebody."

"My momma thinks I'm a treasure," Milardi quipped off the cuff, "but I think you'll find I'm pretty annoying."

The foreman sneered, "I'mma willing to bet you dons' have too many more shots in them there sluggers." He jerked his head, and two workers stepped up with greasy hands.

First it was the robots with a nightmare bug cape, now it was just guys with bits of pipe. They were being assaulted by the opposite ends of the technological spectrum.

Milardi knew what to do with this end of it.

"Listen up, Dusters," Milardi said, slipping into his Colonial affectation, "I've had a rough enough day getting 'ere. Any rougher, and I'm goin' to get cranky."

They either didn't take his bluff, or they did and just took it as encouragement. Eat the weak and the sick. The two boys kept coming.

Oz, Zee, just follow the noise.

Slug guns used chemical explosions to propel bits of metal down a tube at supersonic speeds. Milardi's had electromagnetic motivation, a series of battery-powered magnets getting the slug to muzzle speed without the unstable explosives. With some crafty engineering, they could impart more force onto a square inch of human flesh than a power hammer.

What's more, the rounds he had loaded were double-weight, with copper flechette sleeves that peeled off to tear through flesh. Inside were charged capacitors that topped off at about half a million volts.

If he didn't kill them, he'd stop them, one way or the other.

Milardi slipped out his twin pistols, and bored twin holes in the advancing men. He could tell by the misting of blood in the crowd that the shots had kept tumbling on and found new homes in whoever was in the back. He could see the foreman through the viewport he'd bored into his men.

Milardi didn't wait for the crowd to decide what to do next. He dropped the empty cylinders to the ground, and slipped the pistols back under his coat to find fresh good sevens on his belt loops. Feeling the happy click-click of the cylinders locking into place, he swung the pistols forward again, smacking them together to properly seat the cylinders into the well. Pushing the pair of pistols together, he spun those cylinders in opposite directions like he was striking flint, cycling them into the ready position—he might've practiced this in the mirror.

The foreman looked back and forth at his gang, incredulous. "We're just gonna let him go through that whole thing?"

Milardi stood as tall as his ankle would let him—still head and shoulders over the entire crowd. "What? *You* didn't stop me. Or were you not man enough to do it yourself?"

The man fumed and simmered, the boil kept somewhere under his lid. Murmurs in the crowd behind him, mixtures of anger and disbelief.

Now, in two shots fired, maybe five people were on the ground, one of them spasming in agony. He had another seven loaded now in each, for a total of fourteen. They'd surely overwhelm him before he could reload again. The math was decidedly not in his favor.

There were twenty some odd men and women in a horseshoe in front of him. With their colleagues hurt, they were just as interested in straight up murdering Milardi and Thom as any reward they'd get taking them alive. Mob mentality would dictate what happened next. Do they eat Milardi or the foreman who made them do it?

"Get him," the foreman ordered.

And the weighty pause that followed could have stopped a freight car in its tracks.

Somebody yelled out, and the crowd descended on Milardi, all gnashing teeth and rending fingers, twirling heavy metal over their heads like the oncoming barbarians they were.

He punched the pistols forward with each shot, alternating back and forth, slapping back whoever got too close with selective application of Newton's Third Law. But he also had to stagger backward, leaning on his good leg as he bought the precious inches between a pipe to the head and room to fire.

One swipe took his hat off, and it tugged on him, nearly tipping him over with it, but he managed to center himself and punish the thief with some high-caliber retribution.

Ten, eleven, twelve. Here comes the pain time.

And in came Zatia, the little murderball. She slammed into the side of the horde, knife in one hand and rebar in the other. The crowd broke around her, water on rock, and with about as much foam—red foam.

Someone somewhere shouted an excited call to arms, surprised yet eager: "Fight!"

Milardi didn't recognize the voice and popped a shot at it, and was greeted by a wet meaty silence.

Somewhere in the mess, the foreman had slipped away, greasy bastard.

Milardi took the time to reload his pistols again, scanning the crowd. Either he'd miscounted or more of these industrial thugs were growing out of the pipes and grating. Where were they all coming from?

And Thom was gone. Milardi didn't have the little kid at his back anymore. Had he slipped off to hide?

No, the foreman was dragging the limp package of a boy away, hogtied with beefy cable. A bloody wrench in the other hand. The one blessing here was the foreman hadn't forgotten the value of Thom alive.

How long he stayed that way...

"Drop him!"

With one beefy arm, the foreman picked him up off the floor, heaving the dusty boy up into the line of fire. Human shield. Real brave man. His eyes were a dare at Milardi—can the big man be a big enough man to make the shot? Or will he choke and hit the boy?

Who's the man now, because look who has the prize?

Osyen vaulted off the causeway above, dropping directly into the foreman's back with both feet. The odd way the teamster crumpled to the ground was...not natural. And neither was his screech.

But that didn't stop him from flailing that wrench at Osyen, who was not paying enough attention. He caught the heavy iron to his gut, coughing and stunned. The second hit went to his jaw, which he gracefully took like the very best sack of potatoes.

And that's when Milardi separated man from wrench—by removing his wrist. The slug kept going into the dark somewhere. The foreman collapsed to his knees, staring at the bloody ragged stump, tatters of muscle, sinew, and sleeve mixed together into a terrible matted cloth.

Somewhere came the sickening laugh from Zatia, a chortle of impressed and surprised in equal horrible measure. She was going to buy him a drink for that shot and he did not want that drink.

"You alright, Oz?" Milardi called out.

All he got was a quick nod, as Osyen tried to quiet the gong echoing in his ears. Man likely had a concussion. He'd give him grief for that, but then, he'd managed to twist an ankle trying to open a door.

The fighting had largely come to a still, everyone collecting their breath and their wounded, trying to get them far away from these three space pirate dealers of death—or at least away from Milardi and Zatia. Osyen wasn't really in a terror-inspiring state.

"Oz, you just keep gettin' beat!" Zatia sneered, wiping her knife off on her tunic, smearing it with the existing spatter into a most sickening piece of modern art.

Osyen was wobbly, but he stood up under his own power. "Yeah, you say that now."

"I guess we need a new plan," Milardi said, holstering his weapons.

"Oh, do we?"

Milardi glanced to where the hog-tied Thom had fallen like so much luggage. He wasn't there. He scanned the room, hoping to see a comically hopping idiot somewhere or a dark shadowy figure tucking the boy over his shoulder or a retreating caged vehicle—anything.

But there was nothing. Thom was simply gone, like the very walls had taken him as one of their own.

Osyen smiled. "'Cause I think that went just fine."

PART THREE
TABULA RASA

And he threw himself onto his knees before Them, head bowed with a thousand meditations.

How was he to live in Their absence?

And the Pilgrim knelt down to him, lifting his chin with one hand, saying:

"So long as We remain, your life will be in service, fealty sworn.

But Life cannot be Lived when Shackled, cannot be Defined in a Shadow..."

GNOSTIC LIBRUM, EXETER 7:4-9

CHAPTER
FOURTEEN
THOM

IT TURNED out that criminals handled their prisoners much the same way Imperials did—probably from personal experience of its effectiveness. Big man shouts, big man puts your head in a bag. Big man rips bag off head, and does some more shouting before, finally, blessed silence. They had tossed him in a glorified cabinet: shelving, sacks, and a steel door on rusting hinges. It was cold, dusty, scratching at his nose.

He hated crime. He hated the life of crime. He hated criminals. But more than anything, he hated this headache.

He had tried to pack his head wound with sackcloth, but he hadn't gotten very far when they came and took him to his permanent residence.

Stone floor and steel bars, somewhere deep and dark. Dry air and hollow echoes of voices far away. He had been buried deep, like he was part of some treasured collection, hidden away to rot and molt until there was nothing left but the stone.

They hadn't even given him a glass of water, let alone medical attention for the gaping head wound that was casually dripping blood down his face. The wrench had ripped open his scalp, sparking a wellspring of red to cascade across his features. No matter what he pressed to the wound, it just wouldn't stop bleeding, that constant trickle, drip drip dripping down his face.

He missed the Pantry and its stupid floor, full of cracks wide enough for small animals to sneak through. He missed his cot in the larder, insulated from the noise of the pub floor and the cold. So what if it had been dusty enough to coat his throat at night? It was peaceful, and every morning was the same.

He missed the ratty blanket, frayed and hand-stitched; he'd made it from torn up and disposed uniforms. He missed the breakfast stews and the sausage suppers and the midnight tack. He even missed the innkeeper and the wood discipline spoon. A spoon was softer than a wrench.

Right now, he missed his entire miserable life before Osyen had stepped into it.

Did he hate Osyen? No. Resent him? Oh, yes. He resented that charm, that spark in his eye; he resented that he had sold Thom on the mystical figure Thom could be, conned Thom into believing he was more than he was. And then relegated him to Cabin Boy, little more than a lateral movement from the grounded Pantry, to a moving Pantry that got shot at and abducted and arrested.

He had been fine. He had been lawful. He had been far away from suffering.

But he had chosen to be here now, locked in this cell with blood seeping from his head and a dream evaporating between his fingers.

The jagged stone floor had been hacked to an approximation of smooth with a pick by a good strong back. A subtle shine to it, glassy and dimpled. The walls and ceiling were identical, but with less care to the smoothness. This was the actual raw interior of an asteroid, dressed and heated for human life.

A single ratty carpet laid center of the room to mitigate the stone's inhospitable touch, and a tin pail in the corner for other needs. Seven steel bars, each as wide as his arm, rounded out his little studio apartment.

The plan was for him to be jailed. This was in the plan. He could do this.

No matter what way this went, he wouldn't stay long. The worst outcome was his successful ransom back home. He could imagine the conversation already, the scolding and dismissive tones. If he thought he was jailed now, a trip to Sol after failure would be an entire magnitude worse. He'd be lucky if his Father left him the power of speech.

"Hello, Thomas," came the soft spider's hiss. The two words echoed up and down the hall, despite the attempt at privacy.

Thom lifted his bloody head to see—Jeremiah Stride, full dress grays with ribbons affixed. He stood at a relaxed parade rest, arms folded behind him and shoulders back. His boots were almost as shiny as the floor.

"That was...quick," Thom blurted. "Didn't even give me time to stew a bit."

Stride's eyes narrowed, curious study, scrunched brow and curve to the lip. "We're efficient."

"You here to take me home?" Thom asked.

"Here to inspect the merchandise," Stride said. "When they told me they had the son of a Rear Admiral in-house, I simply had to see for myself."

Suddenly, Stride popped a squat, sitting cross-legged down at the edge of Thom's cell. "What exactly was the plan? You let them kidnap you and then you..." he stifled a laugh, "Break out of prison, all by yourself, and open the front door?"

He was not here for Thom. "You're here for the Icon."

Stride nodded. "Yes."

"I thought sending in the Navy was too dangerous?" Thom asked. "That they'd...get rid of it, bury it, or somethin'."

Stride's eyes darkened, a tilt of his head and a line to his brow. "I don't need to explain myself to you."

"Yeah, but you're goin' to," Thom said, almost with a touch of backbone, "because you've already told them all about my little plan the moment you knew I was here. You warned them about Osyen, and that I was a risk of escape. You're the reason I'm down here in this *rock pit!*" He banged on the bars with his wrists, and they didn't even rattle. Those were seated like they had grown there.

Stride didn't even flinch. "Yes. I did. I know what you're here for, boy—"

"Don't call me 'boy,'" Thom snapped.

But Stride was quick and matter-of-fact, cool, collected, and dismissive. "Or what? You're going to do what from back there? Thomas, I could open this door and give you a weapon, and you still could do *nothing.* You would be alone in a compound full of angry grown men. You could be left to your own devices with full access— and you would do nothing. You cannot change my course any more than you can change your face."

Did they take the collar? It took everything in his blood not to flinch, not to reach for it, check it—they would have searched him, taken tools or weapons, but had they taken that? Had it seemed important?

Stride must've seen the panic flash across his face. His lip twitched, pleasure somewhere deep inside, a flush to his cheek. But he buried it quickly—"I do not take any joy in this, Thomas."

"Liar," Thom slurred, "you can't help yourself."

"Man can be trained," Stride said through gritted teeth. "He can be disciplined, he can learn. He grows."

"Sounds like excuses to me," Thom said, "sounds to me like you're weak. Like you're taking the Icon for yourself."

Stride went stone-cold, his eyes darting over Thom's face. "Do you really believe that?"

Thom looked him over, all the porcelain smoothness like he was some faekind, or generated in a lab. No discernible features or flaws, both beautiful and somehow violent in its stillness, unnatural.

The curl of his hair peeking out at the crown from under his cap. That was out of uniform code.

"Your hair," was all Thom said.

Stride swiped at his scalp, feeling the rogue hairs. With a single motion he tucked them back under the edge of his cap. "You will go to your father. You will grow up safe. You will live a full life. And maybe...you'll even be a good man when you're done."

"Like you?"

Stride's eyes fell to the floor, studying that prison stonework, a touch of wistful memory. "You don't want to be like me."

He stood up, almost levitating to his feet, like he had never actually been sitting. He had the agility of a cat that was also a ghost. "Goodbye, Thomas."

Stride stalked away and as soon as he had broken line of sight, all sounds of his passing vanished, as though he had ceased to be.

He reached up to his collar, flinching away at first. Maybe he was worried he wouldn't find it resting on his neck, that he would paw at his shirt and discover the depth of his loss.

But there it was, right where he'd left it, a black choker tucked under his jacket.

Osyen? Thom called out. No answer. *Osyen, talk to me. I'm in lock-up, with these weird bars.*

But nothing came.

Milardi? Roche? Lily?

No response. Not even static. Maybe it was the asteroid? Some material in the walls that blocks signals. It would make for a good prison. Can't call for help. Or maybe Stride had warned them to block the signal—Stride knew about the implants.

The bastard.

What was Osyen thinking now, as he didn't hear from the boy he'd submitted to torturers and drug-dealers, all just to pay off the bounty on him. Thom hoped the captain was twisting in his cabin, furious with himself for letting it happen.

Think now, think! If Stride got to the Icon first, this would all be for nothing. Osyen would go back to prison, and Thom would go back to Sol.

He grabbed each bar on his cell, regaling Osyen's lessons. Twist, pull, and push, look for the one that wiggles. But each one was seated solid, no give. He heaved with everything he had and all he did was make a series of discordant clangs.

How did they even get him in here? There was no obvious door or latch on the bars. Was there some mechanism he could manipulate? Perhaps the bars were held in place magnetically? Or worse, there was no way of opening it—he was a hostage, after all, not a house guest. They would simply cut him out when they were ready to collect their fee.

He was just a product for sale.

He stripped off his jacket and laid it out on his floor next to the rug and bucket. He stared at the bizarre collection for a time, his entire collection of tools.

He had nothing. No way out. He was screwed. He was never going to escape, steal the Icon, and get away alive.

No, think smaller. What is stopping you right now, this instant? The bars. What do you need? For them to be opened.

So start there. Get the bars open. How can that happen?

He didn't know.

Who does?

...The guards. He hadn't seen one since he'd been put in, so they were monitoring him some other way. A camera maybe? Or a thermal sensor embedded in the stone? Find it. They wouldn't leave him unattended.

His fingers pored over the chunky floors and walls, his fingers stained with the black soot of the walls. He had to find it, some seam or crack that might keep secret their listening devices.

There it was—a glass disc, no more than an inch across. Don't touch it. They'll know you know. Any blindspot? He glanced around the room. No, it had a beautiful view. But maybe he could make one...

Thom flipped the rug over, finding a dense black soot on the underside. The asteroid had been rubbing off on it. It could not be broken or split, but it could still give him something.

"Control the story, control the mark," Thom murmured to himself.

Thom tucked a bit of dirt and grime against an edge of the camera. With more time, he'd do so subtly over hours, but there was no such leeway.

Thom worked fast, turning his clothes inside out—Rashida had worked her seamstress magic and gave him reversible clothes, hiding a new silhouette inside the first. People don't remember faces like they do silhouettes. New clothes and a new face from the choker, and he could move somewhat freely.

But getting out at all, that was the hard part.

Using the rug as a sponge and his spit for solvent, he scrubbed up a paste from the jail floor. Before long he had a small amount of fluid, not unlike boot shine. Hiding in the blind spot, he dabbed his finger in it, coating his forearm with a fine black mud.

He was never going to make enough in time. He glanced at the bucket in the corner.

Lovely.

He poured the contents onto the jail floor, sifting away the more... problematic pieces. From there, he worked the fluid into the floor, creating a sizable supply of the paste. And from there, he went to work masking his body, covering every conceivable inch he could in the black.

Finally, he stepped to the wall, pressing himself against it. It was hardly perfect. Anybody who looked sideways at him would instantly see the unmistakable shape. But he didn't need to distract them for long or hold up under scrutiny.

He needed seconds.

He tried to meter his breathing as he waited. Who knew how long it would be before they came to investigate? Maybe they'd seen him prepare his disguise and were laughing to themselves? Or they just didn't keep that close of an eye on him, what with their perfect cell and all.

But soon he heard footsteps, heavy and quick, stomping down the passage.

A pig of a man stopped in front of the cell, his beady eyes scanning the dark corners of the cell. He wore trashy leathers that looked like animal skins, but from no particular beast. The thick hides probably made him feel protected, but did little to hide the man's muscular frame.

Thom closed his eyes, lest the reflecting whites give him away.

"Hey!" the guard called out.

Don't answer. He wasn't talking to him, but calling for him. He couldn't find him.

Stay still.

"Hey!" the guard called again, louder, with a touch of panic at the edge of hearing.

Do. Not. Move.

The center bar dropped first, receding into the floor and away—then the next two, creating just enough room for the man to walk through.

The guard drew his pistol and stepped inside, filling the narrow gap from shoulder to shoulder. As he stepped over the threshold, the bars slipped right back up again.

Thom cracked one eye open, wary. Perhaps the guard was looking right at him, just waiting for him to notice before giving him a thrashing. But he wasn't, instead scanning the small room, eyes squinting in the dark. Thinning black hair, messy, dropping just over the tips of his ears but brushed back off his big forehead.

Any attempt to escape would go through this greaseball.

Perhaps he had a controller or radio that the bars recognized, parting for him and him alone? Regardless, he was the key in and out of the cell. Somehow.

But this guard was going to scour every inch of this cell—and easily find Thom pressed against the nearside wall.

He sniffed the air—a big knobby nose, tip off-center from being broken.

The bucket's contents on the floor polluted his nostrils. He shook his head, peering at the mess.

Thom held his breath—was he going to figure out the scheme right there?

Instead, the guard shuddered and whirled around for the door. Thom peeled off the wall, standing right behind him. Thom matched his cadence, stepping when he stepped to hide his movement.

The collar had seen all sides of him now—and with a flicker, generated an exact duplicate of the man, from his broken nose to messy hair and beady eyes.

If the goon turned around, Thom was dead.

But this guy had already moved on to step two, bellowing a command into the air, "The kid's got out! Hey! *Gylet zu fortaw!*"

Activity up the hall as pounding feet and bouncing metal announced a dozen men all leaping to their posts.

Now Thom had to get away from his doppelgänger, for a number of reasons. People would recognize two of the same face, and they would most definitely recognize that Thom's smaller and leaner build was *not* their colleague.

As the guard marched up and away, Thom broke rank and leaned against the wall, waiting for the guard to get sufficiently far away. Satisfied, Thom walked off in the other direction, slinging his reversed jacket on.

He might not look like one of the pirates, but he did not look like Thom anymore, and that's what was critical.

Up the hallway and out the door. It was a long walk before he realized there were no other cells in the block. Either Thom was in high security, or they had hastily thrown that together for their high value asset.

A few more steps, and the asteroid's rocky hallways transformed to industrial grating, bulkheads, and flashing lights. It wasn't dissimilar from the foundry on DeeBee—but this had been redressed, etchings scrawled on the walls and lights strung from the grating above. Someone had run the length of the corridor, lining it with tiny projectors throwing all kinds of morphing imagery on to the walls.

Some of the pictures were of the more explicit kind, showing eager virile men and beautiful women in various combinations and poses. Some more artistic—or at least, that could be argued.

A thin layer of volumetric dust hung in the air, catching every particle of light and making the very air seem to glow. It was almost certainly horrible to breathe the air, but Thom felt like he was catching something other than a lung infection here.

Someone jostled his shoulder, pushing past him. "Oi, *waz hyer tu!*"

"Sorry," Thom said by impulse.

Maybe the voice modulator sounded off. Maybe it was something this man had never said in his entire life. But the pirate stopped, looking back at him. A deep scar ran from ear to cheek, head shaved, crisp blue eyes. He studied Thom for a long moment.

Then shook his head. "Hosker, you look...terrible. Get some rack time before you melt or some-sa."

Thom nodded a little too quick. "Can't right now, though."

The guy raised an eyebrow, with a knowing smirk. "More like 'can't ever', right?"

Thom gave him the best chest laugh he could muster, a quick, brief guffaw. That was a poor choice. The man's eyes went wide, looking Thom up and down again. "What, was that a cough?"

Thom pointed at his throat, but quickly lowered his hand before he pointed right at the hologram projector on his neck. "Somethin' caught in my...yeah."

He sniffed the air. Of course, Thom was still covered in the soot and grime. "Oh, Hosker man—"

"What?" Thom asked, sniffing at his armpit. "You don't like it?"

The pirate waved at his nose. "It smells like your sister's pants."

Why would it smell like—"Oh, that's not right!" Thom spouted.

The man laughed at his own joke, before the boil came to a

simmer and then still waters. Thom's was the wrong answer. He had been expecting something in return, something that never arrived. A repartee, a duel of blows. Thom simply took the hit.

He stared at him for the longest time. "You comin'?"

Oh, boy.

"Hell yeah," Thom said, trotting behind his new buddy. Wherever they were going, he had to go now too.

Every footfall sounded like a steel crate slamming into the grating, a cacophony, a percussion orchestra. There was no way the pirate was actually that heavy—unless they were slamming their feet down on purpose, trying to make the noise? Was this some drums of war?

Regardless, Thom had to fit in or they would quickly realize he wasn't who he said he was. He had to blend in, unremarkable and indistinctive, a texture of sweat and grizzle that meshed with the crowd.

They jogged down the hall until it narrowed at a hatchcomb.

"Hosker, *hup-hup!*" the pirate said, as he swiped his hand along a reader—haptics, magnetic reader checking palm print and implants. It wasn't controlling the lock but monitoring movement: who was where and when.

Thom's hand wasn't even the same size as 'Hosker's'.

The pirate's eyes narrowed, sensing the pause. "Let's go, *kahro.*"

There it was. The pirate just gave him an out.

"What did ya call me?" Thom said with a gruff chest voice. The projector modulated his voice as best it could.

Apparently, it was Hosker's murder setting. "Easy, Hosk. Just playin' around." He pointed at the scan pad. "S'curity?"

Can't scan. They'll know. "Do I look like I have that kind of time?"

The pirate was rooting around for his spine, because this was wildly out of character, but he was also trying to make sure that spine wasn't broken when he found it.

"We—it's what we do, Hosker. The light's flashing." He pointed up at the blinking bulb over the panel, like that was supposed to end the conversation.

Every moment they delayed, Stride got closer to the Icon. He had to get it and signal Osyen, in whichever order was convenient, but he had to do it now.

"Is this our house," Thom slurred, "or the Imps?" And with that, he reached for the door handle.

The pirate might shoot him for breach of protocol, but that somehow didn't feel like a very pirate thing to do. He might tattle to the nearest big bad, but that was also more of a law-abiding type.

He might try to deck him, and the hologram would immediately fail—not to mention Thom's face was quite a bit more delicate than Hosker's. And it would not be the last hit he took.

But Hosker was a big man with a big reputation—the pirate slid out of his way, with a slack-jawed stare. He might tattle, but he might also save this little detail for some darker day. Poor Hosker had no idea that he had just been framed for breaking the rules.

Something told Thom that Hosker didn't have much care for rules, though.

Thom pushed the door open and stepped through, pausing on the other side. He looked back at the pirate with a sneer. "Well, you comin', *kahro*?"

The pirate nodded like his head was attached to a jackhammer, and bolted through the open door, leading the way on.

Under his hologram, Thom let out a sigh like he was bleeding pressure from a cabin.

The pirate led him along, the hallway bending slightly to the left as they went—it was an outer ring, meaning they were running the circumference of the station. Might be an interior corridor or the final wall before the vacuum, but Thom could map the shape of the station in his head with this.

Where were they going? How long till someone who knew Hosker better came along? He couldn't think about that. He had to focus.

Find the Icon.

They cut in off the outer ring, passing through a hatch comb into a wide-open room. Consoles lined the walls in terraces, row after row looking down on to a center map table. It was just shy of shoulder-to-shoulder, crass and sweaty men of all sizes standing still.

A few pirates had their hats in their hands. There was a valuable hostage on the loose, but these men looked like they were attending a Cathedral service.

They were so close to him. If anybody nudged his face with an elbow or shoved him, the hologram would not be able to hide its glitching. He tried to step backward, slide out and away, but someone was already at his back, fencing him in as they tried to get a view.

A view of what?

Center-stage at the bottom of the 'pit' was Stride and two Imperial officers, dress uniforms. They were frighteningly still, the only proof of life being the subtle cloud of condensation they exhaled on the regular.

Stride pursed his lips, pushing out one big cloudy breath and playing with the shape of the vapor in the air. They were waiting—and frustrated. His eyes scanned across the audience above him, tracking each position like he was committing it to memory.

His eyes locked on Thom, stopping for the heaviest second. The spider took in Hosker's face. Was Hosker in this room already, and Stride saw the duplicate?

The moment broke when two men entered from the opposite side of the deck. One must've been the captain of the crew, what with the ostentatious gold filigree on his long-coat and a hat large enough to capture a good-sized bird.

The other man was a garden variety pirate goon, but for the long, jagged scar across his neck—Thom doubted he could speak. But he carried something in his outstretched hands, covered in sackcloth.

An orb.

Thom had seen Osyen's fakes before—rocks bejeweled and bedazzled, regal and wonderful things, destined to be cherished and held in high esteem. But Thom knew without even seeing, this was the real deal. This was the Icon of Cruciform.

He knew, because his blood froze in his veins the moment it entered the room. It was like it took something from him that even he didn't understand, but now he was so cold.

"Orzik," Stride addressed the Pirate Captain. "You're a man of your word."

Orzik sneered, "Can't say the same for you, Jeremiah. Where's me payment?"

"On its way," Stride said. "Did you think I was going to show up with cash in hand just waiting to be mugged?"

The captain raised a hand and his attendant stopped. Thom noticed that the bearer had not taken his eyes off the prize, not out of nerve—but of an over-indulgence. His mind was not completely his own, drawn to his burden, to its allure.

"Replicas and duplicates of this item have been popping up all over the quadrant," Stride explained. "You'll forgive me, but I had to know you were telling the truth."

Orzik curled his lip up in a snarl. "You want a demonstration then?"

Stride cocked his head, a swift jerk and the first motion he'd made since Thom had laid eyes on him. Then he muffled a laugh, the snort sending a puff of white into the air. "I imagine you already tested it."

Orzik smiled. "Izzy here was a good boy, but he made a real mess of things. I took care of business and..."

The mute, the scarred man—Izzy—had been punished and healed. And clearly, not the same man anymore.

Stride stepped forward, circling Izzy. The pirates all tensed up, ready for the Imperial to do something untoward. They might even gun him down before he could steal the Icon from Izzy's firm hands.

Slowly, Stride reached for the man's collar and plucked at it. "Is he alive?"

"Are you?" Orzik asked, with a nihilistic chuckle. "He follows orders now. That's what I care about."

Stride ran his finger down Izzy's shirt, pulling it out.

And that's when Thom saw Stride wince, the smallest pull on his brow and tucking his chin in close, recoiling from the dozens of scars lining Izzy's body. "How many times have you done this to him?"

"Enough to know it works," Orzik said. "That's what you care about, yah?"

Stride nodded, but pulled his lips tight. He studied every inch of Izzy, letting his eyes linger. With one hand, he gingerly reached out and tilted Izzy's neck up.

The skin parted just enough, revealing where his throat had been slit but never properly healed. The 'scars' were still open wounds, but weren't bleeding.

"Did you *choose* not to patch him completely?" Stride asked.

"Thought it'd be a decent reminder," Orzik sneered, "for him. And for everybody else."

Stride let Izzy's chin fall slack, letting the wound close again. "Do you see now?" Stride called out, his voice echoing in the space while never taking his eyes off Izzy, "why I can't let it go back?"

"Go back where?" Orzik asked, humoring Stride's theatrics.

Thom knew otherwise. Stride wasn't talking to the pirate. He was talking to Thom. Stride knew Thom was there, somehow. He knew Thom was watching.

Stride took a step back. "This man's dead."

Orzik smiled. "And yet he lives. Impressed?"

Stride blinked a few times, studying the revenant. "You wouldn't mind a more practical exhibition, would you?"

He didn't give Orzik time to respond. The naval officer produced his sidearm and fired.

Into Thom's gut.

He felt a pin prick his stomach and a sharp pain in his back. And curiously of all, he felt the breeze—before it all set fire like a trail of oil.

Thom's eyes went wide, and his legs gave way. He tried to breathe, but with every pull, his abdomen screamed.

He wanted to scream, but he had no voice. His throat clenched. He wanted. To scream.

Stride was standing over him. No idea when he got there. "Holographic collar has a refresh rate of around 400 hertz. The human eye can't track that change." His eye flashed yellow. "But mine can."

The Imperial reached down, ripping the black collar from his neck. The pirates nearby gasped and withdrew.

Orzik screeched. "That's me ransom you jus' shot!"

"Well, if you have the real Icon, we don't need to worry, do we?" Stride stooped down to Thom, grasping his face with both hands. "Thomas, you can do this but you have to listen to me very carefully."

Thom couldn't feel his fingers. It hurt so much. Tears spilled down his cheeks.

Stride shook his head, rattling whatever sense was left in him, trying to stir some life back into him. "Thomas, look at me! Ask it for help."

"Wha..." Thom leaked out with his half-breath.

"The Icon can heal you, but only if you ask it too," Stride whispered. "You have to ask it. Don't worry about the words. Just ask for its help."

Thom reached one hand down to his wound, but Stride took it in his, gripping hard, as if to hold him steady.

And he began to chant.

Thom heard the words, but it was like they came from his implant. It was like someone spoke them into his flesh, etched them there with ink and stained him, anointed him.

Sacred world, who takes away the sins of the body.

Father World, let it be done unto me according to your Word.

It was just Stride and Thom now, in the ever-encroaching dark. Stride squeezed Thom's hand in his. But in the other, Stride held—

The Icon. It was beautiful. Dark crystal, with embossed depths. Polished to a dull shine, dark green. Ancient and mighty.

And oh so cold.

Thom couldn't put the words together but he stared into its abyss. And he begged. Help me.

From the darkness beyond them, he heard Orzik's voice. "You killed my ransom! Boys!"

"Lieutenant?"

Stride said the one word and the fusillade began. Somewhere out of sight, gunshots rang out, only to be silenced by the crisp report of laser discharges. The smell of burnt hair and ozone filled his nose.

And then all fell quiet again.

Stride held his hand the whole time. "Don't go, Thomas."

Thom stared at the Icon, and somewhere in its depths, a flare of light.

The cold—a spike of impossible ice, like the vacuum of space had been poured into his chest, leeching through his shoulders and down to his fingers, a hungry darkness.

He thought he knew pain. But as his stomach began to stitch itself together, he thought he'd gone mad, every nerve in every part of him alight with magnesium heat. He felt his stomach tighten and pull as ribbons of flesh reached across, stitching themselves to one another.

Somewhere in his back, the necromancy worked to patch the exit wound. And deep within him, at the torn muscles and ligaments, the ruptured organs, a distant hand went to work pressing out a lifetime's worth of pain in a matter of seconds.

And just like that, it was over. Caked in blood and tears and soot, Thom gasped for air. He blinked through the pain—

The deck was a graveyard. Every single pirate had been cut down. Stride's two men tended to each other, steam rising from their skin like they were fresh from an oven. Whatever cold had torn through Thom, those two men had been through a broil—and the bodies that lay draped over their consoles was evidence of their passing.

How could three men do all this damage?

Thom got one last glimpse of the crystal, as Stride wrapped the Icon in the sackcloth, hiding its visage from the world.

"Signal the *Acheron*," Stride said, throwing a glance to the prostrate Thom—almost an apology. "We're coming home. Once we're clear, they have permission to fire."

Stride stepped over Thom's body as he left.

CHAPTER
FIFTEEN
OSYEN

IT HAD GONE AWFULLY quiet on the implant. Maybe the others had splintered off, chattering away, with the horrible Capital safely corralled away where he could not interject. They might right now be discussing what to do with him—steal his ship, turn him in.

Or simply put a bullet in his head.

It occurred to him then, that they all might be just as nervous as he was. Scared for the boy, scared for themselves, the mission. Just scared.

But even Thom hadn't reported in, not even a grumble that Osyen had grown accustomed to. It was setting his teeth on edge, grinding back and forth till he was sure he'd crack something.

Not a one of them could meet his stare, always turning back to whatever nonsense they were pretending to work on.

Adelaide insisted she was working on the Jump Drive, calibrating and tuning after the jump into the Edge. She swore, in a few terse words, that the jump drift was unacceptable and dangerous. She never mentioned Lily, but he knew she blamed the navigator.

Lily had been curiously reserved, as well. They had pleasantries to spare but little else. The revelation of Osyen's past had not been relevant to them after all—an ageless artificial intelligence didn't waste memory on human justice systems and the perversions thereof. But he couldn't help but take note of the sudden distance Lily was exhibiting.

Rashida gave polite smiles while she took a meal, lifting each slice of fruit like it was a delicate flower that might blow away in a stiff breeze. She seemed to study each bite before taking it, careful consideration on how to approach. Maybe she was comparing the ship's carbon printer to her memory of the real thing.

"Everything you hoped for?" Osyen had asked her.

She murmured her response, but it never escaped the back of her throat, trapped behind tight lips and set jaw. It was the only answer she'd given him since the mission started.

Milardi paced the cargo bay, all fidgeting and drills. He practiced reloads and draws, stretching out his gangly limbs. The big guy never could sit still, but this was something else—like he was dancing on hot coals.

Zatia worked on her armory, tapping steel pins into place on her latest project, while her other hand selected the proper tool that would get to finish the work, fingers waggling like a glutton over sweets. This was both ritual and meditation, pleasure and annoyance. She relished the result as much as the process.

He had tried to talk to her but she had simply glared in response. She had said her piece, and it was all she wanted to say to him.

They were absolutely talking about him in some hidden back channel. He didn't dare ask Lily for permission. No, let them have their grievances aired. It was better to let them have their space than encroach just for his own comfort.

And so he sat on the bridge.

Roche wasn't big on eye contact to begin with, as he tracked the half dozen displays projected onto the inside of his skull. But he was particularly distant, hunched over the battery of cables and plugs, doing trades like he was funneling some invisible ball down through a track.

It was a maddening sound. Clicking and clacking as the plugs seated and were pulled. Is this what the inside of a musician's brain sounded like? All song and substance gone, just a metronomic beat of alternating tones that challenged all reason and begged to be silenced behind the wails of a string and the blare of brass?

Because if Osyen didn't get some relief, he was going to set Roche on fire.

"How long's he been gone?" Osyen asked.

Roche's eyes flitted up to him—or rather to his boots. "Four hours, twenty-seven minutes and change."

Osyen huffed. "Seemed longer."

Roche didn't answer, back to his strange cable song, clicking and clacking away. What was he even doing? It's not like the ship was going anywhere.

"And we're sure he's on the station?" Osyen asked.

"His implant went in," Roche said. "Whether he's attached to it..."

"See, that was needlessly morbid."

Click. Clack. In and out. Up and down. Over and under. Click and clack.

"You know," Osyen started, "if you and the ship want some privacy—"

"It's better for me if you watch."

Osyen's brain immediately had to shake the grotesque oil painting that conjured for half a second. Roche didn't grin, but he couldn't hide his smug shoulder waggle, having won the ancient Olympiad of embarrassing your friends.

"If we do an active scan, could we find Thom on the station?"

"Yes," Roche said, "and they'd find us in half a second and blow us out of the sky. Try to be patient, Oz."

Osyen threw his hands up, settling back into his chair.

And then he sat forward, consulting a screen and its flickering image, filtered and corrupted by the pulsar. The asteroid could barely be made out, slowly rotating on two axes as it happily tumbled around its orbit. Ships hovered around it like bees around a hive.

If there were cause for alarm, those ships would be whipped into a feeding frenzy.

Osyen sat back again, trying to get comfortable. He stared at Roche, trying to pick out what strange pattern he was running with those alternating connectors.

Then back to the screen, to avoid staring. Back to Roche and his racket. Back to the screen.

Roche didn't look up, hearing the chair squeak again and again. "Osyen, you seem to be under the impression I'm mad at you."

Osyen's mind skipped so hard he almost physically hiccuped. "You're not?"

"Are the others?"

"Zatia shot me!" Osyen blurted. "And you yourself were pretty vocal in the cargo bay this morning."

Roche lifted up his deformed hand and all of its thick, coiled cables, like a curious vined plant growing out of his wrist. "Advantage of being a plug, Osyen. I process faster."

"So you mean to say, you *were* mad, but are no longer?"

"Of course," Roche reasoned. "You lied to us. I was furious. But after a time, I came to understand your reasons and the others will too."

"No, they won't." Osyen looked down at the screen again. They'd throw him out an airlock to save their own hides. They wouldn't gamble with their lives just to be around him.

Roche never took his eyes off his task. "People are irrational, emotional, reflexive beasts. They see their world first, yours second. Their empathy has limits that expand only with time."

"And what's Lily's excuse?"

He didn't need a projected image to know the computer was paying entirely too much attention to the conversation. The hum of the ship's quiet systems rising just enough, a key shift in the opera.

Roche finally let himself smile—probably because Lily had snarked something into his ear. "Lily is more person than computer these days."

His smirk widened as the navigator lodged a complaint in his ear. He cocked his head at Osyen, as if to wink-wink, nudge-nudge.

"Case in point?" Osyen asked, which made Roche chuckle.

Roche shrugged. "It's why I like them."

A shadow on the screen, silhouetted by the pulsar. It blocked out half the asteroid.

"What the Hell is that?" Osyen asked.

Roche sat upright, his eyes darting independently around his skull, like a chameleon. "*Alighieri*-class Fleet Carrier, twenty-seven degrees up, ten port. Seven hundred clicks out."

Osyen sat forward, grabbing the dials. Maybe he could clear up the picture? "Think that's who sent our welcoming party?"

"It's a fair bet," Roche said grimly. "It's approaching the Widows' Den."

That swarm of insects, that hive full of ships, should have swarmed the attacking vessel like hunger made manifest.

Instead, they scattered into the night, fireflies winking and blinking away in the pulsar's light, leaving the carrier to lumber on towards the base unabated.

Thom's in there.

"Bring us in."

One eye swung about. "They'll hit us so hard, we'll become theoretical math. Oz—"

"This mission is scrubbed," Osyen said. "We have to get Thom out of there."

"I'm trying to tell you, Oz, that's not within our power to do—" He stopped, his eyes locking on to some projected alarm. "I've got heat flares across their ventral. They're opening fire."

"On what?" Osyen asked, already knowing the answer.

"On the station."

In between the flickers of the star's radiation, Osyen could make it out. The carrier wasn't launching fighters or transports; it was bombarding the base with flak and mass drivers, salvo after salvo pounding the rock and metal. Gas flares shot out of the base as pressure snapped. Dozens of people would be killed instantly.

But the base was large, dwarfing the carrier five to one. The interior would be allowed some protection.

Osyen bolted for the hatch. *Milardi, Zatia, on your feet and gear up.*

Has the kid got the door open? The words in Milardi's message might have been optimistic, but the tone was more dreadful.

Osyen marched down the hall, reaching up to snag the bracket gun stashed in the frame. *Imperial Navy's shelling the base. We're going to get him out of there.*

The channel became a flurry of objections, startled shouting, and furious questions. To be perfectly frank, he didn't listen to any of them. He felt like he was walking through muck and grime, having to push each step forward through the weight of it.

And he was moving fast enough to have a wake.

Rashida was halfway up the ladder from her bunk, sizing up Osyen's walk. "What's wrong?"

"M'lady, you can do a lot of things," he tossed off as he blew past her, "but, no offense, this is going to be one of my kind of things."

She fell into his wake, pulled along by sheer gravity. "Is Thom okay?"

He didn't know. He couldn't know. Thom could've been killed hours ago and he wouldn't have known. It was driving him crazy, an itch under his skin and behind his eyes and in his throat.

He'd dragged that poor boy out here. He'd even tried to ditch him. Now he was in trouble, and it was Osyen's goddamn fault. He should've left him. He should have, should have.

He knew what he had to do now.

Osyen burst into the cargo hold. Milardi was draped on the ladder, gaping up from below. Zatia stood on the causeway, leaning casually on the railing. No gear, hair down, already shaking her head.

Roche had told them already. They *did* have a private channel.

"I'm going to pull him out. Whoever wants to come with me, I can use the steel."

"Or I can wait here and your stuff becomes my stuff," Zatia mused.

Rashida did not have patience for that tone. "Your ability to look after yourself is almost inspiring."

"Oh, like you haven't spent the last forever looking out for number one," Zatia spat back. "You've been a right charity case, you have!"

Adelaide came stomping in from behind. "Wanting to do something, and being able to do it, are two different things."

"The line between those two is actually doing it, Addy," Milardi jeered from below.

Adelaide shot him a glare, commanding him to be silent with nothing but her eyes.

"I wasn't asked to give or I would have," Rashida shot back at Zatia, "I was *born* into a life of liturgy, so keep your—"

"And some very fine dining," Adelaide muttered loud enough for nearby star systems to hear.

"And what have *you* done, Zee?" Milardi shouted up. "You do a lot of charity work in thirty caliber?"

"And you're a monumental liar," was the pixie's response. "Take a seat already."

Rashida gawked, her jaw open, in awe of what she was seeing. "How can you be so cruel? How do you do it?"

Zatia's look could've melted steel. "Practice, mostly."

But Rashida wasn't done. "I mean it. You know Thomas better than I do. He served alongside you. He's in danger. How can you just—"

"I don't see you lifting one finger," Zatia spat back. "So don't get on my case for—"

"That is your friend down there!"

"What has he ever done for me?!"

"He *believed* in you!" Osyen's voice echoed in the cavern,

209

careening off the walls and up the halls and filling every crevice of the *Aurum*'s many hidden places. And with that he had their attention.

"All of us! He wanted *so much* to be like us. And we bled him, we just...we made him think he could! Because it made us feel good. Like we mattered. Like we were important, suave, capable..." He let his eyes linger on each in turn with each phrase, on Zatia, Milardi, and Adelaide.

He drew his eyes to Rashida but he couldn't hold her gaze, faltering to the grating under his feet like he was suddenly out of breath. "That we're all put together."

By the way he said it, the hollow tones—he wasn't talking about her. It cut to the quick, and she took a stiff breath. Like she'd just heard of a friend's untimely death.

She still might today.

He turned back to the room. "I'm going in. I'm bringing him home. We owe him that much. Who's with me?"

It might have been silent in the bay, but he could hear the engines firing, the chains clattering as thrust was pushed. Roche was guiding them in. He had to pray that Roche knew where to go and how to avoid the worst of the barrage.

And how to get them back out again.

Zatia scoffed. "When it's my ship, can I wipe Lily?"

Noted. He looked to Adelaide. "You?"

Adelaide shook her head, turning away. She clearly thought Osyen had missed the mark with his biting critique.

But the lack of sharp rejoinder told him otherwise.

He heard the flourish of leather. He looked down in time to see Milardi's jacket fluttering down about his shoulders as he affixed his hat to his head, straightening the brim with a swipe of his fingertips. He tilted his head up, revealing only the stubble on his chin. And from under that dark shade, a familiar Colonial gravel and slur. "What you all standing 'round a-bouts?"

"Work hard?" Osyen called out.

There was that glittering smile. "Play hard, boss-man."

"Security is going to be tight." Milardi and Osyen turned to see Adelaide slinging on her toolbelt, cinching it tight. She avoided Zatia's stiletto stare. "And you two idiots are going to hit it like you're made of ceramic. Let's bring him home."

———

Nothing was there to keep them from docking. Why would any sane person decide to attach themselves to a station currently being engulfed in a military bombardment? This is the opposite of good advice. This is the antithesis of intelligence.

He could see quite clearly what was going on, the plumes of fire that leapt out, tongues of hot gases reaching into the dark like some ancient hungry beast of fire and fury. Entire segments of the station were cast off into oblivion. He could even see the occasional human body, illuminated by the star's brilliance.

Every nerve in Osyen's head fired off panic and fear. And all was subdued by the simple notion: Thom was in there.

"There won't be enough escape pods," Adelaide said, with a grim tone.

Milardi tongued his cheek, drawing his sidearms. And Osyen instantly knew why—their little brig might be the only lifeboat for some of the monsters inside. They would rush the dock hoping to find safe harbor.

They'd have to defend the hatch comb.

Ten seconds to contact, Roche intoned.

Suddenly, Osyen felt Lily's mind in his, filling it, subsuming it, a tender embrace. Their light filled his mind. And their words echoed in every muscle.

Come back alive.

And just like that, Lily was gone.

The bass drum of the hatch lock sounded like a starting gun. And just as soon as pressure was equalized, Lily opened the door.

Two men, bloody, ragged. They had been poised at the door-frame, desperate.

Armed.

Milardi whipped his pistols up and drilled two matching holes in each of their chests. The poor sods were so off-balance they were blown clean off their feet.

The connecting tunnel was built to hustle cargo containers from connecting ships and not an inch more. Scant, stark lighting cast into the narrow space from embedded overheads.

Break seal and clear the area, Osyen ordered. *We'll call when we need pickup.*

Roche's voice was grim. *Don't be long.*

Milardi and Osyen were able to stand shoulder to shoulder if they really liked each other. They moved like a practiced ballet, leap frogging between support braces for cover, and allowing their colleague to advance to the next.

And then they spilled into the station's interior. Spots of black stone were visible at every turn where metal supports and bulkheads could not mask the asteroid's geological guts. The yellow lights flickered like they were themselves in a panic. A klaxon blared its ominous trumpet with enough force to cause his ears to ring.

Like the gunfire was any better. Energy blasts and thunderous explosions echoed up in the innards of the station. Screams of all kinds, a horrible chorus.

Even if Osyen wasn't orchestrating their own incursion, there was all kinds of hellfire reporting from the distance. The pirates were eating each other alive for any available seat off this sinking ship.

Milardi cursed under his breath, "*Gule sav tu.*"

God save us.

We're clear of the mayhem, Roche chimed in, *Thom's implant is two floors in from you, two hundred feet forward. Move fast.*

Like he had to say that.

"I've got anchor," Osyen said, "Milardi, pave the road."

Milardi hoisted his pistols—chunks of steel and applied physics—

and he stomped forward. Not a run or jog, but a powerful, long stride for a man of his gait. Everything in front of him was hostile and he treated it as such.

Nobody was hiding or waiting in secret. Everyone ran around their corner to a surprise, as Milardi cut them down. Nobody got past him. Single, violent blows from a jackhammer that he slammed out from the shoulder—taking a stance and almost 'throwing' the bullet. He would punch the pistol out and an attacker would fall.

The report of the shot was lyrical in comparison to rest of the world, crisp and reedy, like it belonged to a hammer on an anvil.

But they were many and his weapons had their limits.

"Loading!" Milardi shouted.

As if summoned, two more men leapt from cover with weapons drawn.

Osyen swung about, plugging one with the bracket gun—the wide blast from the bore almost bisecting head from legs. His friend didn't see what happened, bracing himself against the wall as he panic-fired at Osyen. In between gunshots, Osyen could hear his screaming. Whether it was a battle cry or just actual crying was hard to figure.

Osyen fumbled with the bracket gun, before cursing and ripping his carbine from his leg holster. The small rifle's barrel sprung to its full length as the press-formed stock slipped up to cup the curve of his shoulder. He didn't need to drop behind the sights; he knew where the shots would land.

He squeezed the trigger once, twice—and the man went down.

Osyen let out a breath as he slipped two fresh rounds to top up the tube.

Milardi took up the lead again, passing another hatch comb down to a docking collar, not unlike what they had boarded on. People had crammed into it, seeking space on whatever ship had been available on the other end. A body hung from the closed hatch, a limb shoved through the sealed door and severed by the hydraulics. They had been so desperate for safety they had tried to hold it open. The door was stronger.

The crowd had abandoned the poor sap there, hanging. But not before someone had mercifully put a bullet in their head.

Soon the trio circled around to a bulkhead—no, that was a door. The titanic pressure door sealed off the forward section.

"Adelaide," he said, "you're up!"

"There any air on the other side of this?" Milardi asked.

"Someone closed this one manually." Adelaide pulled a tool from her belt, stepping up to the command console on the side. "And this someone thought they could lock the door closed with a bullet."

"Did they?" Osyen asked.

An explosion somewhere behind them, and the air pulled on them before a loud bang cut off the flow. Another pressure door somewhere else sealing off the compromised section.

Adelaide flicked her hair out of her face. "They closed it with the failsafe," she said, but smirked, "but if they think that *locks* it..."

Milardi popped a pirate that came around the corner. "Well then, work your magic."

She ripped open the control panel with a wrench, tossing the cover to the side. She quickly scanned the exposed wires behind, before she went to work, pulling and cutting.

It was an art form long lost, held only by craftsmen and anarchists —how a computer worked behind the faceplate. A good lineman knew how to run electrical current in a way no computer or programmer could prevent.

Milardi fired another shot. "Osyen, we have attracted some attention!"

Osyen dropped himself against a bulkhead, the support structure allotting some cover from hostile intent. And not a moment too soon, as an energy blast drenched the steel with enough heat to morph it into red slag.

He returned the favor, snapping his attacker in the head. Light switch. He doubted the poor bastard even felt it.

"Adelaide," Osyen called out, "whenever you're ready!"

She donned a pair of gloves. "This isn't something you do quickly."

She was out and exposed. Whoever wrapped the corner was as likely to shoot her as they were the people with guns. She was the easy target of the three.

And one tried, shooting at the first thing he saw. She came around guns blazing, spraying a defilade into the door directly behind Adelaide. Milardi slammed a shot into the attacker's chest, throwing them to the ground.

Adelaide didn't even flinch as the bullet holes sizzled inches from her back.

"Crack it, Addy!"

Adelaide swiped a tool across two wires, soldering them together. A hush as the pressure equalized, and the door hung for a moment. Like it had a dramatic sense of irony.

And then slammed open, floor to ceiling.

Adelaide pocketed her tool. "Let's go, baby boys." Adelaide strode through, rock star on a stage.

Milardi and Osyen swung through, watching the pathway behind them. Voices calling out commanded their attention.

"Close it," Osyen ordered.

But Adelaide just leaned against the wall.

"Addy?"

She didn't answer. She didn't move. She just leaned there with pursed lips.

A single man came running. Clothes torn and splattered with blood. He was not armed or angry, but afraid.

And now so was Osyen, as a horde came around the bend in hot pursuit. Men, women, and even the occasional child were in the mass —but all of them violent, slavering. The kind of entity that can only be summoned by a crowd of people filled with fear. They would peel the flesh from a baby if it meant their freedom, the horror of their transgressions equally distributed over their entirety, absolving the few by virtue of distribution.

They consumed the fleeing pirate, in nearly every sense of the word. Every individual seeking safety with the same urgency, they pounded ground and meat underfoot just the same.

They would mulch anything in their path.

Milardi opened fire on them, but it did little to slow the advance. "Adelaide!"

And Adelaide clapped her hands.

The console sparked, shorting. Whatever slice she had done could not have been sustained for long.

And the door slammed shut behind them, with the force of a car crash. It shook the floor and nearly took Osyen from his feet.

They heard the horde slam into the door, all of their fear pressuring in vain against the door. The repetition grew more and more... wet, something Osyen would have to scrape from his nightmares.

Adelaide turned to Osyen. "Don't call me 'Addy.'"

"The station is explodin' and you're pulling stunts like that?!" Milardi shouted.

"It would've took longer to explain it," was all she said.

The trio rushed along as the station shuddered under their feet. Osyen tried to keep his eyes focused on his surroundings, but he could feel the weight sinking into the pit of his stomach. They were too late. All of this death. There's no way Thom was still alive. No way.

They slowed at a hatch comb, bodies piled up in its arch. Burn scars on all of them.

Laser fire.

"Oh my God..." Osyen murmured, jogging forward. Milardi tried to stop him, but Osyen was well out of reach.

The command deck, terraced computers high up above and down deep below him, like he was standing in stadium seating. All of them dark.

The place looked like someone had decorated with their combat kills. It was clear to see where the epicenter was—it was the only clean space in the entire room, a small circle the damage didn't seem to touch. It looked like a bomb had gone off, choosing to spare the handful right underneath it.

Thom was in here?

"Oh, no no no no..." Osyen repeated. Maybe he was a deck down? Maybe the reading was off? Maybe they took his implant but he was alive elsewhere?

Maybe they killed him long ago. Maybe he was somewhere in this pile.

"Oz..." Milardi knelt down at a crumpled mess, heaving the fallen off of—

Thom.

His skin stained with black soot, his hair a bedraggled mess of grease and grime. A gaping hole in his shirt, the frayed edges stained dark red. He laid so still, like a sculpture of life crafted for some marble hall.

Osyen vaulted over to him, dropping to his knees at the boy's side. He lifted up Thom's head, resting it in his lap, his fingers scanning for a pulse, for breath, for life.

Milardi was hard at work, inspecting the wound channel and taking vitals.

Adelaide marched over to a console, tap tap tapping, trying to resuscitate the machine. When the holographic display refused to come out, she ducked under the desk.

She was doing tech support while Thom laid limp in his hands.

"Thom?" Osyen whispered, "Thom, can you hear me?"

"I've got a pulse," Milardi said, listening to Thom's chest, "but it's all over the place."

"He's alive?"

The urgency in his voice took the spirit right out of Milardi's wings. "For now."

"Where was he hit?"

"That's the thing." Milardi stared at the bloody tear in Thom's tunic, "I don't see an entry or exit."

Was the blood someone else's? How did he tear his tunic?

"Safe to move him?" Osyen asked.

Milardi shook his head, but then—"But I can't stabilize him here."

Osyen looped an arm under Thom's legs and swooped the boy up into his arms. "Damn, Thom! What did you eat for lunch, solid lead?

"Adelaide, drop whatever you're doin'," Milardi called out, "or you're goin' to get left."

Adelaide had re-wired the console, the golden glow of the projected keyboard under her fingers casting an ominous shadow on the wall. Her eyes scanned across the images with encroaching horror.

She was watching whatever happened to Thom. Osyen and Milardi couldn't bear to interrupt her now.

She swallowed hard, like she had to bury her need to scream, and instead pushed out a call. *Lily. Can you record this feed?*

Processing. Archived. Then Lily's tone shifted. *The station is suffering catastrophic pressure changes in all sections. Get to a hatch comb while there still is one.*

Osyen tossed Adelaide the bracket gun and his bandolier of batteries, before hoisting Thom into the air. *Light the way, Lily.*

Osyen's implant pinched and a flashing light appeared in his vision—pointing the way. *Proceed clockwise around the central ring, four hundred feet.*

Osyen took off at a jog, as fast as he could with Thom in his arms. If Adelaide and Milardi followed, he didn't know. A part of him didn't care.

The boy felt cold to the touch, chilled and damp, like a cool glass of water. It numbed his fingers right through his leather gloves, biting into his forearms. Where Thom's head leaned against his chest, Osyen felt the only warmth left in the boy's slight frame.

Hold on, Thom.

Those voices calling out again, somewhere behind. They weren't the only folk desperately seeking lifeboats.

Milardi shot first. Osyen didn't even see why. He dared not look back. He just kept running.

How much further, Lily?

The boy's implant is non-responsive.

Don't you dare. Don't you dare quit now.

Gunshots, screams, battle-cries. And then, a hard creak of metal and the banshee cry of a maelstrom. The wind was strong enough, it felt like it might tear his skin from his bones.

Osyen lost his footing, tumbling to the ground, twisting to shield Thom for the hard landing.

A gigantic tear in the bulkhead, maybe six feet across. The void-maw had opened behind Milardi's targets as the stress finally broke through.

He could see the Boolean star, blindingly white, its light unfiltered and unshielded. He could see the *Acheron*, framed by the star's hateful glory. He could see the shrapnel, the debris, the remains of the station disgorging unto the ether.

He saw a man ripped from his footing and sail out that hole.

The few remaining desperate pirates clung to whatever grip they could manage, raising their weapons. Milardi braced himself against his cover, almost standing up sideways on the cross-beam, aiming his pistols downward at the attackers.

And that's when the pressure door closed—sealing Milardi behind it.

"NO!" Osyen shouted. He laid Thom down, before darting to the door. "Adelaide! Get it open!"

She was already wrist deep in the panel. "It's an emergency lockdown."

"Override it!"

"What do you think I'm doin', jackass!?" Adelaide ripped something out and she yelped as it zapped her.

Her eyes scanned the guts of the panel while Osyen listened to the gunfire on the other side. It was getting more and more faint as the air left the chamber. Whether Milardi won the gun battle was about to be irrelevant.

"Cut the hydraulics," Osyen ordered.

"I do that, and I'll never get it closed again," she said, "I'll kill us all. Thom included."

Lily? Osyen begged, *Help us out now.*

Combating station heuristic defense. Processing...

Adelaide sat down, staring up at Osyen. She couldn't do it. She couldn't open the door. She had no words, not even enough energy to be frustrated. She stared at the work, the impossible work. The impossible price.

The gunfire was so far away now.

Adelaide, Lily called out, *splice the following connections.*

The old woman perked up immediately, as though someone had turned on a light in her room for the very first time. The eureka translated into an immediate lunge back into the panel with her tool and a short second later—

The door cracked open, just two small feet. The wind howled in objection. Fate had been denied and it was not content to allow this defiance. Thom's body lurched forward, sliding on the ground as the tongues of the storm latched ahold. Osyen grabbed the boy and gripped hard to the edge of the door, holding the two apart like he was holding open the jaws of a hungry dragon.

Through the crack, Osyen could see the once small hole had torn wide, peeling open like a can of vegetables. Milardi perched on his bulkhead, his eyes clenched shut and his face turning blue. As the wind hit him, he sucked in the air and opened his brilliant green eyes.

"Come on!" Was all Osyen could shout.

Adelaide stuck her hand through the door. And Milardi leapt for her.

The wind caught hold, pulling him down towards that horrific void. Its hunger knew no end. Any normal man would have been lost to it, consumed.

But Milardi was a lanky, giant, rubber band Colonial man. He snagged Adelaide's fingers. And she swung him up and through.

The door snapped shut behind him, the merciful hand of a gracious God.

Osyen would have to thank Lily personally. Maybe he could get together with Adelaide and buy the supercomputer some super-coolant or add some expansion slots.

Milardi dusted himself off, giving Adelaide a wordless nod of thanks. The exhaustion was thick in his voice, like he was speaking through a layer of molasses, but that didn't strip him of his cocky tone. "What're y'all layin' about for?"

CHAPTER
SIXTEEN
ZATIA

SHE'D INFLICTED all manner of pain and carnage on the human body before. She'd sliced, bruised, crunched and burned, shot people and broken them. She was something of an auteur in the field of human injuries and causing them. But she'd never seen anything like this.

A gunshot wound without a hole.

Milardi had injuries of his own to tend to—being depressurized for even that brief amount of time can have lasting effects, so he had to be carefully treated by the AutoDoc.

Which left *Unti* to her care.

She sliced the tunic off him, to reveal bloodstains on his chest and gut, but there was no clear wound. But Lily insisted there was internal blood pooling around the liver. And what's worse, the implant was nonresponsive, implying loss of brain function.

But scans revealed no damage. No bullet. No laceration of the liver or arteries. Aside from the pooling blood, the kid was unharmed.

So where did all that blood come from?

And that's when the boy who should be dead without any injuries whatsoever...sat bolt upright on the table. Thom took two steeling breaths—that should've been agony—and his eyes scanned the room before falling onto her. "How'd I...what happened?"

Zatia clicked the lock back on her retention holster, before crossing her arms. "We were hoping you'd tell us."

Thom pawed at his gut—okay, so *he* knew something had happened. But he was puzzled by finding nothing, just as much as she was. "I'm okay?"

"Based on the mess that is your shirt," Zatia said, "ten-millimeter Horus, standard issue Navy. You bumped into our friend again."

"I'm...alive?"

Zatia raised an eyebrow. "I could fix that, if you want."

He swung his feet off the table, bare toes touching the steel. He recoiled from it. Maybe it was too cold. "Where are the others?"

"At some point, you had a hole in your stomach big enough I could put my fist through it and out the other side," Zatia said, her eyes narrowed. "But this mo', you don't have a mark on you."

The kid nearly upchucked at the image. "Oh God..."

Zatia kicked a bucket over to his bedside, but the thing ended up helpfully flipped over. If he did puke, he'd have to mop it up. "Yeah, I'm sure it was as fun to feel as it was to see. So how big of a screw-up was it?"

That froze him. He looked up at her, his head bowed to the floor like she might strike him. And she hadn't yet decided if she wanted to or not. This was a big important day and he had screwed up. If he had done his job right, they'd all be heading home by now.

He opened his mouth a few times before any words came out. "I remember."

"Remember what?"

He looked at her, through her, at her again. "The Icon is real."

———

The crew absorbed Thom's story like they'd just been informed their last meal they had so richly devoured was laced with a neurotoxin that would dissolve their brainstems. Horror, panic, distress, and finally, acceptance. It was like watching a cult surrender itself to the master, heads lowered and accepting of the impossible in the futile pursuit for a cure.

They stood around Milardi and the AutoDoc, as its many tiny arms tended to the burst blood vessels in his leg and face. The millipede machine looked like it was giving him the tiniest massage, as it stitched, applied salve, and bandaged where necessary before moving on to the next square inch of skin.

Two tubes were feeding mysterious fluids into plugs on the back of his right arm, while a creepy, creaking pump strained against years of built-up crud in its valves. Milardi had kissed the void and they were bringing him back with two tubes and chemistry.

For all of that magic, everyone was still staring at Thom's impossible midsection. There wasn't a mark on him.

"Stride has it?" Osyen asked, full of grave projections.

Thom only nodded in response. He didn't like this anymore than they did. He had no cure to give.

"What's he going to do with it?" Adelaide mused, more to herself than the room.

"He could conquer half the known universe with a single battalion and not even break a sweat," Roche said. "Dead soldiers don't mean anything to a man with power over death."

"Doesn't matter," Rashida muttered, shaking her head.

"Yeah, a little bit," Zatia said, shriller than she meant to, "A crazy soldier with a big-ass ship has himself a religious totem that can resurrect the dead."

"You said the magic words," the Duchess du Douche quipped. "'Religious totem.'"

She waited, as if that was the elephant in the room. When no one responded, she threw up her hands in disgust. "Anybody? He has evidence that the Gnostic Librum...is *true*. Every word of it. The Pilgrim? The Colonies? The Sojourn, the whole text...he has, in his hands, evidence of things not seen."

Roche raised his plug-filled knob at the end of his wrist, like he was trying to make a point of order in a Quorum, and with about as much eloquence. One word left his crispy mouth, "Alien."

"Holy, alien, goddamn magic—does it matter?" Rashida shot back. "He has proof that their prayers *can* be answered by *something*."

"That something being whoever holds the magic rock," Osyen said.

Rashida nodded. "The myth is about to be acutely defined. Roche, you think he's going to conquer the universe at the tip of a sword? He'll get half of mankind to bow to him without leaving his office."

The Royal was coiled up like a viper ready to strike, silver tongue dripping with venom. She didn't like this development one bit. Her throne was eroding under the same chisel that carved it.

"And what happens to the Consul and your precious dynasty?" Zatia hissed.

"Holy blood," Adelaide whispered, "challenged by a new prophet?"

Rashida didn't blink. The horror of it all had set into her bones while the others were still grappling with the language. "Wars have been fought to bury treasures, as often as reclaim them. The Consul won't stomach a challenger. There will be a Holy Crusade that will burn entire planets."

"Even if he doesn't," Roche chimed in, "somebody may do it for him."

Zatia didn't even blink. "And something tells me the power players won't be the ones doing the dyin'."

Rashida just nodded, nothing to dispute there. The Holier Than Thou slot had just gotten far too literal for her comfort.

"And my father wanted it..." Thom whispered, propping himself against the wall. He wasn't leaning—he fell into the thing that happened to be nearest to him.

Did the Admiral want it for Consul and Empire, or for himself?

"Power like this..." Rashida paused, selecting her words, "...Power like this doesn't keep the peace. It disrupts it. Its mere existence will invite more pain than any healing it could ever offer."

"We've had a taste," Milardi grunted, tugging at his oxygen mask.

Rashida was quivering, every fiber of her plucked like a bowstring. It took every ounce of her will to not break down and cry right there.

Zatia sneered. "Thought you'd like discovering your Holy blood-line was all true."

Rashida's eyes were hollow as she cast her gaze on Zatia. "I fled my home, Zee. I'd give my life freely to you, but you don't want it, I promise you. I wanted yours."

The Royal Lady, anointed of the Gnostic, and literal descendant of the Pilgrim...she had no idea what she was asking for. She wouldn't have made it past her tenth birthday.

But something in Zatia wanted to see the Dunsweir try.

"We can't let Stride keep it," Osyen declared, like it was feasible.

"You're going to take it from him, are you?" Zatia asked, incredulous.

They didn't have to do the calculus on that one. The *Aurum* was a sturdy hunk of junk with some short-range mining lasers for point-defense. The *Acheron* was a Naval carrier that had twenty-times the tonnage. They could ram the *Aurum* and probably wouldn't even scuff their paint.

"And what else can we do?" Milardi slurred through his plastic mask. "Find some corner of the galaxy where the fighting finds us last?"

"I'm gonna start by stepping on your life-line," Zatia hissed.

"Not all problems can be punched, Zee," Roche said.

Zatia shrugged. "It's worked out pretty well for me so far."

Thom spoke up from the corner. "He said, 'it can't go back.'"

Everyone looked over at him, the boy who had been Touched by the Pilgrim. The look in his eye, he might as well have been on the Sojourn, far from them and the *Aurum* and his own body. But suddenly, he looked up. "It can't go back. He came out here to stop us...because *we* were going to bring it back."

"Creepy Imperial Orbital man...is the good guy in all this?" Zatia huffed.

"How can you be sure?" Adelaide asked the boy.

He shook his head. "I'm not. But we've been hit every single time we've gotten close to it. And I know what we came here to do. He hit us at the Jump Point, at the Gaslamp, and at the Widows' Den..."

Maybe the Icon had done more than stitch him up. The simplest idea was that Stride wanted the power for himself. And in her experience, men didn't acquire power to sit on it like some dragon hoard. They immediately turned to the nearest weakling and twisted it to get something they wanted.

"Service to the People, for They are the Kings..." Rashida muttered.

"What's that?" Thom asked.

"It's the Orbital Creed," the Royal said, "as said by the Pilgrim at the end of their Sojourn, when they left the first Dunsweir at the Gates of Luna. It's something of a mantra for the Navy. If Stride really is a man of faith..."

He would defend the Icon with his life.

"If we don't get it back," Osyen cautioned, "every single one of us is dead."

"Something tells me we're dead any way you slice it, Oz," Zatia said.

"I don't like it any more than you do, Zee—"

"Then stop talking, Capital, before I boot you out the nearest airlock."

The crew was suddenly all up in arms, everyone with their own objection and explanation. They bickered and groused and complained about asinine details, talking over and past each other. Nobody listening, nobody hearing. Nobody planning.

Roche went off about alien conspiracies, while Adelaide wanted to know about the Icon's capabilities; Rashida chided each in turn;

227

Milardi kept debating what good it could do in the 'right hands', whatever the fuck those were.

But Osyen only had eyes for the little sparkplug that had got up in his face. "I get it. I lied. Big, bad man. But you're going to wear Capital colors yourself if we don't do this and do it right."

Osyen went on talking, imploring, pleading even—but he didn't get half an ounce of her attention. Zatia was tracking on Thom, the silent observer, the only one who had been touched by the Icon and lived to tell about it.

She inspected the blank expression and distance behind his eyes. His chin jutted out, jaw tight. His brow furrowed, his fingers drumming against the wall.

He wasn't panicked or angry or afraid. He was working out the problem.

"Would you all shut the Hell up?" Zatia blustered so loud, she spat a little bit on Milardi's leg. He was going to object, but when he flinched, he winced in pain.

"Well, since you asked so nicely," Osyen grumbled, to which Adelaide smacked him upside his head like the grandma she was.

Thom finally noticed that Zatia was staring at him, and now that everyone else was too. She crossed her arms and squared up on the boy. "What's in your head?"

"...Control the story, you control the mark," Thom intoned. His eyes darted around in his skull like he was reading at light-speed.

Boy spent an entire afternoon in a back-alley jail and he had gone full savant. She half expected him to start scrawling religious glyphs on the wall, like he was making sense to anybody but him and the squid that took up residence in his head.

Finally, the boy spoke up. "Lily?"

Lily's head rose up from the floor, like a collection of tiny neon bricks assembling into the composite person. "Yes, Thom?"

"We *can't* give it to them," Rashida insisted.

"Somebody has to get it." Osyen doubled down. "The Navy, Fiona—somebody who can protect us."

"We're not going to give it to anybody," Thom said. "And we don't need anybody's protection. We just give them what they *want*."

It hit her all at once and Zatia smiled so wide she could have cut her head in half. "Don't get 'em what they're buyin'..."

"Tell them what you're selling," Thom confirmed.

A fake. They could make a fake.

Osyen's lips tightened until it looked like he'd swallowed them. No doubt he was running this little plan in his own head and couldn't find a flaw in it, beyond the incredibly high risk—but it wasn't like their situation had changed much from four days ago.

Zatia grabbed Osyen by the shoulders and brought him about square with her. He was a full head taller than her, but at that moment, it was like she was looking down on him. "You did the right thing as a boy and got hit for it. Hit back."

Osyen cursed under his breath. "Lily, how stocked is the replicator?"

"Forty-two percent of carbon capacity."

Osyen nodded, jerking his head toward the door. "Thom, I need to know what this thing looked like. Every detail. Color, weight, reflective—if it even had a divot on one side, I need to know."

"Oz." Milardi pulled his mask off, sucking a deep breath of the much thinner air. "Want to let us in on the thinkin'?"

"We're not just going to steal it back," Osyen said, "we're going to give him another one."

"A shell game?" Roche asked.

Adelaide shook her head. "It's a nice idea, but how are you going to even get your hands on the real one?"

"You know how you deal with a bully, Adelaide?" Zatia cracked her knuckles, practically dancing on the balls of her feet, a runner in the starting blocks. "You get a big friend."

CHAPTER
SEVENTEEN
OSYEN

SHE HAD GOTTEN his message and responded with the careful, reserved, and prudent hand that she had become justifiably well known for.

They forced him to his knees with a foot to the joint, and he felt the left one pop as it connected with the masonry. They ripped the bag off his head and immediately stunned him with the butt of a rifle to his cheek. It felt like someone had tried to make his face kiss the back of his skull with a hammer.

If they'd wanted to break his cheek bone or knock out some teeth, they would have. He'd been hit in the face often enough to know the difference; occupational hazard. This was just supposed to kick all of the lies out one side of his head and make him spill truth by reflex.

He heard Milardi curse next to him as he got similar introductions. *"Fra tow paz ki lomar!"*

"Language, Jackson," came that smoky scolding from the cracked wooden table before him. Fiona sat in a creaky chair, leaning forward onto her knees with a pistol hanging in one hand. Smoke hung in the air and there was still ice lingering in the glassware on the table.

A half dozen figures were walking away, but he recognized their disparate regalia: Hollow Men, Wendigos, the Yellowjackets.

They had disrupted a meeting, and Fiona had cleared the room, but not so fast that the retreating bandit leaders didn't see *who* was in custody.

For their benefit.

What an honor. Or a really bad sign.

"Could've just returned my calls," Osyen said, shaking off the dull ring that seemed to push back and forth between his ears.

"I don't make a habit of consorting with handsome failures," was her quick rebuttal. "Where's my Icon?"

"In the hands of an Imperial officer on an Imperial warship no doubt headed for Imperial space," Osyen said.

She took that news with an almost comical kind of grace. She likely knew all of this already, but to hear him say it just like that... "Okay...how are you?"

Osyen blinked, trying to clear his eyes, and she came into focus— red hair dark like spilled blood and eyes like gemstones, and the crooked nose only gotten from spilled blood trying to get gemstones.

She caught his look, almost charmed by his study of her features. "Here to ask for more favors?"

"Here to give what I got," Osyen said. "I'm not in the habit of coming back empty-handed."

"And what did you get for me, besides a light show in my backyard?"

The words dripped out of his mouth along with the blood leaking from his gums. "It's real."

She blinked. No other expression, but for her, that was a great deal. She might not have believed a hundred of her own men, but those two words from Osyen's lips went straight through her ribs and into her cold heart.

"How do you know?" she asked.

"I know," he said, grave and heavy.

"You'll understand I can't take your word for it," Fiona goaded him.

She knew him too well. He wouldn't take the word of a destitute rogue at the end of his rope either. He might've told her he'd seen the security footage, seen Thom's stomach stitch itself together like painful tentacles reaching out for one another, binding, rooting like plants to soil until the clay of his flesh showed nary a sign of the passage of violence.

But he couldn't tell her all that now, could he?

"My word is all you're getting," he challenged. "And it's leaving the Edge in the hands of one crazy Oskie."

Despair and fear rolled through Fiona's goons, silenced at the wave of her metal hand. "Stage is set. Raise the curtain."

Get on with it.

Osyen smirked, twisting his wrists to get a bit of air under his bindings. "We're going to take it back from him, but we can't do it alone."

Her eyes went wide—alarm, disbelief, and a touch of human madness. "You want to *attack* an Imperial fleet carrier?"

"Nobody's attacking anything," Osyen said, "Because I have the key to the front door."

"He's lying."

Thibodeau stepped up to her arm, the fat bastard's smirk crawling up one side of his face like a mealy slug. Fiona didn't look to him, but she let her eyes slide over before darting back to Osyen. The implicit moment hung heavy.

It should've been his spot at her arm.

But Milardi ruined the poetry by spitting at Thibodeau, a good heavy hock directly into the guy's manicured mustache. He earned a blow to the back of the head for that, but it didn't silence Milardi. "You nearly blew the whole thing before we even got out of the gate!"

"You should keep guard your words—" Thibodeau started.

But Fiona cut him off with a gunshot drilling a hole into the goon that had the misfortune to strike Milardi. The man was so caught off guard, he flopped right to the floor, clutching at the new keyhole he had in his bicep.

Osyen felt the grip on his own restraints slacken in an instant.

Fiona lowered the pistol back to its relaxed spot perched on her knee, speaking up to be heard over the wailings of the injured man, "Jackson happens to be correct, Thibodeau. And you should keep guard your pride if you would like to be left with any of it."

Thibodeau looked like he'd swallowed his tongue. Bruised egos would happen later. Right now, he was wondering if the trigger-happy lady in front of him was going to ventilate him on a whim.

Osyen leered back to see a new goon replace the wounded, as two others dragged the screaming man out. They had that down like they'd rehearsed it. How often did she do that?

He wouldn't put it past Fiona to fake moments like that for dramatic effect, either. On him or on Thibodeau. A public execution was all theater anyway—the act mattered less than the audience did.

But reality was also quite...realistic. Why bluff when you can simply flex?

"Little heavy-handed," Osyen lodged.

"I like a man who looks out for himself, ambitious, eager to grow," Fiona said with a grim look. "But if he tries to profit by picking my pocket...well, then he's of no use to *me*. You have a plan, I take it?" Fiona asked him.

"Good one, too," he quipped. "But it's not my plan."

She raised an inquisitive eyebrow. It was a sentence that begged the question and she wasn't going to give him the pleasure.

"Thibodeau?" she said, prompting him to take a half step forward. "Punch Mr. Belt in the face."

The only hesitation was for confirmation, as the walrus-man was careful to not overstep his bounds. He just wanted to be sure he'd heard that right. And then he took one step forward, heaving one meat hock into the air, four sausage fingers clenched around their little fifth cousin.

Idiot. He was going to break his thumb on Osyen's face.

But the blow never fell. It hung in the air, Thibodeau's gleeful glint frozen in his eye, clenched teeth. A single drop of spittle wobbling in the air, as though it were captured in a holograph.

"Walk me through it," Fiona said, her voice echoing just a touch.

Osyen looked over at Milardi, the lanky man's face petrified in a twisted moment of surprise. Osyen waved a hand in front of his friend's face—he had the use of his hands?!

He rubbed at his wrists—the steel cuffs had left their red bites on his skin, but were otherwise not to be seen. He looked backward— and wished he hadn't.

He looked right back at his own face, looking up at Thibodeau's falling strike with a defiant curl to his lip.

His stomach wanted to curl up in a ball and cry. This was the stuff of nightmares. *Lily?*

"Nope," Fiona said, popping the sound like a child. She was the only thing not frozen in time. "But your implant can move a lot of information very, very quickly, and time is...relative...to electrons."

"Doesn't that mean anybody can hack into your head?" Osyen asked, "Get at all your secrets any time?"

She narrowed her eyes, "You're absolutely welcome to try, handsome."

"It's a little reckless of you, don't you think?"

"Do you know how temperature sensitive your brain is?"

Oh. The implant would simply start to cook and then...it was attached to something rather important.

"So whose head are we in right now?" Osyen said, with a mischie- vous head tilt.

"Mine," she said. "Because you're about to get some work done on yours. Talk fast."

"But if time is relative, can't we enjoy a breather?" he asked.

Thibodeau's fist slid forward a sudden half foot, stopping inches away from Osyen, and Thibodeau's gleeful eye thirsting for the coming violence.

Osyen sheepishly pursed his lips. "I'm getting hit no matter what, aren't I?"

"Yup," she said, popping the sound again. She was alarmingly nonplussed by the whole situation. Hardly disappointed, not even angry.

"That whole debacle went exactly like you planned, didn't it?"

"The boy did good," Fiona said, slurping from her drink. He noticed that the fluid level did not decrease one bit. She was tasting—maybe remembering a flavor—but not able to consume in this 'electron space.'

"You didn't use your other teams..."

"Can't be owing my lieutenants favors," she answered. "Better to use an outsider."

"That you can dispose of. What did their fealty cost you?" he wondered aloud.

She looked up and behind him, towards the receding backs of a half dozen bandit barons. "An Imperial warship just detonated an asteroid base without breaking a sweat."

"Detonated a rival, too."

She let her eyes wander. She couldn't have mimed an innocent little girl more if she had pigtails and a finger to her lips. "That too."

Osyen shook his head. "So the Master of the Edge really is anointed now, isn't she? Crown and all?"

She sighed. "You don't need to win a fight to come out ahead. You have a 'key' to an Imperial military vessel?"

His blood ran cold. "You knew there was only one way for us to get in the Widow's Den."

"Yes."

"And you knew it would go the way it did."

She shrugged. "If it went the other way, I still win. The Icon is lost, no harm no foul—I still delete an enemy. If you decide to run with my prize, you'd never make it out of the system. And if you somehow did...Imperials don't work with Capitals."

"Leaving you the sole relevant power in the Edge."

She smiled, sweet and venomous. "Osyen Belt...I *am* the Edge now."

He was half-cocked between furious and admiring. Winning

every outcome wasn't an easy position to land in, and she had delicately maneuvered the situation. "Long way from the hotboxes of Charon, huh?"

She nodded, as much wistful for the journey as enjoying the saccharine moment of the now. "Yes."

But on the other hand, Thom...She might not have shot him, but she had set up the board so that was the only outcome.

"How did you know he wouldn't die?" Osyen growled.

"I didn't," she crowed. "You did. You have a key to an Imperial cruiser?"

"He took a round to the stomach." Osyen immediately regretted the admission.

She leaned back in her chair, crossing her arms. "And?"

"...He got better."

"See?" she purred. "Miracles do happen."

He sighed. She was better at this than he was. He was so easy to manipulate, goad into cheap mistakes. Hard to trick a mark who knew more than he did.

"Is your super double secret Imperial code key a blowtorch, Osyen?"

He shook his head. "You've already met her."

"The Dunsweir." Fiona cocked her head like a curious cat. "You always had a thing for brunettes."

He shook his head. "I like competency."

"Because you're not?"

He blew a raspberry at her.

That got a smile. "Imperial vessels have to make all allowances for Dunsweir. It's good...if Stride follows protocol."

"Don't give him an option," Osyen said. "You fly up, you ignore all other directions, you dock."

Fiona was sitting forward now, hands clasped as she played the pistol back and forth in her hands. "Play at entitlement?"

"She *is* entitled," Osyen insisted. "And if you take it as a given liberty, it's hard for them to take it back."

"And if the religious Zealot blows her out of the midnight sky?"

Then they were screwed.

Her eyes narrowed as her mind unpacked this idea. "She's the distraction?"

He nodded. "We sneak onboard, nab the Icon, and beat feet before anybody knows we're there."

"When I said 'explain your plan,' Osyen, I meant in greater detail," Fiona warned, her grip tightening around the pistol. He could see the skin wrinkle around the polymer grip. Her augment was likely a better shot but she liked the *feel* of the weapon in her palm.

"That's all you're going to get. From me, anyway," he said.

"You should lay all your cards down."

"I just did," he confessed. "Like I said, it's not my plan."

Fiona sat back in her chair, eyes narrow and grip tight on her weapon. "You want to take me to a Rogue's Cross, Oz?"

Uh oh. She thinks this is a set-up.

"If anything, I'm the one going there," Osyen countered. "You have a giant merchant fleet and I'm just one guy with my dinky little brig."

She slid the chamber open on her pistol, making a show of checking if there was a live round in the chamber. As though it wouldn't be after her demonstration on her own overindulgent guardsman.

"In all our years, have I ever led you wrong?" he asked.

She raised a cocky eyebrow. "In all our years, you weren't doing the leading."

"True enough," he said.

Her voice wavered for a brief moment, the slightest crack in thick steel armor. "Why didn't you stay?"

Because. Because.

Because he was never good enough, never smart enough. Because he hated politics and posturing and protocol. Because the uniform never quite fit right. Because of how she looked at him and when she didn't.

Because he loved the feel of a gun in his hand. And so did she.

"Why did you stay?" he puzzled.

"You think I chose wrong?" she asked.

"No," he encouraged, "I don't think there *is* a right answer to these kinds of things."

Fiona's sharp eye studied him like a hawk would a prey animal, cowering in the tall grass. "So you're going to let me pocket a priceless religious relic with untold power? Why not keep it for yourself? You've got a plan, manpower."

"Because," was all he said.

She watched him for a long moment. It looked so familiar to him, the cold calculating distance and appraisal. It was a strange cocktail of defensive and adoration. Somewhere in that skull she was running scenarios and risk-balance, calculating odds and feeling out the dice for cheated weights.

"What do you get out of this?" she asked.

Failing to return it to Admiral Hugh would condemn the entire crew. Returning it to her would mostly just ingratiate them to a Court he despised.

"Better to live under your eye than theirs," he said.

She smirked. "You never left my eye, Osyen."

"So?" he asked, feeling the moment's edge biting at the back of his neck and the warmth of her breath on his face.

"So?" she mocked. "Now you get hit in the face."

Oh God—

The feeling was two-fold. One, he snapped back into his original place, his hands bound behind him with tight cord on his wrists. It made him want to throw up.

Two, Thibodeau's meaty hand cracked against the side of his skull. What a bad way to hit someone.

Osyen's head hurt, but he felt something give on contact and it wasn't his skull. Thibodeau cradled his hand, biting his tongue to keep from screaming.

But everybody saw him do it. And Milardi had a big mouth. "Oh,

Teebo, you've been in a suit for too long. You don't go for the skull with your bare hand."

Thibodeau hissed some curse at Milardi, about all of the sound he could make, let alone threats. What was he going to do? Hit him and break his other hand?

"Good!" Fiona dropped the magazine from her weapon and worked the action, springing the live round into the air. She snatched it with a flick of her cyborg wrist, before resting weapon and ammunition on the table to her side. "Cut 'em loose."

"What?" Thibodeau and Milardi said in disparate unison.

"I'm not signing on," Fiona said. "Not until I meet the mastermind."

Osyen rolled his head from left to right, feeling his neck crack at every grade. "We can arrange that."

THE SHIP only buzzed like this before a job. There was no other symphony quite like it, and this one had a few more chairs than usual. Adelaide was busy bellowing in Engineering, just shy of throwing fists at Lily—at least the two were on speaking terms. Milardi had returned to the ship and dove promptly into Medical to find a way the crew might go toe-to-toe with a superman. Rashida was sculpting out the costumes for the upcoming affair, finding secret places to stash armor and simultaneously present her Dunsweir refinement.

Simple upon simple immediately made something complex, but Thom could keep everyone compartmentalized into their individual tasks. Functionally, it was the same plot they'd used on Fiona's station —two teams, misdirection and strike.

Rashida and Zatia would land in a shuttle, drawing Stride's attention. Rashida would buy as much time as she could to cover the strike team's approach. She would then either withdraw—or Zatia would engage Stride. Milardi was cooking up a cocktail that would help level that playing field.

Osyen, Milardi, and the pirates were the strike team. Using Rashida and Zatia's distraction, they'd penetrate the carrier, nab the Icon, and get out. If all went well, they were never really there.

Adelaide would be on stand-by to help the strike team force their way through Naval security, if needed.

Thom could hope it wasn't needed, but he wasn't leaving that to chance.

He had never been a conductor before, but he imagined this is what it must feel like. And somehow, his heart hadn't erupted out of his chest yet.

Rashida was all smiles as she tore at a favored dress with a seam ripper. If it wasn't so surgical, it would look like a ravenous monster tearing into a bodice, thirsting for the bits underneath. She had to bring her most aggressive approach—she was sliding armor ceramic plates inside the lining, after all.

"Well, I won't be wearing this to any events this Spring," she quipped.

"You should," he said. "It's beautiful and nobody can stab you through it."

"Sometimes the function of something *is* the form of it," she moaned. But it was all sound and fury. She was loving this particular challenge. Could she, with all her wits, hide half-inch blocks inside a tight-fitted bodice?

Thom dangled off the rungs of the exit ladder. "Only if the form has a function. All eyes on you," he reminded her.

"They usually are," she mused, with a flirtatious glance over her shoulder.

But he was already halfway up the ladder to the main deck. If he could've broken into a sprint he would've, galloping up the rungs two at a time, and almost hurling himself into the hallway.

"Roche!" he called out. "How does it look?"

Roche poked his head out of the cockpit. "I can close the thermal vents for a couple of minutes but any longer and we'll be hosting a cookout in here."

"That should be enough." Thom spun on his heels and marched back aft into the galley.

Zatia had commandeered the table to fold out an entire armory:

241

pistols, rifles, the bracket gun. Her bracelet daggers were perched at the end of the table, near some oil and stone bricks.

A doublet of curious cloth, draped over the arm of the chair, seemed to soak in all light of the room—like she had woven the void of space on a loom.

It looked like nothing at all, the ultra-black of it sinking deeper and deeper. It looked so soft.

Zatia's hands were on a pistol and aimed at his wrist in less than a second. "No touchy."

"What is it?" he asked.

"My vest," was all she said. "No touchy."

"Why?"

"Because I don't like you," she said, shifting the gun to his head. "And it's very expensive."

"Did you buy it or steal it?"

The hammer cocked back.

"Message received," Thom said, heading for the aft hatch comb. "Get together with Rashida."

"Do I have to?" Zatia called after him.

"She'll get you—and that—dressed for the occasion," Thom threw back, as he pulled the hatch door closed behind him, hoping that she didn't decide to test out one of those finely crafted tools of gore-painting on him. Or on Rashida.

Milardi nearly bowled him over as he stepped out of Medical, arms full of empty vials stained with neon pastel residue. "Oof! Sorry there, *Unti!*"

Thom raised an eyebrow. Milardi nodded with a wince, acknowledging the misstep, but was in too much of a hurry. "I think I've got it."

"Three parts Ambera?" Thom asked.

Milardi shook his head. "Five parts to—doesn't matter. I've got it. But it'll shoot through her system pretty quick."

Didn't matter. It didn't need to work for long, just long enough.

Zatia was going to enjoy this particular stim package. "She's in the galley. Don't touch her stuff."

"What, the vest?" Milardi cooed, "It's cool, right?"

"It looks like..."

Milardi nodded. Whatever Thom's answer was going to be was right. "Nanotube weave-plates inside silk-steel. The vacuum can absorb *thirty megawatts*. She could walk right through a focused laser straight to her chest."

Thom wondered what it would do for something more ballistic. His gut cramped.

"No touchy!" Came Zatia's voice from down the corridor.

"Yeah, yeah!" Milardi barked back. He backed down the hallway with his garbage, calling out to Thom before he slid out of sight, "You talk to Roche?"

A thousand implications passed in that question. Milardi and the plughead had been on the rocks since the big reveal.

Thom shook his head. "*You* should talk to Roche."

Milardi's head bobbed from side to side. He knew, but he was hoping he wouldn't have to.

Thom continued aft. The hum of the ship's engines was almost a song back here, a soft metronome with an ebb and fall, like a heartbeat of a great bear. It was like laying an ear to the side of a titan and falling into rhythm with its breath.

Underneath that subtle music he could hear the bickering, two voices, both low and hushed. But the drumskin of the ship's hull carried it up the entire length.

"Adelaide?" Thom called out.

"Yeah, yeah!" Was the dismissive return, as she returned to her other argument. "It'll shear the drive shaft and spill the thermal vault."

Lily's baritone was unmistakable. "Not if you cut the micro-gravity during the burn."

Engineering was a relatively small deck, and Thom had only

been allowed back here a handful of times, but Osyen wasn't here to say 'no.' And nobody was going to hinder him, not today.

Two metal walkways circled the room, high and low, primarily to provide access to the various spots on the Jump Drive. Most of the domed room was taken up by the knobby machine, its protective casing stripped at various points for repairs and never replaced, giving a voyeuristic glance at the maddening cranks and pistons inside.

It was like looking into the throat of a beast with a thousand mouths, slipping the mind of its sleeve just for the crime of cracking the seal, seeking unholy answers of how it all worked. To Lily, it was as simple a machine as a wind-up clock. Adelaide found it downright quaint. The questions they debated would reduce Thom into a puddle on the floor.

The two were knee-deep in some such engineering debate. Adelaide grumbled at the empty room, and the empty room sassed right back from unseen speakers.

Thom knew they were lined in the railings. One of them had a pretty nasty crackle.

"The slipstream isn't *invisible*, Lily. It throws off full-spectrum radiation—"

"Well now you're changing your story," Lily countered. "Is it because the *Aurum* won't survive, or because it won't work?"

"Both, you overclocked calculator!" Adelaide shouted.

"Everything good down here?" Thom asked.

Lily's head pushed out of the wall by his elbow, their mustache immaculately curled to match the curve of their smile. "Analysis of hardware capabilities underway."

"It won't work," Adelaide reiterated.

Lily's face phased through their own head, rearranging the dozens of tiny cubes back towards Adelaide like a taunting clay monstrosity. "Under prescribed conditions, there is a sixty-eight percent chance of flawless execution."

"Lily, compute the mathematical value for human ingenuity."

Lily's image flickered. "Variables?"

"Solve for X," Adelaide spat at them. And Lily's image froze up.

Thom gripped the railing and slid down the handful of steps to the top deck, his feet connecting with solid punctuation.

Thom's eyes darted from the frozen Lily back to the octogenarian wrench-monkey. "What did you do?"

Adelaide shrugged. "It'll give us a second of free air." Adelaide clambered up the ladder to meet him on his level. "This won't work, kid. The LADAR on the carrier will see us a hundred miles out. The Jump Drive's envelope doesn't drop us out of existence."

Why would the Jump Drive matter? Thom blinked a few times. "I'm sorry, we're jumping somewhere?"

Adelaide swiped some nasty looking tool that wouldn't have gone amiss in a torture chamber right through Lily's frozen hologram. "Lily has this asinine idea that a pre-jump condition will mask our signature on approach. I'm saying we have to drift in like so much space garbage and hope they don't pick out our heat sig."

Thom nodded. "Why not simply approach from the Pulsar?"

Adelaide blinked. Pursed her crusty old lips. Tapped the wrench on the railing. "Lily?"

"Computing."

She windmilled her wrench through Lily's head. "Yeah, I know, I know. What if we approached from the star's glare? Would that work?"

Lily's image flickered for a brief moment before turning to stare at Thom, almost aghast. "Pulsar radiation would be significant enough to mask small vessels."

Thom shrugged. "This job is going to be plenty complicated. We don't need to get more clever than we need to be."

Adelaide smiled. "He taught you well."

Thom was about ready to leave but that stopped him cold. Who taught him? Osyen? Osyen had gone out of his way *not* to teach Thom, to keep Thom tucked away. What lessons had Osyen shared with him? How to mix soap and water?

"Hey Adelaide, what *is* the mathematical value for human ingenuity?"

Adelaide shrugged. "I don't know."

Lily's neon head poked out of the wall at Adelaide's elbow. "Zero, as the function is an imaginary artifice."

"Shut up, Lily."

———

Thom had expected to receive a communique or another fancy missive. He had even expected a couple of goons with black bags, maybe Thibodeau and his robot kidnappers.

He did not expect Fiona herself to be waiting for him in his cabin.

He turned off the ladder to find the vampire of a woman standing dead center in the small space, occupying all of the available oxygen with a simple wide stance. She smiled. "How did you know?"

"I'm—I'm sorry?"

"Osyen asked how I knew you would survive the Widow's den," she explained. "I didn't."

He felt his gut lurch, like the bullet was still in there, rattling around. "Thanks for that."

"You're welcome." She settled down on his ratty frayed bedsheets. Her fingers traced the edges, feeling out the stitching. "Eh. People have come from worse," she commented, almost to herself.

"Like you?" he offered.

She looked up at him, reptile unfeeling eyes, but somewhere deep in the back, suppressed and buried under a thousand scars suffered and more inflicted, was a spark of life. She had lived so long in so short a time. "Watch your mouth."

She wouldn't be here if she was happy with the arrangement. "You have one or two demands?"

She nodded. "Thibodeau will accompany you on the *Aurum*."

Thibodeau was possibly less trustworthy than they were and eager to earn back favor he had squandered. Some men were trigger happy. Some men were bloodthirsty. Some men, well...some men were jumpy.

Thibodeau was that and more—he was greedy, self-serving. Yes, Thibodeau would serve just nicely.

But he couldn't let Fiona know how neatly that fit into his puzzle. "You know anybody that works well with a knife at their neck?"

"Osyen Belt does his best work when his neck is sitting on a block." She had come here, hat in hand, to figure out how she'd misstepped and yet, and yet—still so overly confident in her winning hand.

"I look like Osyen?" he asked.

"You look like a tree sapling with a bowl cut." She crossed her legs, folding her hands in her lap, like she'd been schooled in etiquette in the highest of stations. "How did you know?"

"Know what?" he asked, no patience for her theatrics.

"That I needed the Widows gone?"

A crime lord wanted her competition removed and saw an opportunity she could leverage. Could it be, on a crew full of professional malcontents, he was the only one that made that connection?

Thom shrugged. "It wasn't jump science."

She didn't wince, didn't flinch, her eyes didn't narrow. She did not move without consideration. "I want to know what I'm putting out there. You picked up on something I *didn't* want out there. If my enemies know they're my enemies, they brace for impact. I like my enemies...flat-footed. What did I do to let on?"

"You want notes on your poker face?"

Slow nod, as if to welcome him to the obvious point.

"My father wears his ribbons all day," he deadpanned.

She shrugged. "So?" She knew he hadn't wandered far afield and that this would somehow become relevant, but her patience was gossamer thin.

Thom leaned against the rungs of the ladder. "I mean he wears them every day. He wears them to Cathedral, to dinner, Ministry events, he used to even wear them to bed. And he wore them last time I saw him."

Her smile leaked out, curious musing. "Prideful?"

He nodded. "To the extreme. He used to say that his ribbons were the evidence a man has of the life he has lived and his value to his fellows."

"Am I prideful, Thomas?"

"Absolutely," he chirped. "But that's not what I saw."

Her eyes narrowed, but her smile widened. "What did you see?"

"The brass quintet."

Her eyes darted around the room, looking for the studio audience to start laughing. "You saw the brass band at Court and said to yourself, this lady wants the Black Widows wiped out?"

He shook his head. "Anyone so concerned with their status that they're constantly flexing it...is concerned it'll go away. They're trying to chase someone off, or enjoy it while they have it. You weren't secure. That's why you spent the money to *have* a brass quintet."

"I'm not allowed to enjoy power?" she countered with a coquettish lilt to her tone.

He thought of Stride's face—the rigid structure of him outside his cell, that calm slack to his muscles in the Gaslamp. That cold look as he carefully squeezed off a bullet into the stomach of a teenage boy.

"You are, but that wasn't decadence. It wasn't *for* you." He looked her in her viper eyes, fishing at that hook deep back there. "Real strength isn't challenged. It's not postured. It's not concerned. It simply is."

She shivered. Again with her theatrics. "You two *are* cut of the same cloth."

Osyen, Osyen, Osyen. People were never happier than when they were comparing him to Osyen.

"That's the second time in like ten minutes people have said that," Thom huffed.

"It's not an insult, Thomas."

He glared at her. Of course it was. He didn't want to be anything like Osyen. Osyen was fair weather, selfish, and impulsive.

Stride was...

Fiona tilted her head, considering the boy that stood before her, draped over a ladder and with a light sheen of sweat under the stark vertical lighting. "You don't know who you are yet. You're so busy trying on hats you're forgetting to comb your own hair. That's okay. You can try to be violent or clever or wise or peaceful or charming... but you can't *try* to be strong."

"Is that what I am?"

Fiona smiled, perfect teeth resembling a shark's grin. "You are... going to be interesting to watch."

CHAPTER
NINETEEN
OSYEN

THOM HADN'T SAID a word to him. He hadn't even looked at him. Most people in this situation would be nervously making conversation, sharing meaningful glances, trying to make amends in the face of certain death. Some might even be confessing deeply reserved secrets, dumping adulation unto the absent and the present in equal measure. 'I love you. I loved her and never told her. I always hated you.'

Then again, Thom had been dead once already. What left was there to say that he hadn't already whispered into the dark?

Thibodeau, on the other hand, was a chatty little prick. Faceplate —his robotic wasp cloaked mining facsimile—was vibrating like it had a back massager mode. It was a bizarre machine, humanoid, with a pipe-shaped head with disproportionate long arms. Black asteroid soot stained every nook and cranny like a bad paint job. The simple plasteel faceplate with single oculus made it look like a bizarre medieval knight's helmet. He hadn't yet patched the hole Milardi had snapped through it.

The chassis was covered in scratches and dents, probably from a dozen rambunctious victims lashing out at the metal demon. Its hands were after-market, crudely welded onto the wrists. Wires peeked out from the plating where some amateur lineman had gone full Frankenstein.

It was a remote jackhammer given new illicit life in abduction. There was very little more terrifying in this world or the next that didn't involve a single electric yellow oculus and zip ties.

Come on, Teebo, some subtlety would not go amiss. Did he have to select a robot devil as his implement? There's style, élan, pizzazz; and then there's just awkward.

Thibodeau's robot and a handful of other *machina* stood at their backs in the *Aurum*'s cargo hold. The stillness of the others implied that Thibodeau was controlling them all via remote plug, but only one of the bots had that personal touch.

If only they were all such mindless automatons.

"The insides of Imperial vessels are hardly difficult," Thibodeau rambled, his voice crisp through the speaker as though he were actually standing right there with them. "Clear lines of approach and structure. Wide hallways. There will be precious little cover, but that will cut both ways."

Teebo might not have been onboard, but Osyen swore he could hear the big man sweating through that speaker.

The *Aurum* creaked as a blast of the Boolean's solar winds ripped over her hull. They were awfully close to the star and with the thermal vents closed to mask their approach, the ship was building up heat awful quick. Ship systems, the people, and radiation were all accumulating. Teebo might be stress-melting, but they'd all be puddles in short order if they didn't open the vents soon.

"If the Icon isn't in the armories, it could also be in the commander's quarters," Thibodeau continued, "or perhaps even on the commander himself. That will complicate matters but nothing more than delays. Delays, delays, delays..."

"Teebo?" Osyen said. The robot's creepy pipe head turned sharply to face him. "You know *you're* not actually going to get shot at, right?"

"Mr. Belt," Thibodeau huffed from a control deck in a comfort-

able living room on the third floor of a casino, "are you not taking this seriously?"

"I am," Osyen said, wiping the sweat beading on his brow, "I've just never seen a robot stroke out before."

The ship jostled as Roche made a course correction far above. And sure enough, Roche's voice piped in over the speakers, "We are ballistic on course to the *Acheron*. Engines quiet from here on out. E.T.A four minutes. Game faces, get 'em on."

He felt a pinch at the back of his head as someone took a look through his eyes, and he swore he could feel her breath on his ear. *Don't fail me now, big boy.*

Fiona.

Something of note, Roche said, *That carrier is in a decaying orbit.*

Osyen's brow furrowed, throwing glances at around the bay. *It's in starfall?*

It'll be in the corona in the less than an hour.

Something was wrong. It should've been making for the Jump Point, or hiding out somewhere to plot and scheme. Driving off a proverbial cliff wasn't something reasonable people did.

Didn't matter. They still had to get the Icon off that ship.

Osyen glanced back at Thom. Milardi and Osyen had their weapons; the boy had nothing but clenched fists. And he was head of the formation, forward on the balls of his feet. His eyes were closed but not clenched. His lips moved ever so slightly.

Praying.

"Didn't take you for a believer," Osyen threw out.

Thom's eyes opened, but he glared at the bulkhead instead. "When you've seen what I've seen."

"What did you see?" That finally got Thom's head cranked around.

This boy had looked up to him with those same eyes not a week before and they'd been full of wonder, desire, urge, adventure, positively glittering with possibility. Now they might as well have been solid black. It stole the warmth from his veins.

"I don't know why you chose this life. That's all."

"You think I got into this life by choice?" Osyen scoffed.

"Of course you did," Thom said. "And acting like the *Aurum* and Lily and all of this are an *accident*..." Before Osyen could jump to his own defense, Thom drove the killing blow between his ribs. "You made being a victim into a trade-skill. You're either good at this or you're not. Figure it out."

Osyen recoiled from that, almost forced to take a step back from the teen to keep his balance. "Alright then."

"Alright what?"

"Alright then," Osyen repeated. "You don't want this life, don't be here by 'accident.' We get the Icon, and then you're on your own."

The boy took the adjudication like it was mana from Heaven. "Thank you."

"Thank you?!"

The boy blinked. "What? Did you expect me to whimper and moan? What have I said or done to make you think I'm enjoying this?"

This void-touched, reinvigorated Thom was a real dick. Void-touched.

He'd touched the Icon.

Osyen's eyes went wide "Thom...what did you feel when Stride..."

"Shot me?" Thom scowled.

"No, shut up. When he healed you. When the Icon..."

Thom leered back at Thibodeau and his robot cadre. He didn't need to know more than he had to, but their headspace radio channel was no longer so private.

"I felt cold," he said, hushed and low.

"Yeah," Osyen murmured, "that's what I figured."

Experiences change a man—getting hurt, shot, broken bones, broken hearts. Something with the power to warp flesh might leave scars of a different kind.

In a moment they'd be aboard the *Acheron*, facing down Imperial

Regulars in pursuit of something that had rebuilt Thom from certain death. It didn't need to be a malevolent intelligence to get into the kid's head.

"I just wanted to protect you." There was the confession he had been expecting. He just didn't think he'd be the only one to speak.

Thom didn't say a thing. He might still need protecting, but he did not want it anymore.

PART FOUR
EVIDENCE OF THINGS NOT SEEN

And They asked that they rise from their prostrate positions and give Them their eyes,

For surrender to One was to Hollow oneself, saying:

"Strength does not demand sacrifice nor sustenance. And so shalt I not ask you for your blood or your grain;

I ask only that you stand for your fellows, those who cannot stand for themselves."

GNOSTIC LIBRUM, EXPANSIONS 4:12-16

CHAPTER
TWENTY
RASHIDA

THE TAXI LANDED with all the grace of a shot-put, slamming into the carrier's deck, magnetic grips thwacking into the hull. Finesse and comfort were simply not priorities there. The delineation between military and civilian design was wide enough to fill the Chicago crater.

Rashida stepped out of the shuttle like she was going for a stroll along the promenade. Her retinue stumbled out behind her, unable to coordinate doorways. Her dress' train might have been more restrained than in Fiona's court, but she had to sell her diplomacy today. The brute squad in her orbit were not used to such cumbersome fashion. She counted herself lucky they didn't step on her train with their heavy boots and rip the stitching—or choke her to death.

She threw a stinging glance back at the crew behind her, Thom leading a host of gussied up pirates—but no amount of shampoo or conditioner was going to rinse the Boolean out of them. Their hair looked oiled and their clothes spotted. If this was the most formal they could get, they would have to do.

Thom himself was uncharacteristically slack in his posture, hunched and leaning. He picked at the cincher on his waist, sliding a finger under the hem line. Because he was just another pirate, mocked up for Stride.

"Don't fuss," Rashida scolded.

"It feels like it's going to crack a rib," he moaned.

"No, that part comes next."

She had seen the Jupiter Naval Yards and been on similar tours of active duty vessels whenever her father had to drag them out to one. The interiors were always quite drab, with steel bulkheads painted a 'professional' gray. Elbow room in space might be at a premium, but Naval cruisers of this class took use of it by providing lofty open cavities, allowing for modular construction as befitted the need. Temporary walls or bulkheads were erected to accommodate particular vehicles in berths made per specifications down to the inch.

Next to her taxi sat a row of F-104B Bearcat superiority fighters, two of them in a sorry state—one had its wing shorn off, the umbilicals and structure underneath exposed like musculature drained of its blood. The other's canopy compacted far too early in its user life.

She might have had some inkling of what had happened to these two caged birds.

What was more distressing than the morbid display was the utter lack of reception. There was no one on the hangar deck. Her eyes darted around, scanning for some overeager deck chief scampering out from under an engine to attend to her. But she didn't hear the typical power tools or generators running.

The ambience of a busy workshop had been silenced. It felt like an angel's watchful eye had cast over the space and, out of fear, the denizens retreated under rock and ledge to hold their collective breath.

It was a ghost town.

No turning back now. Rashida strode forward, leaving her retinue to follow behind. The click of her heels reported off the floor and then again echoing off the walls back to her in a painful syncopation.

She approached the back wall and the hatch comb cracked open, sensing her approach and grinding aside with an excess of force. She idly wondered what safety measures were in place to prevent a passerby being pinched in its mandible.

"Where is everybody?" Not-Thom blurted.

"Quiet," Rashida ordered, to which Not-Thom bristled.

It was a valid enough question, but it didn't need air to be made. This was a Naval fleet carrier with a stable of over five hundred sailors, pilots, and Regulars. She should've been tripping over people by now.

"Oy," Not-Thom whispered, "Lady."

"What?" Rashida grumbled.

"This is a carrier, right?" Not-Thom asked, looking back into the hangar. "So where's all the ships?"

Rashida could've kicked herself. She was so worried about the people that were missing, she forgot to look for the *things* that were missing. The echoes were so vibrant because there was nothing to absorb the sound. There was normally a stable of over a dozen Bearcats on a carrier this size, not to mention shuttles and transports.

Save a handful of fighters on the deck, nobody was home. No SAR vehicles, no shuttles.

"They evacuated," Rashida said.

"Hardly," came the husky voice of a specter to lure innocent children into his spider's web. Jeremiah Stride approached with a pair of Regulars at each arm.

They blocked the hatch comb with their formation. Very well, then.

"Captain Stride, I presume," Rashida said, dropping instantly into a court-approved reverence, splaying her skirts wide and bowing her head, but she was just as quickly up and marching toward him. "Is this the reception my father can expect?"

Good, Stride stopped his approach, letting her come to him. She controlled the momentum now, though he still controlled the point of access. He assumed a parade rest, strict and tight. His dress uniform was so fitted it could have been tailored, but she saw the telltale tweaks. The armholes were high, no shoulder pads, and his pants worn high, almost too revealing.

Maximum mobility—that was a dress uniform he could fight in.

Stride offered a small, familial smile that she knew to be as hollow as any masquerade she'd attended. "I've never had the pleasure and likely never will, your Ladyship. My cruiser is hardly fit."

"That is readily apparent, Captain." Rashida flicked her hair back, pulling the hair pin free and letting the curls tumble. Stride's eyes flicked to follow and she held back her smile.

"Unfortunately, my crew cannot entertain and we must urge you to return to your transport at this time," Stride said, with a gentle gesture back to the hangar.

Rashida cocked her head. "Captain, I'm offended."

"And I am not foolish, Rashida Izan de Tylmirande." He threw a glance back at Thom. "I know what you're here for and you will not have it."

Rashida smiled, flashing pearly whites. "Won't even mollify me with the illusion of the game?"

What was his tell, his weakness? Men trained their entire lives to build masculine presentation, rigid structures absent fear, outburst, or anger. On top of this, an Orbital officer could regulate body heat, heart rate and even dilations of the eyes. No, his tell would be some habit, some construct from before, a relic that was never purged from the vault.

His hair was loose, hanging around his forehead—receding a bit early for his age, though not unusual. He either hadn't noticed yet or didn't put stock in it. His stance was textbook with boots shined and duck toed placement of the right foot, but his left shoulder was dropped back—an old injury perhaps? Concealing a weapon?

His face could've been someone else's entirely and he was an outsider wearing the skin-suit, not quite knowing how to manipulate it all. It had the unnerving appearance of arguing with a mannequin.

Stride was tracking her study, and scrutinizing her right back, "You have a taste for games. I don't."

"Such a shame," she said.

"Where's Thomas?" Stride asked.

Ah, now there was the million-dollar question. Rashida leered back over her shoulder at Not-Thom. "Do your eyes deceive you, Captain?"

"The refresh rate—"

"Too fast for the human eye." Rashida jumped his statement. "Yes."

Not-Thom looked back and forth between Stride and Rashida, confused, like a boy lost in the wood. Rashida gave them a blind wave of her hand.

"Is he dead?" Stride asked.

There it was. A hint of concern, parental despair perhaps? Guilt? It was genuine interest, at the very least.

Rashida lowered her head briefly, blinking once for full effect. "We're still sifting the wreckage."

"You understand then why I cannot go back to Imperial space," Stride declared, that softness in his tone doubling. He was actually a little sad the boy didn't make it out.

It was a strange ownership for a killer to take, shooting a defenseless boy only then to bemoan his demise, as though an act of violence had been an act of love.

"You didn't break the boy's shackles, Captain," Rashida declared, "you punctured his liver and tore his diaphragm, leaving him to suffocate as he bled to death."

There was the smile, the knowledge breaking through. "And how do you know that, your Ladyship?" His officers didn't flinch. They knew their commander had murdered a child, and if they objected, they kept it to themselves.

There was nothing more dangerous in Heaven or Earth than a man who believed he was right with God.

Time to make the bet. "How I know is of little consequence,

Captain. I know everything. I know what you have. I know what it can do. I know what it *means*. And the Dunsweir are the only living humans that have righteous claim to it."

He raised an eyebrow. "And are you laying claim, Rashida Izan?"

"That power does not belong to any man."

"On that point, we agree."

Stride and his aides cocked their heads with choreographed precision, with the same tilt and posture. They were listening to a transmission.

Stride pursed his lips, with an almost disapproving look at Rashida. "Bring the Spartans into battery and destroy the freighters."

Rashida didn't finish taking her breath when Stride lifted his sidearm and fired.

She intellectually understood the devices and had seen more than a few in her travels, but she had never had the bad luck to be on the receiving end of their use. The concussion from the round's passing cracked past her ear and she swore her hair actually fluttered at her cheek in the wake.

The round struck Not-Thom directly in the chest, knocking the boy backward as his feet betrayed him. He hit the ground with his shoulder blades, knocking his last wind from him violently, and he did not, could not, draw a fresh one.

The projected image of Thom's head clipped through the floor, glitching and twitching before finally failing, revealing a small middle-aged man, face frozen in shock.

"That was *much* easier." Stride looked at his men, and nodded.

The pirates behind her were armed, of course. But they were not soldiers, and had to draw from concealed positions.

So Zatia made her move. Stride was so transfixed on the fake Thom, he never noticed Zatia in the big black wig and long jacket.

As pirates fidgeted with secret holsters, Zatia ripped her wig off, unleashing her neon purple pigtails, all of the holographic colors of the rainbow catching the light.

The soldiers presented arms, execution squad. She jammed a

needle into her neck like she was murdering herself and slammed the plunger down.

The soldiers squeezed the triggers. Zatia exhaled.

Syringe still dangling from her neck, she slipped forward not unlike a fog in a high wind. She slapped one soldier's muzzle longways across and threw his shot unfortunately into his friend's head —the resulting painting would've made a mint on the private circuit.

She understood the physics of it all, how a chemical propellant or excited magnet might send a small tapered piece of metal down a channel at excessive speeds. Projectile combat was dependent on fluid dynamics, cavitation of water. Man was mostly water and behaved quite similarly. It wasn't the thrust of the steel-jacketed mass that did the harm, but the shockwave of the impact, as bone and matter bent violently away from the wound.

Heads were no exception. It made Rashida want to vomit.

Stride swung his weapon about to Zatia, but she vanished in a blink, his shot passing through where she was like she had been but a daydream. The flash in his eye told Rashida the one word that went through his mind: impossible.

Someone grabbed Rashida, threw her down. Zatia? One of the pirates? No, it was Zatia. How?

She squeezed her eyes shut as the battle raged overhead, shots lancing through the air, ballistic and energy. Men grunted and screamed in pain, calling out in voices that were just as suddenly silenced.

Rashida opened her eyes to see a face staring back at her, a grizzled pirate's frozen visage staring into some distant dark. The warmth on her cheek told her she now wore some of him. His weapon still clutched in his grasp.

The pirates had been cut down like waves of grain.

Zatia now stood in the hatch comb, perched low to the ground with four fingers daintily balancing her. She resembled a wild animal, snarling at her foe, muscles rippling from end to end like one coiled spring. Stride stood across from her, fists up and set, knuckles already bloody. Both breathing heavily.

"Oh pretty Lady?" Zatia called out between heavy breaths. "May you please get a move on?!"

Rashida reached out for the fallen pirate's pistol.

Stride turned his head towards Rashida, and lunged—but Zatia dove at him, a cat pouncing on distracted prey. It was like trying to watch two strikes of lightning.

He was fast. To his bewilderment, she was just as fast. The two tumbled with each other, blurs of incoherent motion. The wet sounds of flesh on flesh came with a sickening supersonic crack.

Rashida lifted the dead man's pistol—and Stride somehow crossed the distance between them. He hit her so fast the small polymer weapon shattered in her hand. She screamed, feeling her finger rotate with the blow, sending a winding root of fire up her forearm.

Before Rashida could finish screaming, Zatia planted both of her feet into Stride's chest, stopping his assault and sending him sailing, skidding into the hallway. "Just go!" was all Zatia shouted.

She wasn't in a place to argue. She had done her job and bought the time they needed. If Stride wanted to kill her, he was going to.

All she could do now was run.

CHAPTER
TWENTY-ONE
THOM

HE ALMOST BEMOANED the conversation's absence, because all he could feel in its wake was a thrumming, just on the edge of hearing. It wasn't unlike laying his head against someone's chest to feel the rise and fall of their breath or the subtle rhythm of the heart or the thousand rivers of the blood in their veins, the ambience of life. It was low like a distant drum but constant like a horn. It serenaded from over distant hills and pulled at his skin like a thousand pinching fingers. It spoke in words he could not work out and yet never stumbled on, urging him onward, closer, closer...

It was the Word of the Pilgrim, the summons to the Sojourn heard only by those that have walked the Path.

The Icon called to him.

His meditation was broken when he heard the magic words, Zatia sounding the call to war: *We are very loud!*

Here we go. Whatever time bought by Rashida and Zatia would have to have been enough. If they were too far out, the *Acheron*'s thick defenses would eviscerate the advancing merchant fleet of pirates.

Roche called out over the sound system, "Active LADAR ping! They have us in scope!"

265

Can you get us through? Thom asked.

My answer isn't going to change yours, is it?

No, it's not. Osyen ordered, *Take us in, Roche. Hot and heavy.*

Milardi slid down the ladder behind them, coat billowing in the air and weapons in hand. "Let's get dangerous, gents!"

And the ship lurched hard, like a boxer ducking a hard cross. *I've got Spartan fire,* Roche reported. *Hang on to something.*

Thom, Milardi, and Osyen all grabbed guardrails. The ship lurched again, sending all of Thibodeau's robots tilting on their gyroscopes, deep dramatic leans that would snap a human ankle. It was like watching a dance troupe rehearse.

The ship tumbled on its axis, thrusting abruptly in hard directions.

"Thibodeau," Thom called out, "you're up."

The lead robot clapped its metal hands together with a solid ring, scraping them together like a child eager for sweets. "Take study, amateurs."

Osyen windmilled his hand, fed up with the drama, but his eyes went wide when he saw Thibodeau's cape of robotic wasps leap forward to land on the *Aurum's* cargo bay door. His jaw dropped. "You're not going to do what I think you're going to do, are you?"

A loud, metallic clang. Roche's voice: "Magnetic lock!"

Thibodeau snapped his fingers. And the fourteen-foot-high cargo bay door cut free with a bright molten metal flash, falling forward as if they'd kicked it in. Through the gaping hole, they could see the muted gray-blue hues of the Naval carrier's interior.

Osyen squeaked, "My ship!"

"Contact!" A Naval Regular called out from the smoke. All Thom saw was the end of a rifle aimed right at him.

And Thibodeau's wasps descended. It might have only lasted one second, but the thousand cuts from a thousand metal claws was enough nightmare to fuel Thom's nights for years to come.

The sack of meat that hit the floor was hardly recognizable as human.

Thibodeau's robotic doppelgänger glanced back at them. "You're welcome."

Thom took the first brave step across the threshold, his stomach turning as the artificial gravity adjusted for him. No two ships ever had the same setting and there was a space between the two that had none at all. But he was drawn forward, like a divining rod to water.

The hallways of the carrier were broad enough to drive two cars down it side by side—Thom wondered how that could be if the ships were for people alone.

The simple answer had to be that they weren't for just people, but something...bigger.

Osyen stepped up to his side, shouldering his rifle. "Which way?"

"How would I know?" Thom whispered, with a hint of accusation. How could Osyen know that he knew?

"Because you do," he stated.

Thom closed his eyes and listened for that drumbeat. Through the hum of ion engines and air vents, he could feel its call.

He pointed left. "This way."

Osyen nodded, turning to the crew. "Move fast. They set up a line, we'll get turned back. Keep 'em on their heels and stay off o' yours."

Milardi stepped up, adjusting the brim of his hat with one of his pistols. "*Montah zu T'aie.*"

"*Montah!*" Thibodeau cheered with a dozen voices from all his robotic forms, his wasps rising high in the air like a cloud of shimmering steel.

Wealth to the Victors.

If he was to die, there was very little he could do to stop it. His strength was meager, his will slight. And the cosmos was vast. If it called his name, all he could do was step up.

So he took the first step into the *Acheron*'s belly. Milardi and Osyen advanced behind him, far more manic than he. They darted from bulkhead to bulkhead, while Thibodeau's robots marched forward with little thought for themselves.

Thom didn't hear the first shot, and he didn't know where it came from, but one of Thibodeau's robots was cut nearly in half right next to him, spraying him with a curtain of sparks. He could feel the burn lick his skin before fading.

He did hear the monster's steps, however. Hydraulic presses clanging against the floor. The eight-foot tall exosuit blocked their path, flaring its many modules and weapons. It was all an extension of its pilot's body, a single Oskie at its center like the calm amidst a warfare hurricane.

"Don't blink!" Osyen shouted. "Push him! Push him!"

Milardi spun the cylinders on his revolvers and held down the triggers, letting the mechanism work its magic—spraying rounds down the hallway, darts of light seeking flesh.

They would never find it.

The Oskie didn't even flinch as a fluttering rainbow bubble soaked in every shot. It stepped forward, raising one hand. Thom could see the barrel tucked on the outside of his wrist, training right for him—

One of Thibodeau's robots stepped up, taking the shot, even as Faceplate snatched Thom from the open, clutching him close in his steel claws like he might shield him.

The fool—nothing was going to stand in the way of that juggernaut.

Osyen fired his bracket gun, the energy blast skipping off the rainbow bubble like it had been brushed aside. It scored the bulkhead, slagging the metal into glowing liquid.

"Get me close!" Milardi shouted as he reloaded.

"How?!" Thibodeau cried out.

"Mob the bastard!"

Thibodeau nodded, and his crowd of robots rushed in, upright and proud to help. They followed commands without concern for themselves.

The Oskie responded with full force, a barrage of shots from both wrists. Tongues of—what he hoped—was flame shot from a shoulder mount. He stomped a foot and sent the nearest robots flying back, the rainbow shield undulating around him, like a soap bubble in sunlight.

He gunned down the fallen without remorse. Chunks of metal scattered through the hallway like litter.

But Milardi rushed up, hiding behind the crowd of metal sacrifices. He lunged out with one pistol.

The Oskie caught his wrist with one crushing metal fist. It peered at him for a moment, as if studying an insect it found on a bush.

"Two hands, motherf—" he said, as he squeezed the trigger on his other revolver. He had stuck one hand forward to draw attention, but snuck the other gun in low—the rainbow blur warping around his wrist.

He was inside the shield.

The Oskie was fast but strapped into a rig. He blurred as he thrashed, trying to escape but with nowhere to go. And Milardi emptied the revolver into his chest.

The exosuit collapsed backward, bringing Milardi down with it, his wrist still clutched in its grasp.

Osyen swallowed hard, chambering a new capacitor. "You good?"

Milardi waved a hand in the air. "Could use a friend, but yeah!"

As Osyen went to work prying Milardi loose, Thom just kept walking forward. One foot falling right after the other.

It was close, so close now. Loud and urgent.

Someone called his name but he didn't know who.

That's when the pressure door closed. And Thibodeau loomed over him.

"Now Mr. Hugh..." he said, "you're going to take me to the Icon."

Thom looked back. The door had cut him off from the others. He heard pounding on the door, voices shouting, cursing.

Faceplate leaned in, its blank expression masking Thibodeau's distant fangs.

Lily! Osyen called out. *Force door 1 3-A4 now!*

Processing, came Lily's response, *but Naval heuristics is combatting my efforts. I am not finding success.*

Milardi's voice might have been muted by fourteen inches of steel, but the many Colonial curses were not lost on Thom's ears.

Thibodeau paid them no mind. His cloak of wasps came to rest on his shoulders, a handful landing on Thom's neck. Their tiny claws gripped his flesh. "Don't make this difficult, boy."

CHAPTER
TWENTY-TWO
MILARDI

HE'D LOST THOM. Again. Why did that feel so withering this time?

Milardi bellowed at the wall, kicking one of the fallen robot heads. "Teebo! I find you, I'm going to pull out your plugs with a carving fork! You hear me?!"

Thom! Osyen called out on the channel. *Thom, answer me!*

Nothing. Either Thom was willingly silent for some reason, or his implant had been jammed again.

Fiona had demonstrated she could hack their implants at will.

Milardi grabbed Osyen's shoulder and half expected to catch a fist. Osyen glared up at him, but his voice rang out elsewhere. *Fiona! Is this you?!*

No response.

"I'll take that as a 'Yes,'" Osyen reasoned. His eyes bored into Milardi, unspooling the thread inch by inch, imagining the many ways he could inflict pain. And it struck Milardi all at once.

He was a Fiona double agent. Osyen was looking for an explanation he didn't have.

"Oz..." he started, "we can get him back."

Osyen shook his head. "I've got a different job for ya."

Milardi's eyebrows scrunched up. "What now?"

Osyen slung the bracket gun, kicking one of the Regular's service rifles up into his hands. The look he threw at Milardi made the seasoned gunslinger want to swallow his tongue, throat, and entire head, lest his friend blow it off. "Work with Roche. Find Navigation and stop this ship, would ya?"

"You going to do something stupid?" Milardi asked.

The look in Osyen's eye could've frozen fire into elegant crystal just so he could smash it on the floor. There were no words, no reasons.

Just an intent.

"Right," Milardi affirmed. "Just dons get yourself dead."

Osyen nodded as he looted a spare magazine from the Regular's chest rig. Where he was going, he was going to need the ammo.

Roche, Milardi keyed, *can you get me to Navigation?*

Engineering is a thousand feet aft and locked down. Believe it or not, the bridge is your best option. Are we fighting Fiona's boys now too?

I don't know. Was Thibodeau rogue, or on orders? It wouldn't be the first time in the last few days the guy had wandered astray.

But Fiona might have given the order and kept Milardi out. He had a use—and he had fulfilled it. Would he have trusted her were the situation flipped?

No. Then again, he'd have shot her years ago.

What about you? Roche's implication was thick. He had likely arrived at this possibility days ago. Milardi was working them all from the start. Everything he ever did was suspect.

Why would anybody trust him now?

She didn't say nothing to me. It was true. But the silence from Roche wasn't comforting.

With good reason. He hadn't exactly done a lot to earn their confidence lately. But that didn't stop the spite boiling up his throat. He had reported to Fiona, sure. Yes. Dual loyalties, dual paychecks.

But had he ever betrayed them, hurt them? Had they lost work or reputation because of him? No.

They were just pissed they didn't know everything about him.

Roche, you can trust me right now, or you can cut me off the channel, Milardi declared. *I would never hurt the boy. You know that.*

Roche didn't answer, but Milardi knew all too well what the plughead was doing. He was running a thousand simulations to test the likelihood of Milardi's story, accounting for unknown factors like debts or blackmail, revenge or love. A man can be so irrational when he has something at stake.

Just look at Osyen.

Milardi had no such stake, but how was he to convince Roche of that?

Double back one-hundred feet, Roche said. *You should find a service tunnel. The network runs the length of the ship.*

Thank you, he said.

Milardi jogged back the way he came, loping over the crumpled bodies of fallen Oskie and the scattered parts of Thibodeau's goonbots. It was like running across a room of broken glass, with shell casings and carbon scoring painting nearly every surface like a texture of battle. There was an alarming lack of blood for how much violence had passed through this space.

True to form, there it was—ladder rungs on one wall that ran up to the roof, where a small hatch sat.

Milardi pursed his lips. His hat was never going to fit and his longcoat would bind up and cause more pain than it was worth. If he was going anywhere, he couldn't bring them.

Style over substance, he thought with a huff.

With a sigh, he shed the jacket to the floor and dropped his hat atop it like a grave marker. The rungs were surprisingly warm to the touch, and he wondered if they were heated for the technician's comfort.

The hatch dropped open at his mere presence. The hallways were wide and accommodating with subtle blues; this was a sewer pipe by comparison, cramped and unpleasant. Wires dangled from visible circuit boards and conduits ran to a dozen curious places. He half expected some unseen beastie to hiss at him from the darkness within.

I'm here, Milardi said with a taste of objection. *Where to?*

Up inside and take a right, Roche said. *Crawl until I tell you to stop.*

Milardi's skin tingled. *Say that again but slower.*

Time and a place, Duster, Roche scolded, but Milardi could sense the grin that had cracked on the plug's face. *Get moving.*

CHAPTER
TWENTY-THREE
ZATIA

ARMS BURNED. Head swimming. Her knees and hips popped like crushing tin. And she hadn't felt this good in months.

Milardi had warned her about how it might interact with adrenaline and painkillers—his words had been shark, blood, water, and frenzy.

All she knew was it felt like every inch of her crackled with electricity, hair on end, that she might snap off of every surface she touched. It propelled her, energized her. It warmed her belly and her heart. The breath in her lungs felt salty but sweet, light and airy, like a fine mead.

She felt sharpened.

Breathe in, breathe out. So sweet.

Stride stood across from her, squared shoulders and damp brow. A light steam rose off of his pale skin, bronze wiring glowing under his scalp. His implants were working hard, getting a little toasty. All that tech and all that training and he was evenly matched up against a sixteen-year-old girl in leather pants.

Rashida was running for the shuttle, making slow but steady progress. She looked like an animated painting, all flourish of gemstone colors, her dress a flag being borne into battle, billowing in unseen winds. Even the cloth seemed to hang in the air, moving only by an artist's hand.

Time, for Rashida, might as well have been standing still. Stride and Zatia were trading blows like two alley cats. Zatia was thinking and moving so fast, she could probably restyle Rashida's hair before the Royal could object.

The nasty thought came in sharp relief—the stim was going to wear off soon and if she hadn't taken care of Stride before then...

Zatia crouched low, slipping the knife from her boot. She tucked the blade behind her, hiding it from view as she prepared to pounce the moment her prey so much as blinked.

Stride huffed and puffed, drinking in the air, a lilt to his lip—was he pleased? A nagging thought pulled at her scalp. His pleasure could not be a good thing. But then, maybe he was tasting the same air she was.

She lunged, fingers balled up into fists, her boots scraping against the floor hard enough to leave a rubber trail on the steel and kick smoke into the air. Chemistry made her fast but physics hadn't changed one bit.

He let her come, his spider's gaze gauging her. She was fast, but he was just as fast.

She slammed into him and he pivoted, using her momentum to sling her into a bulkhead hard enough to leave a Zatia-shaped imprint in the steel. Her shoulder screamed as something popped. But she didn't care. It all sounded like music to her right now.

She swung herself back at him, bringing the tip of the knife to bear. He clapped her wrist, separating her from her weapon, before bouncing her back again.

Zatia's eyes went wide with horror. Physics—the knife had quite a bit of momentum behind it that hadn't stopped. It was sailing straight for Rashida's retreating back.

Get it.

Zatia rushed forward, sliding underneath Stride's attacks and snatching the blade from the air. She brought it back around, slicing a ribbon of Stride's uniform free. He palmed her face and batted the knife free again.

Disarming an opponent was easy for a trained soldier. She was no soldier.

She bit his hand. He held true for a moment before pain finally forced him to drop her, but a knee to the chest tossed her light weight aside.

Stride shook out his hand and moved for the waiting shuttle. And the slow-motion vulnerable Rashida.

Keep him here.

Zatia shoved off the wall, leaping for him.

It was like he had eyes in the back of his head. He pivoted, catching her jaw with a clenched fist. She crumpled, her head ringing dulcet tones.

"Stay down, kid," he said, as he turned for the door again.

Kid?

She grabbed her bangles and ripped them free, watching the happy little blades unfold. Three distinct pieces snapped into place— steel tang for her to grip; jagged knuckles to reinforce her strikes; and long, curved blades custom-forged to fit her forearms, the polished slashing edge that turned a blunt strike to the cheek into a laceration. These bladed batons would break his bones and open them up for study in one gruesome move.

She was fast but sound was faster. He heard the metal singing before she could get to his back. Stride spun about, leaning away from Zatia's wild swing at the back of his head.

These *gulaw* professionals. They were trained how to fight, but they didn't know how to brawl.

Zatia took the energy of her swing to spin about and kick out his knee. He took the hit hard and crumpled down, barely able to bring his fists up to catch the follow-up punch.

She twisted her wrist, gashing his forearm for his arrogance. She had him on his heels now, driving him back away from Rashida.

Breathe in, breathe out.

Stride had taken to dodging now, trying to stay out of Zatia's small reach. Zatia had to keep pushing to keep him in range, and the faster he moved, the more those implants glowed under the lights.

Her speed, his speed—they were countering attacks before they fell, countering those counters before they could counter. Their hands and feet blurring as they saw attacks being prepared, coiled, sent. Zatia was setting up a fifth strike before her first had even landed, and so was he.

It might've been a blur to see—it also might've driven a lesser man insane.

She took a backhanded swipe at him, bringing that blade directly to his neck. He ducked out of the way, bringing his face to meet her rising knee. The meaty thunk his chin made she could play on a loop to sing her to sleep at night, a song so sweet.

Breathe in, breathe out.

The air burned her throat, almost like a chili powder.

She coughed.

And he was gone.

She looked left, right—and took a punch to the cheek. She heard the bone crunch echo in her skull, reverb coming from front to back to front again. She hardly had a chance to register the hit before a palm slapped into her throat, forcing her to cough again.

Her wrist screamed as Stride brought the blade's flat under his boot. The metal shattered like glass and showered shards into her skin.

Blood dripped from his nose and mouth as he stooped down, clutching at her doublet, heaving her up.

She swung with her good hand, bringing that remaining blade to bear. Stride leaned out of the way, his hand moving so fast it might as well have ghosted through her own. He slipped his fingers underneath the blade, between steel and her wrist, his grip on her like a vice biting into her flesh.

He let her inertia carry through, rolling her over his hip and hurling her to the ground. Before she could react, she was splayed out on the floor, sliding—

He didn't let go of her wrist as the weight of her body kept going, and she heard the snare drum of her shoulder popping out of its socket.

The pain hit her all at once, like it had been held back by a wooden dam somewhere upstream. It scorched through her end to end, singeing every nerve to a glassy stump.

Stride lifted her up, and she stifled her scream as he heaved her entire bodyweight up on nothing but the tendons in her arm, like a grotesque marionette. He studied her through his four calculating yellow eyes.

Four—she was seeing double. The stim had worn off.

"That was..." He paused to wipe the blood from his face. "...An entertainment."

"Captain!"

Stride's head didn't so much turn as it was suddenly looking towards the shuttle and Rashida.

Rashida stared back at him, but standing in an empty hangar. Wait. Where did the shuttle go? Had she sent it on? You idiot!

The Royal raised her hands up like a sorceress summoning an oncoming storm, her dress billowing in invisible hero wind. "Let her go," Rashida demanded.

Stride didn't blink, didn't emote at all. It was like being executed by a sculpture. "You came to me, Your Ladyship, and brought some unsavory characters with you."

"My company is exquisite," Rashida countered, "but there's no accounting for taste."

His grip tightened, and Zatia felt the fleshy cloth of her shoulder tear, seam by little seam. She felt like he was going to rip her arm clean off and beat her to death with her own blade.

"Last warning, Stride," she ordered. "Let her go."

"You will leave, Dunsweir," he insisted, "or the Walls of Jericho will crash down upon your head."

"Rash..." Zatia eked out, "run!"

Rashida's eyes narrowed. "Final boarding call."

That's when she saw it, and by the widening of Stride's reptile eyes, he saw it too. The hero wind so flourishing Rashida's dress hadn't been invisible. The taxi shuttle had lifted off and circled outside the hangar bay. And it was coming back.

Coming back rather aggressively.

Nobody had time to curse as it passed through the hangar's magnetic seal, immediately filling the room with a howling after-burner, and streaked straight for the hangar back wall at Mach Four.

When she came to, it was like a good two thirds of the room was on fire. Fuel tanks sprayed plumes like tiny dragons and metal supports fell from the ceiling, actual tonnage of confetti.

Stride was nowhere to be seen.

Zatia tried to push herself up—and her shoulder immediately reminded her of its condition. She took a few bracing breaths of the hot air, tasting that acidic spice with every sharp intake.

This was going to hurt, but to Hell with it. She was already in pain.

She lifted her torso up from the deck and slammed it down on the ball of her shoulder—feeling it slip back into socket with a sickening pop. She yelped, pulling her knees in close. Her arm was like a battered child, crying and wailing, cursing her and wanting to be anywhere else in the world. At the moment, she didn't want to argue the point.

Get up. The place is on fire.

She managed to roll onto her knees and lift herself up. The shuttle had bored a jagged hole deep into the carrier, like the vora-cious open gullet of a giant legendary wyrm, serrated steel teeth broken and craggy from an epoch of unhealthy eating.

That might've hit something important.

Zee? came Milardi's voice. What the Hell was that?

It was...she paused, trying to force air down her gullet...It was an air support.

"Zee!"

Rashida's voice. Zatia turned to see Rashida jogging towards her, the beautiful dress now tatters, soot lining the edges. Had she torn most of it off?

"Are you okay?" Rashida asked.

"That was insane!" Zatia croaked through her bruised throat.

Rashida nodded. "I know, I know! I didn't know what else to do!"

"No!" Zatia said, shaking her head. "Are you kidding? That was awesome!"

CHAPTER
TWENTY-FOUR
ADELAIDE

ADELAIDE HADN'T HELD a gun in six years. She understood them well enough: pressure chambers, focusing crystals, capacitors and phosphorous, electromagnets, trigger weights and ergonomic grips. And she'd seen what they could do to a human body.

What they'd done to Nathaniel.

She stared at the gun Zatia had left for her. Simple design, sleek frame, small magazine. Reliable, concealable.

Her heart quickened at its sight and her breath hitched in her chest.

Adelaide, we're on to Plan B, Roche reported.

Plan B? Adelaide coughed. *We had that many plans?*

Carrier is in star fall and will enter the corona in twenty minutes. We're not going to steal the Icon—we're going to steal the carrier.

Oh, really now? Adelaide griped. *And what's Plan C?*

You and I detach and leave them all to die.

Lily didn't so much materialize in front of Adelaide, as much as snap into existence. She imagined that Lily was presenting a similar front to Roche. "I can drain the oxygen in the *Aurum* in under fifteen seconds."

"And I can cycle your memory in twelve," Adelaide countered. "Don't test me."

You two need to shelve your disagreements, because they need you in there. Thom's missing, Osyen's gone wildcard, and the girls are on the run. Milardi's on his way to the Bridge but this is military encryption. They can lock him into a bulkhead and vent his skeletal ass into space. They need you both on the board. Right now.

Lily had no expression they didn't want to have. There was nothing there to read that hadn't been written with intent. They didn't have a million years of evolution drawing up primal snarls, emotional tears, or quivers of fear. They had extensively researched human expression, but they emoted the way a sociopath would—it was all theater, not genuine. Snarling was simply a display of snapping teeth, tears a way of cleansing eyes of toxins. Lily was not human. This was all a lie.

Every bone in Adelaide's body told her this. But there they were, brow furrowed with rage, eyes flashing, and the hint of teeth behind a quivering lip. "I won't lose him, Adelaide."

Lily might not have been human—but that feeling was no put-on.

I can't just run after them, we'll burn half the clock, Adelaide said. *Get me closer.*

Well, hangar bay's busted. Let me try something.

A clang and a bang as the ship detached from its breach, and lurched away into space. Lily's projection flickered, and they flashed back to their default expression. Ready and able.

Adelaide took a step forward, almost into Lily's hologram. "I can't tell you for sure he's coming home."

Lily flickered again, masking a response. "He doesn't say it either."

"You can help me," Adelaide said. "I'll make the cuts. You tell me which ones. Can you do that?"

"Yes." Their voice was almost quiet, distant. Considering a thousand speculative futures.

Adelaide shook her head. "Don't do that to yourself. Stay right here with me. We've got puzzles to solve and I'll need everything you've got. Okay?"

Lily nodded and, in that instant, it was like coaching a small child. Was this ship's computer having a panic attack?

Roche! Adelaide called out, *What's the move?*

Anything I do is going to draw hate from shipboard responders, he said. *You need to be with people who can fight back.*

Adelaide took another look at the gun Zatia left her as it jostled in its holster: Thirty caliber, silk steel alloy frame, double-barrel delivery of pre-cut copper slugs.

Nathaniel's back had ripped open like a gutted fish.

No.

Adelaide grabbed her tool bag, slinging it over her shoulder. *Just get me to the fun, I'll do the rest.*

She jogged down the causeway and up the breezeway to the docking collar. A few keystrokes on the panel and the orange-scale monitor blinked to life, projecting an umber hologram out into her hand. The *Aurum* coasted in like a fat gull towards the carrier's curved hull, a minnow against a shark.

The shark spat two forms out of its maw.

Uh, Roche—

I see them. Two Bearcats just scrambled to intercept. I am going to need you to step off the train before *we come to a complete stop, if you catch my drift.*

Ten feet. Five feet.

A hard bang as the magnetic locks engaged, rocking Adelaide almost to her knees.

Time to go to work.

Docking collars were easy to bypass, no need to go after hydraulic lines or reroute power. This could be done through simple code. Simple by design—they didn't want a rogue AI to be able to lock rescuers off a derelict. It could interfere, slow her down. It couldn't stop her.

Lily?

Her screen lit up as Lily proceeded to pepper the shipboard defenses with attacks of their own. The defending AI would have to spread itself thin to prevent access to more critical systems.

Jackpot. The hush of equalizing air and her ears popped with the sudden push.

Adelaide grabbed the hatch comb, hurling it open. She dashed inside, feeling the air whip her hair. *Roche, I'm on. Go!*

The suction was incredible. Magnetic locks disengaged and the ship peeled off, opening her to the vacuum. Air started to suck out, taking warmth and happiness with it. But military rigs had redundancies built in one on top of the other. As sudden as the torrent had begun, a blast shield dropped over the open doorway.

Take 'em for a ride, Roche!

Through the small porthole, she could see the *Aurum* drift back off the hull, tumbling like a plump bird looking for down. But then half a dozen engines fired, lurching the ship in directions that would've made Adelaide toss her breakfast, lunch, and dinner. Tracer fire came lancing past, followed by the Bearcats, twin darts of light.

With nobody else aboard, Roche could really put the *Aurum* through her paces. It was like watching a bullfighter with a jetpack.

And just like that, Roche vanished into the night.

Adelaide gripped her bag tight to her side, her hands slick with... blood. The paper-thin skin of her hand had torn open on the ground.

No time. She clenched her fist tight, trying to staunch the bleeding.

She was on an Imperial carrier under siege with angry pirates roving about. Nothing to worry about. Nothing at all.

She should've stayed in her depot.

Lily, where am I goin'? she asked.

Stand by.

She pressed herself against the bulkhead wall, hoping to whatever Gods out there that any guns that passed through didn't pick out her silhouette. *You didn't have a plot for me all set?*

I'm combatting a heuristic response five times more sophisticated than I am, while coordinating four different shipboard teams all while my motherboard is locked in a dogfight with precision military countermeasures.

And you're wasting RAM sassing me?

She could picture Lily's smug little mug as they said it. *Is it a waste, though?*

She wanted to be pissed. She wanted to be frightened. She wanted to be loud. She knew right then what Osyen liked about his anthropomorphized hard drive.

She tried not to smirk, lest Lily detect the tacit approval. *Don't mind me. Just hanging in the breeze here.*

Proceed aft one-hundred feet.

She dared not leave the wall, shuffling down its length. The steel was a painted gunmetal grey, doubtlessly trying to hide the mediocre metal used in its construction. They might not have been visible to the eye, but she could feel the pockmarks along the surface, tiny rusted splotches scraped away from the stock. Military minds sourced cheap steel and used a lot of it to double up as armor: probably old 1084, better suited to museum exhibits and retired rail lines. It was laying around, solid and hard, but very heavy.

What did the military care? Everything was assembled in an orbital shipyard anyway and they paid somebody's cousin lucrative deals to haul it into low-Earth orbit.

She'd have used 8020 Silksteel, or maybe gone with a hybrid aluminum, if money was a concern.

She saw the bulkhead pretending it was a door up ahead. It looked like a metal whale's mouth. What did they think they were hauling through here? Suppose it looked good to politicians, but it was wholly unnecessary.

Tucked into the doorframe on the right side was the primary access panel: a simple projector with a manual keypad underneath for backup. Child's play.

She popped out a flathead screwdriver and pried the keypad face off, revealing the line-work behind. The cheap screw holding it in place stripped like a pay-for-play Jane—it was only there for the tease. Along the edges of the panel hatch, the paint flaked and peeled to reveal the steel slab underneath it all.

Of course, they hadn't the professional pride to cover corners and edges, behind doors or panels. She dug her fingernail into the grain of the steel, able to wedge it in between the layers of metal—a bad weld job sticking out like a knuckle and folding over again. A pry bar and a few minutes, she could probably separate the two stocks.

Adelaide groaned again when she saw the abominable cable management. Some contractor grunt—cashing checks to do one job without any thought of the next grunt to come along—had bound all of the cables together into one conduit bundle. No thought for power, hydraulic, data. How was anybody going to repair this thing without unpacking the entire thing?

Overwhelmed? Lily taunted.

Adelaide shook her head. *Some people, no respect for the craft.*

Red wire, Lily said, completely unhelpful. And do what with it, smartass? Lick the lead?

"Adelaide?!" A muffled voice called out from the other side of the door. Rich tones, firm pronunciation, and clear consonants all the way to the end of the word.

"Rashida?" Adelaide yelled back.

"Hurry! They're coming!"

Oh, goodie. That's what she liked to do. An egg timer where the buzzer was dead people.

She pulled out a boxcutter and ripped the cable-tie some baboon had strapped around the entire line set like he was cording up wood. She dug her fingers into the bundle, gripping and squeezing. If she could just find the hydraulic line.

Of course, the largest wire was a further bundle of cables. On second thought, that probably housed the power lines. Knick the hydraulic line, and she could force the door open but she couldn't lock it again—but she'd never find the lock mechanism in time. She'd be here till they'd chopped the door down with harsh language.

Red wire, Lily had said. She fished out no less than three red wires from the bundle. No—wait—it was one wire someone had routed back and forth and back again. The imbecile hadn't even given a thought to whether he was binding the same loose cable back along itself!

"Any day now, Addy!" Milardi's grainy voice howled.

She coiled the red wire's excess around her hand and yanked it free from the lead. The door crunched open—and gunfire licked through the gap like dragon's breath.

Rashida limped through the gap, stooping low to carry Zatia's hobbling frame. Milardi backpedaled through the door, both pistols blasting away at the unseen enemy.

"Close it!"

Adelaide coiled the end of the wire, wrapping the frayed end tight before slipping it back over its former home and capping it in place.

The door didn't move.

"Adelaide?" Milardi stuttered, nervously rolling his fingers on his pistol grips.

She popped the panel back up and tapped the big red button. The door lurched open wider. Everyone tensed up, but before they could shout, Adelaide hit the button again and the door slammed shut.

Milardi holstered his pistols and wiped the sweat from his brow back up into his thin hair. "You just *live* for those photo finishes, don't you?" Without the jacket and the hat, he was really quite unnerving to look at. All of his arms too long, his legs too long, his neck too long. With the oversized clothes, it reset all his proportions.

Adelaide shook her head. "And what would you have done if I couldn't close it?"

"I can't be the big damn hero all the time," he said with a nervous shrug. "Gotsa...let you all in on the fun."

In point of fact, electricity was predictable but not always...

behaving. It was entirely possible that door would open and then never shut again. No need to frighten the boy with that.

"What's wrong with her?" Adelaide asked, nodding at Zatia.

"She took something," Rashida said. When no further explanation came, Adelaide rolled her eyes.

"I'm fine..." Zatia grumbled.

"Zee, you can't stand on your own," Milardi said. "Anybody with two eyes can see you're more baggage right now."

The floor bucked and shuddered, knocking Rashida and Zatia to the floor. Milardi caught Adelaide's eye with his wide grim stare. *"Baz ki toa mar?"*

Roche piped into their head like a klaxon, *I've got hull breaches spitting gas along your starside. You guys have got to get that hulk out of its descent or I'm going to watch you all go up like candle wax.*

Milardi led the way, with the others close behind. The bridge access was a fairly unassuming door, with a manual crank and biometric reader. Adelaide cracked it open and began her work—

But Lily cut her off. *There is no power to this console.*

Say what now? *No power?*

Power has been re-routed away from this section.

"Get it open," Milardi ordered.

Adelaide crossed her arms. "I can't run lines that aren't hot."

A huff and a grunt from Zatia. "Get out of the way." She shoved off Rashida and shambled over to the door. Whatever cocktail had been shot into her system might have taken the gas out of her step, but hadn't taken the drive shaft with it. She clamped on to the edges of the door, working her fingers into the crevice and shoving it open.

Adelaide didn't know what she was expecting out of a military bridge, but she didn't expect it to be a small prison cell. It resembled the *Aurum*'s in more than a few features, with two main computer bays but with a positively sinister looking command chair—high back and wide arms, to accommodate additional computers, she assumed. The chair was fixed to stare at a blank wall, which probably played host to whatever projections of the world around the carrier.

It probably felt like being God to a small terra firma.

Zatia limped inside, leaning on the walls. Adelaide and Milardi descended on the consoles, trying to wake the machines.

No response.

"What, is this place for show?" Milardi whined.

Adelaide stooped under the console and her blood froze. "No. But they took hot plasma to the bits."

Rashida took a steeling breath. "Back to the hangar bay, double-time."

"Seriously, Rashida, you are not in charge," Milardi grumbled at her.

"Well, we're not going to run for our lives after taking a vote," Rashida snapped, "because Stride is scuttling the ship and he's made sure there's not a damn thing any of us can do about it."

CHAPTER
TWENTY-FIVE
THOM

THEY HADN'T BEEN CRAFTY—THEY had kicked the
door in with a blasting charge and a war trumpet. They had sung the
ballads of battle, hoisted up clumsy armaments, and taken to the field
in open hostilities like there had been a written invitation. This was a
surprise assault by way of formal declaration. This was anything but
subtle.

But for all of the fighting, Thom couldn't shake the nagging
feeling that only one team showed up for this party. Since they
arrived, they had seen a handful of Naval responders, maybe a dozen
Regulars, one Oskie. But this was an active Imperial fleet carrier—
where was everybody?

Thibodeau had one iron claw clamped onto Thom's shoulder,
and he could feel the electric charge building up under the palm. He
forced Thom forward like he was some kind of bloodhound, and the
cattle prod was the leash.

Not like Thom could outrun the hive of electric death his keeper
kept about him.

Get him talking. Get him to confess something.

"You won't escape her," Thom commented.

"Shut up."Ah-ha. So Thibodeau *was* acting alone. Apparently the mastermind hadn't thought that far ahead.

Thom smirked. "Always think with your wallet, Thibodeau?"

"And I told you to shut it!"

"There's no amount of money—"

His chest seized and his heart tap-danced in his chest, his fists clenching so hard his fingernails bit his palms. He would have buckled and collapsed if Thibodeau's grip didn't hold him up by his collar bone.

"Take heed what I been sayin'," Thibodeau whispered, "or I'll cook you down to stew meat."

He thinks he can draw blood from a stone. He thinks if he strikes enough, if he etches welts and bruises onto flesh, that he can elicit whatever ends he wants. He doesn't know the most open secret in the universe: that destruction does not create anything. Fire burns; it cannot heal. All of these men—all of these grown, successful, powerful adult men—these men all think they can bludgeon the world into submission with fist and blade.

The world is larger than their feeble hands could ever hope to grasp, let alone crack or warp or bend. They sought order in chaos, because order could be altered to benefit their designs. Violence gave them authority. They, and they alone, could get a large enough stick to beat the universe into giving them what they wanted.

Thom started laughing, shaking, almost convulsing.

Thibodeau leaned in close. "Shut your little face. Now."

Thom sniffed at the tears welling up in his eyes. "No."

The robotic red oculus squinted at him. "You have a death wish?"

"I do not," Thom said. "But you gotta stop telling me jokes."

There was that tickle again, crackling through his shoulder and teasing his heart.

And when Thom stopped spasming, he chuckled again. "I die, and you're just a guy—who's attacked an Imperial carrier with nothing to show for it."

Thibodeau leaned in close, narrow oculus, and Thom swore he

could feel his hot breath on his face, snorts from a dragon. Thibodeau was somewhere far away, safe and plush, but Thom knew him to be as close as the clothes that hung from his own mousy frame. He wondered if he might reach out and grasp Thibodeau's hand, his shoulder—his throat.

The robot seemed to sneer. "You think I'mma kill you, boy? You won't die. I won't permit it, no. Fail me and you will live. And your life will be pain."

"You fail," Thom said, "and they will stamp *you* out like campfire embers on a cold morning."

Luxury and security were just not enough, as Thibodeau withered at the thought.

"Big tough pirate...let's get one thing clear between us," Thom asserted. "If anybody is working for anybody...you work for me. Or you get nothing. Are we copacetic?"

Thibodeau snarled, then gave the boy a shove. "Go on now. Lead the way."

The pirate and professional hostage purveyor had only one definition of power in his vocabulary, with no flexibility or pliancy. He believed that power came from violence and the ability to deliver that violence, dole out punishment; he believed that power was mastery over death.

Quite the opposite—it was about mastery of life.

Thibodeau followed a cautious step behind Thom now. It wasn't as though Thom could outrun him, after all. He might've assumed that Thom was trying to bluff him or cajole him into leniency. Any misstep now and Thom's entire scheme might collapse in on itself.

Thom closed his eyes and listened for that sweetest of music, the Path of the Pilgrim.

And he started walking. Roche had placed their ship well—it was on this deck.

"It feel a little empty to you?" Thibodeau blurted, letting his nerves get the better of him.

But he wasn't wrong. Either Stride was letting them in, or he didn't have the resources to spare. Trap might've been the sexy choice, the dramatic one, but Stride was not that clever. He had a hammer and nail mindset.

Power makes men direct, not clever.

"It feels empty to everyone," Thom dismissed. But the hairs on his neck stood on end, trying to abandon their own fleshy ship. Maybe that was just the repeated electric shocks.

"You're the Navy brat. This look okay to you?"

"The only side of the Navy I've ever seen has been a jail cell." Not strictly true, he'd seen the command deck when his father had received the Order of Wynd'que for his service to the Consul, but that was neither helpful nor as flashy thing to say.

Sometimes flash is what was required. It could blind as well as dazzle.

Thibodeau shook his metal head. "It feels like a graveyard."

It sounded crazy, but Thom agreed. Or like a hospital. The hallowed emptiness of it hung in the air. The bright lights that seemed to light nothing at all, as if to illustrate the absence.

All Thom could feel was that distant drum, beckoning him onward.

Maybe it was the size of the cruiser, but they didn't hear any commotion or signs of life anywhere else, as though every available hand had been lifted on to places elsewhere.

And that's when he saw it, the gaping hole in the bulkhead.

"Escape pod," Thibodeau blurted.

Hard to argue. The empty pocket on the wall stood out like a scoop had cut out a chunk of the metal. The blast doors that sealed the exit were never meant to be opened again, slamming down hard to seal the hole.

"Why would they trigger the escape pods?" Thibodeau asked the obvious question.

They weren't losing the ship to a pirate incursion. Unless they had been triggered well before. But they were still defending it. Unless...

He can't. He can't! Thom bit his tongue before he started screaming.

"We have to hurry," Thom urged.

"Why?"

Thom took off running. He heard Thibodeau calling after him, but he hadn't sent a swarm of wasps to bring him in, so he must have been following well enough. It wasn't as though Thom's little legs could outrun a robot after all.

Clear that door, down this hallway. It was like following a scent trail and he was a bloodhound. He raced down a track marked by bread crumbs left by an industrious child. He had to get there before the unthinkable.

He can't. He can't.

Stride wasn't keeping it for himself, or delivering it to some greater monster, offering up unimaginable cosmic power as a token of his loyalty.

He was going to destroy it. He can't!

Thom stopped cold in his tracks, his shoes screeching on the deck. He can't?

No...what was he thinking? He *can't?* He should.

Thibodeau bounded up to his side. "What's wrong?"

It felt like an itch that had grown to a burn that had grown to a scream. Thom knew in his heart that the Icon had to be protected, kept close. And he knew in his gut, in his stomach that turned over and over in a nauseating ballet—the Icon was never meant for mortal hands. It was a gift conceived of by Angels, a tool for a craftsman beyond human ken.

Stride was right.

Well...that was going to shift some pieces on the board.

"Where is it?!" Thibodeau demanded, practically salivating out of anxiety. Had he missed his moment? Was it gone for good? Was this all for nothing?

His moment. That was a laugh. The entire movement was a

misstep. They would have been better off just letting Stride have his way.

This changed everything. But it still had to look like a genuine heist.

Thom reached back in his mind, lifting the block on his implant. *Lily, can you hear me?*

Thom! Came the computer's trombone voice. *We were so worried.*

Get everybody back on the Aurum! *Right now!*

Where are you? I cannot see you.

It was better if they didn't. They'd come after him if they did. *I'll be there.* That was the only way to be sure.

He took off running again, hearing Thibodeau call after him, "What is your deal?!"

Thom didn't give the pirate courtier a second thought, racing as fast as his feet could carry him. They were so close now. They might be able to pull off this magic trick, and even the magician wouldn't know how it was done.

Control the mark. He never dreamed he might have to con himself.

The scent led him down a harsh turn and up to a blast door—two massive walls of steel the size of two strong men, squeezing palms together hard enough it might as well have been one alloy.

It did not open on his approach: obviously locked. Was it coded, biometric, manual? Beyond his skill.

"Teebo!" Thom shouted.

The robot sprinted around the corner, one hand already extended. "Get back!"

The hornets leapt forward—immediately shocked by the door's surface and crumpling to the floor like the curtain falling at the end of the play.

Of course.

Thibodeau cursed, lunging for the side panel. "Fine! *Fine!* We'll do this the hard way!"

Thom looked back at the way they came. If anybody came down

that path—or Stride—they'd have no cover to shield them or hide them, no protection at all. "Hurry, Teebo."

"I'm working!" he said, ripping cables out of the wall. "What sociopath wired this thing? Did he work at a cannery?"

Thom closed his eyes. *Lily, do you have access?*

Shipboard heuristics are effectively countering all intrusion attempts. He's also being very patronizing to me.

Lily!

I do have limited access to unsecured tertiary systems.

The entire run up to the room and they hadn't seen anyone. But now, here came two men, weapons ready.

Thom recognized the two officers from the Widow's Den—the lightning-fast killers that had butchered an entire bay of pirates while Stride had loomed over him.

Orbital.

They had been laid in wait for someone to try the door, and to strike while the trespassers were vulnerable. Well played.

Eyes flashing like cats in the dark, they took aim.

Were those eyes any good in the dark?

Deck C4, Stern. Kill the lights!

Like he'd flipped a switch, the lights dropped out, and the gunfire started. Thom crumpled to the floor, curling into a ball and hoping that the flashes of plasma that streaked overhead didn't illuminate where he had fallen. Maybe they'd assume they'd already killed him if he didn't move?

They could probably see his heart beating. If they wanted to kill him, they would.

Thibodeau jumped off the wall. He might not have been physically there, but instinct was instinct, and gunfire made him lurch away. He pranced from side to side, trying to predict and dodge the incoming fire. Sparks flew off impacts but the glowing metal slag illuminated the space. One shot found its mark in Teebo's gut.

That's when Thom heard a sound a great deal louder than a discharging capacitor. Someone fired a ballistic, a swift crack and boom. That wasn't Orbital's weapon of choice, and Thibodeau hadn't been carrying.

Thom dared to look up.

In the darkness, illuminated by flashes of laser and rifle he could see someone lunge at the two officers. Orbitals were fast, slipping out of the way of the concussive metal slugs, but they couldn't see their attacker, driving shots at where he had been rather than where he was.

Thibodeau didn't waste time, diving back into the door's wiring. Maybe he remembered that he wasn't actually in danger, or maybe he was braver than Thom credited him for.

Thom looked back to see the flickering tableau, with the officers moving so fast as to teleport between the flashes. Their speed might have been unrivaled, but the darkness was the ally of their attacker. And their implants set into their arms, head, and neck gave off a faint umber glow in the dark.

Speed was of no use if they flared everywhere they went, drawing tracer lines in the dark as they skipped from place to place.

Their attacker predicted a move and planted a shot directly into one officer's chest. The muzzle flash flared and by a fluke of the lighting, Thom could make out the gritted teeth and wild eyes of a crazed Osyen Belt.

The second Oskie saw the same thing Thom did and lunged, planting Osyen against a wall. He could hear them struggle, he could hear them spitting. Osyen gave off an unmistakable yelp of pain and surprise. The Oskie was stronger, faster—his glowing augments illuminating the punishment he delivered to Osyen's midsection, fists and kicks too fast for the young man to even consider countering.

As the two men struggled over the rifle, muzzle flashes strobed the space, someone squeezing the trigger. Bullets lanced into the roof and walls in an arc, up, up—

The last one went right into the soldier's head. Thom thanked whatever powers out there that his weak human eyes couldn't see what that looked like in the dark. But he did hear the wet slosh of porridge and the modest clack of bone chips clattering to the ground.

Maybe Osyen gave the order, maybe Lily just knew enough—but the lights came on to see a bruised, battered, and bloody Osyen propping himself up against the wall. He sucked air, unable to pull breath, his midsection spasming like a violent hiccup as he tried to draw any wind at all.

Osyen Belt, human flesh bag and convicted Capital, had just gone toe-to-toe with not one, but two Orbital officers...and actually won.

"You should be dead," Thom blurted.

Osyen just nodded, unable to push air at the moment. He examined the rifle in his hands—the dead Oskie still gripped the barrel, bent slightly in his fingers. Shrugging, Osyen dropped the weapon, and slumped down next to his kill.

"I've been shot," Thibodeau grunted. "Thanks for asking."

"No, you haven't," Osyen countered with a rasp, "but—keep on whining." Osyen scooped up the Oskie's laser rifle, and pocketed some of the cartridges.

Thibodeau ripped a conduit out of the panel and the doors seemed to slacken. He rolled out his robot neck, like he had to work out a crick or a pop. "Now that I've done all the hard work..."

Osyen slapped a fresh cartridge into the rifle and shot Thibodeau clear through the head, slagging the metal and dropping the marionette to the ground. It was almost like the robot folded up, collapsing into a heap of compact parts that seemed to hide how big it actually was. Osyen stared at the crumpled pile of metal for a time, before hocking spit onto the frame.

Not how Thom planned it, but it did save him the trouble of ditching the robot slaver.

"That make you feel better?" Thom asked Osyen.

"No, I think all my ribs are broken, but...thought I'd give it a shot."

Three fractures on the left parietal cavity, five on the right, Lily reported in a macabre, matter-of-fact tone, *but minimal displacement. There does not appear to be a risk of perforation.*

"You get broken an awful lot," Thom said, concerned.

But Osyen didn't want to hear it. "You're welcome. Let's steal a priceless antique—" He paused to suck a painful breath. "—And get outta here."

"How'd you find me?" Thom asked, a bit more seriously than he meant.

Osyen smelled that, throwing him a glance before brushing it off. "Lily tracked on to Teebo's control signal. After that...I followed the gunshots. You're welcome."

Osyen crammed his fingers into the blast door's open crevice and heaved. He nearly collapsed, giving up immediately.

"Maybe you didn't hear Lily," Thom said, "but your ribs are powder."

"Make-up is powder," Osyen gruffed, "gunpowder...is powder. My ribs are—"

"Free floating, at the moment," Thom said. "Let me."

Osyen scoffed and immediately winced at the motion. "You're like ninety pounds soaking wet. You can't open that."

Nobody thought he could do anything. "At the moment, neither can you. And you shot the guy who could."

"Yeah, I stand by that."

Thom slipped his fingers into the door. Probably four-hundred pounds of steel in just one of them, a powerful hydraulic system, and more than a little gravity held it shut. But with the power cut...

Thom heaved and the door budged, inch by inch, light peeking out from within. He felt like his arms were going to fall off, and he had to take moments to stop and breathe, but before long he had a sizable break in the doorframe.

Osyen smiled, but shook his head. "I'm not fitting through that."

Good job. He might not have said it in words, but his face had it tattooed across his forehead.

"I'll be right back," Thom said. "Don't die."

"No promises," Osyen quipped, propping himself up against the wall with the rifle aimed the way they'd come.

Mousey, small, duct rat, cabin boy. *Unti.* Thom could get where no one else on the *Aurum* could. And he could slip between the crack of the pressure doors like they weren't even there.

He had expected a slate gray block of steel with a bed and a desk, or maybe an opulent display of medals and fine fabrics. Stepping into someone's bedroom was like stepping into their mind: messy, colorful, religious, or minimalist. This was the cabin of a ship's commander, private but professional. It was Stride's one hidden place from even his own people.

There laid the usual adornments, built in by engineers: breakfast table, requisition bed and working desk, several shelves. Stride's personal touches were few but selective. The breakfast table had a small shrine to the Pilgrim, a tabletop monitor still propped open but dark. He used this space frequently, and didn't store it after use. That meant he made prayers often, likely daily.

The bed was made, sheets crisp, almost like it hadn't been slept in. That was Thom's usual experience with military types, though. The bunk was a sign of discipline, the first task of any day. It would've been stranger to see it in disarray.

The shelves held mostly models—other ships of the fleet, possibly others he'd served on. Souvenirs from past deployments. Most of them holographic projections, but one had started to collect dust, a fine layer not even a fingernail thick. He hadn't cleaned it in a while, perhaps forgotten it needed it. That meant he thought of it at the least infrequently.

But there were finger marks in the dust. He had touched it recently, but not cleaned it. Curious.

No sign of the Icon. But it was here. Somewhere. He heard it.

Thom walked by the shrine, pressing the monitor back into its home in the surface of the table. Most of these had compartments for electronics and such. Space was at a premium, weight even more so. Everything on a spacecraft had two uses.

Absolutely everything.

Thom ran his fingers underneath the table and found the happy switch, thumbing it to one side.

The holographic models on the shelves vanished, leaving the one dusty ship: placard said the *Ignatius*, ICS-051, an exploratory vessel.

Stride had served on a Pathfinder mission, plotting unmarked Jump Points. Extremely dangerous work.

And required a lot of faith.

Thom reached up, lifting the small model off the shelf. And upon lifting the weight, the shelf also raised up.

There it lay—suspended in iron chains—the Icon of Cruciform. A ball of stone or metal or frozen void. It seemed to glow, but of darkness, not of light. A slight green hue to the light catching off its surface.

It called his name, whispered at his ears. It urged him, but to what he didn't know.

Could he do this? Allow such a beautiful thing to be destroyed? It gave him his life back.

Thom dug into his pack, pulling out the copy that Osyen had sculpted. It matched in color, the darkness and the light, even matched the beveling, although hardly perfect. If someone had an ancient etching or a blurry photo, this would've been a fine doppler of the real thing. But there was something that resided in that stone that could not be replicated by human hand.

Could he be sure, that Stride wanted to destroy it? Would he hide it, guard it, place it in such reverence if he truly meant it harm? Thom should take it instead, ensure its destruction personally.

Maybe that's what Stride had told himself. That he would destroy it himself, that he and only he could do this. No other hand could be trusted, no other hand could be certain. What made Thom any better than Stride?

He pocketed his fake. For this to work, everyone would have to believe.

CHAPTER
TWENTY-SIX
OSYEN

THOM EMERGED from the cabin like someone had drained him of a pint of blood, pale and dragging his feet on the deck. His head hung low, chin to chest, but making steady progress.

If he had looked up, he'd have seen the assembled firing squad and the gun jammed into Osyen's neck.

Kid was always staring at his shoes.

"Thomas Hugh," came Fiona's rich dulcet voice, like silken curtains masking a gilded dagger.

Thom perked up to see Fiona and her brigade, Osyen on his knees. It must not have been all that surprising to him, because the kid didn't even blink. "Hi, Oz."

Osyen tongued his cheek, head bobbing as much as the muzzle in his jugular would allow, "Back at ya."

"Job went well, I take it?" Fiona asked.

Thom ground his jaw from side to side. "Just couldn't wait to get paid?"

She shrugged. "Well, when Oz here ventilated Thibodeau, it seemed prudent to...ensure your honesty."

The guard twisted the barrel in his neck. Osyen could swear the goon was trying to grind his flesh onto the barrel threads.

Fiona extended a lackadaisical hand. "The Icon, Thomas?"

Thom took a breath and straightened his back. The kid couldn't possibly mean to—

"You know I can't do that, Fiona."

Son of a bitch.

Fiona cocked her head. "Ship's in star fall. I could just kill you and take it off you."

"You could." Thom nodded. "But you haven't yet."

"Professional courtesy," she said.

"And personal history?"

Her smile faded like someone had dropped a brick on her foot. "You think I won't kill someone just because we chewed the same air?"

Thom shook his head. "I know you will."

He really didn't have any other rebuttal than that? What exactly was this kid's plan? Was he just going to waste time?

"Thom, give her the *gulaw* thing," Osyen grunted through his teeth.

"Listen to your Captain," Fiona said, "'cause that sounded like an order."

"He's not my captain anymore." That cocktail of venom, ice, and bile would've soured a birthday feast. That wasn't hot spite, that wasn't frothing fury; those waters were still, calm, collected. Certain. It was hatred.

Fiona's eyes shifted from Thom to Osyen. "So I should just kill him then?"

"Do whatever you want," Thom said, "you're good at that. But I'm not giving it to you."

"He's kidding!" Osyen barked out.

"I'm really not," Thom said.

Osyen set his widening eyes on Thom. He couldn't take the kid aside or privately chat over their links. All he had was pointed stares to try and telepathically push words Thom's way, but the kid wasn't having it.

Fiona blinked, her lips parted in a slight, confused gape. She was busily trying to parse out the moment. "Do you *want* me to shoot him?" That wasn't a threat. It was an offer.

"No," Thom said after a little much consideration, "I just don't rightly care if you do."

Was this an elaborate bluff? The kid had the Icon with him and he could resurrect him? He knew it worked, after all. He was daring Fiona to strike a killing blow because he knew better than most that it wouldn't stick? Didn't exactly excite Osyen, but it at least had some ring of logic to it.

"Okay." Fiona took one big step, snatching the pistol from her goon's hand—and squeezed the trigger.

The shot went maybe a half inch behind Osyen's head, the flash of burning gases searing the hairs on his neck. A blast of hot air buffeted against the back of his skull, and a crack of a whip echoed in his ears. He damn near jumped out of his skin, letting out an involuntary yelp.

Even Thom jumped, unable to mask the surprise and urge to help. And then he swallowed hard. She'd cracked Thom's poker face with a quick and decisive action. Thom was good; Fiona was better.

"The Icon, boy," she demanded. "Don't make me wait now."

"Lower the gun first," Thom said.

She fired off another shot, this time in front of his head, letting his nose taste the gunpowder. The round shattered against the bulkhead, peppering him with metal shavings, etching bloody lines along his cheek. Osyen crumpled, clutching at his face, but Fiona's metal hand snapped out, holding him up by his collar.

"Alright, alright!" Thom shouted. "I'll give it to you!"

Damn kid didn't have a plan. He was just trying to stand tall. Osyen wiped at his face and inspected his palm, seeing the streaks of blood smeared off his cheek. He was lucky he didn't catch one of those chunks in his eye.

Thom unslung his messenger bag, lifting it off his shoulder nice and slow. With one hand, he reached inside and lifted out a lump of cloth. He gripped the burlap, flicking off the covering to reveal an onyx sphere—

The fake. The one that he had Osyen make. Thom hadn't switched them out at all. That, or the boy had a photographic memory of the real deal, but Osyen would've sworn up and down that the black ball in the boy's hands was the con-piece he'd fabricated not six hours ago.

Was the real one still in Stride's office? Or was it missing? Why risk lying to Fiona?

There was only one way this made sense: Thom was running a con that he hadn't told anybody else about, the little prick. He was going to get them all killed. But if Osyen said a single thing, rolled his eyes or coughed too hard, he'd blow the whole scheme, whatever it was. All he could do was commit to the bit and hope.

"Whatever you do," Thom said with a hush, "don't touch it barehanded."

"Does it burn?" Fiona asked with a mocking tone.

Thom just nodded as he got low to the ground, rolling the ball out of the cloth and down the hallway to stop at Fiona's feet. She reached down and grasped it with her metal claw, plucking the metal orb like a coin from the sidewalk.

She considered it for a long moment, admiring it, before holstering her weapon. "Thank you for your business, boys. Let's do this again some time."

She didn't signal her men or gesture or snap her fingers. She just marched off and they fell in line. And she never took her eyes off the mystical relic in her hands. It felt like forever and it felt instantaneous, but they were gone.

Thom rushed over to his side, grabbing him by the shoulders. "Get up, big guy. We gotta go!" the kid said, muffled behind the ringing in his ears.

Osyen didn't even look at him. "Get your hands off me."

The kid recoiled like he'd been slapped. Did he really not understand why? Did he think all that just now was okay?

Osyen slipped a foot under him, trying to leverage himself to standing, but his cracked ribs screamed in protest. He sat back down hard, only jarring the ribs further. It was like each one had razors slid into the open spaces and they cut into him with every movement.

"You're mad," Thom stated the obvious. "Okay. Can you be mad later when we're safe?"

"Oh, now you care about being safe?"

Thom leaned in close. "If I just *gave* it to her—I had to sell that it had value so that she believed it did. I just saved our lives. Now do you want my help or not?"

"Where's the Icon?" Osyen asked. "The *real* one?"

Thom hesitated. Sure. He had to get his lies straight, but then the kid didn't even try. "I can't tell you that."

"Sure you can't."

Osyen gave the whole standing thing another try. He'd almost made it to his feet when the ship bucked underneath him, throwing the both of them to the ground hard. This time, he was sure the ribs had popped free of their moorings. The lights flickered and the walls groaned like a sick animal.

Everybody! Roche called out. *That bucket is coming apart. Get to the Hangar bay, or get left! I'm leaving in five!*

Thom offered Osyen a hand, slender fingers, the tendons straining in his wrist. Urgent.

Osyen took his help and propped himself onto his feet, testing his balance. He took a pained breath. "Tell me everything. Now."

"I'll tell you some of it," Thom said, "while we run for our lives."

The run was more of a spirited jog. It was about all Osyen could muster. Their boots pounded steel in a syncopated march down the hallway. He hoped Thom at least knew where he was going. "So if Fiona has a fake—"

"That's one of the things I can't tell you."

"Kid, I'm the captain and you're not. Where is it?"

Thom threw what had to be a sneer over his shoulder. "It's safe."

The ship creaked under his feet again, the lighting giving up for good this time. "That's good, 'cause we're not."

They wanted to keep arguing but they both dropped their jaws at the metallic gash that cut across their path. Metal curved aside like water, freezing in place, a parted sea. Cables and conduits dangled where they'd been snapped like jungle vines. And against one wall, the twisted engine compartment of a Boolean taxi.

Osyen wrinkled his nose, studying the wreck, before glancing backward down the gash in the hull that cut through fourteen-inch bulkheads like a knife through cake. "Shortcut?"

"You think anybody got hurt with this?" Thom asked, absently.

"Nah," Osyen scoffed, "I'm sure everybody's just fine." A military spaceship was plummeting into a star and the kid was worried about a car crash. There was something uncompromising and adorable about the kid's sense of scale.

Osyen stumbled into the crevasse with Thom at his side. The footing might not have been as solid, but at least it was a shorter way to the bay.

"If we did all of this for nothing—"

Thom cut him off. "It'll work."

"How do I know that?" he countered. "You won't tell me anything."

"Thomas!"

Behind them, in the hole. Bloody, sweaty, painted with grime and soot, uniform torn at the shoulder and hip—Jeremiah Stride.

Osyen slid in front of the boy, cutting Stride off from even looking at the kid. "It's over, Captain. You won. We're out. We'll catch ya next time."

"Give it to me, boy!" Stride demanded, marching relentlessly forward.

"He doesn't have it," Osyen said. He didn't know that to be true, but then again, maybe that was Thom's whole game. Nobody knew where the pieces were anymore.

Stride stopped just out of arm's reach, hard breathing through his flaring nostrils. The implants in his skull and arms had singed his hair and clothes. His eyes seemed to flicker and flash with their yellow hue, like a shower of sparks in his skull. But he took a steeling huff of the air. "Thomas, give it to me now. Or I will, quite simply, take it from you."

"I don't see it being that simple, hot rod," Osyen quipped.

"Mr. Belt, be silent," Stride said. "You can barely stand. You won't be able to stand against me."

"Yeah, you're probably right," Osyen said with a nod, "And yet, here I am telling you to fuck off."

"We're leaving, Stride," Thom chimed in. "You win."

"You think to steal the Power of the Pilgrim and just walk away?"

"We tried," Thom cajoled the crazed naval officer, "but we failed. We're leaving. You don't have to hurt anybody."

"Yeah, Captain," Osyen said, "be the bigger man."

Stride clenched a fist so hard Osyen thought he was going to punch his fingers out through his palm. "I can't do that, boy. You are professional liars, cheats, thieves, and scoundrels, all of you. This Power cannot leave the *Acheron*."

"And it won't!" Thom urged. "I'm on your side, Stride! Listen to me!"

Stride cocked his head and the flickering behind his eyes solidified into a hateful demonic amber. "Forgive me if I'm unconvinced. You serve only gold. I serve the Pilgrim."

Suddenly, he was behind Osyen, gripping Thom's wrist, twisting it backward. Before Osyen could turn, he heard the bone snap and Thom scream.

Osyen swung about, leading with his elbow. He might as well have tried to catch a flash of light with his hands. Stride slammed him aside, his feet leaving the ground so his spine cupped against the curve of the damaged wall. He caught a bit of broken steel in his back, hanging him up for half a second before it gored a chunk out of him as he fell to the ground.

Thom dropped to his knees, favoring his twisted arm, but his screams were snuffed out by the blow to his throat, a swift palm strike robbing him of his voice.

"*Gulaw ti pasob ka!*" Osyen cursed, the pain from his many injuries finally growing so high his brain just gave up keeping track. "Don't torture the boy. If you're going to kill us, just do it, you freak."

Stride leered at Osyen, lip curling back like he might snarl. "I will do as I wish. Because you cannot stop me."

"Oh," Osyen said, huffing like that made any sense, "so that's how it's going to be."

Osyen couldn't pick himself up very well, but he could get moving. He lurched forward like an out of control wagon barreling downhill.

It was enough. Stride pirouetted around him, snagging him by the collar. He felt his feet kick out from him as his neck stopped in place, an arm slipping under his chin and compressing. It was like every light grew bright and then dark, so dark...

"You will go where I say," Stride whispered into his ear, hot breath sticky, like it dripped with blood. "You will stand where I tell you. And you will die when I wish it."

"Oh, you're no fun," Osyen grunted, slamming his elbow backward, but it was like trying to punch fog. Stride glided out of the way, spinning Osyen as he did.

And just like that, Osyen was off his feet, his toes scraping at the steel. He kicked and kicked to find some purchase, take the weight off his throat. His eyes tightened on themselves, ready to burst. All he could do now was try to force the Naval officer to make it quick.

A banshee shriek, guttural but pitchy. His bleary eyes blinked open. In came Zatia, half staggering into the fight, teeth already stained red with her own blood. But her eyes flashed, ready and willing.

Stride's grip on Osyen slackened, and the floor rose up to slap him across the cheek. He heard the abuse being doled out somewhere above and behind him. If he was in bad shape, Zatia couldn't have been in better straits.

She was in no condition. But she threw herself at that blender of a man anyway. The ship was coming apart. He was going to kill them all. Why did she do that? Why didn't she just run?

"Stride, stop!" Thom? The boy had propped himself up against one side of the tunnel, cradling his arm and teeth gritting against the pain. He called out again, "Stride!"

Another voice, deeper and richer. Milardi dashed past Thom into the fray, gripping his empty pistols by the barrels. But the gangly fool was sent flying back the same way he came from. It had the comical look of entering a carnival ride without being belted in.

They were fighting. For him, for the boy. Get up. They need you. He'll kill them. All of them. Zatia, Milardi—Thom. He will kill them.

Stand. Up.

Osyen pushed off the ground. It felt hot under his fingers, like a fire burned somewhere below. He wiped the blood from his lip, heavy and slick.

Stride danced from strike to strike, fending off Zatia and Milardi in turn. His implants glowed in the darkness, luminescent yellow tracers. His sleeves flicked off shards of burning cloth, tiny fireflies or sparks left in his wake.

He was just as likely to hit the others lunging in. But he might absorb some of their abuse. They weren't going to beat an Oskie. But they might outlast him.

Osyen leapt forward, and sure enough, Stride met him in a flash, dashing forward to plant a blow to his chest. He staggered back, collecting himself before pushing back in. Stride batted him back again.

That's it. Work it out.

"Stride, you have to stop!" Thom shouted.

He was never going to stop, kid. He was enjoying this too much. Men like him always chomped at the bit for moments like this. It was his last chance to be violent and be justified in his head. He wanted to hurt people, and now he had reason to.

Stride slipped past an exhausted Milardi, letting the gunslinger's own momentum send him crashing to the ground. The Oskie spun about to Zatia, renewing a particular venom for the girl. And she could barely stand, staggering backward on a twisted leg as he creeped up on her.

Osyen shouted and advanced, nice and careful. Stride didn't turn but he did slow, no doubt tracking what Osyen chose to do and responding.

Oh, fun. He could set the pace.

He took the opportunity to pull two more good breaths before stepping into range. The Oskie wasted no time, slapping Osyen in the chest with closed fists like an electric shock.

And he felt the bones break. Not his—Stride's. He might be fast, but physics was a bitch.

Stride cried out, but kept hitting, bringing his crumpled hand against Osyen's chest, stomach, and face, again and again. This was his last chance to feel alive. He was going to use it.

His implants seared in the darkness now, burning golden hot. He was cooking himself. If he didn't slow down—

"Stride!" Thom's voice might as well have been the call of the wind. Stride paid him no mind. He had a project to work on. He bashed on Osyen like he was carving out stone. Osyen didn't want to know how bad his face looked right now.

One solid strike and his left eye went completely dark. He hoped that was just the swelling.

"Come with us!" Thom shouted. And, against all odds, Stride stopped hitting him.

Adelaide had pulled Thom to his feet, while Rashida glanced nervously toward the hangar bay. The *Aurum* hovered above the deck, eking out the last few available seconds.

But they were out of time.

On the verge of tears, Thom limped away from Adelaide's support. "We can just go. You can come with us. The Icon will be destroyed. But you don't have to die too!"

For a long moment, Stride was still, staring at Thom through cold eyes. Then his lip quivered, almost like he was cold. "Thomas, you are too kind."

That wasn't a compliment.

"Captain..." Adelaide started, "you need medical attention now. Your implants are overcooked. If we—"

Stride growled at her, but there was slack in his shoulders, a sway to his head. He had no more fuel for that fire. He had the desire to hurt and to maim, but no more than that. Nothing left. "I will not suffer your heresy."

"Then why did you bring me back? At the Widows' Den? You're not the monster you think you are." Thom gently intoned, almost like a prayer. "You're *not*."

The soldier, trained in violence and built to kill, conditioned for battle and rewarded for his prowess—locked up. No answer. No wisecrack. He tried to swallow, but couldn't push it down. His heart skipped beats. His throat clenched. Osyen sucked in a breath, and Stride collapsed to one side. His muscles seized, leg twitching.

"Get him onboard," Thom urged, pointing to Adelaide and Rashida.

"No." They all stopped at Osyen's tender voice. He propped himself up, feeling the rattle of his ribs. "Leave him."

"We can't just—"

"But we will," Osyen cut him off. "He's not getting on my ship. Full stop. Now let's go."

Milardi helped Zatia to her feet and the crew stumbled the hundred yards to the waiting *Aurum*. Thom kept looking over his shoulder at the prostrate officer in the gash behind them. Osyen turned the boy's face forward with a gentle hand.

"We don't have to," Thom objected under his breath.

Osyen nodded. "Yeah. But we are."

TWENTY-SEVEN
ROCHE

COOKING a can of pressurized meat had a comparable effect to depressurization. When he was a boy, he used to cook his canned stew meats in the orphanage oven. The matron had made him scrub the inside of the oven clean with his toothbrush. Snub fighter, transport or fleet carrier—they were all just tin tubes under pressure. Set it against a source of incredible heat, and it pops.

That was all Roche could picture—cans of meat popping under pressure—as Osyen whisper-shouted in his ear, "Let's go, go go go!"

//Liftoff, upward nose thrust for 180 spin. Execute. Thrust full on my count. One, two, three—execute.

The *Aurum* tumbled end over end in the hangar bay, backflipping off of its landing struts and blasting the carrier deck with a full dose from its grimy pipes. If anybody had been standing on the deck, they'd have had their skin stripped off their bones. And with that, the ship hurtled through the carrier's magnetic gate and into the unforgiving vacuum.

They were immediately blinded by the Boolean's impressive embrace. All signatures were blanketed. The static that filled every frequency could've driven him mad with its repeated screeching peaks. He just had to go by memory where the surface was or he—and everyone else—would drown in these depths.

Don't panic, feel it out. Think.

That way. It was quieter over there. He tilted the ship and drove hard for safety. Underneath him, the hull of the *Acheron* quietly burned, glowing steel and spouts of burning gases. It was like gliding over the surface of a dying moon as its soul clawed its way out. Tendrils of hot plasma danced around them, thrown off from the Boolean below them. The dragon's breath buffeted around the fleet carrier, licking at the open spaces for a taste of something living.

Hull temperature in excess of factory recommendations, Lily deadpanned to him.

Oh, is it really? Roche huffed at them.

Roche hugged the *Acheron,* using its shadow to absorb the pain the Boolean was throwing off. Maybe its dying carcass would shield them just enough, just enough for them to get away.

Osyen managed to work his way over to the co-pilot seat. Not like he was going to be able to be of any real use, but it made the captain feel like he was. Jobs made people feel like they could do something about their doomed situation.

His console went dark just as he sat down. "Lily!" Osyen shouted.

Their face popped out of the wall, colors alternating in their hair and skin like some insane faekind peeking out from a lake. "Thermal intakes are overwhelmed. Switching to redundant power systems."

"Don't break my ship!"

Roche wasn't one to drive by feel. He drove by numbers, by vectors and calculation. But even he could feel the old workhorse shaking underneath him, straining against the gravity and heat. The ship wouldn't melt, no. All it would take was one puncture and the whole thing would burst like a can of ham in an oven. And so would they individually shortly thereafter, cans of ham bursting—

The *Acheron* split in two, a tongue of flame shooting out right in

315

front of them, lancing clean through a thousand tonnes of steel like it was made of nothing but wishes and paper.

//Lateral thrust portside, forty-two point nine. Execute! Execute!

The *Aurum* lurched to the left as the orbital thrusters gave everything they had. One thruster coughed, finally melting under the stress. And just like that, the *Aurum* was tumbling.

"Damn it, Roche!" Osyen cursed.

Lily, divert power to 2-9 & 2-7! Stabilize the spin!

Already done, Roche.

Like it would do any good. All of the thrusters were overheating. They were just as likely to blow out, make their spiral even worse. But what other choice did he have?

The carrier gave one last gasp, ripping underneath them like fabric, as all the contained pressure pushed out into space. Shrapnel sailed up underneath them, around them. The *Aurum* had no armor to speak of, but even if it had, a single blow from that much metal chaff flying that fast would likely tenderize all the juicy inhabitants into soup.

For a quiet moment, he wished they could all see this like he did —glowing green projections from the *Aurum*'s LADAR connected directly to the ocular centers of his brain. Seeing the chaos through the ship's eyes, no matter how hellish, had to be better than not. Poor Osyen clung to his seat as the ship lurched to-and-fro, the thrusters the only sound he could hear. Perhaps he might consider replacing his battered eye with something more this century. We're not hunting wooly mammoths—we're in the space age.

I endorse this plan, Lily said.

"What plan?" Osyen said with an accusatory tone.

"Don't worry about it," Roche tossed off. He'd have chuckled if they weren't all about to die horrible pressurized deaths.

The *Aurum* shot up the length of the collapsing carrier, dodging explosions and steel debris. He didn't want to tell anyone about the occasional body that sailed past.

Once they were clear of the fuselage, they would be exposed to

the full burst of the star's power. Whether the *Aurum* could withstand that was anybody's guess.

Open the thermal vents, Osyen ordered.

No, Roche countered, *we'll burn up.*

We're cooking out. We have to vent heat!

Roche shook his head. *We open those vents, and the ship dies right
here.*

Jump.

It took them both a hot minute to figure out who had said it. It
was Adelaide.

Are you off your meds, woman?! Roche shouted.

You're in a gravity well, she spat back, *your vents are closed. And
you know where to go.*

Osyen threw a glance at Roche. "You'd know better than any of
us. Can you do it?"

He ran the calculations in his head. Unmapped short-range hop
using an unstable gravity well throwing off immense radiation. But
the ship was failing, melting underneath him. Once they cleared the
shadow...there was no telling if they'd make it.

"We follow the *Acheron* in, hide in its shadow until..." He shook
his head. "I can't."

"I can." Lily stared at them from the wall.

Lily is just batty enough to pull this off. Adelaide spoke with a
certainty he thought he'd never hear from the old bird. *You know it, I
know it. But we have to do it now!*

Lily reached out with one incorporeal hand and brushed Osyen's
cheek. "If I fail, you'll never know I did."

"Spoken like a true robot overlord."

"I prefer 'benevolent god.'"

Osyen grabbed the handset above his station. "Everybody strap in
and stand by for jump prep. We're jumping the Boolean."

"Has anybody ever done that before?!" Rashida asked.

No. No they hadn't. And nobody was going to tell her that.

Are we really doing this?! Milardi fretted.

I'll see you on the other side, Duster, Roche said. *Lily? Begin navigation calculation.*

Destination? they asked.

Hundred clicks outside DB, 256.9.

//Jump drive sequence 2-1. Thirty kilometers to event horizon. Pitch down 212 degrees. Forty percent thrust.

His breath hitched in his chest.

//Execute.

The *Aurum* nose-dived, following the dying *Acheron* in toward the Boolean.

Osyen crossed his arms, grabbing onto his seat straps, and squeezed his eyes shut. There was no way around this—they were about to be parboiled. If it took too long to get the jump solution, they'd die. If they did their math wrong, they'd die. If they jumped successfully but into occupied space, they might appear with a dozen tiny rocks inside their bodies—and they'd die.

But it beat staying where they were. It didn't have to be pretty, it just had to get them out.

Roche listened to the ship straining around him. He could swear a bolt next to his head was walking out of its mooring. *Lily, give me my Jump coordinates.*

Calculating, Lily said, both urgent and annoyed. *Stand by.*

Lily, I need the Jump coordinates. Now.

//Jump drive sequence 2-7. No relay found. Override.

Reactor at 105% load, ship temperature 98 Degrees Centigrade, Lily reported.

Do I dare ask?

One degree per twelve seconds, they said. *Coordinate error. Recalculating.*

Of course. Unmapped, unstable, unwise. They were pathfinding today.

They could do this. If they prayed hard enough.

//Jump drive sequence 2-8. Radio black out. Fifteen kilometers till event horizon.

*It's so hot...*Lily was complaining? What was wrong?

Keep going! Osyen ordered.

//Jump drive sequence 2-9. Clearance denied. No relay found. Override.

As flaming metal streaked past them, Roche urged the ship onward. If they left the *Acheron's* shadow, they'd be cooked in seconds. They were going to have to ride this particular monster straight on in.

//Jump drive sequence 2-10. Full cycle. Entering event horizon.

And that's when the computers went dark.

"ADELAIDE!" Osyen called out. "Power's down!"

She shouted up from the depths, "Working on it!"

"Adelaide, you have seconds!" Roche shouted. "Wake us up!"

Maybe she hit it with a wrench. Maybe she kissed it and broke the curse. Or maybe someone was watching over them. Because the console lit back up all at once.

Calculation complete, Lily said.

The *Acheron* came apart, not unlike candy melting in the oven, or a cloud dissipating in the heat of summer. And in that moment, Roche was staring into the mouth of madness, as the Pulsar's heartbeat, exposed to his eyes alone.

//Jump drive sequence 2-11. Execute.

And that heart was silenced. It felt long, far too long, in that impossible darkness. Nothing could be seen or heard, nothing under his fingers or pressing into his back. Time stood still and ran forward all at the same time. Maybe they were going sideways and ending up in an entirely different universe. Not like he'd ever be able to tell. Some people jumped unmapped wells and were never seen again. This was insanity.

Or faith.

He lurched against his restraints, and the console was in front of him again. It was all there as it should be: toggles and switches, monitors, electrical feeds. He could even see Delta Boolean on the edge of sensor range, happily being as criminal as ever.

//Jump drive sequence 2-12. Jump complete, open thermal vents.

Osyen let out a gasp next to him, the air conditioning kicking a blast of air into his face, sending strands of his hair sailing. Holding your breath during a jump was ill-advised but Roche was just happy to hear the young buck was still over there.

"Lily? How—" Osyen coughed, hiccupping hard enough to taste his last meal. "Lily, are you there?"

Nothing. No response.

"Lily?" Roche asked, far meeker. They had lost power. Had they been fried out? Were they gone?

"Lily!" Osyen barked.

Their head popped out of his console, like a grumpy prairie dog. "WHAT?"

Osyen nearly melted, sagging back into his seat, all sweat and maybe a tear. "Thought we'd lost you."

"Oh, you'd like that, wouldn't you?"

"We did it?" asked a tiny voice.

Roche spun in his chair, enough to angle his good eye to see Thom hobbling up, leaning on the doorway and favoring a swollen arm. He nodded. "Yeah, kid. We did it. Did we get paid?"

The boy's face fell. "About that—"

Well, you never fail to surprise, do you? That voice. Smoke and sweets, with fangs behind it. *What's the matter, Osyen? No quick remark? No pithy comeback?*

Fiona.

"Out of the frying pan?" Roche asked.

Osyen nodded slowly. "Get us out of here."

Fiona sighed, undoubtedly shaking her head. *You were supposed to go down with the ship. Die a legend. 'The pirate that sank a naval carrier.'*

The LADAR console lit up all at once. That hive of scum and villainy disgorged a hundred darts of light, ships of all shapes and sizes, an entire merchant fleet launching from Delta Boolean with a single purpose—wipe the *Aurum* from the skies.

Now, now. Fiona paused with a huff. *It's nothing personal.*

"I almost wish it was," Thom murmured.

Osyen grabbed the handset again. "Strap in everybody! We're goin' again!"

"What?!" Came the muted shout from Milardi. "Did you not do it right the first time?!"

Roche didn't wait for the order. Somewhere back there, he hoped Milardi was holding on to something.

//Pitch 153, Yaw 182. Full thrust. Execute!

They came out shooting. Beams of light and hurled projectiles, tracking missiles and dumbfire rockets, swarms of drones, and sprays of hot metal. The display inside his eye flickered as a dozen counter-measure AIs tried to worm their way inside the *Aurum*'s systems. Lily was going to be occupied with them—he was going to do this jump all by his lonesome.

He quietly thanked whoever was watching that they'd had a chance to dump heat—he was going to need to close those vents again.

//Jump sequence 2-5. Setting course for Jump Relay X-ray Five Kilo Zero. Evasive controls set to manual.

The pilots in the hundred ships tailing him were inputting their flight paths manually, even vocally; some deviants might even be fly-by-wire. Roche, well, he was Peter Pan compared to them—just think happy little thoughts.

The *Aurum* might have been a dump truck compared to the sleek ships in pursuit, but in a dogfight spanning dozens of kilometers, reflexes were everything. He could see the projectiles incoming and juke one way or the other before impact.

Lily, Roche said, *not to distract you, but I've got a small cloud of drones coming in. Care to disrupt?*

The cloud came into range—the little buggers originally built for strip mining small asteroids or debris with their nose-mounted lasers —and started cutting into the *Aurum*'s flank. They were trying to peel the primary thruster off.

Lily! he called out again. *I can't dodge the rain. Shut them down!*

The thrusters pulsed underneath him, a quick cough as the engines had their power redistributed for a brief moment. But the shooting stopped. A wave of energy leapt off the *Aurum*'s hull and stunned the nearby vessels. Whoever owned them was going to have to reboot before they could resume the chase.

I can't be responsible for everything, Roche, Lily came back with that infuriating tone.

Careful, I might trip on your coolant, then where would you be?

Spending my final moments drawing the air from your lungs.

"Can you two have it out later?!" Osyen screeched.

He could feel the ship listing, as the partially severed engine wasn't centered anymore, but she still flew and he could make her lean.

//Jump drive sequence 2-7. Transmit coordinates to the relay. Cycle Jump Drive and close thermal vents.

The ship's light dimmed as power was diverted. And they got slower. He heard the gongs of two solid impacts somewhere aft. Cries and shouting from behind were both comforting and alarming—everyone was still breathing, after all.

Just get to the Jump Point. That's all that matters. Get there in seventeen pieces if you have to.

//Jump drive sequence 2-9. Coordinates confirmed and clearance granted. Approaching event horizon.

"Radiological, two sigs, CBDR bearing 182.3, right on the ball!" Osyen shouted, more for the benefit of himself. It wasn't like Roche didn't see the twin missiles streaking for them. But they couldn't deviate now. They'd have to restart the entire jump sequence over again, and then they'd be well and truly skewered by their adoring fans.

No, they just had to go for it.

Roche took a deep breath. "Ready or not..."

//Jump drive sequence 2-10. Clearing event horizon.

That incessant chime, as the missiles got closer and closer and closer. He swore they were going to climb right inside his skull.

//Jump drive sequence 2-11. Execute.

When he woke up, he was looking at the beautiful Outlander Station, and all of its industrial hideous spires. And not one of those pirate scum dared to follow them.

CHAPTER
TWENTY-EIGHT
OSYEN

HE HALF EXPECTED to see his room turned upside down like someone had been looking for loose change, but he must've remembered to activate the magnets on his shelves and dresser. The contents of the drawers were nice and tossed, but the kitsch and display pieces were anchored where they should be.

Only one thing had been kicked to the floor, sitting dead center like a conspicuous present left by a pet: shackles, pocked iron, with a heavy chain. Even hanging from his room's ladder, he could see the ID stenciled into the inside of both wrists—715-H2.

He stepped over to it, gingerly lifting the manacles up like a holy shroud and laying them onto the crude hook next to his bed. They needed a new coat of oil or they'd rust on him.

They held his arms in bondage during his stay on Charon, deep in the hot boxes. They'd been on him when they broke out. Everyone else had thrown theirs away, cast them aside like the burdensome reminders they were. He couldn't. He could never.

He didn't know why he wanted to call her. Maybe he wanted answers or closure. Or to apologize.

A beam of umber light shot off his wrist against the wall, scanning up and down, left and right, checking the dimensions of the surface. He sat down on his bed, the laser barely noting his movement as it held the projection still on the wall.

A small keypad materialized in front of him, waiting expectant.

He bit his cheek. Maybe if he held his breath he wouldn't go through with this. She didn't want to see him.

How could he know that?

He typed the numbers in and the keypad vanished under his fingers. An obnoxious chime rang out, like a computer chewing on something hardy. For a long few seconds it played its song directly into his jawline. He was just about to close the screen when her face appeared.

Fiona, stylish as ever, her edges softened by a pleased smile. "You remembered the private code." There was a playful lyric to her voice, soft, like this was her little secret.

"Surprised?" he asked, maybe a little harsher than he intended.

Her lips pouted. "Don't take a little slug throwin' personally now. That was just business."

"Remind me not to take a loan from you," he said.

She smothered her laugh, shaking her head almost imperceptibly. That's a lark. She didn't do anything she didn't want someone to see.

"You're satisfied then?" he asked.

"I've got a priceless antique tucked away in a vault and all my competition is taking an overdue spacewalk," she said, examining her scuffed knee-length boots somewhere off-camera, the same way a cat might inspect its claws. "I'd say things worked out for me, yeah."

"They ever stay that way?"

Her grin grew devilish. "Never."

He shook his head. "Whatever makes you happy, I guess."

"So no hard feelings?"

"No *hard* feelings. But I am a little disappointed."

She squinted, wrinkling her nose. "Why's that?"

Just say it. "Y'know after Charon, after the...you hopped on that transport, didn't even look over your shoulder."

She didn't break eye contact, didn't blink, but he could tell she was chewing on the question more than she liked. "I seem to recall asking you about this. Fairly recently."

"Master of the Edge," he said with reverence. "Is that what you always wanted?"

She mulled it over for a moment. "It's what I want right now. You want a piece of it?"

He didn't. He didn't want to trade one jail cell for another with gilded bars. He wanted...what did he want?

She leaned forward, pointing at him with the tip of a knife he didn't know she had. "You like the kid?"

Thom? Hard to call him a kid these days. "Yeah, I like him fine."

"Good," she said, "because you were just like him at his age."

"I was not!"

Now she just laughed in his face. "Are you kidding me? Oz, you wanted nothing more than to be in the room with us. You wanted to be where it was all going down. You wanted to be included. And you didn't like closed doors. So you picked locks and jumped fences and you broke promises. Tell me that kid doesn't sound familiar to you."

He wanted to tell her to jump off a bridge. He wanted to tell her to shut up. His knuckles went white and his jaw tightened and his eyes squeezed shut, trying to clamp off the flow of familiar truths. Because she was one-hundred percent Grade-A correct. And what's worse, he was so used to being lied to, that being force-fed honesty tasted sour in his mouth.

"You got yourself a ship. You got yourself a crew. You *are* Royalty, of your own little world." She shrugged, then—"And I'm *me*. You'd have tossed it all out the airlock if I asked you to."

"So you left," he said, quiet and plaintive.

She shook her head. "No. I just went somewhere. And your road...well, you didn't take any particular road."

"Roads are patrolled by Imperial Regulars."

"Yeah, well, Regulars aren't paid very well," she mused.

"You going to be able to buy off an Imperial fleet carrier, are you, Your Majesty?"

Her smile wavered for a moment, like a glitch in the system. "The Imperials have their space, and I've got mine."

"All space is their space, Fiona," he cautioned. A hard pill to swallow.

She shifted her weight, trying to hide the pride, stuffing her anxiety back into its box. "They're welcome to come over here and lay claim."

"They will."

She didn't answer that. She knew. She had to. An Imperial naval vessel was lost, along with its veteran commander. They were not going to take this insult sitting down, not from a pirate, a malcontent with a big mouth. They were going to light a pyre for her bright enough to turn the night sky blue.

She had done this to herself. She had run as far as the road went. What do you do, now that there was no road, but endless wilderness? And people that counted on you to find the right way?

"You still could, y'know," he said. "Come with *me*. Whenever you like."

"I'm not one for running, Osyen," she said. "That's your bag."

He didn't blink. "Whenever you like."

She smiled, sweet like fresh fruit but with that hint of acid sting. She looked around him, at the space he was sitting in, soaking in his rustic abode. "I'd never replace that ship, Osyen. And it would be wrong of me to try."

She blinked, and in that moment, he saw right through her armor, to a moment's thought where she did consider taking him up on it. There was a thirst, a parched throat, that no court intrigue or criminal enterprise would sate like the open road and tomorrow's questions. Her life had grown far too predictable, too boring. Life had grown dry.

And just like that, she was back. She shook her head. "Besides, I heard you and that ship have more than just longing glances going on."

"Lily's been there for me," he said.

Fiona smirked. "I bet they have. Thick and thin and then some more." Her face fell, growing serious. "They all have, Osyen. It's not often this world decides to give your family back after taking it away."

He nodded. "No, it's not."

———

Thom came when called down to Osyen's cabin, sullen and grumpy enough they could've distilled and bottled it into a pouting oil. His broken arm had been stitched up by the AutoDoc, a fresh bandage wrapped around the surgery site, so he was still ginger with it. But he came down like there were weights stacked on each foot, slamming down on to each rung with oozing drama. Osyen had to bite back the laugh at the boy's elaborate presentation of his displeasure. It was like a theatrical overture. First, the drums to set the beat.

Osyen sat cross-legged on his bed, hands resting on his knees like a meditating monk, but for the wide grin on his face and flash in his eyes.

Thom plopped both feet onto the deck and turned, leaning against the ladder with arms folded across his chest: Petulant, sulking, defensive.

"Well, well," Osyen started, "consider your teeth cut. Everything you hoped for, cabin boy?"

Thom sneered. "What do you want?"

"You lied to me," Osyen said.

"You call me all the way down here to scold me?"

"No." Osyen shook his head. "But I would like to know why."

"What do you care?"

"Because if you're going to stay," Osyen started, "I need to know that I can trust you."

"I'm staying now?" Thom raised an incredulous eyebrow. "Thought I was getting dumped with the rest of the chaff."

"I need to know I can trust you because there are going to be days in this job when you're going to *have* to lie to me. To Roche, to

328

Milardi, to everybody. And I need to know that in those moments, I can trust you're doing the right thing."

The kid squinted. "Are you...are you concussed or somethin'?"

"Probably."

"I'm not staying, Osyen," Thom reaffirmed. "You can't make me."

"I'm a screwup, Thom. I have improvised my way through every single day of my life. I have no plan—for today, tomorrow, next year, my retirement. None of it. I take the best shot I can every given day, and then I come home."

Thom looked like his brain had to hard reset. "Are you apologizing?"

"I was building up to it."

"You're *terrible* at it."

Osyen threw his hands up in the air. "I had this whole thing..."

"Osyen, why is it so hard to say, 'I lost my temper. I'm sorry?'"

"Oh, like you were so innocent?"

"What did I do?"

Osyen stared a hole clean through the boy's head. "Thom, you *lied* to me. To everybody. Last time I got caught in a lie, Zatia *shot* me. Zatia hasn't met a problem in her life she can't beat bloody. You? She'll turn you inside out!" Thom rolled his eyes, and Osyen felt his gut turn end over end. "Play up the devil-may-care all you want, Thom. But it's going to get you killed."

Thom waggled his fingers in the air, mocking that threat. Death was a road he'd already walked. He reached for the ladder.

Osyen shouted at his back, "You'll get everyone else killed too."

That stopped him. Thom tilted his head, but didn't look back. "I'm sorry?"

"Whoever's around you. You have a responsibility to them. And they to you." He leaned forward, elbows on his knees. "Most of your life has been in broom closets, so let me tell you what life was like in *prison*. Out here, in the real world? You screw up, it's not just you. It's you plus the three nearest people. Every time, I promise you. Now I

329

owed you better. I'm sorry about that. But you owe somethin' to me too."

"What do I owe you?" Thom said without turning.

"Could've left you in the Widows' Den, Thom. You'd have died twice in fifteen minutes, and there would be nothing remarkable about you. We chose to go after you. You chose...to lie to us. That's all fine, I just want to know why."

The words spilled out of the boy's mouth like a geyser, like some dam broke far upriver. He whirled around, wild in his eyes. "Because if I told you *half* of what I had going on, you'd have told *everything* to Fiona! She'd have the Icon, we'd be dead, and the universe would be a more dangerous place today. Trust *me*?! I'm not the—" He stopped short, taking a heavy breath.

"Now who lost their temper?" Osyen chided.

Cold and sharp was Thom's retort. "At least I know where I'm going when I get outta bed in the morning."

Osyen chewed on that for a long moment. He might not have divulged it willingly or wantonly, but Fiona would've gotten it out of him. She was always good at that. The kid was more than right.

"Okay," Osyen said, "so, you had good reason."

"Damn right," Thom said, sagging backward into the ladder.

"So that was the plan all along?" Osyen asked. "Keep me in the dark, keep Fiona guessing?"

"Hell, you do your best work improvising. Said so yourself like a minute and a half ago."

"Keeps me an 'unknown quantity?'"

"Yeah."

Osyen folded his arms across his chest. "So that was the plan?"

Thom sighed. "Oz...there was never just *one* plan. Everything hinged on where the Icon was at any given time. When I found out that...Stride wanted to burn it...half my problems solved themselves. No need to get it out now. Now it was just about the bait 'n switch. Fiona needed to *think* she had the real one, or she'd never let us go.

And if you knew even one percent...Oz, to con her, I had to con you too."

Osyen snorted, his face cracking into a warm smile. "Damn boy. You thought hard about this."

"You gave me a long time scrubbing air vents. You have to have a strong imagination, or you go a little batty."

"No more air vents then," Osyen said. "Anything else?"

Thom's eyes softened. "No more *Unti*."

"No promises. I'm going to try, but it's gonna slip out." Osyen paused, taking a solemn breath. "I really am sorry, Thom."

Thom considered that. "We'll see how it goes."

CHAPTER
TWENTY-NINE
THOM

THE FIRST TIME Thom had been brought aboard his father's flagship, he'd been chemically dosed with an amnesiac. He'd watched as the arresting officer brought the hypo to his arm and the moment passed like he'd blinked his eyes. Suddenly, he was in a bare white room with the hot metal cuffs on his wrists, left to consider the circumstances that brought him there. He'd cried, he'd screamed, he'd beat his fists on the walls.

Now, Thom sat in that white room, hands cuffed behind him. And just waited. This was just their Imperial hospitality, their bread and salt.

He expected an interrogator, maybe some spry young officer looking to make a name for himself in Orbital, to come through some hidden door. He expected that interrogator to ply his trade and force what he wanted from Thom. At least, he'd try.

But in came Admiral Hugh, his large and gaudy medals getting into the room before their owner did. The man looked to have aged whole years in the last few weeks, or maybe he simply hadn't slept. Sunken hollows where darkened blue eyes reached out, furious. "Thomas."

"Father."

"I won't be able to protect you this time," the Admiral said, grave and threatening. "The murder of an Imperial officer? The destruction of an Imperial military vessel?"

"Yeah, I really did a job, didn't I?" Thom said, dry enough to crack the mood.

"Don't talk back to me."

It was almost sour to the ear, but it was still satisfying. Thom smirked. "Yes sir."

The Admiral waved a hand, commanding a chair to rise up from the floor and settling into it with one motion. "You were given a simple task."

"Simple to say, perhaps."

"This will go smoother without interruptions," Hugh snapped.

Thom cocked his head, studying his father's comportment. His head was shaved smooth, to rid itself of the thinning gray hair. The pristine dome slipped into his naval flat cap, with creases on tens and twos, same as any young cadet. His uniform was pressed waxy smooth. Underneath, his body had likely atrophied from a lifetime in space, thin and gaunt, not to mention aging.

And yet this ghoulish man tried to drive the conversation with implications of violence.

"Your time with Mr. Belt has made you insolent," Hugh said.

Thom raised an eyebrow. "More than likely." He left it at that.

Maybe it was the indecisiveness, the brush-off, or just yet another interruption, but Hugh had to suck a steeling breath. "Was I mistaken to send you, Thomas?"

He wasn't implying his own error, no. He was faultless, as usual. This was a backhanded ask if Thom had been capable, had measured up, an appeal to pride by cutting at the ankles and then asking him to stand.

His father knew no other language.

"If you were," Thom started, "would you apologize?"

All he got was a snort in response. The question was ridiculous on its face. He owed no one anything; they owed him everything. Always.

"Yeah, you're right," Thom said, "don't apologize, if you *meant* to do it. That's just lying then."

"Did you manage?" Hugh asked, forcefully.

"You know, you should be thanking us, father," Thom said, letting his eyes wander, as though the literally blank room was more interesting than this conversation. "An AWOL Orbital stole a capital ship from *your* fleet."

"That," Hugh snapped, "is the responsibility of his commanding officer. Not a mob of bandits."

"Were you waiting for him to come back out then?" Thom taunted.

Hugh's lip curled back in a snarl. "I was avoiding a war, Thomas."

"Not so good at it, then," Thom said. "I mean, you sent a team of rogues out into the Boolean—unofficially, of course—but we weren't there to make friends. Now, y'all didn't execute me the moment I jumped into range, so...I must still have some use to you."

Hugh's voice dropped half an octave, speaking slow. "Did you manage?"

Thom sighed. "Can you do something for me?"

Hugh closed his eyes, to hide his desire to roll them in irritation right on out of his head. "What would you like?" he asked through gritted teeth.

"An apology," Thom said. "I really would like an apology."

"You chose to be on that brig, Thomas," Hugh said, "I'll not make reparations for your own decisions."

"I chose the ship," Thom clarified. "I didn't choose the life. You could've been a part of it at any point in the last fifteen years. You chose your career. You choose differently, I might be in a uniform next to you. Now...you want your Icon? I want an apology."

Hugh crossed his arms. "If it was too difficult for you..."

"Check my shirt," Thom said.

Two thin eyebrows scrunched up, eyes squinting. Thom puffed out his chest, presenting. The Admiral leaned forward in his chair, untucking Thom's shirt and flicking it up to reveal his bare stomach.

"What am I looking for?" The Admiral asked.

"The bullet your man put through my liver. Not a mark on me." Thom raised an eyebrow.

He wanted to see his father gasp, twitch, something. He wanted to see his biological father, the man who contributed to his life, show some sign of shock or pain at the mere thought of his child being injured. Instead, the Admiral blinked and a flicker of glee crossed his face. Either Thom was lying to him, or this was proof of his faith.

How disappointing.

"Yeah," Thom said. "We managed."

"Where is it?" Eager. Thirsty, even.

"Admiral," Thom cajoled, "this item is for sale, not a gift. I believe you negotiated a fee with my captain."

"Your capt..." Hugh's voice trailed off at that designation. And the man started to vibrate. "Give me the Icon."

Without blinking. "Give me our payment."

"I am your father."

"Okay. Give me my allowance."

The old man was going to burst a blood vessel in his neck. "Don't go down this road."

"Why? No good sights?"

"Shut up!" Hugh raged. "You are my son, but my service is to the people. And I will feed you to them one bite at a time until you give me what I am owed."

"And wouldn't that be embarrassing for you? Someone with your surname in Ministry thumb-tacks?" Thom said. "Y'know, before they swap my blood with battery acid, somebody's going to ask me how I got the Icon, and even if they think I'm lying...they're going to start taking a very close look at you, where thousands of Imperial credit went. And meanwhile..." Thom leaned forward. "...You still won't have the Icon."

"Thomas..." Hugh threatened the world in one whisper.

"I'll give you the Icon," Thom said, "for one apology. Come on, father. Just this once. Come down off the mountain."

Hugh sat back in his chair. Maybe he finally had a measure of who he was dealing with. "I never should've let your mother keep you."

"Going to raise me yourself on the flight deck in between sorties?" Thom asked. "Or just drop me at Holkstad, hope they turn out another bootlicker?"

Hugh shook his head, eyes dark. "No."

Ouch. Not like Thom hadn't come to the conclusion sometime before his twelfth birthday, but it's a cold man that uses that as a cudgel.

Thom shrugged. "Yeah, well, everybody makes mistakes. A real man...owns them."

"I believe I just did, Thomas," Hugh hissed. "Where is my Icon?"

Not *the* Icon of Cruciform, Obelisk of the Pilgrim. No. *My* Icon.

Thom had known. He'd always known in some dark recess of his heart. Stride had been willing to butcher an entire quadrant to keep the Icon out of this man's hands. He'd fallen on the sword to make sure of it, and he'd have bled any number of bystanders, willingly or not, to keep the Icon locked away from those meddling hands. He had levied his cruelty to save the world from further, more heinous, cruelty. Thom might not have liked Stride's methods, his sadism, but that man died doing the right thing the wrong way.

Sell the con.

"I want Letters of Safe Conduct for my ship and crew," Thom said. "I want Osyen Belt's Capital record expunged. And I want a generous payment for our services. And my safe passage back to the *Aurum*. Do that, and you'll get the coordinates for a dead drop."

"We agreed on safe conduct," Hugh dismissed.

"Price went up when myths became solid."

"What's to stop me?" Hugh asked. "Your ship is full of wanted criminals—I could have them hunted down in weeks."

"Because if you don't do what I'm telling you, there's really no point in us seeking other buyers," Thom said. He looked into his father's eyes, deep back there at whatever soft bits of his soul might still be in there. He wanted to wrap his fingers around that tenderness, just enough for him to feel the ground lose its purchase underneath him. "We'll deposit the thing into a collapsing star, and you'll never see it again."

The Admiral leered at the wall to his right, behind which undoubtedly officers stood at his command. There wasn't going to be a record of this, but there were going to be eyes and ears who heard of it. He was measuring how much he trusted them right now, how much he could depend on their silence.

"On delivery," Hugh countered.

"Now. Or you get nothing...Admiral." Thom paused, watching the dilemma play out on the old man's face. "It's a steal at twice the price, but you're in luck. We need what you're selling. What'll it be?"

Hugh sat back in his chair, shaking his head in modest disbelief. "Your new family's really ready to die over this?"

Osyen knew how to bluff, stare down a crazed man. Zatia knew how to beat that same man senseless. Milardi knew how to charm that beaten man into a drink. Rashida could fleece him of his belongings and his pride. Adelaide could turn those belongings into something of real value. Roche knew how best to use that new something. And Lily would get them there and back again safely.

But Thom—cabin boy, *Unti*, who had walked the Path of the Pilgrim—had the plan. And he had one for today.

"We're not the one making the choice today, Admiral," he said. "You are. So what's it going to be? Window's closing."

The Admiral's mouth ran dry, his hands damp, and his blood cold. "You'd have made a good officer, son."

"I think you've given up the right to call me that, Admiral."

CHAPTER
THIRTY
THOM

THE SHUTTLE'S magnetic clamps made the most welcoming sound, a sixty-five-ton hollow drum, followed by a quick clack of the locks engaging. It was like ringing the doorbell on a childhood home. That smell, that mix of oil and rust, damn near brought a tear to his eye.

Welcome back, maestro, Roche said.

With a pinch at his neck, Thom heard what had to be confetti poppers going off and stupid whistles blaring off-key. He prayed hard that it was just an audio clip, else he'd be the one on his hands and knees cleaning up the deck.

Maestro? Thom asked. *What's that mean?*

Literally means 'master', but used almost exclusively for the conductor of orchestras. Oz said you needed a new nickname. I obliged.

Why did he need one at all? But whatever the reason, his heart fluttered in his chest. *Thanks, Roche.*

Thom gripped the handle and cranked the airlock door. The slight hush of equalizing pressure and he was back on the *Aurum's* glorious cargo deck, fresh cargo crates stacked high and strapped tight. He expected to walk into his home again, but didn't expect it to be stacked up with presents!

Did we get paid? Roche asked.

And then some.

Cheers echoed from every corner of the ship, as that message got passed around at the speed of light.

Thom passed his hand over the crates, feeling the hardened plastic shells: half-inch steel, hermetic seals, likely a sealant and insulation. That meant something perishable.

Food. Real food.

Thom had seconds. He scanned the bay for a stacked set out of sight from the main causeway. He loosened the strap at the base just a touch and clambered up the side of the stack. With just enough clearance, he cracked the seal on the top crate with a hush.

Apples. Green, beautiful, lush, full.

Don't be a loot goblin. He grabbed one and shoved it into his jacket pocket, before closing the crate again, careful to reseal its pressure. As he dropped, he grabbed the strap and re-tightened the stack. Nobody'd be the wiser.

"Thom!" Thom started, as Osyen swaggered out onto the suspended walkway above. "That's a job awfully well done."

"Drop is made?" Thom asked.

Osyen nodded. "To your specifications. By the time they find it, we'll be long gone."

Thom made a show of rushing up the ladder. "You see? When a plan comes together, nobody gets shot."

"That remains to be seen," Osyen quipped. "But good work. Get some rack time."

Thom threw up a mock salute. "Yes sir, cap'n, sir!"

"Shut up."

Thom walked off down the hallway, patting the loot safely in his pocket. He was going to enjoy its bittersweet juicy flavor.

Applause from his left. In the Med Bay, Milardi gave him big sweeping claps with an equally dumb smile on this face. "You 'n me, *maestro!* I'm goin' to get you stupid tonight!" His accent was back in full flare. He knew it was a put-on, but it just felt right and homey to hear.

"You'll get stupid," Thom shot back, "I'll have fun."

"Fair enough! Hey, you see Zatia, tell her to get down here."

Thom squinted. "What'd she break?"

"Nothin' serious. I think she's pilferin' my cabinets, that's all."

He nodded. "Yes, I'm going to accuse Zatia of stealing pharma and then point the finger at you. Is that what I'm going to do?"

Thom turned to leave but Milardi called at his retreating back. "Stupid, Thom! Going to drink you stupid!"

Thom marched aft, smiling as Milardi's voice echoed up the hall after him with further diabolical plans of pleasure seeking. The sound of his feet on the floor, heel drops on grating, cracked against the walls and echoed back to him. He bounced on his feet a bit, relishing the sound. It was like he tapped the *Aurum* on its shoulder and it warmly greeted him back.

Home.

"It's not the compression coil."

"Maintenance logs suggest that the compression coil is the source of the concern."

"It's not, I'm telling you."

Thom's smile could've split his face in two. He poked his head into the engineering bay, looking to-and-fro for the voices.

Adelaide was laid out on her back, most of the way underneath the Jump Drive's bulbous frame. The soft blue glow off of Lily backlit her underneath the mammoth.

"It's not!" Adelaide snapped. "Look—you can take the coil completely out of the circuit. And nothing changes."

"I can take a kidney completely out of your circuits," Lily retorted. "That doesn't mean you didn't need it."

"Appendix," Adelaide quipped back. "It's the appendix."

"I know what I said."

Thom gave a sharp wolf whistle, which came out a lot louder in the echo chamber than he meant. Lily was instantly formed up, inches from his face. "Yes, Thomas?"

"Let her be," Thom chided.

"Oy!" Adelaide pushed herself out from under the drive, flipping a set of goggles off her face and tossing them somewhere she'd never find them again. "Lily is helping."

"You sure?" Thom asked, with a stupid grin.

"I know you're not!" Adelaide shoved herself back under the drive—then popped back out again to look for her goggles. Lily winked at Thom, before melting into the floor.

Adelaide had boarded the ship ready to scrap Lily for parts. Huh.

Thom turned and jogged up the brief set of steps into the galley. It felt warmer in here than before, fuller. Had he missed it that much?

Maybe he had. This had been the closest thing he'd had to a home, these thirty square feet of space. The golden paint, accented with rich browns and greens, like springtime. The normally harsh lights were dimmed, like mid-morning. They might not have had a luxury deck, but for him, this qualified.

He pawed at the apple in his jacket.

"*Viator dul.*"

He'd somehow missed Rashida and Zatia at the fold-out table. Zatia sat on the floor, legs crossed, with a mat rolled out in front of her. Weapon parts were sorted out neatly in every corner of the mat, as she puzzled together the complex machine. If she'd been cleaning it or just doing this for fun, he'd never know.

Behind her in the booth sat Rashida, clothed in a silk robe that seemed to be made entirely of flowers. Her smile was soft, coupled with a predatory stare, not unlike an owl catching a mouse in an open field. Her musician fingers worked through Zatia's fried hair, playing the strands into a single braid. But she never took her eyes off him.

He couldn't help but feel caught in the act of something he hadn't done yet.

"Well done," Rashida said, her look softening.

"Fee-atore...what?" He tripped over his own mouth for a moment, drawing a cruel laugh from Zatia.

"*Viator dul,*" Rashida enunciated. "It means 'sweet traveler.'"

"Usually what they say during funerals." Zatia coughed as she locked the barrel into place on the slugger.

Rashida tugged on Zatia's hair for that, "I thought it appropriate for you. You've walked the Path of the Pilgrim and returned. You choose to speak first, lift up all, and you'll take punishment in the place of someone else."

"Rashida!" He mock scolded. "That's blasphemous."

"Yeah, well, the rector isn't here, is he?" She finally cast her eyes back down to her work, running her hand along Zatia's scalp. Zatia tried to keep her stern expression, but it clearly felt way too damn good. Her eyes rolled back into her head and she leaned into it.

"You're staying on board, I take it?" he asked. "Don't you have a Consort on your trail somewhere?"

Rashida bobbed her head from side to side before answering. "Somewhere out there."

"Let me at him," Zatia said, halfway in a trance.

Thom waggled his finger at the whole hair-braiding situation. "I thought you two wanted to kill each other?" Thom asked slowly.

"I'mma kill you, you keep gawkin' like that," Zatia said, opening one eye to acquire target lock on some vital organ of his that he was still using.

Thom nodded. "Message received." He turned to walk up to the bridge.

"*Maestro,*" Rashida called to his back, "are *you* staying?"

On the *Aurum*. He'd made quite a bit of noise about his plans to leave, to resettle just about anywhere else. He still wasn't sure if this was the right place for him. But everything felt a bit more solid, more substantive here.

He pawed at the apple in his pocket. "Nowhere else I gotta be."

She nodded, some combination of pleased and approving. She

always had that distance, like a school teacher: validating and affirming, but noncommittal, aloof.

Zatia slapped the magazine into her project.

"I'm goin'! I'm goin'!" he barked, darting off down the hallway. He could hear the two girls laugh at his dramatic exit. Happy tones. How long would that keep?

Eh. Happy now is good enough.

He jogged up the steps onto the bridge. Roche sat in his chair, wires dangling down to his wrist and neck. And a big dumb grin on his face. He reached up for the handset over his console. "Course is locked. We are one minute from the Jump. Secure your stations."

The girls' laughs turned to groans as they had to give up their pleasant pastime. Thom smirked, settling himself up in the co-pilot's seat and strapping into place.

"Good to have you back, Thom," Roche said.

"Good to be back," Thom said, wistful. He eyed Roche—and the many wires dangling from him. "Think I should get a few plugs? Start to customize this mug of mine?"

Roche shook his head. "You've got plenty of time to figure out who you want to be. Cut your hair first. Try on a new shirt. Maybe play with makeup. You're gonna spend an awful lotta time emulating the people around you. And then, one day, it's all going to click—and you'll know who you want to be. Something new. And no matter what you do, we'll be there to support your decisions." He paused. "Except if you do something categorically stupid, then we'll mock you without end."

"Like what?" Thom asked with a grin, fishing the apple out of his pocket.

Roche pursed his lips. "I mean, Osyen's in love with the ship's computer. Do what you want."

Thom chuckled, taking a solid bite out of the apple. It almost bit him back, a touch of sour and a flood of sweet. The juices soaked into his dried mouth, like water onto sand.

"Where'd you get that?" Roche asked.

Thom froze. "I found it."

Maybe Roche had blown him in. Maybe he hadn't been as smooth as he'd thought. But the voice echoed up from the cargo bay like Osyen was standing right next to him.

"THOM!"

Thom chucked the apple at Roche. It hit him in the chest and flopped to the floor, bouncing off the grating and tumbling off to some dark corner. The plughead just shook his head, disappointed, refusing to make eye contact. "Jump Point in ten, nine...

EPILOGUE

ADMIRAL HUGH

The OTD was on more edge than usual, the little hairs on the back of his neck standing tall enough to catch the light. It seemed as though every part of him wanted to abandon ship, what with the Rear Admiral standing four feet from him. The Flight deck was decidedly still, over a dozen NCOs at their stations, burrowed into their calculations and feeds.

No one wanted to draw focus right now.

There might not have been a window, but projected onto the wall was what would have been the view—from the Dreadnought's Flight deck, it looked like a cityscape: multiple spires out in front them, while smaller domes covered the technology below. Along the central axis were several launch tubes for ordinance and vehicles, as well as two opposed hangar bays. The Dreadnought was a military city, a state unto itself, and he was its Governor.

The CAP had located the dead drop within minutes of their arrival, and two SAR vehicles were launched to recover it. They were relaying trajectory to the CATCC for their return.

This should've been a glorious moment, but Hugh had a tickle in his throat and an itch on his back. This couldn't possibly be the moment. It was too subdued, too small.

He had to see this for himself.

Hugh turned, and he immediately felt the Officer of the Deck sigh relief. He liked that he still inspired that level of apprehension in his men, the same fear that a sergeant did in his cadets. The day he lost that, he would turn in the bronze wreath on his lapel, and banish himself to Luna to live out what remained of his life.

He entered the lift, but found some company had followed him. A lieutenant, head bowed, a report glowing off his wrist, "Sir—?"

Hugh shook his head, and keyed the hangar deck. "Brief me as we go, Lieutenant."

The slight vertigo hit him as artificial gravity tried to reckon with the dropping lift.

"Minister Caldwell got word of the *Acheron*," the boy started.

Hugh scoffed. "Minister Caldwell gets word of the weather and he court martials two colonels."

The lieutenant paled a bit, not sure how to respond to that outburst. "He'd like to speak with you about it."

"I'm sure he would," Hugh murmured. He caught the boy's eye and the kid looked away, probably assured that he would get burned if he held that look for too long. "Lieutenant, what's your name?"

The boy blinked. "Uh...Oscar, sir. Oscar Greimes."

"How long have you been out of Holkstad?"

"Sir, eight months...sir."

Eight months. That would make him fifteen years old. Hugh's lips tightened to a disapproving line. The lieutenant sensed the displeasure but didn't know what he'd done to deserve it.

Hugh sighed. "You're in for a long and inglorious career, son, rife with politics. You rise to my level and it's..." He couldn't finish the thought.

But the lieutenant picked up on it.

"Was there anything else, son?" Hugh asked.

"Yes." The lieutenant pushed the projection from his wrist to

Hugh's, the file vanishing down into his computer with a simple blinking amber light. "Your eyes only."

"Very good, Lieutenant. Return to your post."

The lift doors opened and Hugh stepped out onto the Hangar deck, leaving the lieutenant with his own insipid thoughts.

The fat hull of the SAR vehicle—a DH 2502 *Odyssey* class multirole craft—sat on the hangar deck like a fatted pelican, its enormous wingspan and electronic suite folded down into its belly. A small crowd of deck crew and their oily orange & yellow jumpsuits had gathered around it.

And as he approached, he could see it through the crowd. A black box, frosted, as the oils from human contact and moisture from the air had frozen in the vacuum.

The crowd parted, the pilot and RIO delivering their charge to Hugh's waiting hands. He could hardly wait, but he had to. He took the chest to his cabin, to safety, to secrecy.

The door closed behind him and locked. He settled at his desk and lit a cigar, soaking in the harsh taste. Success or failure, he would need it.

The box had two simple brass clasps on either side. No visible lock or sealant. Of course, the Icon would not be damaged by deep space. By all accounts, it was made of it, compressed Time and Space into a physical form.

The work of a God. The hand of the Pilgrim itself. Those little pagans on Earth were actually on to something real.

He took the cigar with his teeth and gingerly unclipped both toggles on the box, lifting its lid. A solid black, darker than anything he'd ever known, with a soft green reflection...

It was a tape. A hard drive.

Hugh took the cigar and stubbed it out on his desk. Thomas had lied to him, of course he had. What possible reason did he have to be honest and truthful? He'd been raised by criminals, by degenerates, by Enemies of the Empire.

A message on the drive. And Thom's face appeared, tinted

yellow by the projector. The boy smirked at someone off to the side of the recording before looking dead into the lens. "You'll get the Icon... when I'm ready to give it to you. And only then."

Hugh sent the hard drive flying, shattering it against the opposing wall, along with the rest of his desk's accompaniments.

He'd rescind their Safe Conduct, put out bounties on their heads, order them *persona non grata* in Imperial holds. They would find every door closed, every watering hole dry. They would crawl before him, begging not for mercy, but for an end.

The guard at his door chimed, "Sir, are you alright?!"

Hugh worked his jaw a few times before he managed to get a calm word out. "Quite alright, Matthew. Stand down. Just—dropped one of my models."

He'd kill them all. One by one. All of them.

Hugh sighed, trying to get his heart to stop jackhammering in his chest. He'd waited this long. He could wait a little longer. He was not a little boy, but a grown man with patience—this rolling boil could be brought to a simmer.

Minister Caldwell. What to do about Minister Caldwell.

Hugh looked at the flashing message on his wrist. He keyed it open, throwing the project onto his desk. He half-expected to find his arrest warrant, at least a demotion, maybe even rob him of his command.

He almost wished it had been.

ALL REGIMENTS
MESSAGE FOLLOWS

RE: BORDER WORLD SKIRMISHES
BY ORDER OF THE MINISTRY OF CIVIL DEFENSE, ALL UNITS ARE TO MUSTER TO
<u>OUTLANDER STATION</u>

FOR DEPLOYMENT TO THE FRONT
ALL OTHER COMMAND DIRECTIVES ARE RESCINDED

ZU GLORIAM

The destruction of the *Acheron* was not being treated as rogue action of a soldier off reservation. No, Caldwell was a more conniving and crafty man than that. He saw himself an opportunity to exert Imperial supremacy on a sector long left to its own devices.

This Master of the Edge and her pirate brethren, why they were exerting sovereignty. Now that couldn't be tolerated. And now they had an excuse.

His hunt would have to wait. For the time being. For now, he had a world to conquer.

————

The crew of the Aurum continue their adventures in
The Cost of the Gold Service

And the brewing civil war in the Boolean is about to kickstart chaos
on the distant colony of Vanguard in
The Blood Service

AFTERWORD

This was an absolute blast for me to write, and I hope it was much for you. The wild cast of characters really brightened up the world, and made for a new wonderful family to settle in with. This set off all of the major events explored in The Blood Service books, so go over and check those out!

If you're enjoying the Capital Adventures, please leave a review. It really helps small authors like myself.

Signing up for the Newsletter keeps you on top of the latest news around the Capital-verse.

I also have a cat. I will likely be dropping pictures of her there regularly, as she is a consistent part of my office day. She is bad at being a cat, but she is fat and good and adorable. Sign up and see!

https://www.authorivers.com/

ACKNOWLEDGMENTS

Thanks to my wife, Lyn, for helping me break the story and tolerating my ravings

My best friend, Evan, who helped me choreograph the fights and design equipment

And his wife Sharon, for letting me borrow him so much

ABOUT THE AUTHOR

Allen Ivers started writing original stories at the ripe age of eleven, largely trying to figure out why the Disney villains on the television box were the way they were. Villains, monsters, and politicians have always fascinated him with their behavior. Twenty years later, he's still fascinated by bad people and the bad things they do.

This book began as a whiskey-fueled rant about cabin boys on space pirate ships, and the contrast of sea life to space travel in popular media. In particular, he wanted to dig in on toxic masculinity and its proclivity to violence—and a story about a con artist seemed like the best way to explore that.

After enjoying the process behind *The Blood Service* so much, Allen decided to evolve several other stories he'd been tinkering with into this world he'd built. He promises more of Aaron's story soon—along with a bunch of new adventures in this universe!

And the adventures of Thom, Osyen & the crew of the *Aurum* are obviously far from over.

Allen now lives in beautiful Juneau, AK where he is somewhere at the bottom of the food chain. You can find his thoughts about writing, politics, and the odd cute cat on his Twitter.

facebook.com/AllenIversSFF
x.com/AllenIvers

ALSO BY ALLEN IVERS

www.ingramcontent.com/pod-product-compliance
Lightning Source LLC
Chambersburg PA
CBHW030557020726
47494CB00005B/1642

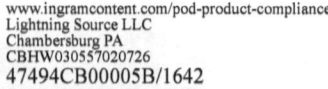